The Alex Craft Novels

Grave Witch
Grave Dance
Grave Memory

Grave Visions

An Alex Craft Novel

KALAYNA PRICE

A ROC BOOK

ROC
Published by New American Library,
an imprint of Penguin Random House LLC
375 Hudson Street, New York, New York 10014

This book is an original publication of New American Library.

First Printing, February 2016

ISBN 978-0-451-41657-5

Printed in the United States of America
10 9 8 7 6 5 4 3 2 1

To Jason,
for picking up the pieces

ACKNOWLEDGMENTS

As always, I cannot possibly express all of my thanks to Jessica for her guidance and patience. This book wouldn't be what it is without you. And thanks to all of your team at Roc who made getting this book to readers possible.

Thank you, Lucienne, for all you do. I wouldn't be here without you.

Special thanks to my friends and family who have been there for me through everything.

And of course, thank you, the very awesome reader who waited for this story and is joining me for the continuation for Alex's adventure. I hope you enjoy it!

Chapter 1

The first time I raised a shade for profit, my client fainted. Since then, I've tried to better prepare clients for their encounter with the dead.

It doesn't always work.

"You son of a bitch," Maryanne Johnson yelled as she slammed her palm against the edge of my circle. "I knew you were sleeping with her."

The shade of her late husband didn't respond. He sat motionless above his grave, his face empty and his gaze distant. That seemed only to irritate the woman more, and she slammed her hand against my circle again.

"Ms. Johnson, calm down. He can't understand your anger. He's dead."

If she heard me, she gave no indication, and I shuddered as she hit the circle again, the impact vibrating through my magic. The circle wouldn't hold much longer, and if it failed, I'd be standing in the middle of a graveyard with my shields wide-open. Not a good thing.

"If you don't take a step back, I'm going to have to end the ritual," I said, moving around the grave so that I partially obscured her view of the shade.

She didn't listen.

"This is between him and me." She rummaged through her purse, muttering curses under her breath. When she looked up again, her smile was dark. She lifted a small revolver, leveling it at the shade. "How long were you with that hussy?"

And that's my cue to end the ritual.

I didn't repeat the question to the shade, because he would have answered. He would have had no choice. Shades were just memories with no will or consciousness. Matthew Johnson might have kept his mistress a secret during life, but he couldn't hide the truth in death. And I had the feeling, regardless what his answer might be, it could only make this situation worse.

I didn't need that.

"Rest now," I whispered under my breath as I reached out with the part of me that sensed the dead and reversed the flow of magic that gave the shade form. The words weren't strictly necessary, but I'd used them for so many years, they were now part of my ritual, producing a near-Pavlovian response with my magic. The shade dissolved, the life heat I'd imbued in it rushing down the well-worn path of my psyche.

"No. No. Bring him back." The woman railed against the edge of my circle. "He died too easy the first time." Without her target of choice visible, she swung the gun in my direction. "I paid for this ritual. Now bring him back."

I was seeing the land of the dead overlaying reality, but even if the revolver looked rusted and ruined in my sight, I had no doubt it was in fine working order in mortal reality. Ms. Johnson herself might have had enough innate magical ability that my circle stopped her from crossing into my ritual space, but unless her gun was loaded with charmed ammo—doubtful—my circle would do nothing to stop a bullet. Which meant I had to defuse this situation. Fast.

"Ms. Johnson I think—"

She cocked the gun.

Right. *One shade coming right up.*

I plunged my magic into the unseen corpse and pulled Johnson's shade free again. He emerged looking exactly the same as the moment he'd died, right down to the bit of tomato soup in his beard.

As soon as the shade appeared, the woman's rage refocused on her deceased husband. The bullet she fired passed through the shade with no effect, but that didn't diminish her fury. She fired off two more shots and I crept to the edge of my circle, trying not to attract attention as I dialed the police.

I seriously needed to start screening my clients better.

"Alex, tell me you didn't sleep here last night?"

I jerked upright at the question and my chair rolled away from my desk. The coins I'd been analyzing before I'd nodded off scattered; several rolling over the side of the desk to fall with loud *plink*s onto the floor. I frowned at the sound and blinked bleary eyes as I tried to focus on the speaker.

Rianna, my once-lost-now-found best friend and business partner, stood in the doorway of my office, her arms crossed over her chest as her green gaze swept over first me and then the mess that comprised my desk. At her side, the barghest who acted as her constant shadow huffed through his large jowls and shook his shaggy head.

"Morning," I said around a yawn. My neck and back ached—no doubt from sleeping in a chair—and I stretched, trying to work out the kinks. "What time is it?"

"A little after eight. You have a . . ." She pointed to her temple and I placed a hand to the side of my face.

One of the coins clung to my skin. I peeled it off, feeling the slightest tingle of a spell in the metal. Great, one magic coin in the whole lot and I'd slept on it. Of course, maybe it would do me some good. The spell felt like a fortune charm and goodness knew I could use a little luck.

A glance over my desk turned up a blank form. I taped the coin in the provided box and jotted down my initial analysis. I'd do a more in-depth check on the spell later.

After setting down my pen, I looked up to discover Rianna still standing in my doorway, her expression somewhere between concern and disapproval.

"What? I had a lot to do." I waved a hand to the mess of coins and forms. She cocked one dark eyebrow, clearly unconvinced. With a sigh, I slipped out of my chair and focused on gathering the escaped coins. Even through the solid wood of the desk, I could feel the weight of her stare.

"Oh, yes," she said, drawing out the words for emphasis. "That looks like an important case. One so pressing, it warranted working through the night."

I didn't answer. Rianna and I both had our private investigator licenses, and as grave witches, our specialty was finding answers for our clients by questioning the dead. Analyzing charmed coins didn't exactly fall within the typical Tongues for the Dead case description, but peering into the land of the dead to raise shades did nasty things to the eyes. So, I'd been searching out cases that wouldn't make me blind before my thirtieth birthday. It didn't pay nearly as well as raising shades, but it covered some bills without burning out my vision.

"My last client got arrested before paying for her ritual," I said, as if recouping the income justified working overtime on a simple spell-identification case we both knew wasn't pressing.

We also both knew exactly why I hadn't gone home last night. He had a name.

Falin Andrews.

The Winter Queen's knight was currently crashing in my one-room loft. Considering we were occasionally lovers, that might have been okay, except that it was the Faerie queen's royal decree placing him there and saying I suspected her motives was more than an understatement. He suspected them too—which was why he himself had told me never to trust him while he was under her rule. Oh yeah, and he'd told me that while holding me at dagger-point. Just after saying he loved me.

Our relationship was complicated, to say the least. In the two weeks he'd been staying at my place we'd barely spoken, by mutual consent. And besides, I was sort of seeing someone else. Can we say awkward? Yeah.

The office was a better option.

When I remained quiet, Rianna joined me on the floor. Together we gathered the coins, the only sound the clicking of my dog's nails on the wood as he moseyed over to see what we were doing—and if we had food.

Rianna shot a glance at the small Chinese crested and frowned again. "PC is with you, so I take it you never planned to go home last night? I thought you arranged to stay in Caleb's guest room until you could figure out what to do about Falin."

"I did." And it wasn't so much that I'd worked it out as that Caleb, my landlord, had insisted. The problem was . . . "The guest room isn't soundproof and I don't think Caleb and Holly ever sleep."

"So they've officially hooked up?"

"Who knows if it's official, but they go at it like bunnies."

Rianna gave me a sympathetic glance as she passed me the last of the coins. "I'd invite you to my place, but . . ."

But she lived in an enchanted castle in Faerie. Well, actually *my* enchanted castle, but I'd never been inside it. I'd inherited the castle in a rather grisly way and the whole thing creeped me out. Besides, I'd have to pass through the winter court to reach limbo, where the castle currently resided, and with the Winter Queen determined to add me to her court, it wasn't worth the risk of her finding a reason to detain me. So yeah, not currently a viable option for a place to crash.

I shrugged. "I'll figure out something." Climbing to my feet, I dumped the coins into a magic-dampening bag—my client thought they were cursed, and though I'd found no evidence of any malicious spells, better safe than sorry—before straightening. Rianna rose slower, levering herself up with the edge of my desk. She teetered when she reached her full height. I looked at her then, really looked at her.

When I'd first rescued Rianna, she was a wasting shadow of her former self, but in the last few months, she'd reclaimed a soft glow of health. The glow was missing today, her cheeks pale and dark smudges ringed her eyes.

"Are you feeling okay? I'm the one who passed out at her desk, but you look worse than I feel." Though I was definitely feeling the weeks of gradual sleep deprivation.

Rianna gave me a feeble smile before shrugging. "I think maybe I caught something."

"I didn't know changelings could catch a cold."

Another shrug. "Apparently. It must be going around. Ms. B. won't be in today. She said something about the garden gnome being unwell."

If I wasn't frowning before, I definitely was now. When I'd inherited the castle, I'd also sort of *acquired* the people—well, two fae and one changeling—living in the castle. Like I said, creepy. The garden gnome I'd never met, but Ms. B was a brownie who'd tended the castle for longer than anyone seemed to remember. She'd taken a liking to me and recently decided to claim the role of receptionist at Tongues for the Dead—I hadn't had a say in the matter. She was gruff on the phone and some of our clients balked at her diminutive size and inhuman appearance, but I'd gotten used to having her around the office. I'd never heard of a fae getting sick, but honestly, despite the fact the fae had come out of the mushroom ring seventy years earlier, or the fact I'd recently discovered I was more fae than human, I didn't know all that much about the day-to-day life of fae.

"Well, I hope he recovers quickly. And you too," I said, my frown deepening. Rianna was all but leaning on the barghest. The large doglike fae stared at her, concern clear in his red-rimmed eyes. "Do you have any rituals scheduled today?"

She shook her head, swaying slightly with the movement.

"Good. Maybe you should keep it that way."

She gave me a half nod, as if completing the movement would have taken too much energy. "I think I'll go sit down."

"Do you need a healer? Or a doctor?"

"No, I just . . ." She trailed off as she turned, swaying a moment before taking a breath and putting one foot very purposefully in front of the other. "This'll pass in a minute. It's happened a couple of times in the last week. Let me rest a moment."

I walked around my desk and helped her into one of the client chairs. She collapsed gratefully, but I didn't get a chance to question her because my cell phone buzzed on my desk and I had to rush back around to grab it.

The displayed number wasn't one of my saved contacts, but I recognized the Central Precinct extension, so I guessed the caller. It had been a while since I'd heard from my favorite homicide detective, and our last few encounters hadn't gone all that well, so I was relieved he was finally calling.

"Hey, John," I said, tucking the phone between my shoulder and ear and heading back to Rianna.

"Craft?" a gruff male voice asked from the other side of the phone.

It wasn't John.

I stopped in my tracks and briefly considered playing it off as a wrong number. If this was a client, professionalism was way past gone. But there was something familiar about the voice, I just couldn't put a name to it. After an uncomfortably long pause, I confirmed he'd reached the right number.

"This is Detective Jenson. I need you at the morgue in an hour."

He disconnected as soon as the last word escaped his mouth, leaving me no time to accept or deny his request. I pulled the phone away from my ear and stared at it like it might morph into something venomous. Because of my—largely unexplained—involvement in several major cases, John and I had suffered a falling-out. But his partner Jenson? We'd never been close. And since my fae heritage had manifested, he'd been downright hateful toward me. Well, most of the time at least. It had been made clear to me that the police department wouldn't be hiring me for a case anytime soon, so why did Jenson want me at the morgue?

"Alex?" Rianna made my name a question, concern mixing with curiosity in her voice.

I shook my head as I redialed the number Jenson had called from. The line rang four times before going to voice mail. Frowning, I ended the call without leaving a message.

"Well," I said, shoving the phone in my back pocket. "I either have a job . . . or I'm about to walk into a trap."

Chapter 2

I arrived at Nekros City Central Precinct fifty-five minutes later. Fall had finally realized it was running late and overcompensated with a cold front that knocked the temperature from the mid-eighties to the mid-forties overnight. Half the city seemed to have raided their stash of winter clothing, so for once no one gave me a second look when I pulled a jacket from the passenger side of my car before heading into the building. I might not have been particularly cold now, but once I embraced the grave—assuming that was why I'd been called—I'd have a chill it would take me hours to shake.

Central Precinct was an austere multipurpose building holding most of the city's important law enforcement entities, from the crime lab and DA's offices on the upper floors, to the main police station on the ground floor and the morgue in the basement. I passed through security without issue, which despite the fact I'd done so a hundred times since I first started working on retainer for the police, was a relief. I'd half expected to be stopped in the front lobby. While nothing had officially ended my retainer status with the NCPD, I'd been told in no uncertain terms that my services wouldn't be requested unless the brass decided it was absolutely necessary. Add to that the fact that John had always been my first contact, and I wasn't sure what I might be walking into. I just hoped this sudden call from Jenson was the start of something good.

I took the elevator down to the basement. Fluorescents lit the long hall leading to the morgue, flooding it with a harsh light that simultaneously washed out color while making everything still seem cast in shadows. The thud of my boots on the linoleum bounced along the walls as I walked, making the area feel hollow and abandoned. I'd never liked the ambiance of this hallway, and as on edge as I was now, if zombies had shambled out of the large morgue doors, I wouldn't have been surprised. Though zombies weren't likely. What I was really afraid of were faeries.

Oh, I know, who is afraid of Tinker Bell, right?

Me, that's who.

Okay, so I wasn't afraid of all fae, but ever since I'd learned *I* was fae and I'd gained the attention of the Faerie courts, life had gotten a lot more complicated. I was currently unaligned, something that just didn't happen in Faerie, and the courts didn't like it. I was also a planeweaver, which meant I could not only see and interact with multiple planes of existence, but I could tie those planes together. I was the first since the age of legends, and every court wanted to add me to their numbers. Personally, I was more interested in maintaining my freedom, so I reserved a healthy amount of caution when it came to fae and Faerie.

And Jenson was fae.

Or at least half fae.

I'd assumed Jenson was independent fae, but you know what they say about assumptions. If he was court fae . . . this could end very badly for me.

Alex, you're freaking yourself out. After all, if one of the courts was going to snatch me away to Faerie, they surely wouldn't do it in front of dozens of cops at Central

Precinct. Besides, as far as I could tell, Jenson hid his heritage even deeper than I did.

With that thought in mind, I took a deep breath and pushed open the morgue door.

Jenson waited in the center of the room with his back toward the door. It was early, so I expected at least one medical examiner and some morgue attendants to be present, but the room was empty aside from the plainclothes police detective.

I stopped, frowning. Tamara Greene, the lead ME and one of my closest friends, wasn't there, of course—she had the next few days off to prepare for her wedding and then she'd be off on her honeymoon—but I'd expected *someone* else to be there. After all, people didn't stop dying just because the ME took time off.

"Jenson," I said, not trying to hide the suspicion in my voice. At my calf, the enchanted dagger hidden in my boot buzzed lightly, either sensing danger or just responding to my own nervousness. The magic imbued in the fac-wrought weapon made it somewhat aware and reactive to my surroundings, which had saved my neck in the past, but it was also bloodthirsty, so I was never sure if it could warn me of danger or if it just liked to be drawn and would use any excuse it found. I didn't draw it now, at least, not yet.

Jenson turned. He wore the glamour that made him look human, hiding the oversized jaw and tusks that marked him as part troll. Surprisingly, he looked relieved when he saw me, though all he said was, "Craft," as he gave me a curt nod and then headed for the cold room where the bodies were kept.

Okay, if he planned to pull out a body, he'd definitely called me here for a ritual, but this was not the way these things worked.

"What's going on, Jenson?" I asked, but I didn't move any farther into the large room. "And where is everyone."

"Mandatory seminar." He emerged pushing a sheet-topped gurney. "We have only about forty-five minutes, so do your thing fast."

My thing?

"Uh, back up. One, there is paperwork that needs to be signed before I begin, and two, why do we have to complete the ritual before the seminar is over?" I didn't add that I hadn't yet agreed to take the case. "And where is John?"

Jenson's jaw locked, his lips screwing together in a scowl. I met the expression with my own level stare. Until I knew more about what was going on, I wasn't raising any shades. I didn't like the situation. It felt wrong. And the hurried secretiveness worried me.

Our silent stare down lasted only a moment before Jenson growled, a low rumbling that didn't sound like it should have emerged from anything human-shaped. Then he shook his head and let go of the gurney.

"There is no paperwork, and there can be no witnesses. As you might have guessed, I didn't invite you down here for a sanctioned ritual." He sighed. "I walk a fine line here, Craft. And this case . . ." He shook his head.

"You think fae are involved?"

He winced and looked around as if afraid someone might overhear. "Let's just say I have a bad feeling, but I hope I'm wrong. You going to raise this shade or what?"

I frowned at him. Jenson was not quite asking me for a favor. One that could be dangerous on several levels. Without approval of the family or authorization from the cops, raising a shade at the morgue was illegal. Also, I was attempting to limit myself to one ritual a week for the sake of my eyesight. The previous day's ritual may have ended up being a short one—the police tended to respond quickly to shots fired—but even a truncated ritual did a number on my eyes. I'd be willing to break that self-imposed—and rather new—rule of one ritual a week to begin mending fences with NCPD, but for an unsanctioned ritual for Jenson . . . ?

"Does John know about this?"

Jenson shook his head. "My fears aren't a human concern."

Right. Great. I worried my bottom lip. Jenson could get into as much trouble as I could if we were discovered, so clearly he thought questioning this particular victim was important. And goodness knew the firm could use the money.

"Okay . . ." I trailed off and took a tentative step into the room. Jenson didn't strike me as a big risk taker, so I had to admit to a certain amount of curiosity. Reaching ever so lightly with my senses, I let that part of me with an affinity for the dead stretch to the corpse on the gurney. It was a female, a couple of years younger than me, but if I wanted to know more about who she'd been or how she'd died, I'd have to raise her shade. Or ask. "Why her? What is it about this case?"

Jenson's frown deepened. "Things aren't adding up at the crime scene. No sign of a break-in. Doors and windows locked from the inside. No disturbance or blood outside the apartment, but dozens of bloody tracks inside that don't lead to any exits." He stared at the sheet-covered figure, as if she might sit up and explain what had happened. Which, if I performed this ritual, she would. Or at least, her shade, a collection of all the memories from her life given shape by my magic, would.

"The killer could have had a key and locked up after he or she left. Maybe showered before leaving?"

Jenson's head shot up. "Don't you think we've considered that, Craft? Something is off about this case. I should alert the FIB, but no one wants the case hijacked over speculation. And besides, we don't need any more bad press in this city."

It took me a second to realize the "we" Jenson referred to was the fae, not the police. And he was right. The fae, or really any of the magical community, definitely didn't need another mysterious case laid at their feet, which was exactly what would happen if the media caught wind of the FIB—the Fae Investigation Bureau—taking over a murder case.

In the last several months Nekros had seen the mysterious death of a governor, grisly ritual murders, rips directly into the Aetheric plane, disembodied body parts, ghouls, and a series of murders disguised as suicides. The city was teetering on a precipice. One more blow and the whole city might topple into chaos. Well, maybe at this point, it would be better to say *further* chaos.

"So if her shade indicates the fae are involved . . . ?" I started.

Jenson met my gaze. "I'm duty-bound to alert the FIB, but let's hope that's not the case." He looked tired, but earnest. If this was anything other than what he'd indicated, I'd seen no hint of deception from him. "Now what do you want in exchange for raising the shade?"

"I have a standard fee if you want to hire me." I'd even be willing to do it at the rate I charged the Nekros City Police Department, which was less than a ritual for private clients, but I didn't add that. Not yet.

At my words, Jenson's eyes widened ever so slightly in surprise, and for the briefest moment he cocked his head to the side as if he was the one looking for a catch. Then his features went carefully blank—the expression of someone who thought he was cheating the other out of a good deal. Digging his wallet out of his back pocket, he pulled out several large bills.

I didn't cross the room. Not immediately at least. *Something here doesn't add up.* In folklore, fae would sometimes pass glamoured leaves or rocks off as money. At sunset or dawn the glamour would vanish. That practice was, of course, illegal, but Jenson was acting rather suspicious. I had to check.

Cracking my shields, I let my gaze travel through planes of reality. I'd recently discovered that I could pierce glamour when my shields were down. Unfortunately, I hadn't yet learned how to discriminate which levels of reality I peered into, so as my shields opened, colorful tendrils of magic from the Aetheric plane popped into view and the room around me appeared to decay as my psyche touched the land of the dead.

I glanced at the money Jenson still held toward me. It withered in my gravesight, but it didn't change into anything else, so it was real. Slamming my shields shut, I pushed the other layers of reality away. The momentary touch made the room dimmer, but that might have been more a reaction to the loss of Aetheric color than damage. Or at least I hoped so. Stepping gingerly across the room, I accepted the money.

Jenson studied me as I folded the bills and shoved them in my back pocket. He still looked like he'd just dodged a bullet by paying me in cash—what did he expect I'd want? Of course, the currency of Faerie was largely debts and power, so maybe he'd expected me to ask for a boon. But I lived in mortal reality.

And I planned to keep it that way.

"There is still paperwork to sign."

Jenson scowled. "We don't have time to waste discussing all the reasons that is a bad idea."

As this was an active police case, my raising the shade could be seen as interference. Without either police or family authorization, it was my ass on the line if we were caught. There was no way I was going any further without paperwork.

My expression clearly spoke for me, because after a moment Jenson let out a breath and said, "I'll sign something acknowledging I hired you. *After* the ritual. My word. Nothing official or specific, mind you, but something that will cover you legally. Now can we get moving?"

As a fae's word was fairly well unbreakable, I accepted with a nod, but then Jenson looked uncertain as he glanced first at the gurney in front of him and then around the room. He'd seen me raise shades before, but only once or twice. Like I said, John was my typical contact with the police. Or Tamara, if I had family authorization to see a body in the morgue.

"The center of the room would be best," I said, nodding in that direction as I dug through my purse for a tube of waxy chalk.

Jenson pushed the gurney to the spot I'd indicated. "There might be a second one," he said, stepping back.

"A second what? Body?" I asked as I duckwalked, dragging the chalk along the linoleum floor to form the physical outline of my circle. "Another shade will cost more."

"Fine, we'll sort that out if it comes to it. Can you do that any faster?"

I didn't bother answering that question. "Are you going to set up the camera?"

"I don't want any record of this. Things get out sometimes."

I cringed. Yeah, I knew that firsthand. I'd become infamous a couple of months back because of a leaked recording made right here in the morgue.

I finished the circle and stood. "Well, then, I'll get started." I tapped into the energy stored in the obsidian ring I wore, intending to activate my circle, but as I began channeling magic into the circle I stopped and looked around. "Detective, mind your toes."

Jenson glanced down at where his shoes crossed the thin chalk line. Then he backed up, color crawling to his cheeks. Nodding, I closed my eyes.

Channeling energy into the waxy line, I activated my barrier and it sprang up around me. The barrage of grave essence fell away so that I could feel only the essence lifting from one corpse, the girl in the circle with me. I kept additional shields in charms on a bracelet I wore, so I removed it first, then I opened my personal shields.

I'd always imagined my outer shield as a knotted wall

of vines—maybe I'd watched *Sleeping Beauty* too often as a child—but I'd always found a living shield helped guard me from the touch of the grave best. I let those thorny vines slither apart now, opening the shield, but simultaneously I envisioned a thin, clear barrier springing up between my psyche and the world. This shield was new, one I'd had to fashion after I'd begun accidentally merging reality. It helped keep my powers from reaching out and pulling layers of the world into contact with one another, but the real trick was keeping it thin enough that my grave magic could still pass through it.

A cold wind picked up around me, whipping my hair. It wasn't anything that existed in the mortal world but blew across the chasm between the living and the dead. I opened my eyes and focused on the sheet-draped form. My power rushed into it, filling the corpse with my living heat as the chill of the grave swept into me.

The woman's shade sat up, out of the body. She wore a tank top with a faded cartoon character on it and a pair of men's boxers. Sleepwear, I guessed. The shade made no sound, showed no emotion. She was far past alarm at being dead, and felt no pain despite the fact she appeared to be covered in small puncture wounds. She was memory given form. Nothing more.

I frowned, studying the wounds. There were several different sizes of punctures, but all were circular and appeared on her body in pairs. *Like fang marks.*

I glanced at Jenson. "How did you say she was killed?"

"I didn't."

Obviously. It was impossible to tell if the wounds were the cause of death, and if they were, if that was because she'd bled out or been injected with something. Vampires, to my knowledge, were a myth. Of course, seventy years ago fae were just myth and folklore, so maybe there were bloodsucking entities out there. But, if she'd been killed by some sort of bloodsucking creature, it—or really they— would have to have been small. Some of the punctures were only a few centimeters apart, others were upward to an inch.

"What is your name?" I asked the shade.

She looked at me, her eyes empty and dispassionate. "Emma Langley."

"And how did you die, Emma?"

"I was giving myself a pedicure in my room and I heard Jeremy scream," she said, and I glanced over at Jenson. His face gave away nothing, so I wasn't sure if the Jeremy she'd mentioned was the killer or another victim. "I went to the living room to see what was wrong and there were snakes, everywhere. He was buried under them. I ran to the kitchen, grabbed the fire extinguisher, and tried to clear a path to him, but the snakes wrapped around my legs. I fell, and they were everywhere. Biting me. Pain shot through my arms, my chest, and . . ." She trailed off.

And she died. Or at least lost consciousness. The shade would have stopped recording as soon as her soul left her body.

I studied the bites covering her. They were literally everywhere. I couldn't have pressed my hand to her skin without touching at least two at once. I shuddered. I'd always had a healthy respect for snakes, but never a fear of them. Emma might change that.

I glanced at Jenson. "What did animal control make of the snakes? Venomous, I'm assuming?" But where would that many snakes have come from?

"There were no snakes when the bodies were found. And there is no trace of venom in the bodies."

I blinked at him. *How —?* Well, he'd said he had a bad feeling about this case. That was why I was here after all. I turned back to Emma.

"Do you know where the snakes came from?"

"No."

"Did you hear anyone enter the house before Jeremy screamed?"

"No."

Okay . . . I looked to Jenson to see if he had any guidance of where he wanted this interview to go, but he only stared at the shade, frowning.

"Did Jeremy like snakes?" I asked.

The shade shook her head. "He was terrified of them."

"When was the last time you were in the living room before you heard Jeremy scream?"

A living person would have had to think about it. The shade answered without hesitation. "About forty minutes earlier."

"And did anything strike you as odd then?"

The question required the shade to extrapolate on the memory, so there was a chance she wouldn't answer, but I lucked out. Or, more likely, she'd noted the oddity at the time. "Jeremy was anxious. He had two half-started projects laid over the coffee table and was channel surfing. That was why I went to my room early. He was all over the place."

It sounded like Emma wasn't the body I needed. I turned to Jenson. "Is Jeremy the second body?"

"Yeah." He glanced at his watch. "You'll have to be fast."

I didn't bother pointing out that if he'd brought out both bodies in the first place it would have been faster, but instead went through the steps of putting the shade back in her body and reclaiming my heat. I didn't release the grave. Not yet, at least. Nor did I drop my circle. I'd have to break the barrier to allow the boy's body into the circle, but with my shields down I needed the circle to protect my psyche.

So I waited.

Jenson emerged a few moments later pushing another gurney. I waited until he was almost to the edge of my circle before dropping the barrier. The cold wind that had been contained with me inside escaped as the circle fell. Jenson stopped, his eyes going wide as the wind rustled his short hair. Equipment rattled somewhere farther off in the room and I could distinctly feel that there were eight bodies still in the cold room—three females and five males. I pushed back against the grave essence clawing at me from those corpses. If I let too much of my attention touch them, we'd have a whole lot more shades than we needed.

Jenson had stopped moving when my power escaped the temporarily released circle. I focused on him. "I recommend getting that body in here so I can finish," I said between gritted teeth.

The detective hesitated like he wasn't sure he wanted to get any closer. Then he seemed to shake himself and he pushed the gurney until it was beside Emma's. I nodded in acknowledgment and waited for him to retreat from the circle. But he didn't move.

"Behind the chalk line unless you want to be locked in here with us."

Jenson looked from me to the faintly drawn circle, and then scurried safely behind the line. That was all I was waiting for. Tapping into the power in my ring, I siphoned it into the circle, making the barrier spring to life around me once again. I all but sighed with relief when the essence clawing at me cut down by well over half. Jenson also looked considerably relieved as the spillover from the land of the dead was once again contained.

I turned my focus onto the new body—Jeremy, theoretically. Letting my senses stretch, I reached with my power, letting my magic seep into the corpse. What I found made me frown.

"He hasn't been raised before, right?" I asked, taking a step closer to the gurney.

"Of course not. Who the hell would I have gotten to raise him, and why would I be talking to you now if I had another witch?"

True. On both points. Jenson and I were not friends, and Tongues for the Dead boasted the only grave witches for at least a hundred miles, but . . . I siphoned more magic into the boy's body.

Shades were just memories given shape with grave magic. In the same way that every cell held a complete strand of a person's DNA, every cell held a complete lifetime of memories, but it took either a whole lot of magic or a massive amount of those strands of memories woven together to form a shade capable of communicating. As bodies deteriorated so did the number of those strands available to use.

This body had so few I'd have believed it was little more than ancient bones if I hadn't been able to *feel* that it was a fresh corpse. The only other way I knew of to lose so much of what made a shade a shade was magic. Every time a shade was raised, it wore out some of those strands of memories, which made it terribly irresponsible for grave witches to raise shades for entertainment reasons and why there was currently a bill in front of the Senate making such rituals illegal.

But if Jeremy had never been raised . . .

I closed my eyes and poured more power into the body, letting magic fill in the gaps in the shade. The cold in my body sank deeper, like ice moving through my blood, freezing my bones. Still I pushed harder, feeding the body more magic.

A shade sat up from under the sheet, thin, weak, even in my vision that was so far across the chasm stretching between the living and the dead. Outside my circle Jenson leaned closer, squinting at the nearly transparent shade.

"What's your name?" I asked the shade.

The shade's mouth moved, but the only sound inside my circle was the whisper of distant wind and my own heartbeat. Reaching deep inside myself, I pulled on my reserves of power, forcing them into the shade. He solidified ever so slightly. I asked my question again.

"Jeremy Watts." Even packed with as much magic as I could summon, his words were a barely audible whisper.

"Why can't it speak?" Jenson asked from outside the circle. "And why is it so see-through?"

I frowned, shivering. Apparently while the shade was barely audible to me, for those not in touch with the dead he was completely silent. Not much I could do about that though. I had nothing left to throw into the shade to strengthen him. I was already expending as much of myself as I dared. If I tried to make the shade any more visible, I was afraid I wouldn't have enough strength after the ritual ended to walk out of this room.

"The shade is weak. Faded. Whatever happened, it . . . drained him," I said to Jenson, and then turned back to the shade because I wasn't going to be able to hold him long. "How did you die?"

"Snakes. I was covered in snakes."

Well, that confirmed what Emma had said, and I repeated it to Jenson before continuing. "And where did the snakes come from?"

"Everywhere. The couch. The electrical socket. The windows. Then the hammer in my hand transformed into a snake and wrapped around my arm."

I turned to Jenson to see his reaction before remembering he couldn't hear the shade. I repeated what Jeremy had said, and Jenson's face darkened. I could guess what he was thinking. He'd been afraid fae might be involved, and snakes that appeared out of nowhere and then disappeared just as mysteriously—not to mention objects that transformed from inanimate to a deadly creature—sounded a hell of a lot like glamour.

I questioned the shade for several more minutes, asking questions Jenson threw at me in rapid succession and repeating the shade's answers. Jeremy confirmed that—to his knowledge—no one besides him and Emma had been in the house when the snakes appeared. It was his day off work, and he hadn't gone anywhere that day or even seen anyone besides Emma in the twenty-four hours prior to his death.

By the time Jenson ran out of questions and turned away with a discouraged sneer, I was trembling so hard I nearly fell over my feet standing still. I reached out with my mind to put the shade back, but then paused.

"Emma said you were anxious and distracted before the snakes appeared. Why?"

Despite the fact I hadn't yet pulled back my magic, it was starting to wear thin and the shade had faded further, so I had to strain to hear him over my chattering teeth.

"I took Glitter."

"Glitter?" Like the sparkly craft supply? That didn't make sense. I glanced at Jenson, who turned back toward me, an equally confused look on his face. "What is glitter?"

Jenson just shrugged, but Jeremy answered me. "A drug. A guy gave it to me at the club Art Barn. He said it would up my creativity and focus."

I repeated this for Jenson, whose frown only deepened. My expression matched his. "You said they ran a tox screen?"

He glanced at the file in his hand, scanning pages before nodding. "Yeah, none of the usual suspects popped in his blood work." He closed the file. "I'll have them rerun it—to look for both more exotic venoms and this . . . Glitter."

I nodded. It sounded like a plan to me. I was just turning back to the shade when outside the morgue and down the hall the elevator dinged to announce it had arrived in the basement.

Jenson's face drained of color, a hint of panic making his eyes a little too wide.

"Shut it down," he said, stepping forward, but my circle stopped him, denying him access to the gurneys.

I shuddered as he collided with the edge of my barrier and sent magical shock waves through me. Withdrawing my magic, I released Jeremy, but I couldn't help feeling we should have gotten more information from him. We would never get another chance. As flimsy as his shade was this time, I doubted I'd be able to raise him again, regardless of how much magic I summoned.

As the depleted shade sank back into the body, my living heat followed the well-worn path back through my psyche into my very being. For a single moment it filled me with warmth, and then it seemed to freeze, falling like an icy rock into my center. I cringed, knowing what was coming. Focusing on my shields, I let the vines grow closed around my psyche again. As the gaps closed, the world went black, my vision fading and then winking out altogether. I fumbled blindly for my charm bracelet and my extra shields. With my shields in place, I dropped the circle, and then hesitated. I hated having to rely on my other senses as my eyes were useless, but with as much magic as I'd expended, I wouldn't be seeing anything for several hours—not with my natural eyes, at least.

I heard Jenson approach and push one of the gurneys out of the circle, one wheel squeaking as it rolled. Outside, in the hall, high-pitched voices spoke animatedly, drawing closer.

"You want to glamour yourself invisible until you're out of here?" Jenson asked, his voice a hissed whisper.

"Uh . . ." I started and then stopped. Jenson knew I was fae. He'd realized it before I had. Hell, he'd sensed the change as soon as the spell my father had bound me in had first started breaking down. He could tell I was Sleagh Maith—the ruling line in Faerie—but I had no idea how much more he knew. From his comments over the last few months, it was clear he thought I'd intentionally been hiding my nature. But the truth was, despite Sleagh Maith's reputation for being great at glamour, I had no clue how to do anything with my fae heritage.

When I didn't answer—or, presumably, disappear from sight—Jenson growled under his breath. "Well, then, help me with that gurney so we can get out of here."

I frowned in the general direction I assumed the remaining gurney sat. While my friends were aware of the consequences my grave magic imposed on my eyes, I didn't exactly advertise, and complete blindness meant I'd really pushed myself. Still, I had my pride, and the main room of the morgue was far from cluttered. It was a straight shot from the circle to the cold room. Jenson had a head start on me, so if I moved carefully, he'd be back out to take the gurney before I ran into the doors . . . Hopefully.

With that thought in mind, I reached out, groping for the push bar of the gurney.

The steel was cold against my palms. And then scorchingly hot.

Then the world fell out from under me.

Chapter 3

"Craft." A voice said, piercing the darkness. "Craft, can you hear me?"

A stinging pain flared along my cheek. I flinched, or tried to, but my eyes were already closed and something cold and hard was behind my head. No, not just my head. All of me.

Another sting—someone slapping my cheek.

I pried open my eyes, but couldn't see anything beyond the contorting mix of colorful energy swirling in front of my face. To make matters worse, grave essence clawed at me from all sides, threatening to overwhelm me as the chill searched for a place under my skin.

Squeezing my eyes closed against the chaos, I focused on my shields. Whatever had just happened, it had blown through my outermost shield. Not good. Concentrating hard, I imagined my barrier growing to an impenetrable wall once again. As the gaps closed, the cold wind tearing around me died, the grave moving farther away. When I opened my eyes again, the room was eerily black, but then it had been before I . . . what? Fainted?

"What the hell just happened, Craft?" Jenson asked at the same time a woman asked, "Are you okay?"

"Not sure," I said, answering both.

My brain felt thick, like my head had been stuffed with cotton. I struggled to a sitting position, releasing an embarrassing grunt with the effort, and the room spun around me. Pulling my knees to my chest, I groaned, and pressed a hand to my forehead. What *had* happened?

I groped blindly for the gurney so I could steady myself and stand, but then I froze, palm inches from where I guessed the parked gurney sat. The skin across my hand tingled painfully, like electricity was jumping from the metal.

"Hey, Jenson, what is the iron content of stainless steel?"

The detective's answer came slow, like he wasn't fully following why I asked. "Pretty high, but it's an alloy."

Which, by his tone, I took to mean it shouldn't have the same effect on fae as pure cold iron. It was universally known that iron was the most effective weapon to use against the fae. What most humans didn't know was why. I'd recently discovered that iron interrupted the magic between a fae and Faerie. Short-term result was usually sickness. But a long-term severing? Death.

I flexed my hand without closing it on the gurney. Pain shot along my skin, and I pulled back. The steel might be an alloy, but it was definitely affecting me.

The two women I'd heard in the hallway were in the room now. I didn't recognize their voices, and I wasn't about to push the topic of iron when I was trying my best to pass for human. Scooting farther away, I staggered to my feet, the effort leaving me dizzy and breathless.

"You gonna make it?" Jenson asked. He stepped closer until I could feel him hovering, but he didn't offer me a hand.

I nodded, sucking down air like the oxygen content wasn't quite enough to sustain life. *What is happening to me?* I didn't know, but if I had to guess, I'd bet it had something to do with Faerie.

The two women were talking softly, too quiet for me to make out what was being said, but I could guess my untimely swoon was the topic. I hated being blind, and the added confusion of having passed out in the middle of the morgue didn't help. Frustrated, I cracked my shields. My physical eyes were currently useless, but with my shields cracked, my psyche looked across the planes. It created a confusing jumble of realities splashed with colors and pitted with decay, but I could see enough to navigate.

It also made my eyes glow with an unearthly light. Strangely, no one gasped or stumbled back, which was the typical reaction to this particular trick. That was a refreshing surprise, but a surprise nonetheless. Then I remembered the necklace I wore. It was a fae-wrought chameleon charm, bound to me with blood magic. Unlike a witch-made perception charm that would allow me to control exactly what people saw—but would have to be targeted and would burn magic quick—this charm simply made people see what they expected to see. I needed it on a daily basis to prevent people from noticing that my skin shimmered—it was a fae thing and as I hadn't figured out glamour yet, one I couldn't control. It apparently also masked my glowing eyes. No one expected to see it, so they didn't. Definitely an added benefit.

It took me several blinks to work out the mess of information my psyche had turned into a type of *sight*, but I was getting rather used to seeing across planes, so after only a moment, I scooped my purse from the floor and turned to Jenson.

"We were going somewhere?" Because I still needed him to sign paperwork, and I wasn't letting him slip away until he did.

Jenson shot a glance from me to the two morgue techs who were both watching us. Then he nodded. "Let me put Mr. Watts away and we can grab a coffee."

That sounded like a plan to me.

* * *

There was a café down the street from the precinct, so we walked. Which was a relief, as I didn't feel like explaining why I couldn't drive. I might be able to see well enough to walk around, but I definitely wasn't trusting myself behind the wheel.

Once Jenson had signed my client agreement, and thus I'd covered my ass legally for any fallout from my ritual, I closed my shields and let the darkness surround me. I hated being blind in public—it made me feel vulnerable. But I was just sitting in a booth nursing a coffee, and Jenson seemed to be in no hurry himself. If I needed, I could always open my psyche again, but giving my eyes some time to heal would be best.

So, we sat in silence. Me with both hands wrapped around the hot coffee as I tried to encourage some of its warmth into my body, and Jenson on the other side of the booth, most likely still staring into his mug, which was pretty much all he'd done since we arrived. It was almost companionable. Almost.

"Will you turn over the case?" I asked once the waitress refilled my mug for the second time.

"I should. No good explanation outside of magic for a horde of serpents showing up like that and then vanishing just as mysteriously. The hammer, especially, is damning, isn't it?"

Admittedly, glamour had been my first thought. But that didn't explain what had happened to the boy's shade. Both Emma and Jeremy had been killed by the snakes, but only his shade had been damaged. He'd also been the first attacked. That seemed significant.

"How about that drug, Glitter. Have the police run across many cases with it before? I've never heard of it."

The table thrummed as Jenson drummed his fingers over it, but he didn't answer immediately. I wished I could see his expression, or if he'd nodded or shook his head, because it didn't seem like I was going to get a verbal answer. Then he grunted and said, "I can talk to narcotics, but new street names for the same old designer drugs pop up on occasion, so it might be nothing. But you'd think the blood panel would have caught that."

I could almost hear his frown. And I had to agree with his initial assessment that something was off about this case. I set down my coffee mug. Damn, I was brooding over the circumstances of the case. This wasn't *my* case. While I couldn't deny that the strange circumstances piqued my interest, my part was over. I'd raised and questioned the shades. That was all I'd been hired to do.

"Well, I should—" I cut off as a commotion broke out in the front of the café. Loud exclamations of what sounded more like amazement than fear rose from several voices all at once, followed by scooting chairs and pounding feet as people rushed toward the windows.

I cursed my eyes as I twisted in my seat, but I didn't stand.

"What's happening?" I asked, straining to hear what people were saying. There were too many voices and I was catching only snatches that didn't make much sense.

"Not sure." Jenson's chair screeched as it scooted back, so I guessed he stood, but with all the other noise, I couldn't tell if he went to check it out or not.

Cursing under my breath, I cracked my shields and opened my psyche. The café snapped into distorted focus and I looked around. Jenson had, in fact, moved to the front of the café where all the patrons were gathered at the large windows. I stood slowly, still trembling from the combo of overused magic and grave chill, and then I made my way toward the crowd.

I stopped before I reached the window, gawking.

Jenson turned toward me. "You seeing a unicorn? Because I am."

I nodded, dumbfounded. Outside the window. In the

middle of main street, a man in dirty clothes that had seen better days sat on the back of a large white horse with a spiraled horn sticking out of the middle of its head. But while I could clearly see the unicorn, I could also see *through* it.

"It does look like one." Superficially, at least.

"Then it can't be a unicorn because you sure as hell aren't a virgin."

I raised an eyebrow but didn't peel my gaze off the spectacle in the street. Jenson had made more than one disparaging comment about my sex life in the past. This time though, it was applicable.

"Yeah, and you aren't exactly a maiden," I shot back, and received an amused grunt in response. For that matter, the guy riding the mythical beast was far from a virginal maiden either, and if folklore was to be believed, only young ladies pure of body and heart should be able to see a unicorn, let alone touch or ride one.

Jenson stepped back from the crowd and dropped his voice. "You think it's real or glamour?" The last word was a whisper.

As I could see through the mythical beast, I was fairly certain it was glamour. But why? And who had created it? The man riding on its back was clearly human, his soul, while a little dim was the yellow I associated with humans. He might have been a witch—that didn't change the color of the soul—but he certainly wasn't fae. So he couldn't have created the unicorn. *Then what is he doing on its back?*

Jenson was staring at me. I'd never answered his question. With a forced smile, I gave him a noncommittal shrug. After all, the unicorn wasn't doing any harm. Just making a spectacle in the street. Now if it turned carnivorous and started eating the man, that would be a problem, but as it was, what was the harm?

As I watched the unlikely pair trot out of view and

vanish around a corner, I wished I could truly believe that it really was just an innocent spectacle, but in my experience, nothing good ever came from glamour.

By the time I left work, the unicorn was already an Internet sensation and speculation about the man riding it was running rampant. Dozens of cell phone videos had captured the beast trotting down the street, but the pair had vanished before reporters arrived on the scene, so most of the footage was shaky or shot from a far angle. I'd followed some of the coverage, but nothing provided any clue as to where the glamoured beast had come from, or why, so I'd eventually gone back to the less than thrilling task of cataloguing the not-so-magic coins I'd been hired to analyze.

Rianna had made me promise I wouldn't sleep at the office again, so after putting it off as long as possible, I finally packed up the coins, gathered my dog, and headed to the house I shared with two housemates and one uninvited house-crasher.

The lights in my one-room efficiency over the garage were all blaring bright and cheery behind the blinds when I arrived home. Falin was in. I stared at the lights as I parked. Then, picking up PC, I bypassed the steps on the side of the house that led to my private entrance and headed toward the door to the main house. Back when I'd first moved in, Caleb had given me a key to the main house in case of emergency. I dug in my purse for that key now. It had been getting quite a workout in the last few weeks.

As I searched for the key, the sound of a movie playing drifted through the door, and I hesitated. Both Caleb's and Holly's cars were in the drive, which meant they were likely watching something together. A few weeks ago, I might have plopped down on the couch beside them and asked someone to pass the popcorn. But a lot had changed recently. For one, Holly and Caleb were likely not just watching a movie, but cuddling while doing so—and hopefully nothing more than cuddling. You'd think they were a pair of love-struck teenagers the way they were suddenly all about each other. Dreamily gazing into someone else's eyes while wearing a smile you just can't contain might feel great during new love, but it was damn awkward for the third wheel living with the couple.

Also, there would be no popcorn.

A few months ago Holly had been forced to eat Faerie food, which for whatever reason, is addictive to mortals. And not the kind of addictive that any number of anonymous group meetings in a basement was likely to fix. Once a mortal ate Faerie food, they could sustain life on nothing else. Human food turned to ash on the tongue. There was no cure. It was Faerie food or starve, and Faerie food couldn't be removed from Faerie without disgusting—and inedible—results.

So, no popcorn or any other form of movie snacks. Also, with the floor plan of the house, I couldn't even subtly nuke a TV dinner without her being very aware of it from the couch. She rarely complained directly about anyone eating in front of her, but I knew her dietary restrictions pained her. Add to that the fact that it was sort of my fault she was in this mess as the deranged changeling who'd given her Faerie food in the first place had kidnapped Holly to use as bait for me . . . and yeah, I didn't eat mortal fare in front of her.

I glanced down at PC in my arms. "Which awkward is more uncomfortable?" I asked him in a whisper.

The little dog cocked one white tufted ear and wagged his tail. Which wasn't an answer. Not that the dog would have cared even if he had been capable of answering. As long as he had food and a bed, he was an easygoing kind of guy. I, on the other hand, would rather not have to choose between the weird tension between Falin and me, or the awkward intrusion into Caleb and Holly's budding romance and the guilt I'd feel if I made even as little as a cold sandwich with Holly around.

With a sigh, I set PC in the grass so he could do his business. Once he was finished, I turned away from the main door and headed toward the stairs to my loft, hoping it was the right choice.

When I opened the door, Falin was in the kitchenette loading steaks and cheesy mashed potatoes onto two plates. He didn't look up as I entered, or when I set my purse down on the one chair in the room. He didn't even say hello. He just grabbed silverware before depositing one of the plates on the far side of the counter, not quite in front of me, and then taking his own plate and leaning against the stove.

"Hi to you too," I said, frowning at the plate of food. "How did you know I'd be home for dinner?" Because the steaks had just come off the pan he'd seared them on, and looked perfectly cooked, not like he'd been waiting. Which was odd, because I certainly hadn't told him when I'd be home. Last night I hadn't come home at all and the previous two nights I'd come upstairs only to grab a change of clothes, so he couldn't have been expecting me.

Falin didn't look away from the food on his plate. "I always make enough for two."

Right. Maybe barging in on Holly and Caleb would have been the less awkward choice. Too late now. Grabbing the plate, I retreated to my bed. It wasn't much of a retreat, if you discounted the bathroom, the loft was only one room. But at least, with Falin in the far side of the kitchenette and me on the other side of the room, it was slightly less weird that we were in the same room ignoring each other, right? Okay, maybe not.

Sighing, I dug into the food. It tasted as good as it smelled. Which didn't surprise me. Falin was an excellent cook. I felt contrary enough to try to be annoyed by that, but it's damn hard to be grouchy while eating an amazing steak.

But even focusing on an exquisite meal couldn't overcome the level of awkward resounding in the small space. Setting my plate on my pillow, I leaned over and pressed the power button on the TV remote. The shabby old television flickered to life. Lusa Duncan, the star reporter for Nekros City's most acclaimed witchy news station, Witch Watch, appeared on the screen. Behind her the image of a man, whom I originally thought was quite old but then realized had most likely simply been worn hard by life, was superimposed on the screen.

"—would not confirm cause of death," Lusa said as I bumped the volume. "But it is believed that Murphy was the same man seen only hours earlier riding on the back of a unicorn in downtown Nekros."

A second image, this one a pixilated close-up of the bedraggled man from earlier today appeared beside the first image. I squinted at the two images. My vision wasn't quite back to what passed as a hundred percent for me, so I was far from certain, but the two men did bear a striking resemblance to each other.

"Did you hear about this?" I asked, looking toward Falin.

He glanced at the screen, but he didn't answer as his focus returned to his plate.

Did that mean yes? No? Or was he just avoiding speaking to me. I frowned at him and turned back to the TV. Lusa went on to mention that the body had been found in an alley earlier in the evening, and that while the police weren't releasing any information, witnesses said the man who'd found him had tried to resuscitate Mr. Murphy, who had no obvious wounds, but to no avail.

By the time she moved on to the next story, my fork lay on my plate, the forgotten food cooling. I hadn't confirmed to Jenson that the unicorn was pure glamour at the café because I didn't like admitting I could see through glamour. Now I wished I had. The rider—if it really was him—ending up dead a few hours later was too much of a coincidence.

I slid off the bed, but as I stood, dark spots filled the corners of my eyes. I swayed, dizzy for a moment. I pressed my hand to my forehead, ready to sink back down—I had no interest in hitting the ground for the second time today. The sensation passed as quickly as it hit. *Did I catch Rianna's cold?* I shook my head. I didn't have any cold-like symptoms, so most likely it was just the exhaustion of too many days of poor sleep mixed with the massive amount of magic I'd used today.

Dropping the rest of the uneaten steak into PC's bowl, I trudged over to the sink with my plate. That put me directly beside Falin, a proximity that made my shoulders tighten, my whole back going rigid. I tried not to let the tension show as I all but dropped my plate into the sink, but it didn't matter. Falin's gaze remained locked on his own plate, and I retreated back around the counter. Too fast.

The dizziness struck again, and I clutched at the counter as darkness filled my vision.

When the black dots cleared, Falin was staring at me. "Are you all right?"

"Fine," I said, jerking my hand back from the counter as if that was the damning evidence of the dizzy spell. "I think I caught something."

Falin set down his plate and crossed the small kitchen area, but he stopped, still two feet short of actually reaching me. "Fae do not 'catch' illness."

I shrugged. "Well, my heritage is rather questionable."

Lines of concern cut deep around his mouth, drawing down the edges of his eyes. The expression looked genuine, but how could I be sure? At the Fall Equinox he'd made a point of proving he couldn't be trusted—a very cutting point, as in with the edge of his blades. That happened right after he tricked me, then said he loved me, and then warned me to never trust him. His display of emotion now could be some ruse conjured by the Winter Queen in which he had no choice but to play out his given part. I couldn't believe anything where he was concerned.

But, oh, I wanted to.

It wasn't his fault he couldn't be trusted. It might have made me a fool, but I really did believe that he cared for me. Of course, him caring didn't make him any less dangerous. That was one reason this sucky situation was so awkward.

"Alexis . . ." He reached out, stepping forward to close the gap between us.

I retreated, dodging around the one chair in the loft, a stool, so it blocked his path. Not my bravest move, but necessary. "What do you know about the unicorn from today?" I asked, as much to redirect his attention as a general wish to know.

He stopped, and for a moment I thought he wasn't going to let it drop. Then he seemed to draw back into himself and the concern on his face vanished as if it had never been there, his features going remote, icy.

"The one on Main Street? We received reports about it, but by the time agents arrived, it was nowhere to be found."

That didn't surprise me. If the media hadn't made it in time, there had been little chance the FIB would.

"It was glamour."

If my words surprised Falin, he didn't let it show. He also didn't ask how I knew. He was aware I could see through glamour.

After a moment's hesitation, he nodded. "I assumed as much. There hasn't been a verified unicorn sighting since the Renaissance."

Now it was my turn to look surprised. *So they really do exist.* Or at least, they had at one time. Maybe they would again. Stranger things had happened. The point was, this one hadn't been real.

"The man riding the glamour was human. The news thinks he's dead."

Falin frowned again. Glamour meant Fae involvement, and we both knew it.

"I heard," he said, nodding toward the television.

"Are you looking into it?"

He gave me a blank look, his features giving away nothing. He was the head agent of the local FIB—surely they were looking into it, right? His focus moved to the dishes in the sink. There was nothing companionable about the silence. It was a force that filled the small room, choking out the possibility of more conversation.

How long had I been home? *Surely Holly and Caleb are finished with their movie by now.*

"I'll just grab a change of clothes and get out of your way," I mumbled as I headed toward my dresser.

There was a clink as Falin set a still-soapy plate on the sink and turned around. "Alex, you realize I'm ordered to live with you. If you aren't living here, I have to go wherever you are."

I froze, a camisole slipping from my fingers. "You mean . . ." If I kept sleeping in Caleb's guest room or made a habit of staying at the office, the queen's order would force him to follow? Caleb was already furious about Falin staying in the loft. He'd probably evict me if Falin moved into his guest room. I closed the dresser drawer much harder than needed. I hated this, but there was no human authority I could turn to, and the highest Faerie authority was the queen—at least in Nekros—and she was the one who'd given the order in the first place.

My nightclothes clutched in my hands, I turned away from the dresser. "Are you actually ordered to sleep in my bed?"

"I haven't been, have I?" He pointed to a neatly folded pile of bed linens in the far corner of the room. I hadn't noticed them before. Two pillows sat on top of the bedding.

"Right. Well, then, my room is part of the greater house, so if you are simply ordered to live with me, that should meet the requirement," I said, and glanced at him for affirmation. When he frowned but didn't disagree, I nodded. "Good. I'll be downstairs. Come on, PC." And with that, I left the awkward ambiance of my loft.

Chapter 4

❖

Ever wake to that feeling, before you even open your eyes, that you are no longer alone in a room? It's one of the creepiest sensations, doubly so, because in the middle of the night, in a dark room, I couldn't see a thing. My eyes were too damaged.

Blood pounded in my ears and I strained to hear over it, searching the quiet night for sounds that someone was there. I heard nothing but PC snoring at my feet and the slight buzz of the house wards. Even Caleb and Holly were finally silent. I should have been relieved that the wards hadn't been disturbed; after all, they were meant to ensure nothing malicious and no one uninvited got inside, but too much had happened in the last few months for me to feel truly safe, even behind wards.

I had a moment of indecision. If someone was in the room and I opened my eyes, they might notice, and it wasn't like my eyes would do me any good in the dark. But it was a reflex. My instincts demanded I *try* to look around. I fought the urge as I instead listened for something disturbing the darkness and wished my dagger was closer, like under my pillow. I hadn't quite gotten that paranoid yet, but maybe I should have. Unfortunately, the dagger was in my purse somewhere on the floor by the bed. Fumbling for it in the dark would definitely give me away.

"You're cute when you pretend to sleep," a deep and wonderfully familiar voice said.

My eyes popped open, my fear washing away in delight. Normally, with the room so dark, I couldn't have seen someone leaning against the closed guest room door, his thumbs hooked in the loops of his faded jeans. But Death wasn't a normal guy, and I wasn't exactly seeing him with my eyes. The smile that tipped his full lips was both relaxed and suggestive, and he watched me with hooded hazel eyes, his dark hair falling forward to brush his chin.

"What time is it?" I asked as I rolled into a sitting position and stretched. A yawn caught me unawares in the middle of the stretch, and I pressed the back of my hand over my mouth to cover it.

"Late or early, whichever you prefer to call it."

I nodded at the answer. There was a clock beside the bed, but I couldn't make out the numbers.

I smiled at Death, but it felt awkward and I clutched at the edge of the comforter where it still bunched at my legs, pulling it self-consciously higher on my thighs. I'd seen Death only once in the last two weeks, and we hadn't gotten much of a chance to talk. He was my oldest and closest friend, but during a case involving a creature from the land of the dead who'd been riding mortal bodies, we'd become more. A lot more. I wasn't sure if we were exactly dating—did adults really date? That felt like such a high school term—but we'd become lovers and I'd promised I wouldn't freak out because of the change. I didn't do relationships well.

But now? Well, he'd kind of disappeared on me again, and since we'd switched essences back, I was once again mortal and he was a soul collector. The relationship was forbidden. And he was just leaning against the door, watching me, not saying anything.

I tugged the comforter up higher, until it covered most of the thin silky cami I'd worn to bed. Death watched the movement, one eyebrow lifting, and then he pushed away from the door. My breath caught as he strolled across the room, his gait casual but his presence seeming to take up more space, so that by the time he stopped in front of me there seemed to be no air left in the room. I wanted to reach out to him, to fling myself in his arms, but I also had the urge to scoot back, putting more distance between us. I'd like to say it was a compromise between the two that I did neither, but in truth I just froze, waiting.

Death, on the other hand, had no hesitation. He reached out and trailed one finger down my cheek.

"No running, remember?" he whispered. His finger traced my jaw and he tilted my chin so I had no choice but to look into the fathoms of his eyes.

Then he kissed me.

It started light, just a teasing brush as much breath as lips. My hesitation melted away. The comforter fell from my fingers, and he deepened the kiss, drawing me into his arms. I met him eagerly, almost greedily, standing and lifting onto my toes as my hands slid up, over his shoulders.

I nipped at his bottom lip playfully and his mouth pressed a smile into mine. When he chuckled, the soft sound rippled over my flesh, sending a surge of excitement through me. Turning, he sat on the bed, dragging me down with him until I was straddling his lap.

The heat of his body passed through his jeans into my bare thighs and I was extremely conscious of how very short my silky shorts were. That of course, didn't stop me from kissing him again.

We were both breathless when we broke apart and from where his body pressed against mine it was obvious he was happy to be exactly where we were. Still . . .

"Isn't this against the rules?" I asked, pushing back slightly so I opened the smallest of gaps between our bodies.

He made a sound that could have been anything and leaned forward, pressing a kiss against my shoulder. He brushed the strap of my cami aside and kissed the spot it had covered a moment before.

I pressed a hand against his chest, stopping him. "I'm serious. What happens when your boss finds out about this? He's psychic, maybe omnipresent." And I'd met the Mender, who seemed to run the soul collectors. He was freaking scary.

"He doesn't know everything. And there have been others who have hidden things from him."

"You mean the Reaper?"

"Among others."

I frowned, my body cooling. Several months past a grave witch changeling and her soul collector lover had nearly torn reality and the world as we know it apart in an attempt to be together. I didn't like the parallel.

Pushing back, I stood. The second I lost contact with Death, my innate planeweaving ability stopped pulling him into reality and he scrambled after me before the bed became unsubstantial under him. I turned from him, wrapping my arms over my chest, my hands balled into fists. The movement must have been too sudden because black dots gathered in the corners of my eyes, a wave of dizziness crashing over me. I'd have fallen if Death hadn't caught me.

"What's wrong?" he asked, and once my vision cleared, I could see the concern written across his face.

I shook my head, but didn't push out of his arms. "I think I'm coming down with something. Don't worry about it. Now what will happen if the Mender finds out you've been with me?"

His frown matched mine. "You know many of our secrets already. Our relationship hasn't been expressly forbidden recently."

Which so didn't mean it wasn't forbidden. Nor did it answer my question. "What will happen?"

"He might reassign me to a different area. Somewhere that will make it harder for me to see you."

Might? I stared into his face, searching for what he was hiding. "And worst-case scenario?"

He sighed. "He might strip my powers and I'll move on like any other soul."

I swallowed and forced my nod to be slow, controlled. To not let the frantic panic show even though he'd just admitted being with me might be a death sentence for him. He'd pass on and be gone forever.

"Alex . . ." He started, but trailed off. His gaze flickering over my face as if he was memorizing every pore in my skin.

Then colors swirled in his irises. Once I hadn't known why that happened or what it meant, but now I did.

"You have to go," I said, and even to my own ears, my voice sounded distant, guarded.

His nod was reluctant but definite.

Somewhere, one of the souls in his care was at a pivotal moment in their life, or their death. His eyes did that when he saw possible lines of the future, at least one of which would lead to a soul that needed to be collected.

I lifted up on my toes and kissed him, but it was a chaste kiss compared to all the ones that had come before. When we broke apart he wove his fingers into my hair and pressed his forehead against mine. It was more friendly than intimate, with a hint of sorrow that hung like an albatross between us.

"I'll return when I can," he whispered into the heavy silence. "No running."

He didn't give me time to protest, but in the next instant vanished, leaving me alone, staring at the darkness where he'd been. I stood there a long time. Until PC whined from the bed. Then I slid back under the covers, but it was a long time after that before I finally fell back asleep.

*   *   *

When I woke next it was to the sound of bells. Wedding bells. Coming from my phone . . .

I totally hadn't set that ringtone. Which meant it was likely the work of my self-appointed ghostly sidekick. He was getting poltergeist good at manipulating objects on the living plane.

"Roy, when your insubstantial butt appears again, I ought to . . ." I muttered, rolling to the edge of the bed, but I didn't finish, suddenly winded just from the effort of moving and attempting to fish my phone out of my purse. My body felt heavy and sluggish with more than just clinging sleep. I was exhausted. If not for the thick block of sunlight peeking around the curtain alerting me to the fact I'd overslept, I may have believed I'd gotten no rest last night at all. I felt more tired than when I'd gone to bed. *I definitely caught something.* My hand finally landed on the phone, and I pulled it free so I could read the display.

Tamara.

Well, at least the wedding bells made more sense. She was getting married this weekend. I hadn't missed any duties, had I? There were no more dress fittings, and all the prep work that could be done beforehand had been finished. All that was left was the rehearsal dinner tonight—and a glance at the clock proved I hadn't slept *that* late.

I hit the TALK button.

"Hey, Tam, what's up?"

"I can't go through with it."

Please don't be talking about the wedding. Because I was *so* not the person to give advice on committed relationships. "With what?"

"What do you mean, 'with what'? What do you think, Alex? The wedding, of course."

Oh, shit.

"What happened?"

Tamara sighed, the sound rushing through the phone. A slight catch at the very end betrayed that she was either on the edge of tears, or she'd already been crying. "Nothing, exactly. Everything. Oh, hell, I don't know."

This was not good. I slid out of bed and padded across the floor to the guest room door, hoping I could enlist some girl-talk reinforcement from Holly. I stepped into the hall, but found it quiet, both Holly's and Caleb's doors open and their rooms empty. Holly was a morning person and had probably left hours ago. Which meant I was alone. I slunk back to the bed and sank into the mattress.

"Well, you have until you exchange vows to back out of the wedding," I said, and Tamara made a strangled sound that was probably a sob. Crap, I was no good at this. Why hadn't she called Holly?

Tamara was one of my best friends. We'd met on the very first case John had brought me in on, and while we'd been far from instant friends—she'd just been appointed head ME at the time and was less than thrilled about some college freshman with no credentials being brought in to examine a murder victim—she was a witch as well as a scientist and eventually mutual respect grew into a friendship. But while we had many shared interests, our view on relationships was drastically different. She'd been with her fiancé, Ethan, for about as long as I'd known her. If all she was suffering from currently was pre-wedding jitters, I definitely didn't want my relationship-phobic advice to influence her into something she would regret for the rest of her life. Which meant I needed to proceed with extreme caution.

She hadn't said anything, and I could still hear soft snuffling sounds despite the fact I was pretty sure she was muffling the phone with her palm. Which meant I needed to say something that didn't drive my foot in my mouth.

"You love him, right?"

"More than anything."

"And you were waiting for how long for him to pop the question? I'll be honest here, after he did, you were rather annoying with the sheer glee of being engaged."

"That's just it, Alex," she said with a catch in her voice. "It took him forever to propose, and then after he did, I couldn't get him to nail down a date until . . . And what if he is only marrying me because . . . And we don't even know if . . ."

She trailed off again, but I knew what hadn't been said in her pauses. I knew what had finally prompted Ethan to agree to a date, as well as why this wedding had been planned in a little less than a month. Tamara had unexpectedly begun expecting.

To complicate matters, Tamara had been attacked in the morgue several weeks ago, and had nearly transformed into a ghoul. We'd stopped her life force from being drained away before permanent damage to her had occurred, but no one was quite sure what damage might have been done to the baby she carried. She was still a month short of finding out the gender and seeing if all the organs and bones were forming properly, but we did know the baby was a fighter. He or she had stuck it out, and the baby's heartbeat still looked good. But while the baby had measured right on time in early ultrasounds, the little one was now falling behind and measuring small.

Tamara was stressed. And who could blame her? Brides were always stressed, and she also had all the uncertainty involved with an unplanned pregnancy and concerns for the health of the baby. And yeah, Ethan may have dragged his feet a little, but the man adored her. He'd proposed long before the baby arrived in the picture.

"Tam, I have no doubts that Ethan loves you and wants to be walking down the aisle with you tomorrow. Even if there wasn't a baby to consider—"

A sharp sob cut across the phone. *Shit.* I hadn't meant

it as such, but I'd just broached the fact that the baby might not make it to the point of being a consideration. Foot meet mouth. Geez, I was bad at this.

After a long moment of helplessly listening to her sob, I said, "Is it too early in the day for me to go buy an un-birthday cake and show up on your doorstep?"

She laughed then. It wasn't exactly a happy sound, but at least it was a laugh. "I'll pass on the cake. Food still isn't agreeing with me. Besides, we have a wedding cake and a groom's cake in two days. I'm going to be stuffed with cake by the time I leave for my honeymoon." She sighed. "And I'm meeting Ethan for an early lunch soon, so I should probably go get ready. I'm doing the right thing, right? I mean, if you were me, you'd get married Sunday, right?"

I tried to imagine being in her situation. I couldn't picture it. Of course, my boyfriend was a soul collector other people typically saw only during their last moments of life, and I'd just learned his being with me might lead to his soul crossing over to the other side. I definitely didn't foresee all our friends and family gathering to watch us get married anytime soon. Besides, vows would be tricky considering I didn't even know his name, and then there was that whole "until death do you part" complication. Yeah, even if I didn't have commitment issues, that would never work out.

"I think only you know if it is right for you. If you decide it isn't right, I'll support you," I finally said. "But in that case, I'm totally keeping your wedding gift — it would be amazing in my kitchen."

"Oh really? Well, I guess that is fair." Again she gave a weak laugh that sounded a little raw from tears. "Thanks, Al. I actually feel a little better. And it means a lot to me to know you'll have my back if I borrow your running shoes and turn tail."

I cringed as her thanks caused a debt to open between us, but only said, "I hope that's a metaphoric loan because I favor boots, and I can assure you that running is neither fun nor easy in them. Besides, they wouldn't go with your dress."

Now I got a more genuine-sounding laugh. Then she said she needed to go to meet Ethan and I promised not to be late for the rehearsal dinner before I said my good-byes and ended the call.

"Well, that was painful but hopefully not a complete disaster," I said to PC as I dropped my phone back into my purse. The little dog just cocked an ear and tilted his head. He was waiting for one of his favorite words, like *food* or *out*. And he probably needed both of those after how late I'd slept.

Dragging myself off the bed, I trudged across the room again, gathering my things as I went. Then, with PC prancing around my feet, I left the main portion of the house and climbed the stairs to my room, expecting it to be empty.

It wasn't.

Falin didn't say anything when I opened the door, but I could feel his eyes on me, watching. He said nothing as I filled PC's bowl, gathered clothes, and slunk off to my shower. He hadn't moved by the time I emerged from the bathroom. If he would have headed to the station, I likely would have dismissed the day as a sick day and rested for the rehearsal tonight—I didn't want to be sick for Tamara's wedding—but he hadn't left, and that huge weight of silence that had chased me out of my room last night still hung in the air between us. I had to get out of the house, and my office was as good a place as any.

By noon Rianna hadn't shown, nor had Ms. B. I had no clients on my docket for the day, and I was seriously considering locking up and taking a nap on the love seat in the waiting room when the chime on the front door sounded.

I reached with my senses as I stood, my magic sensitivity scanning the unseen visitor for spells. Nothing. The lack of magic confirmed it definitely wasn't Rianna, but didn't tell me much else about my visitor. Stepping out of my office, I found a man in a dark suit standing just beyond the doorway. He looked vaguely familiar, but I couldn't place his face.

"Ms. Craft?"

I nodded, summoning my professional smile as I crossed the room. I made it only halfway before he spoke again.

"Governor Caine requests your presence at his estate."

I ground to an abrupt halt. *That* was where I'd seen him—he was one of my father's drivers. The smile fell from my face and I crossed my arms over my chest.

"You can tell him—" I started, but the man interrupted me.

"He was most insistent. You have been dodging his calls."

My shoulders hitched, just a notch, because it was true. And as it was true, I couldn't deny it. My father wanted me to come by for more glamour lessons, which I desperately needed to learn to control, but I wasn't sure I wanted to learn from *him*.

My father was an enigma. He played the long game, and apparently had been doing so for quite some time. I wasn't sure exactly how old he was, but I did know he was once Nekros's first governor, and at that time he was openly fae. Fifty years later he was once again the governor, with a new name and face, only this time he was with the Humans First party, an antiwitch antifae organization. He'd disowned me when I was younger, distanced our known association as much as possible, and I would have said hated me for being a wyrd witch. Now I knew it played into his long game. I just didn't know how.

Even scarier, I'd also recently learned he'd had me spelled most of my life, which was why I hadn't known I was fae until the spell began breaking under the Blood Moon. I'd washed away the remaining effects of the spell at the Harvest Festival when Falin had tricked me into drinking Faerie wine. Which was when I'd started shimmering like a glowworm and I'd had my first glamour lesson with my father. I'd agreed to call him to schedule another lesson, but I never had.

The man opened the front door, motioning me to exit. Beyond him, I could see a black town car idling at the curb.

I hesitated and the driver turned toward me. "I'm to remind you of his promptness in responding to your recent calls."

I wasn't sure if that was meant to guilt me or was a threat that I might owe my father a favor, which he could call in at his discretion. Either way, it was a true enough statement. I'd called him several times when all other avenues had closed on me. With a sigh, I retrieved my purse.

It looked as if I was off to see daddy dearest.

It wasn't until the driver showed me into the house and led me all the way to the second floor to stop in front of the suite that had, until recently, belonged to my sister but now contained an accidental pocket of Faerie, that the nagging suspicion at the back of my brain beat through my exhaustion and screamed that something was off. Cracking my shields, I studied the driver's profile. Under the generically familiar face was another, stranger, more striking face. A face that hung in a place of honor at the statehouse.

My father's face.

"I should have known," I whispered as he opened the enchanted locks on the door. "You never would have sent a staff member to retrieve your witchy daughter from the Magic Quarter. Tongues might wag."

My father glanced over his shoulder and grinned. It was one of the most genuine expressions I'd ever seen on him. "You do have a bad habit of seeing through glamour.

I simply wanted to test the ability. I take it by how long it took that you have to *See* intentionally."

I didn't answer. I don't think he even expected me to, because his grin only grew at my silence.

"Come in, come in," he said, ushering me into the room and shutting the door behind us. I felt the magic in the door relock as it closed.

I shuddered at the feeling. I didn't like being locked in this room. Well, honestly, it wasn't this room that was the problem. It was the next. Formerly Casey's bedroom, it was now the scene of some of my worst nightmares. Mostly because a few months ago I'd nearly died there. As had my sister. Oh yeah, and I'd nearly been the trigger that could have ended the world. Nothing big, right?

It took more effort to cross the sitting room and enter the bedroom than I'd like to admit, each step twisting my stomach as my clenched fists shook by my sides. But when I crossed the once-invisible line that marked the circle, everything changed.

I'd been here a few weeks back, so I already expected the maddening mix of merged realities. The pockets of Faerie and the land of the dead that spilled into human reality were splashed around the room like a Pollock painting, the realities bleeding and merging in ways they were never meant to do. But no, that was no surprise to me. What stopped me in my tracks was the sudden lightness I felt. Like my exhaustion had fallen from my shoulders and I could float if needed.

I don't know if I made a sound or if it was simply my expression, but my father stopped and his grin fell away. He didn't just look at me, his eyes scrutinized me, a frown growing across his face.

"You're unwell. You should have answered my calls earlier," he said after an agonizingly long moment.

"Because that would have prevented a virus?"

"Alexis, you do not have a virus. You're fading. I did not expect it to happen quite this quickly, but from the looks of it, you're teetering into the second phase. I imagine you've been feeling rather exhausted for weeks now."

I had been, but that was because I hadn't gotten a good night's sleep in weeks, wasn't it? I couldn't be fading. Could I?

The fae were said to have been fading before the Magical Awakening. Lack of belief was literally erasing them from the world. That was no longer an issue. In fact, there were rumors of old legends awakening in the few wild spaces left in the modern world. The fae were no longer fading, and surely I, in particular, wasn't.

His eyes scanned my face and I could feel him noting my doubt. "Have you ever asked yourself why there are no unaligned fae? All either belong to a court or have taken the vows of the solitary fae."

I shrugged. "Because the ruling monarchs take exception and make their lives miserable?" Or at least, that was what was happening in my life currently.

"Do try to take this seriously," he said, the reprimand in his voice clear. "Fae must join a court or be granted the vows of the independent fae because it is through their court Faerie sustains them. The more powerful the court, the more fae it can maintain. Without a solid tie to a court, there is only the most tenuous tie to Faerie and the fae will fade."

I swallowed, digesting the words. "You're saying that I'll die if I don't join a court?" I reeled under the idea. I'd been told for months I'd eventually have to choose a court, but I'd been avoiding it. If I joined a court, I'd be bound to stay inside the areas it controlled. Nekros was currently inside the winter court, but the doors moved. No one knew when the doors to Faerie would shift, rearranging which court held which territory, but when they did, all fae within that territory would have to follow.

The courts had a scary amount of power over their subjects, even the independents within the court's boundaries, but much more over those who'd sworn fealty to the court itself. I hadn't interacted with all of the courts, but what I'd seen thus far was enough to let me know I didn't want my life bound to one. Especially not the winter court. But if I joined a different court, I'd have to move. My friends, my business, my whole life was in Nekros—I didn't want to leave. When Falin had first been ordered to move in with me, I'd sent a petition to be declared independent, but the queen had denied my request.

And so, I was court-less.

And that could kill me.

My thoughts flew to Rianna, whom I'd assumed was sick because she'd been weak, dizzy . . . I didn't even know what else. "What if other people are bound to an unaligned fae? What happens to them if she fades?"

My father cocked an eyebrow, interest gleaming through his concern. "Like changelings and lesser fae? What have you gotten into, Alexis?" He rubbed his chin between two fingers and his thumb. "That would explain the acceleration of your decline."

"Yes, but what happens to them?"

"Their tie to you would normally be what ties them back to Faerie. Without that, they will drain you until your self-preservation naturally cuts them off. Then they would fade fast, very fast. Especially if they spent large amounts of time outside of Faerie."

Great. My indecision was killing my friends. I had to join a court, and soon.

Chapter 5

"I need to sit down," I said, though this time the sick feeling surging through me had nothing to do with fading.

My father led me around the patches of decay hanging in the air where reality touched the land of the dead, and deposited me on a large stone bench in the center of the room. Once I sank onto it, I just sat there, staring at nothing.

I had to join a court. No more waffling. No more hoping if I ignored the issue long enough that it would go away. I had to make a decision. Now. Well, maybe not right this second, but soon. Very soon.

Fading. I hadn't even known that was possible.

"What court are you in?" I asked, the words tumbling over my lips messily, like I was too numb to form them properly.

"That isn't your concern."

My head jerked up, but my gaze was too sluggish to snap to my father. Finally my eyes found him, but he wasn't looking at me. He was staring at the far corner of the room.

I knew he was court fae, not independent. He'd told

me that much, but not to which court he belonged. He wasn't winter court, which meant he shouldn't have been in Nekros. He was in deep hiding, but I had no idea how he defied one of the basic laws of Faerie. If I could figure out how he was doing it . . .

My father's hand shot out and twisted, as if to snatch something out of the air. But he didn't. At least, not with his physical hands.

Something moved in the shadows—the same shadows he'd been studying so intently. I hadn't noticed it when I'd first entered, but the room was bigger than the last time I'd been here. It had been a large but still rather normal bedroom before that fateful night under the Blood Moon, but glancing around now, I realized that there was far too much space for the room's original dimensions. This pocket of Faerie was growing. *And there is something in the shadows.*

A chill swept cold fingers across my nape, and I squinted. My eyes worked better in Faerie than in the mortal realm, and while this small pocket was a mess of planes that shouldn't have touched, my sight was clear here. Still, the thing in the shadows was so out of context, at first I couldn't make sense of what I saw. There were wires and wings and limbs . . . I blinked. No, the *wires* were actually vines, bound tight around a figure I finally identified as a harpy. My father lowered his clenched fist, and the vines drooped downward, lowering the suspended fae.

She thrashed, the talons at the crooks of her wings straining toward the vines, as did the beak that took the place of her nose and upper lip, and the large talons on her toes. Her efforts gained her nothing. She was well and truly caught, her wings and legs stretched to their limits by the constraining vines. More vines curled around her waist and throat.

Since the vines appeared to be growing directly out of

the wall, I assumed they had been simple glamour initially, but my father must have been very, very good, because this little pocket of Faerie had accepted the vines as real and even with my shields cracked, they looked solid. The vines lowered the harpy until she hung in the air a mere yard ahead of my father. He studied her, shaking his head.

"Your master's impatience is noted," he told her after she finally stilled to hang limply in the restraints.

"He wanted to be prepared when you returned with the girl," she said, her voice a harsh squawk.

I raised a questioning eyebrow at my father, as I was most definitely the girl in question. He didn't spare me a glance. I did not like where this was going. I considered walking out right then and there, but I had my doubts that I could make it past the magical lock on the door.

"I appear to be here. Where is he?" My father asked, but while the question was delivered lightly, there was an edge to his voice. He opened his hand, flattening his palm, and the vines fell away from the harpy.

She touched the ground for only a moment before jumping back into the air, her large wings stirring up gusts of wind as she took off. She soared toward the shadows and they ate her form, swallowing her from sight. I frowned. The unnatural sky where the ceiling should have been showed the night sky of Faerie, the stars so close it seemed that if I stretched I might be able to reach one, but the moon was missing. Either it had set already or it was in the new-moon phase. As it was probably about one in the afternoon in the mortal realm, it was hard to guess what the moon cycle in Faerie might be. Regardless, as the only light filtered in from the stars, the room was darker than the last time I'd been here, but the shadows the harpy had dived into seemed too deep for the length of the room.

I'd seen harpies before, during my brief visit to the

shadow court, so I wasn't shocked when three figures stepped through what must have been a magical door hidden in the shadows.

I recognized one of the figures immediately by his oiled black armor, the dark, pointed goatee, and the un-concealed blood coating his palms. The Shadow King. Two steps behind him was a smaller figure, who I guessed must have been the planebender. He would have been the one who opened the hole between this normally closed pocket of Faerie and the shadow court. As with the first time I'd seen him, his small form was obscured by an all-encompassing cloak, a hood pulled down over his face. The third figure I didn't know. Sleagh Maith based on his striking features and inner glow that made him shimmer despite the shadows around him. His long dark hair hung loose around his shoulders and he wore gray armor similar to the king's.

I managed not to scowl at the small group, but it was a near thing. Last time I'd seen the Shadow King he'd fol-lowed a rescue from the winter court by locking me in a lavishly decorated room. Circumstances had prevented me from having to find out what the king had planned for me, but now here we were again.

"I understand you're acquainted with King Nandin?" my father asked as he ushered me toward the newly ar-rived party.

My first instinct was to bark out a curt *yes*, but even if he wasn't *my* king, he was still a Faerie monarch, old and powerful. So I inclined my head slightly and simply said, "Your majesty."

"Dearest niece," he responded, lifting his arms to en-gulf me in a hug.

Oh, did I mention the shadow king was my great-granduncle on my mother's side? I didn't return the hug, but I didn't pull away either. As soon as he dropped his arms, I stepped back, out of reach. If he noticed, he didn't point it out, but instead turned to the stranger with him.

"Alexis, this is Dugan."

The gray-armored Sleagh Maith bowed, which made me wonder if I was supposed to curtsy or something. As I was in leather pants and knee-high boots instead of a skirt, I decided that would look ridiculous. Instead I lifted my hand in a halfhearted wave.

"Uh, hi?" I said, and then turned a questioning look at my father.

He smiled, but it was his politician smile, the one that looked genuine, even crinkled the edges of his eyes, but wasn't real. "Dugan is prince of the shadow court."

Good for him? I didn't say it aloud though. Instead I said, "So does that make you my cousin?"

Dugan jerked, as if my words had stung him. It had seemed an innocent enough question.

The king chuckled, shaking his head. "No, my dear. You share no blood, nor I with him. The title is honorary, and indicates to the court that one day I may step down and make him king."

Okay. I glanced between my father, the king, and Dugan. I'd thought my father brought me here for a glamour lesson, but apparently not. I had a growing suspicion that he wanted me to join the shadow court—that was the only reason I could think of for the king and prince to be here.

A moment passed before Dugan turned to my father. "She doesn't know?"

My father gave the other fae a nonchalant shrug. "Your king was impatient."

Dugan's brow knotted, and then he stepped forward. He bowed again, taking my hand. "My lady, it is a great pleasure to see you again."

I frowned. "Have we met?"

"It was a long time ago."

I tried recalling having ever seen Dugan before. It was possible that I had caught a glance of him at the fall equinox, but that was recent and I certainly hadn't interacted with him. He had to mean when I was a child. If so, I had no memories of him.

My father stepped to my shoulder. He pitched his voice in a low whisper, his words meant only for me. "Dugan is your betrothed."

I jerked my hand out of Dugan's and reeled back, away from the group. No one tried to stop me. All three fae watched me, expressions inquisitive but distant.

"You have to be kidding," I said, focusing on my father.

"I would never joke about such things. You have been affianced since birth."

I laughed, I couldn't help it. Between learning I was fading and taking my friends with me, and learning I was betrothed, I'd had too many shocks in a short period of time. It was laugh or scream.

"Dugan has an impressive pedigree," my father said, his tone making it clear he disapproved of my behavior. "His many times great-grandfather was a planeweaver, so there is a higher than average chance your child will inherit the ability."

I thought about that. About what I knew of my father. About what he'd said the last time I was here when he'd told me Casey was none of his, simply a backup of my mother's genetic line.

"And engineering planeweavers is what this really boils down to, isn't it? You think I want to be part of your little breeding program? Well, think again."

My father lifted his hand in a placating gesture. "Be reasonable, Alexis. The fae have gone without planeweavers too long. There are kinks and knots in the fabric of Faerie's reality and planeweavers are needed to unravel and mend the damage. You have an opportunity to help all of Faeric." He must have been able to tell by my expression that I wasn't buying any of it. He sighed. "You have to join a court anyway. Entering, say, a twenty-year union with Dugan would solidify your position in fae society as well as give you a companion who can guide you in the intricacies of court and help you master your glamour. The child produced by such a union would be an extra bonus."

I just blinked at him, not sure what to say. So of course, what fell out of my mouth when I opened it focused on only the least important point. "You mean marriages among fae expire?"

"Of course. Fae are near immortal. Divorce would get very tedious otherwise."

Right. Of course. Why not? I shook my head, trying to jar my thoughts into something akin to order. It was no use, I had too many things vying for attention. I needed to get away from here. To think things through. To plan my next step.

No one planned to give me that opportunity.

"Listen, Dugan," I said, turning toward the prince. He was tall, which wasn't surprising as most Sleagh Maith were, and I could admit he was nice to look at, but I just wasn't interested. Besides, I had a boyfriend already, of sorts. "I'm sure you're an interesting guy and all, but I don't know you—"

Dugan stepped toward me. "I had not anticipated the need to court you, but of course I am willing."

Gee, how romantic.

The shadow king whispered something to Dugan. I couldn't hear what was said, but my would-be suitor's face darkened even as he nodded.

"I am a master of glamour. If it is easier on you, I can look like this." In the space of a heartbeat, his dark hair lightened, the angles of his face changed, and no longer was a handsome stranger standing in front of me, but now an even more handsome—and intimately familiar— figure.

I gawked at the prince, who now looked exactly like Falin. A mix of fury and sick surprise surged through me. Fury that he—or really, *they*—thought they could manipulate me so easily, but also shock that an obviously proud fae would submit to taking the likeness of another man to entice a girl to his bed. What could my father possibly offer as a reward to be worth that? As was often the case when my father was involved, I felt like I lacked several key pieces to even begin to guess the shape of this particular puzzle.

Still, before this stunt my answer was a resounding no. Now? Yeah, now it was a hell no, not ever, not even if I was as immortal as they claimed.

"I have to get back to work," I said, turning from the group and heading for the door.

"Alexis, you still have to join a court." While my father's voice didn't exactly sound smug, it did sound as if regardless of what I did, he was confident the ultimate outcome would be of his preference.

"Yeah, I'll work on that. But it's not happening today." I reached the doorway and stepped through, back into mortal reality. Leaving the pocket of Faerie hit me harder than I expected as the exhaustion that had vanished while I was inside once again crushed me as soon as I left. I almost stumbled under the weight of it, but I didn't and after a moment I turned back toward the door and called out, "Are you giving me a ride back to my office, or do I need to call a cab?"

Chapter 6

❦

My father did give me a ride, though neither of us spoke during the trip. As I slid out of the car in front of my office, he leaned across the seat.

"Be very careful, Alexis. My spell no longer binds you to Faerie. You do not have much time before you fade from this life. The shadow court is a good choice for you, at least for now. Come to me when you are ready to accept it."

"Right," I said, and slammed the door. While I had no intention of marrying Dugan, I also wasn't going to doom Rianna, Ms. B, or the little elusive garden gnome. If I couldn't find a ruler to grant me independent status, I'd have to join a court. I didn't think it would be shadow, but that might be a slightly preferable choice to winter.

With my thoughts ruminating on everything that had happened in the last two hours, I stuck my key in the lock, but it didn't turn over. I frowned and pulled open the already unlocked door. *Did Rianna come in after all?*

I got my answer quickly enough.

Leaning on the reception desk was one familiar blond-haired fae. After everything that had happened, I double-checked to make sure his appearance didn't change when

I cracked my shields. Nope, no more glamour than he normally wore to tame down his Sleagh Maith traits. It really was Falin.

"I could have sworn I locked that door," I said, jerking my head toward the aforementioned door.

He gave me a half shrug. "I got tired of waiting outside."

Right. So he broke into Tongues for the Dead. Honestly though, with everything else going on, this fact didn't seem important enough to bother with, so I let it drop.

"Do you need something?" Because aside from the unavoidable interaction of living in my room, he'd done his best over the last two weeks to avoid me.

Falin nodded, but didn't answer immediately. Finally he pushed off the desk. "We have to go. You've been summoned by the queen."

The first time the Winter Queen had summoned me to Faerie, the FIB had issued an arrest warrant and Falin had attempted to hide me. This time, he'd accept no argument: I'd been summoned to Faerie and as a fae living inside winter court boundaries, I was going. He did permit a small detour, which was good with me—anything to prolong the time before appearing at court—except the reason we stopped was so I could find something more appropriate to wear.

Falin frowned at the slacks I held, shaking his head. "In all likelihood, if you show up to court in pants, the queen will change them into a gown."

Great. There was exactly one dress in my closet. My bridesmaid dress for Tamara's wedding. And I had no intention of wearing that monstrosity before the event Sunday because if I ruined it, I didn't have time to have another tailored.

But I didn't doubt him about the queen. The first time I'd gone to Faerie I'd lost one of my favorite outfits when the queen glamoured it into a ridiculous ball gown and Faerie had accepted the transformation as true.

Speaking of that gown . . .

I hurried to my linen closet and pulled out the boxes on the bottom shelf. The gown had been shoved unceremoniously in a bag in the back, complete with layers of petticoats and small ice flowers that had never melted. It was rather worse for the wear from the storage, and I shook it, trying to release the wrinkles.

"I can wear this," I said, holding up the dress.

Falin grimaced at its condition. I couldn't blame him, now that I really looked at it, the dress was in worse shape than just wrinkles. It had survived a hard night the only time I'd worn it, including a trip to the realm of dreams where I'd been carried off by dozens of clawed, scaled, and otherwise monstrous nightmares.

Okay, yeah, the dress wasn't at its best, but at least I wouldn't lose another outfit. With that thought in mind, I excused myself to the bathroom and changed.

Falin looked less than convinced when I emerged. I couldn't blame him. The gown was ratty and I felt rather like a child playing dress-up in the thing. To make matters worse, I didn't own any dress shoes. I needed to buy a pair of heels before Tam's wedding, but shopping for a pair hadn't made it to the top of my to-do list yet. Thankfully the gown hit the ground, so my boots wouldn't be immediately obvious under it.

Crossing the small room, I sat on the bed and strapped my dagger into place. The semicognizant blade crooned in my hand. It responded to my nervousness with a type of excitement that betrayed how badly it wanted to be drawn, used. A disturbing sensation, but it was a good dagger, fae-wrought with enchantments that let it cut through almost anything. Its ever-fight-ready eagerness had scared me off from carrying it for years, but now I never left the house without it—I'd needed it too many times over the last few months.

Of course, if I needed it today, it was going to be a bitch to draw. I'd wrestled the dagger from under this gown before, and there just wasn't an elegant—or more important, fast—way to hike up the multiple layers of tulle to reach the holster. But it wasn't like I could walk into the winter court with a blade strapped to my waist.

"Try this one," Falin said, holding out what looked like a larger version of my boot holster.

I took it from him and examined it. "A thigh holster? I doubt that will be easier."

"It is when you're wearing a gown like that," he said. I had my doubts, which he clearly read in my expression because after a moment he continued. "You'll have to make a small modification. You need to . . ." He trailed off, gesturing at the full skirt. Then he sighed. "I can show you," he said, but the words seemed to pain him.

After a moment's hesitation, he stepped forward, and forward, right into my personal bubble. In the last few weeks we'd barely spoken—his choice as much as mine—and he hadn't come within an arm's length of me. In fact, the last time he'd been this close, he'd kissed me, told me he loved me, and then pulled his knives on me and told me to stay far, far away from him.

I'd listened, and I would have stumbled out of reach now, except I was blocked in by the edge of the bed. I considered throwing myself back and trying to somersault over the bed. It was the kind of thing an action hero would do, probably drawing her weapon in the same move and having it locked on her target by the time she straightened. Me? I'd likely tangle myself in the huge gown and end up in a helpless pile. So I held my ground. Besides, Falin was clearly trying his hardest to look nonthreatening.

He knelt in front of me, lifting the edge of the gown and gathering it up, over my calf, my knees, up to my thigh.

"Uh, Falin, what are you . . . ?"

Without a word he picked up the thigh holster I didn't remember dropping and slipped it around the exposed skin of my right thigh. His fingers moved with absolute efficiency, not lingering or caressing, but regardless, heat still rose to my cheeks as his gloved hands worked over my thigh. He pulled the dagger and hilt from where they were mostly concealed in my boot and slid them into the new thigh holster and then checked that the straps were secure. I stared at the ceiling, reminding myself that there was nothing—could never be anything—between Falin and me. Besides, I had a boyfriend.

A boyfriend whose being with me was a death sentence to him and who I couldn't contact. Hell, I didn't even know his real name, but he was my oldest friend and I cared about him. And at least he wasn't likely to betray me at word one from the Winter Queen, unlike certain fae.

By the time Falin dropped the gown I was scowling, mostly at my own thoughts. When he stood, I nearly sighed in relief.

Then he drew his own dagger.

This time I did stumble backward, my calves slamming into the bed hard enough that my knees bent and I barely caught myself before falling onto the mattress. Falin frowned at me, and then down at the dagger in his hand.

"I mean you no harm," he said, and while his face was blank, his voice was rough, like all of his emotions had caught in his throat. "My word, I mean you no harm."

He was fae, so he couldn't lie. He'd given his word, he wouldn't harm me. At least, not right now. He reached out and I pressed myself harder against the bed. His frown deepened, but he didn't say anything else. He'd already given me his word—what else could he offer?

I forced myself still as his fingers landed on my hips and traced downward until he felt the hilt of the dagger on my upper thigh. He studied the hang of the gown a brief moment, fingering the gathered folds, and then, faster than I could react, he raised his dagger and sliced a long slit into the material. Despite his word, I winced, expecting pain to blossom in my leg. When it didn't I pried open my eyes in time to see him make similar slices through the layers of petticoats. Then he stepped back with a self-satisfied nod.

"Reach in the hole," he said.

I couldn't see the slit between the folds of the gown, but I knew where it was. Reaching with trembling fingers, I slipped my hand into the slit, and brushed the hilt of my dagger. *Nice.* I began to draw the dagger, but Falin caught my arm, stopping me midmotion.

"It's a lot harder to get it back in the holster, and with a dagger like that . . ." He trailed off, but I knew exactly what he meant. The dagger liked to draw blood. Usually it reserved that thirst to urging my hand against someone threatening me, but if I gave it the perfect opportunity, I wasn't sure it wouldn't take a little of mine.

Releasing the hilt, I pulled my hand free and studied the gown. The slit closed nearly seamlessly, not completely, but you'd definitely have to be looking for it to know it was there.

Falin wasn't finished yet.

He reached out one more time, his hands moving over the fabric without actually touching it. "Now for a thin layer of glamour and . . ." He stepped back, gesturing to the mirror over my dresser.

Not only was the slit now invisible, but the gown no longer looked wrinkled or ratty.

Cool.

"Ready?" he asked, but he looked away from me as he spoke.

"If I said no would it make a difference?"

He headed for the door, motioning me to follow. "You don't want to keep the queen waiting."

*   *   *

The drive was far too short. I used most of it texting Holly and Tamara and letting them know I'd been summoned to Faerie. They were both aware of my ongoing struggle with the Winter Queen's attempts to add me to her court and that I wouldn't have chosen to visit there. They also knew time and doors worked a little funky in Faerie, so Tamara was understandably pissed. I reassured her I'd do everything in my power to make it to the rehearsal dinner and wedding, but I didn't promise. I couldn't. I didn't know why I'd been summoned or if the queen planned to let me leave Faerie without a fight.

Falin parked the car, and I was out of time to text. I left my phone and purse in the car—technology didn't tend to work in Faerie anyway—and moments later was bustling down the sidewalk of the Magic Quarter, feeling very overdressed in the ornate gown. Of course, that all changed once we reached the Eternal Bloom.

As the one and only fae bar in Nekros, the Bloom had a reputation as a tourist trap. A handful of unglamoured fae were contractually required to frequent the main bar so they could be seen by the mortals. It was good PR and mortals catching sight of fae reinforced the belief Faerie magic required. That said, there were never more than three or four fae at the bar at any given time, the menu was overpriced and limited, and aside from the opportunity to stare at unglamoured fae, the bar itself was rather mundane.

The VIP room was different. Hidden through a door humans couldn't perceive unless they knew to look for it, the VIP area was a pocket of Faerie. The fae who worked the mortal side of the bar were doing just that, working. They were required to be seen, so they put themselves on display. Most of the fae on the VIP side were there to relax. They let down their glamour because it felt good to be unconfined, and a single glance around the room revealed shapes both beautiful and monstrous of every shape, size, color, and element. The food was served in magnificent feasts unlike anything I'd tasted elsewhere. Granted, it was Faerie food and if you tried to smuggle any of it out, the food transformed into toadstools that quickly rotted away. And the bar itself? Well, despite the fact I'd been in the bar at least once a week for the last few months, entering still took my breath away.

The furniture was deceptively simple; all wood but without nail or seam as if each piece had been carved from a single trunk. The room was much larger than what should have been possible for the building to contain. Not that the confines of the rest of the building mattered. The roof was missing, the sky of Faerie stretching above the bar. The sun was up now, high in the sky above, but the branches of the giant tree growing in the very center of the room shaded the bar, making it comfortable.

The tree itself was possibly one of the most magical things in the room, as well as one of the more dangerous. The amaranthine tree, which gave the Eternal Bloom its name, held flowers of every sort and shape on its many branches, but as I'd learned on my first trip to the Bloom, studying the flowers could lead the unwary to be hopelessly entranced. And that was hardly the only danger in the bar. It was a magnificent place, but a potentially deadly one.

I sighed as we passed through the threshold. The relief I felt wasn't quite as profound as when I'd stepped into the pocket of Faerie at my father's mansion, likely because that pocket had been created by my magic pulling chunks of reality into Faerie, whereas the Bloom was a space where Faerie and reality both bled over and mingled, but it was still an intense change. Falin spared me a momentary frown, and then led me past the fae scattered among the tables. They fell quiet as he approached. Most of the fae in the bar were independents and Falin was not only an agent of the winter court, but the queen's knight. Her assassin. Her bloody hands. He wasn't popular, not even among his fellow court fae.

By the time we reached the trunk of the amaranthine tree, the bar was silent aside from a distant thread of music. I ignored the sound—it might have been coming from the endless dance. The dancers jumped and twirled and writhed in the corner of the bar, but I knew better than to get too close. Once you joined the dance, you had to dance until the music ended. The previous dance had lasted over half a millennium—until I'd cut the fiddler's strings on my first visit here—and I had no desire to get caught up in the "merriment." Besides, even if I was better on this side of the door, I was still exhausted.

Falin paused. His gaze skittered over my face but I couldn't read his expression. He could have been memorizing my face because he thought this was the last time he'd see me, or simply judging if I'd make a dash for it rather than follow him into Faerie. Either way, it wasn't reassuring.

He didn't ask again if I was ready. Which was best, as I wasn't but didn't want to admit as much. I'd been to the outlying pockets of Faerie like the Bloom and the one in my father's house numerous times, but Faerie proper? I'd been there only a few times and two out of three hadn't gone particularly well for me. Seeing the queen also wasn't at the top of my list of fun—or safe—things to do.

Falin held out a hand. I stared at his gloved palm for a moment. I could turn and try to run, but that would be rather pointless. I could shrug off his gesture and walk into Faerie all on my own, but doors tended to be strange in Faerie. While I might walk through only a moment after him, it was possible for us to arrive on the other side of the door hours apart. Contact guaranteed we'd arrive together. So, after a moment of hesitation, I placed my own gloved hand in his.

Then we walked around the tree, and though I couldn't see the door, between one step and the next the world slid out of focus. The bar vanished, as did the dappled sunlight, the thin strands of music, and the tree itself. In its place was a pillar of intricately carved ice. The floor and walls were also ice, though there was no chill to the air nor was the surface slick. Above us stretched an inky black sky, broken with pinpoints of glistening white specks though I wasn't sure if they were distant stars or falling snow that vanished long before it could reach our heads.

Entering the Bloom had made me feel slightly better, but entering Faerie proper felt like I shed a hundred pounds of exhaustion that had been attempting to drown me, and my vision cleared, the magic that damaged my eyes ineffectual here. I almost smiled as I looked around. Almost. Even the sudden physical relief wasn't enough to stem my general anxiety of being in the winter court.

I expected Falin to lead the way, but he simply stopped, waiting. It didn't take long to learn what he was waiting for. Two guards in snowy white cloaks and armor that looked to be carved from solid ice stepped out of seemingly nowhere into the hall in front of us.

"Knight. Planeweaver. Her majesty awaits you," the one on the right said. His hand hovered over his large sword, but he didn't draw it. I took a step closer to Falin, but when the guards turned and led the way through the maze of ice caverns, I followed without comment.

Though I'd been to the winter court before, I couldn't have navigated the caverns on my own if my life had depended on it. They all looked the same: endless corridors lined with countless doorways and ice-carved sentinels that I knew from experience would come to life at the queen's will. I glanced at some of the doorways as we passed, but they told me nothing. As far as I could tell, unless you knew where you were going, it was impossible to know what was on the other side of a door until you stepped through it. The last time I'd been here I'd stepped into what looked to be an empty storage closet and ended up in an enormous ballroom filled with courtiers. The time before Rianna had led me through what appeared to be a solid wall into limbo. Yeah, Faerie was not my favorite place.

I'd lost count of how many turns we'd taken when the two guards finally stopped in front of what appeared to me to be another indistinguishable door. While it may have appeared so to me, the choice caused Falin to lift one eyebrow, his critical gaze studying the guards. They bowed ever so slightly and backed away without a word, leaving us alone in front of the door.

"Is something wrong?" I asked as quietly as I could and still be heard.

Falin frowned, but after a moment shook his head. "No. This is not where I expected to be taken, but if this is where the queen wishes to have an audience with us, then it is her choice. Let's go."

He stepped through the doorway, vanishing the moment he passed the icy frame. I glanced around. Aside from the ice sentinels, I appeared to be alone. The two guards had disappeared down another corridor and there was no one else here. I once again considered turning tail and running, but where would I go? I had no idea how to get back to the pillar that marked the exit, nor any idea what lay beyond any of the doors in this or any other corridor.

Taking a deep breath, I stepped through the threshold.

Chapter 7

A hand caught my arm as soon as I emerged from the threshold and, before I could get my bearings, dragged me downward, into the . . . snow? Falin was beside me, kneeling low. I eyed the snow under my feet. It glistened in a fluffy white sheet all around me, but though it looked deep, my boots remained on top of it, not making an impression. Still, I didn't want to kneel in it, so I let Falin tug me into a low curtsy, but not all the way to the ground. My knees protested the less than familiar pose, but Falin didn't release me, so I was forced to hold the curtsy. While his grip kept me locked in the awkward position, it didn't prevent me from looking up.

What I assumed would be a room, wasn't. We were in a small clearing. Pale trees, their bare branches weighted with snow, ringed the clearing, including behind me. Which meant the door I'd passed through had vanished. *Great.*

The Winter Queen paced several feet in front of me. She was a vision of Sleagh Maith beauty. Tall and lithe, her snow-white gown clung to her, accentuating her understated but feminine curves. Her dark hair hung around her heart-shaped face in perfect ringlets, glistening ice crystals kissing the curls. She was entrancing, either her magic or her presence making those around her wish to please her, to admire her. I'd had to fight the pull of those enchantments the first time I'd met her. Today it was simpler as she was making no attempt to dazzle me. In fact, I wasn't sure she'd noticed we'd entered the room. Her full red lips were tugged downward in a scowl and her movements were jerky, her fingers clutching the skirt of her gown as she paced.

Behind her, a long mahogany table was out of place in the snow-covered clearing. Four fae sat around the table. One I recognized on sight: Ryese, the queen's nephew. Saying he smiled at me when he caught my gaze would be an overstatement. It was more a smug glower. He lifted a crystal flute filled with golden liquid in a silent toast, and my stomach made a painful twist.

Ryese had spent the last couple of months trying to seduce me, and while he was handsome enough—most Sleagh Maith were unearthly gorgeous—arrogant entitlement didn't appeal to me. My continual rejection irritated him, and more than once I'd glimpsed a very nasty cloud of anger behind his pretty features. His eyes, with irises so light they almost looked white except for a pale blue outer ring, gleamed in the fae light, and the mocking greeting made me fear the worst about why I may have been summoned to court.

Beside him sat a female Sleagh Maith. Her chestnut-colored hair was piled high on her head and woven through with mistletoe, the white berries hanging down like gems around her face. Her gown was the color of an evergreen dusted with snow and decorated with more mistletoe accents. She studied me with inquisitive eyes as green as my own, but her features were carefully placid, controlled.

Across from her was a blond-haired fae. At first glance I assumed he was just another Sleagh Maith, but something about the arrangement of his features made me second-guess that assessment. It was nothing I could point to and say that one thing made him different. It was the height of his forehead, the width between his eyes, the shape of his ears, the angle of his jaw—nearly every feature—was just a little off, a little *more other*, than the other Sleagh Maith I'd met.

The last fae at the table was another male Sleagh Maith. He had dove-white hair pulled back in a stern knot at the base of his skull. His brown frock coat was austere and unadorned aside from holly leaf buttons and cuff links. He gave me only a cursory glance before his attention returned to his queen.

My gaze also slid back to the queen, who still paced the length of the clearing. She whispered something under her breath in that chimelike language I'd heard other fae use in the past, but while the language might sound pretty, by her tone I guessed it was a curse.

"My queen?" Falin said, his head still bowed.

She whirled around. Her ice blue gaze landed on us with the weight of a glacier. She radiated power, anger, and . . . distress.

The last caught me off guard. I let my eyes wander to the fae at the table again, but none betrayed anything.

"You took your time, Knight." The queen shoved the skirt from her hands and turned to me. "Lexi, I require your abilities."

I cringed inwardly at the nickname, but it was the request that made my spine stiffen. My abilities? She couldn't think I'd merge realities for her, could she? Hell, even if I could fully control the ability, I wouldn't use it for the queen.

I cut my gaze to Falin, trying to read his take on the situation. He still hadn't moved and I couldn't tell anything from his posture. My legs shook from curtsying so long, my knees locking. Shrugging Falin's hand off my arm, I straightened. The queen lifted one perfectly sculpted eyebrow as I moved, but she didn't comment on the break in protocol.

"Your majesty, I think there has been some mistake."

"Oh, there have been mistakes. I'm confident that you will ensure this is not one of them," she said as her eyes bored into me, sending ice down my spine. "And it is not something you can refuse. You may dismiss my offer of kinship, but as long as you reside within my borders you may not refuse my summons."

"And I am here, as requested." I tried to keep my voice light, but the ache in my jaw betrayed the fact I'd been clenching my teeth. I focused on pasting my best professional smile on my face. "But, I have no training in my planeweaving ability. I doubt I can accomplish whatever task you desire."

It was the truth, and she knew it as I couldn't lie, but admitting the weakness to her stung. In this situation though, I hoped admitting the shortcoming would prevent her from commanding me to perform whatever task she had in mind.

The queen cocked her head to the side, studying me. For a moment I thought she'd laugh, like I'd done something childish, but she only pressed her palms against the front of her skirt. "That is a matter that must be addressed some other time. Today I don't require your planeweaving, I seek your grave magic. I am told you often hire yourself out for this purpose?"

"I—er, yes." I glanced at Falin, who finally straightened, the movement smooth despite his extended bow.

"My queen, may I inquire—" he started, but she whirled around, eyes going wide, angry, and cut him off.

"No. You may not. Knight, had you been here, this . . ." She took a deep breath and squeezed her eyes closed. When she opened them again she was once again calm, cold, and as deceptively harmless as an iceberg. "Yes, Knight, you need to see this as well. I must know your thoughts." She turned back to me. "What you see today, you may not discuss with anyone outside this clearing. It is court business. *My* business."

Her tone held authority and just a touch of power. I could feel the command on my skin, but her words didn't sink through my flesh like an oath would have. They didn't bind me. Would they have if I'd been part of her court? *And does she realize she's not binding me?* I kept my mouth closed. I didn't know what it was she wanted to hire me for, but I'd rather not end up oath bound not to speak of it—that always ended up inconvenient. Still, I'd keep her command in mind. I had no interest in aggravating the queen further than my refusal to join her court already had.

"And who is in this clearing?" I asked, my gaze moving to the fae at the table.

The queen frowned and glanced back at the table. "This is my council. Had you attended the revelries I have thrown in your honor, you would be familiar with them already."

I waited. I wasn't going to be baited into defending my choice to decline all her invitations. She would introduce her council, or she wouldn't.

She studied me and then nodded over her shoulder.

"Ryese, you know. Beside him is Maeve and then Lyell." She pointed first at the woman and then at the man, whom I was still unsure whether or not was Sleagh Maith. Finally she turned to the last fae. "And that is Blayne." Introductions done, she nodded at the fae gathered around the table. "Come, all of you, follow me."

Without another word she swept past me, her gown swishing lightly over the snow. No footprints marked her path as she strode toward a group of trees to my left. A doorway appeared between a small gap in the trees, and she vanished through it.

That door couldn't have been the one we'd entered through—I had made it barely a step before Falin had dragged me to a curtsy and the door the queen had just used was a good half dozen yards away from where we stood. Of course, this was Faerie, maybe the door had moved. I glanced at Falin. He gave me a half shrug that told me nothing.

The council members stood quickly and silently, following their queen. All except Ryese. He slid out from his large chair near—but not at—the head of the enormous table, with leisurely ease. He drained his flute before setting it down and heading for the door after the queen. The movements were casual, in no apparent hurry.

"What is going on?" I asked, but he only smiled a cruel-looking smile and gave a half shrug. Either he didn't know, or he didn't care.

Falin motioned for me to follow him, and I did, stepping through the new doorway. The others were waiting on the other side, the queen tapping her foot in impatience. Once I'd cleared the doorway, she turned, striding down the corridor.

The queen didn't exactly stomp down the ice-laden halls, but she also didn't move with the seemingly effortless grace I'd seen her exhibit on previous occasions. Her movements were sharp, almost harsh in her haste. Once a small hawthorn fae stepped out of a doorway ahead of us, but he took one look at our odd procession and the branches on his head stood on end before he turned and ducked back the way he'd come. The queen didn't even seem to notice, but led us onward. We entered a corridor with two ice-armored guards standing at attention in front of a large double door. I wasn't surprised when that door was where we stopped.

"No one attempted to enter?" The queen asked, as the guards stepped aside. She received a twin chorus of reassurances before she nodded. "Good. Remain at your posts."

She passed through the door. I knew I was expected to follow, and somehow I'd ended up in front of the council members. I could feel their stares on my back, pricking along my spine. Still, I studied it dubiously, unsure what I'd find behind it. I really hated the way doors worked here. Falin pressed his palm against my back, not shoving me, but definitely urging me forward. Well, it wasn't like I had a choice.

I stepped through the door.

On the other side I found myself in a huge chamber. It might have been the same ballroom I'd visited the last time I'd been to the winter court, but this time there were no dancers, no music, no buffet tables. Pillars of solid ice broke the space every few yards, arches and flying buttresses extending from the walls. The thinnest layer of snow led a narrow path up the center of the room, like a rolled-out carpet leading to the glistening dais at the heart of the room. On top of the dais, a throne of ice.

And sitting on the throne, as if holding court, sprawled a bloody skeleton.

Chapter 8

It took a moment for my brain to catch up to what my eyes were seeing. Meat still clung to the skeleton in places, dried blood flaking off white bone. A few clumps of hair hung from the skull, and on the top of the head, a delicate tiara carved of ice.

I spun away from the sight, back toward the door just as Ryese stepped into the room, followed by Maeve. He raised an eyebrow at whatever expression of horror my face betrayed; Maeve only studied me, her expression evaluating. I squeezed my eyes closed, not waiting to see their reactions to the gruesome scene. I gulped down air—a calming reflex. A stupid one around a rotting corpse. Or at least, typically, but my lungful of air didn't bring with it the sickly sweet scent of decay. Blayne and then Lyell entered the room, and I dragged down three more deep breaths, before I realized that the air should have been gagging me. Yes, the room was large, and the corpse was more bones than body, but with the amount of gore hanging to it, the smell should have been pervasive. But there was no scent of rot. In fact, the air was as sweet as any in Faerie.

A jolt of shock ran through me. I couldn't *feel* the corpse either. There was no grave essence reaching for me. No sense of the body at all.

I glanced over my shoulder, uncertain. The skeleton still sat there, grinning down from the throne. It certainly *looked* real. But I couldn't feel it.

"What happened?" I asked, fixing my gaze on the back wall again.

"That is most certainly the question." The queen sounded like she said the words through clenched teeth, but she'd moved farther into the room and I wasn't about to turn around again.

"My queen, have you received any other threats?" Falin asked, but he didn't approach the corpse or follow the queen. Instead he remained by my side.

"Do I need more than one? That is my circlet on its head." Her heels clicked on the ice-crusted floor. "Lexi, whose body is that and who did this, this grotesque display?"

She made it sound as if the body would tell me just by being in the room. I forced myself to turn, to look at her, all the while trying to keep my gaze away from the corpse. Her council members had moved farther into the room. Lyell had approached the skeleton, but his body language was casual, as if he was studying a museum piece rather than a desecrated body. Blayne and Maeve both had their gazes locked on me, no doubt waiting for me to do something odd and witchy. Ryese leaned on one of the large pillars, watching the queen, not the corpse. Not that the corpse was doing anything, and it wouldn't either. Not here in Faerie at least. There was no land of the dead here. I'd known that fact, had even enjoyed the release of pressure on my shields. But it meant my grave magic offered me nothing.

"I'll need the body moved outside of Faerie."

"No." The queen clenched her hands in her skirt again.

"No one outside this room must know about this. You will find the answers and then the body will be destroyed."

I frowned at her. "It doesn't work like that. The land of the dead doesn't touch Faerie. You want me to raise a shade, that body has to be moved to the mortal realm." I left no wiggle room in the statement. If she wanted me to raise the shade, we'd have to move the body. With the thought, my gaze flickered to the skeleton. *How are we going to move that?* I shuddered. I definitely didn't want to be anywhere near it. I might have an affinity for the dead, but I didn't do decaying bodies or blood. Or, apparently, skeletons.

The queen released a strangled sound and Falin took a step toward her, his face betraying his concern. "My queen?"

I caught her movement only out of the corner of my eye, but it was fast. Much faster than I would have assumed the aristocrat could move. By the time my head whipped around the queen had a large blade of ice pressed against Falin's jugular.

"Are you behind this, Knight? You are the only member of court with blood on his hands."

Falin tilted his head back, but he made no attempt to defend himself. The queen was shorter, but that made her no less deadly. A trickle of blood welled around the frozen blade, trailing a red line down Falin's throat.

My gaze shot around the room, to the other fae present. All were focused on the conflict, but none moved, offered to help, or even objected. While I saw some startlement in their expressions, the overall impression I got was that they were each relieved the queen hadn't turned her accusations—and blade—on them.

Falin lifted his hands, palms outward in supplication. "My word, I have no part of this and no knowledge who is behind it."

He couldn't lie. The queen knew he couldn't, but she

didn't immediately lower the blade. She stared at him, the blade pressed against Falin's flesh. My hand crept to the slit in my gown. My fingers brushed the hilt of my blade. It buzzed against my flesh, emitting a confidence that we could take the queen. I had my doubts, enchanted blade or not. Falin's eyes flickered to me, and I wasn't positive, but I thought he gave the smallest shake of his head.

The queen took several deep breaths and then stepped back. Her blade dissolved into mist and she rolled her shoulders, taking on a regal posture once more. I eased my hand away from my own hilt. Ryese was watching me, a knowing look in his eyes.

I ignored him.

"That is reassuring, I suppose," the queen said, and from her tone, you'd never known she'd just considered slitting the throat of her knight. "Then we'll have to move the body. I don't want anyone to see it. Pack it as discreetly as you can." A large leather knapsack appeared at her feet. "Be quick about it."

I glanced at the knapsack and then at the skeleton. A chill that had nothing to do with all the ice around me ran down my spine. I pressed my lips together and turned to Falin.

"She wants us to . . . ?"

"I've got it," he whispered, scooping up the bag.

In another situation I might have insisted on helping. Not this time. Losing my lunch on the queen's throne wouldn't be helpful. So I relinquished the job to Falin, with only the slightest tinge of guilt at leaving him to the grisly task. Not surprisingly, none of the council members made a move to help Falin.

As Falin approached the corpse, Ryese pushed away from the pillar and turned to the queen. "Dear aunt, are you sure about this? Perhaps we should destroy the body. If rumor of this . . . display were to be whispered about court, you will look weak. And there will be no keeping it from other courts if even one whisper escapes."

"Would I not look weaker letting this action stand? I will find who is behind it and make a very public example of them."

Blayne's eyes cut to me, the move slow and exaggerated. "What if she cannot get that information for you? She is . . . untested. Is it worth the risk?"

As if her gaze were tied to his by a string, the queen looked at me. The frown that tugged down her red lips was uncertain. Half of me wanted to defend my credentials as a grave witch, but another part knew that getting tied up in this likely wasn't good for my continued health and freedom. Unless, of course, I could swing this to my advantage.

The queen clenched her fist again and began to pace, just as she'd been doing when we'd first entered the snowy clearing. Her movement was jerky, her anger and worry barely contained. Her lips pursed, and she turned at random moments and just stared at me. I straightened my shoulders, trying not to squirm under her assessing gaze.

Finally her pacing brought her directly in front of me, and she stopped. "Can you do this, Lexi? You can question this corpse if we take it to the mortal realm?"

It took all my will to keep my gaze locked with the queen and not let it wander to the skeleton Falin was packing away. A skeleton I couldn't actually feel.

"If it's real, I should be able to raise a shade."

"Should?" Her perfect eyebrow arched.

I left that alone. I'd never actually raised a fae before, not a full-blooded one at least, but I knew it was possible. "As long as the corpse is really a corpse."

The frown tugged her lips down farther, until it dragged at the edges of her eyes, but she nodded. The body looked real, but Faerie often accepted glamour as real. If it had never truly been alive, there would be nothing I could do.

She started to turn away, but I took a step forward. I pasted on a smile I didn't feel, trying to look confident. Not an easy task in the froufrou gown. Still, I was about to take a gamble, and confidence was key.

"Of course, you'll have to hire me to raise the shade."

"Hire you?"

"That is how these transactions occur."

She stared at me, her frown giving way to a scowl, but it was Maeve who asked, "Are you threatening to refuse to question this corpse for her majesty?"

And onto thin ice already. "No, I'm simply trying to negotiate the terms."

The queen crossed her arms over her chest and the abrupt silence in the room told me Falin had stopped bagging the body to listen to our conversation. The council members also watched with a little too much interest. Inside my head I cursed Maeve, but I held my tongue, and kept my chin lifted.

The Winter Queen's eyes widened. She was shorter than me, but somehow came off as looming. It would have been a neat trick, if it weren't so freaking frightening.

"I am the queen and you are in my territory," she said, her voice cutting through the suddenly frosty air.

I acquiesced with the smallest nod. "Yes, and as the law requires, I came to your summons. But if you would like to employ my skills, we must negotiate a fair bargain." Or, at least, that was my understanding of Faeric law. I'd had a crash course over the last few months, but the finer points escaped me.

The queen studied me for a long moment before giving a hiss of disgust and dropping her hands. "What is it you desire in exchange, Lexi?"

"Independent status."

"No."

She said it with rigid finality, and the hope inside me deflated. I needed to create a bond to Faerie for my own and my friends' survival, and I'd thought I'd been handed a way. Two little letters crushed that chance. I tried not to let it show as I gave her a small shrug.

"Well, then, I wish you the best of luck discovering who is behind this." I waved in the general direction of the skeleton.

"You cannot walk away now. Negotiations have already begun. We must continue until they are complete."

Crap. *Seriously?* I glanced to Falin for confirmation I didn't actually need—it wasn't like the queen could lie. He gave a small nod and shoved a long bone into the bag. I tore my gaze away.

So we were locked in negotiations now. And that was why it was dangerous to jump into a situation with the fae when you only halfway understood how things worked. I sighed and considered my words carefully. Fae couldn't lie but they could twist the truth so backward it was a near thing, and they always tried to get the better end of a bargain.

"So then, little planeweaver, what is your next offer?" the queen asked, smiling at me in the way a predator might grin down at cornered prey. And I doubted the fact she'd dropped the false-familiar nickname she'd given me was a good sign.

From the other side of the room the rustle of the knapsack closing was loud in the too-quiet space. Falin joined us a moment later, the bag slung over his shoulder. The tanned material bulged in odd places, and it was too small. If I hadn't known a body was in there, I wouldn't have guessed, but I did know, and the half-masked shapes pressing against the edges made my stomach sour.

"We are ready," he said, heading for the doorway.

The queen shook her head. "No, we are in the middle of something."

"Your majesty, can it not be discussed on the way?" he asked without pausing. He passed through the doorway and vanished a moment later.

The queen frowned after him for half a moment, but seemed reluctant to let the corpse get too far. "Come along," she said before hurrying out of the room as well.

By the time I made it to the hall, the queen had taken the lead, Falin several steps behind. I caught up to him and fell in step beside him.

"Is she always this unpredictable?" I whispered the question as quietly as I could and have any hope he'd hear, but the look he shot me told me I shouldn't have chanced saying anything.

I didn't think he'd answer, especially when his gaze darted back to where Ryese and Lyell trudged along several steps behind us, but after a moment he whispered back, "No."

I glanced at him, but he was staring at the queen's back, and his features held both caution and concern. I didn't really understand his relationship with the queen. He'd been her lover once, I knew that, but from what he'd said, that time was long past and he held no love for her now. There must be something between them though—his expression was too complex for him to care nothing about her. I hated that realizing that fact made my chest constrict, ever so slightly.

We turned a corner and reached the corridor with the carved ice pillar. The world fell from focus as we stepped between Faerie and the Bloom, and my steps became heavier, the world darkening slightly. It wasn't bad though. Noticeable yes, but not even so bad as leaving the pocket in my father's house.

Which was why I was completely unprepared for actually reentering mortal reality.

When I stepped through the door leaving the Bloom I stumbled, gasping under the weight of reality as it slammed down on me. The world spun, my knees locked, and I pitched forward. Falin caught one arm, the startled-looking bouncer—a green-skinned goblin—caught the other. They were the only reason I didn't hit the wooden floorboards headfirst.

"What is wrong with her?" the queen snapped.

I couldn't see her, my vision hadn't cleared yet, but she sounded close.

"She's fading." Falin's hand supported me physically, but his words were hard, unemotional.

My vision was clearing—at least to the point it ever did in mortal reality, I always missed the clarity of Faerie after leaving—so I had no trouble seeing the queen as she stormed over to Falin and grabbed a handful of his hair, pulling him down to her height.

"And this is the first I'm hearing about it? Why did I even bother sending you to watch her?"

Well, I guess that explained why the queen had gone from preventing Falin from speaking to me to ordering him to live with me. Not that it was any great surprise; I'd assumed he was there to spy for her.

I stepped out of the hands supporting me. I nodded to the goblin, but I didn't thank him. You didn't thank fae. Now that I'd gotten used to the achy exhaustion that had crashed on me upon reentering reality, it no longer seemed so crippling. I rolled my shoulders, already growing accustomed to the feeling.

"Are we going to do this thing?" I asked, moving for the door.

The queen hadn't released Falin yet, so he stooped at what looked like an uncomfortable angle as she studied my face. Anger still flickered around the edges of her features, but there was concern there as well. I wasn't foolish enough to think it was concern for me as a person, more concern for her potential asset. If I faded she couldn't have her own pet planeweaver.

Her lips pursed, as if she was about to say something, but then her gaze slid to the short goblin who shuffled nervously in her presence. She released Falin and stepped back, smoothing her dress. "Yes. Knight, take us somewhere we will be undisturbed."

Chapter 9

As we walked to the parking garage where Falin had left his car, I wondered if the queen or any of her council members owned a car and if it was parked in Nekros. *Maybe she'll just conjure a minivan from glamour.* Because seven people and a body in a knapsack were not fitting in Falin's car. I was almost disappointed to learn the FIB kept a small fleet of cars in the garage for instances when fae who didn't spend much time in mortal reality decided to pass into Nekros for a visit. We split up with the queen, Ryese, and me riding with Falin, while Lyell, Blayne, and Maeve followed in a loaner. I tried to arrange for the skeleton to go with the councilors, but the queen wouldn't let it or me out of her sight. Which meant I was stuck with it, and now that we were out of Faerie, I could *feel* the body, my grave magic having to be held in careful check to keep it from slipping into it.

The car ride was uncomfortable, in more ways than one. I hadn't bothered trying to call shotgun, and wasn't the least bit surprised when the queen slid into the front passenger seat. That left Ryese and me in what there was of a backseat. When I'd first met Falin, he'd driven a flashy red sports car that had gotten totaled during our first case together.

This car could have been that one's twin.

Unfortunately, when it had been designed, the backseat had clearly been an afterthought, with absolutely no consideration for legroom in the event someone actually wanted to sit there. So, I ended up with my legs practically pressed to my chest and the knapsack of gruesome remains wedged between Ryese and me. Even the arrogant fae couldn't make the seating arrangement look comfortable, and he scowled at the back of Falin's head for the extent of the ride. At least Falin left the top down and the wind roaring by pretty much prevented any extended conversations.

The house would have been the most private place to conduct the ritual, but I refused to have a body lugged into my bedroom so we were headed for the forest just out of town. The drive wasn't long—the Quarter gave way to the suburbs and then out into the wilds. I'd hoped that the trip would give me time to form an argument that would force the queen to grant me independent status, but no brilliant revelations had hit me while crammed in the backseat with a bagged body pressed against my thigh.

We found a small clearing far enough off the road that we couldn't be seen, and I used my dagger to draw a circle for my ritual. The huge skirt made the task difficult, and I used several colorful curses as I tripped on the hem for the third time. If the gown hadn't been ruined before, it likely was now, though Falin's glamour still hid the damage. By the time I completed the circle, I was breathing hard, mostly from fighting with the damn layers of tulle in the skirt.

The queen frowned at me. "Do you have the energy to complete this task?"

"Today? Yeah, but I apparently need a tie to Faerie

sooner rather than later. I request independent status in exchange for this ritual." Okay, I'd been turned down once, but if I refused to ask for anything else maybe I'd wear her down, right? Probably not.

"I could offer you a place of honor in my court. Riches. Power. A place on my council. A union with my beloved nephew." She motioned to Ryese.

I resisted a groan, but it was a near thing. The council members began chittering at the queen's words, likely at the idea of adding me to their lot or perhaps about the proposed marriage to Ryese. I didn't care which. I wasn't interested in either, but especially not the latter. I pointedly avoided looking at Ryese. Still, I could imagine the haughty look on his face that was part a dare to accept the offer and part anger already guessing I wouldn't.

"I will accept nothing less for the ritual than independent status."

The queen frowned at me and we stood in silence for several minutes, glaring at each other. She took a step closer. I had the urge to back away, but I held my ground.

"Find out who killed my subject and created that monstrous display in my throne room, and I will grant you independent status for a year and a day," she said, and I nearly laughed in a mix of relief and surprise—I'd demanded it three times, but I guess I hadn't really expected her to grant the request. She wasn't quite done yet. "During that year and a day, you will agree to continue to reside in my territory and at the end of it, you will inform me before swearing allegiances with any other court."

I almost blurted out "deal," but bargains with fae are binding, so I forced myself to examine the conditions she'd laid out. A year and a day wasn't much time in the grand scheme of things, but it was more time than I had now and I was unlikely to get another Faerie monarch in the position of needing a favor from me before Rianna and I had faded out of existence. The extension would give me time to arrange something more permanent. And while she'd stipulated that I inform her if I'd be joining a court other than hers, she hadn't said I'd need her consent. Of course, if she learned I was leaving her sphere of control, she might just have me killed when I told her, but what was my choice? Die now or die later? At least I'd have time to try to come up with a better plan.

I nodded and held out my hand. "I agree to your terms."

"It is settled then."

"Witnessed," Falin said from where he stood. Each council member also repeated the phrase. It was a formality, as I could already feel the small binding our agreement had created. The queen pressed her palm against mine in a surprisingly firm but not crushing handshake. I realized it was the first time I'd ever touched her and her skin was cold, even to my low body temperature.

With that settled, I focused on the matter at hand again, namely the ritual I had to perform to finish this deal. I motioned for Falin to place the knapsack in my circle. He was frowning, but he said nothing as he placed the bag where I'd indicated. He opened it, clearly intending to lay the skeletal corpse out.

"Just leave her in there," I said, glancing away before I caught sight of the ghastly bones again.

"Her?" The queen asked.

I nodded. Now that we were back in mortal reality and I was once again in touch with the land of the dead, the corpse sang soft lullabies just outside my range of hearing, as if tempting me to listen in and learn all her secrets. Without even thinking about it, I could feel that she had in fact been female. Usually I could guesstimate the age a corpse had died at as well, but not with fae. The body felt old, very old. But what did that mean for a fae? Two hundred years? Two thousand years? I didn't have the experience to gauge how long she'd lived before someone had done . . . Well, whatever had happened to her.

Falin retreated, leaving me alone beside the bag. I glanced around, ensuring the thin line of the circle hadn't gotten scuffed or broken. It looked complete, and I tapped into the raw magic stored in my ring, channeling it into the line in the grass.

The magical circle sprang up around me, strong and solid. Satisfied, I removed the shields on my charm bracelet and opened my mind. I kept my eyes closed—while touching the grave I tended to see the world slightly rotted away, and I didn't want to catch a glimpse of the bones crammed into a decaying bag. Besides, I didn't need my eyes to reach with my magic.

I could feel the corpse in my circle, but the grave didn't claw at me as viciously as expected. Cold wind danced across my skin, but it didn't rip at me, didn't try to crawl under my flesh. I'd never raised a fae before. A couple of feykin, but no full-blooded fae. So at first I thought that might be the difference.

Then my magic touched the corpse and I knew I was mistaken.

My eyes popped open, and through the rotted material of the bag, I could see what I already knew I'd find: a silver shimmering soul clinging to the now-dismembered bones. A shiver crawled down my flesh, making my hair stand on end. Her soul was still in there, trapped in the bones. Aware.

I swallowed around the sick taste that crawled up the back of my throat. I knew nothing about this fae, but I ached for her. I'd never considered the full ramifications of the fact the collectors couldn't enter Faerie. How long had a living soul been stuck inside a dead body? How much of what happened to that shell had she been aware of? I cringed again, catching sight of how very small the bag was where her bones had been shoved.

But guilt and sympathy were not the only issues I had to deal with. Her soul presented a very big complication.

I couldn't raise a shade while the soul was still inside the body—my magic just didn't work that way.

As long as the soul was inside the body, it was somewhat alive and protected. I could eject the soul, but it would become a ghost and be stuck inside my circle until I broke the barrier. Ghosts couldn't interact with the mortal world, but I was a crossover point for realities, and they were very physical to me. I didn't know what kind of fae I was dealing with, or how well she'd cope with being dead. But even if she didn't go all poltergeist on me, to eject her, trap her in a circle with her desecrated body, and then raise her shade in front of her would be a type of torture.

I turned to where the others waited outside my circle. "We have a problem. She's still . . . *in* there," I said and the queen raised one dark eyebrow, not understanding. "Meaning her soul hasn't been collected and moved on yet."

"So?"

"I can't raise her shade unless I eject her soul and force her to become a ghost."

Ryese scoffed under his breath. "See. I told you this would be more trouble than it's worth."

Lyell nodded in agreement, but the queen ignored both men. She looked more harassed than concerned. "Ghost. Shade. I don't care what you have to raise as long as I get my answers."

Right. I wasn't actually suggesting questioning the ghost. "Ghosts aren't reliable witnesses. Unlike a shade, they have an ego, their own motivations, and they can—" I cut off because I'd been about to say a ghost could lie, but fae couldn't lie during life so it was unlikely being dead would change that fact. Besides, while a shade might be an ideal witness, a ghost was basically a person minus the fleshy bits, and most eyewitness accounts came from the living. I might value the blunt honesty of a shade, but most people were accustomed to dealing with the living, and aside from the obvious corporeal limitations, ghosts weren't all that different personality-wise from a live witness.

So maybe questioning the ghost wouldn't be the worst thing, if she cooperated. The problem was, I had no idea what kind of ghost would emerge from that bag. How long had she been dead? Nothing decayed in Faerie, so she might have been a savaged skeleton for centuries—and aware of it the entire time. She clearly hadn't died of natural causes. What tortures might have been inflicted on her premortem? And speaking of torture, Falin had disassembled her skeleton and shoved her in a bag. This ghost might emerge insane.

And I'd be trapped in a circle with her.

I eyed the bag with the glowing soul trapped inside. Whether the ghost could be questioned or if I'd eject her from the body and then have to try to get her out of my circle quickly so she could wander until a collector found her, was uncertain, but I had to get the answers for the queen if I was going to get my independent status. I palmed my dagger again. If the ghost emerged enraged, the dagger was not the best of weapons, but it was better than nothing.

Taking a deep breath, I reached with my magic. I didn't usually use magic to manipulate souls, but honestly, I was surprised it hadn't self-ejected yet. A soul clinging to a fairly well-preserved corpse was one thing, but this one was barely a body anymore. I lifted my empty hand, and gave a small shove with my magic.

The soul moved under my magic's touch, and it felt kind of like tugging saltwater taffy apart, as though the soul clutched to the bones with every bit of strength it had left, unwilling to give up the body that had sustained it. But it did move. I drew on more magic, and shoved harder. A shimmering shape sprang out of the bag, the glow fading as it transitioned to the land of the dead, until a pale figure stood in the grass before me.

The fae woman was shorter than I expected, at least a

foot and a half smaller than me, and her frame was thin, delicate. I hadn't noticed those details when she'd been just a skeleton sitting on the throne, but then I hadn't been looking too hard. Her eyes were dark, with no distinction between pupil and iris, and no white areas. They were her largest feature, dominating her face and overshadowing a very small pointed nose and a thin slit of a mouth. Her hair, if you wanted to call it that, swept back from her head in long crystalline projections, like icicles exploding from her scalp. From my angle, I could just barely catch sight of wings growing from her back, but I had no idea if they'd actually carried her in life because what I could see of them had dozens of holes in the gauzy flesh, like lace. *Or a snowflake.*

Now that the body was empty, the grave tugged on me hard, trying to draw my magic and heat to it. I closed my shields, blocking it out as best I could. I didn't need the distraction right now.

The fae ghost hadn't moved, and she looked more shocked than anything I'd categorize as angry or enraged, so I took a chance. "Hi, I'm Alex. What's your name?"

Her enormous, dark eyes moved to me, rounding out as she studied me. I kept the dagger pressed by my side, hidden in the folds of the gown where I hoped she didn't notice. I didn't know if it was her small stature or huge eyes, but she looked very childlike and more than a little scared. I didn't want to come off as threatening. But I wasn't going to put the dagger away. Looks could be deceiving.

She wrapped her twig-thin arms around her chest like she was hugging herself, and her bottom eyelids quivered. I thought for a moment she might start crying.

"What happened?" she asked, her voice high-pitched and clear as a bell. She looked down, where the knapsack slumped by her ankles. She didn't have eyebrows, but her forehead creased, and now I was sure she'd start crying any second. "What is that?"

"Give me your hand," I said, holding mine toward her.

She didn't. She wasn't even looking at me. She was staring at the bag. I didn't know exactly what she was seeing—it really depended on how close to the chasm between the land of the dead and the living she was, but I guessed she could see her bones through the bag. That couldn't be good. I was pretty sure if I were in her shoes, the last thing I'd want to focus on would be my own desecrated body. I had to get her attention.

Besides, she seemed rational so it was quite possible she could answer the queen's questions. Making the ghost manifest in reality would be a whole lot simpler than raising a shade from mere bones—and take a lot less energy. As exhausted as I already was, expending less magic definitely sounded like a plus. I wasn't sure if questioning her would be kinder or crueler than questioning her shade, but the horrified way she stared at her own bones made me think seeing her shade would not be good for her mental health—not that I thought it would be for anyone. I took a step toward her, my hand still extended, and she pushed off the ground, her snowflake wings fluttering into motion behind her as she lifted three feet in the air.

Well, I guess the wings aren't just decoration.

She shot upward, but the circle I'd drawn wasn't very large, so she hit the ceiling and bounced off. My teeth chattered with the impact, the magical vibration jolting through me.

I doubted she could see the magical barrier as it was Aetheric energy and most fae couldn't reach that plane, but she definitely felt it because she turned and beat both small fists against the barrier. Each pound of her fist made me cringe. I squeezed my eyes closed and channeled more magic into the circle to reinforce it.

"Stop," I yelled at the phantom. If she'd been a shade she would have had to obey me. But she wasn't, and she took no notice of my command.

"Alex?" Falin said from outside the circle, sounding concerned. He couldn't see the fae, didn't know what was happening, but my reactions were enough to tell him something was wrong.

I could have made the ghost visible without touching her, but it would have used a lot more energy. So, forcing my eyes open despite the pounding in my brain that reverberated with each slam of her fists, I rushed across the circle and grabbed her ankle. Power surged out of me, flooding over her through the contact. She screamed, writhing in my grip. I'd pulled this particular trick with multiple ghosts, and only once, when I'd lost control, had I been told it hurt, so I doubted her scream indicated pain.

But scream she did, her voice going shrill and piercing the air. I almost pulled my hand back to cover my ears, but I held on, dragging her close to the mortal realm.

"Be silent," the queen commanded, and even through my circle, there was power in her words.

The thrashing fae went still. Her head jerked around, and she seemed to become aware of the world beyond the circle—and the people just on the other side of it—for the first time. Her scream died in her throat, and she floated back to the ground. I switched my grasp from her ankle to her elbow as she moved, but I doubt she noticed. Her entire focus centered on the queen.

She sank to her knees in the tall grass, all but dragging me down with her.

"My queen," she said, her head bowing.

The queen stared at her, studying her wings more than her face. "You are one of my handmaidens, are you not?"

"Yes, my lady."

"What is your name?"

"Icelynne, my lady," the little fae said, and the queen nodded.

I didn't say anything, but I wondered exactly how

many handmaidens the queen had that she only vaguely recognized and didn't even know the name of this fae who had served her. Had she noticed she was missing? By the queen's frown, I guessed she hadn't, and just maybe, that fact bothered her.

No one spoke for several minutes. The council members huddled together a small distance from the queen and Falin. They stared at the ghost with naked horror. Ryese shook his head, and Lyell and Maeve kept shooting furtive glances back the way we'd come. Blayne's mouth moved, but nothing audible escaped from behind his lips. Apparently they didn't like ghosts. Likely this was the first they'd seen. I remembered something Falin had once told me—*Fae don't like reminders of their own mortality.* And Icelynne was undeniably fae and dead.

Finally Falin broke the silence. "What happened, Icelynne?"

His voice was surprisingly gentle. His tone that of a cop who had questioned victims before. I sometimes forgot that while it was true he did a lot of the queen's dirty work, he was also the head of the local FIB office and dealt with the fae equivalent of what any other cop did.

Icelynne rolled from her knees to rock back on her heels. She drew her legs against her chest, hugging them tight to her. If she'd reminded me of a child before, now she did so doubly.

"I felt it. I felt it all. He . . . He *ate* me."

"Who did?" the queen asked, taking a step closer to the outside edge of the circle.

The little frost fae shook her head. "I . . . I don't know. I couldn't see him. But I knew. I knew he was eating me."

"Were you blindfolded or was he glamoured?" Falin asked, his voice gentle but demanding. "And could you tell anything else about him? Did he speak? Could you smell anything?"

"I don't know. I can't remember. He was eating me.

That's all. I couldn't see or hear him. I—" She broke off in tears.

"How can you not remember something like that?" the queen asked, balling her hands into fists. "Surely you must have been trying to get a sense of him so you could identify him later."

The little fae just continued to cry, her ghostly body shuddering. I'd moved my hand to her shoulder and I squeezed it lightly, trying to comfort her. If she noticed, she didn't show it.

"He ate me," she said between sobs. "And, and he took me apart." She shot a tear-filled glance back at the knapsack.

Blayne cleared his throat. "The knight disassembled the skeleton. Are you stating the Winter Knight ate *you*?"

Her eyes went very large as she looked first at the council member and then focused on Falin. Everyone's attention followed.

I cleared my throat. "No. She's not. She's listing traumatic events that she was able to sense but has no coherent details on," I said, and then hesitated. I didn't want to explain in front of the ghost, but they needed to understand why she didn't remember anything about whomever had eaten her and why she'd lumped the person who'd eaten her and Falin when he'd put her bones in the bag under the same moniker. "I think Icelynne was already dead when that happened. Her soul was present, so she experienced what happened to her, but had no functioning systems like hearing or sight to interpret it through. We need to move on."

They stared at me in disbelief and Icelynne cried louder, gulping down ragged breaths between her sobs. Normally what happened to a body after death was of little consequence to the soul that had resided in it because death occurred the moment the soul left the body. Oh, sometimes full physical death took another minute or two for all bodily functions to shut down, but if I raised a shade, those minutes would be missing because the record button on life had already been clicked off, and of course, the soul wouldn't remember them because it was no longer connected to the body. But Icelynne's body had ceased living and her soul had still been trapped inside. Her brain had shut down, her senses dead, but her soul still experienced what happened to her flesh on some level. She hadn't been eaten alive, exactly, but it was the next worst thing.

"Icelynne," I said, trying to keep my voice soothing, but I usually questioned shades who had no emotions, not traumatized ghosts. Still, I tried. "Can you tell us what happened before that? What is the last thing you remember seeing?"

She sniffled and wiped her nose on her arm. For a moment I didn't think she'd answer, but then she said, "I was tied to a chair. And I had these tubes coming out of my arm . . . I was bleeding. I mean, the tubes, my blood was being carried away in those tubes."

I glanced at Falin, but I couldn't read anything in the dark expression clouding his face. I thought about the skeleton as it had looked in the throne room, but so much had been done to Icelynne after her death, and I didn't have the experience to know if she'd died of exsanguination. How would you even tell when most of the flesh was gone and only bones were left?

"How did you get there?" Falin asked. "Do you know where you were?"

Icelynne's face scrunched, though if from deep thought or painful memories, I couldn't guess. "I was still in the court. The sky was ours. But I don't know where I was. I remember being in my own rooms. There was a knock on the door. Two people were outside in white cloaks, the hoods pulled down. But I don't think they were guards. One was very short and almost as wide as tall. The other was too slight to have been wearing armor under the cloak. They . . ." She trailed off, a fresh wave of tears escaping from her. We gave her a moment to collect herself, and after wiping her eyes, she continued. "Everything happened so fast. They grabbed me, and I struggled, and then everything went dark. When I woke up, I was in the chair, the tubes drawing out my blood."

When she stopped, no one spoke for a long time. Finally I asked, "And the two cloaked figures, you never saw their faces? Did you see anyone else while you were held?"

"I never saw them. I don't even know if they were male or female or what kind of fae they were." Her shoulders shook under my hands, but she didn't stop speaking this time. "There were other fae in the room with me. Also tied down. I could only see two—another handmaiden named Snowlilly, and a rowen fae I didn't recognize. I don't think he was a member of our court. There were others too, but they were behind me and I couldn't see them. I don't know how many. I only saw the short and the lithe fae one more time. They came and . . . They came and took the rowen's body and brought a tree nymph to take his place. She wasn't familiar either."

Others? It sounded like at least four, most likely more. I glanced at Falin and saw the same thought on his face— this was bigger than just one body staged to scare the queen.

"Did you see anything else? Did you hear anything?" Falin asked. "How long do you think you were held?"

"Days? Weeks? I don't know. It seemed to go on forever. I was so tired and my whole body hurt. Especially when he'd connect the tubes and drain away my blood."

"Wait—he?" I asked and the little fae cringed under my hand. She wasn't telling us everything, and she clearly hadn't meant to say "he." This was why I didn't like questioning ghosts. "Who was he? What did he look like?"

"I don't know," she sounded miserable, but evasive. This wasn't the same desperate cry of ignorance she'd used earlier. She was hiding something.

I wasn't the only one who heard the difference.

"Tell us what you do know, handmaiden," the queen said, and there was unmistakable command in her voice. There was also fury, the cold kind that could patiently and with clearheaded calculations drag out horrible torture. I was glad it wasn't directed at me.

"My queen, I can't —"

"Now."

The little fae seemed to collapse further into herself, but she answered. "I never saw his face, and he only whispered when he spoke to me. He told me that my sacrifice was for the good of all and that big changes were coming and I'd be helping." She paused, but the queen cocked one dark eyebrow and the words stumbled out of her again. "He was, or at least I think he was, Sleagh Maith, my lady." She drew back with the last, as if she thought the queen would reach out and grab her for accusing one of the noble line of fae of being her captor. Of course, my circle still separated the ghost from the queen, so even if the queen had wanted to throttle the ghost, she couldn't have.

For her part, the queen rocked back slightly on her heels, as if Icelynne's words had delivered a physical blow her body had absorbed. She turned, hands clenched at her sides, and paced the edge of my circle.

"Do you have any idea who he was? This captor of yours, was he of my court?"

Icelynne sniffed loudly, her body trembling. "I do not know, my lady. I swear I do not know. He never took off his cloak, and he only spoke to me when he brought food or hooked or unhooked the tubes. Most of the time when he was in the room he was fiddling with an alchemy lab."

"Alchemy? Like turning lead into gold?" I asked.

The little fae shook her head, making the ice crystals shimmer in the afternoon light. "No. I think he was distilling the glamour from our blood."

Chapter 10

We continued to question Icelynne for what felt like another hour, but there wasn't much more she could tell us. She'd been held by three fae, one of whom she thought might be Sleagh Maith, but she'd never seen any faces. They'd drained their captives, but slowly. They'd fed the prisoners, presumably so they'd gather as much blood as possible from each. Oh, and just maybe they were using the blood to distill pure glamour. Why? I couldn't guess, and it seemed no one else could either. Not yet at least.

The queen was the most persistent in the questioning. Continuing to try the same questions from different angles long after everyone else had fallen silent. Icelynne dutifully attempted to answer, but there was just no more information she could provide.

By the time the queen turned away, disgust curling her lips, I'd consented to sitting cross-legged beside the ghost. It didn't take much energy to keep her visible—certainly much less than a ritual holding a shade for this long would have cost me—but the interrogation had still taken more than an hour, and I was exhausted. I was also getting rather anxious about the time. Tamara's rehearsal dinner was in a couple of hours, and I wanted to have this all tied up in time to make the event. Ethan's family had booked a reservation at one of Nekros's nicer restaurants, and I needed enough energy in reserve that I didn't fall asleep on my very expensive plate.

It was a relief when I finally released Icelynne's shoulder, slipped my extra shields back in place, and dropped my circle. The evening sun hung over the horizon, all but obscured by the surrounding trees. Fall was progressing quickly, so despite the growing gloom it was still relatively early in the evening. Early or not, I wanted to go home and sleep. I couldn't, but oh how I wanted to. On the plus side, I could still see. No ritual meant my eyes had taken minimal damage.

"Where will you take that?" Icelynne asked as Falin retrieved the knapsack holding her bones.

Since I no longer had contact with her, he couldn't hear her, so I repeated the question. Falin paused, the bag not quite slung over his shoulder. The look on his face was half grimace, half embarrassment, as if he'd forgotten the connection between the fae he'd spent the last hour questioning and the bones. Or as though he hadn't realized she was still there watching now that she was once again farther across the chasm between the living and the dead.

"My lady?" he asked, turning to the queen.

For a moment I thought she'd brush off the question, unconcerned. Then she frowned, and addressed an empty space to my left, not quite where the ghost-fae stood, but close. "Icelynne, you served me as my handmaiden. What is it you would like done to honor your body? We could bury you here where you would become part of the wild."

That sounded like something Icelynne should answer with her own words, and likely nothing I'd want to try to repeat. So I reached out and gave her a bit more energy. When the queen's eyes snapped to Icelynne, I knew the ghost had solidified.

The little fae's face scrunched in thought. She'd clearly never considered what should be done with her body after death—most near-immortals didn't dwell on such mortal details. "I hate this place. It is decaying all around me," she finally said. "I want to be in the beauty and magic of Faerie. I want to be returned to the winter court."

The queen nodded and turned away, satisfied the conversation was over. I had no idea what they'd do with her bones once they got them back to Faerie, but Falin carried the bag toward the car, so I dropped my hand from Icelynne's arm.

I trudged after the queen and Falin. Ryese and Blayne had apparently gone ahead of us while I was breaking my circle, but Maeve and Lyell followed me, leaving a wide stretch between us that I could feel their suspicious gazes filling.

"Wait," Icelynne called after me, her wings fluttering as she crossed the distance I'd already covered. "I'm uh, dead, correct? And they can't see or hear me, but you can."

I nodded.

"What happens now? To me, I mean?"

I opened my mouth, but then closed it again as I found I had no words that could offer her comfort. I'd seen the plane of light and life the soul collectors existed on, but that wasn't where souls actually went after they moved on. I wasn't even sure Death knew what awaited a soul on the other side. Telling Icelynne that likely wouldn't reassure her. While most ghosts crossed into the land of the dead by the soul struggling against collector, Icelynne hadn't chosen to stay behind, to become what she now was. I'd freed her from the prison of her bones, but only to release her into the purgatory of the land of the dead. Looking at her panicked features, that seemed like less of a kindness than it should have been.

"I'll help you find a soul collector," I finally said. From what I understood, souls were assigned to collectors at birth, but those born in Faerie didn't get collectors because the collectors' realm didn't cross over with Faerie. Now that she was a ghost in the mortal realm though, any passing collector could help her cross over. At least, that was my understanding from the fact Death had promised he'd come for my soul when I died. He'd sort of adopted me. Kind of creepy in a way, considering he was my boyfriend, but reassuring to know that I wouldn't end up wandering for eternity or get eaten by something nasty in the land of the dead. I assumed he wouldn't have an issue with taking Icelynne the next time he visited. "He'll help you cross over to whatever comes next."

Shimmering tears rose again in her dark eyes. I'd have thought by now she would have run out of moisture. But one fat tear escaped, running a fresh trail down her cheek. "I don't want to cross over. I want to go home. To Faerie."

She was hovering eye level to me, but she still looked small, childlike. I almost wanted to hug her. I didn't. She wasn't a child. In fact, she was probably hundreds of years older than me.

"I don't think you can," I told her. Faerie didn't have a land of the dead, or the realm of souls where the collectors existed. I'd seen one ghost in the Bloom before, but the Bloom was a bleed-over point between the planes, and I had no idea what happened to him once he passed into Faerie proper. I'd never seen any ghosts during my trips in Faerie.

In the distance, the sound of a car starting up roared through the trees and Falin called my name. I didn't know what else to tell Icelynne, so I started walking again.

"You can't just leave me here," she called after me, her high-pitched voice thin, desperate.

I hadn't planned to. And besides, even if I'd wanted to leave her behind, she was a ghost. I couldn't have stopped her from following me. But she was new to this ghostly gig and didn't realize that yet.

"Come with us to the Magic Quarter," I said, beckoning her to follow.

She didn't move. "You will not take me to a . . . collector?" The way she stumbled over the title betrayed her unfamiliarity. Of course, even among humans, whose life spans were tragically short compared to fae, the idea of a soul collector, angel of death, or grim reaper — whatever title you wanted to give them — was often more than people could accept.

I started to promise I wouldn't take her to a collector before she was ready, but the words wouldn't form on my lips. While it wasn't a lie, it was too close to an oath I couldn't guarantee I'd be able to keep. With as much contact as I had with collectors, the longer she hung around me, the higher her likelihood of encountering one. "I occasionally keep company with collectors, but I have no intention of slapping a bow on you and presenting you as a present. I work with a ghost and he's managed to haunt me for months despite my other associations."

She studied me for several seconds before nodding and fluttering up beside me. I turned in the direction of the road again, and began trudging back along the path we'd followed.

"Do you know many ghosts?" she asked as I stumbled over yet another tree root.

"Not exactly," I said, ducking under a tree branch but then had to stop to catch my breath. "Ghosts aren't rare, per se, but they aren't common." I straightened, still breathing hard. I'd never been a marathon runner or anything, but I wasn't typically this bad off just from hiking in the woods. I guessed this was another side effect of fading. I needed to catch up to the queen and find out how to cement my tie to Faerie as an independent fae.

Icelynne seemed as though she had more questions she wanted to ask, but I was in no shape to answer them, so thankfully she let me trip through the woods in peace. By the time I reached the road, everyone else was already loaded up in the cars. The queen showed no inclination to get back out or even lean her seat forward, and for a moment I considered trying to climb into the back over the side of the car. My exhausted limbs were not agreeable with the idea. Falin slid out and motioned me around. I expected Ryese to slide over and take the seat behind the queen, but he just smiled, forcing me to climb over his lap. I may have "accidentally" stepped on his foot. Twice.

I all but collapsed in the backseat, not caring that I was so scrunched my knees touched my chest. Icelynne regarded the car skeptically. I wasn't sure if that was because she'd never seen one before—some fae hadn't left Faerie for centuries—or because in the land of the dead the mostly plastic car probably looked as if it was melting onto a pockmarked road. Still, she crawled in, cramming herself on top of the knapsack between Ryese and me. She then spent the entire ride staring mournfully at the bag under her. Not that anyone besides me noticed. I felt for her, but had no idea what I could do, so instead stared out at the growing darkness surrounding the car.

With evening approaching, the street parking in front of the Bloom was packed with tourists' vehicles. Falin took a side street and pulled into the small underground garage he'd parked in earlier. It wasn't marked private, but most of the cars were the plastic and carbon fiber fae preferred—traditional cars had far too much steel and iron—so if I had to guess, I'd put money on the entrance being spelled so that only those who knew about the garage could see it or enter, much like the VIP door at the Bloom. That door was likely part of the reason this lot existed. Metered parking wasn't great when the doors sometimes spit you out hours or days later than expected. I'd have to ask about getting a parking pass.

Once the car was parked, the queen immediately started toward the Bloom. The clip of her pace and the swing of her arms said she was done with the mortal world—or maybe she was about to go tear her court apart searching for an alchemist's lab full of fae being drained to death. Probably both.

I jogged after her, and if it was anyone else, I would have grabbed her arm to stop her. But I had no interest in laying a hand on the Winter Queen.

"We have a bargain to resolve," I said, already out of breath from the minimal exertion. I needed that tie to Faerie and I needed it now.

The queen swiveled on her heels and frowned at me. "You didn't complete your part of the bargain."

"I—"

"You agreed to find out who killed my subject. We still don't know."

I could have cursed myself. I'd worked enough cases with the police to know the victim didn't always know who killed them. Sometimes they were blitz-attacked from behind, blindfolded while held, or the perp wore a mask. And even if they did get a good look at the attacker and a sketch artist rendered a drawing from the description, the shade couldn't give any feedback on how accurate the sketch was. Of course some victims knew their attackers and could identify them by name, but definitely not all. And I knew that.

I should have paid more attention to the queen's wording. Phrasing is important in a bargain. If I hadn't been so focused on the stipulations she'd made, and how badly I needed my independent status, I'd have realized Icelynne needed to identify her attackers. The fae hadn't been able to do that. Now I was stuck with an incomplete deal.

I expected the queen to be smug. After all, she'd gotten hours of free use from my ability. Instead she sighed, her shoulders sagging as if she almost regretted not being able to bend the deal we'd made and give me my year and a day. "I can still make you a member of my court. It would stop you from fading."

Did I have a choice? There were other courts. Other rulers. My bargain with the queen wasn't complete so I wasn't bound to inform her if I went to another court.

Maybe some other ruler would let me become independent. *But what will I have to trade to them?* I wouldn't know until I tried.

The queen's eyes narrowed, obviously reading the resolve on my face. She sighed. "At least come back to Faerie with me. You'll fade slower there," she said, and then something else occurred to her, and she smiled, the curl of her lips sly. "And in Faerie you still have a chance to complete your side of the bargain. Help me find this killer, and I will be bound to grant your status."

She had a point. Maybe even a good point. But what good would blundering around Faerie really do for me? My grave magic, while neither offensive or defensive, was the one power I was really good at, and I had no access to it in Faerie. My witchy spell casting was dismal at best, my sensitivity to magic didn't do a lot in a land where almost none of the residents could channel Aetheric energy, and I didn't understand my planeweaving abilities—or the planes in Faerie for that matter—well enough for it to be helpful. I'd be like a child blundering around in a world I didn't fully understand. What chance did I have there to find the alchemist?

But what chance did I stand here?

"How many Sleagh Maith are in the winter court?" I asked.

"Too many to remand all to my dungeons for questioning."

And the fact she'd considered that a possible option was exactly why I had no intention of joining the winter court.

I rubbed my temples with a finger and thumb. I wasn't sure when my head had started hurting, but the headache was to the point of pounding now. I needed some sleep, and a clear head. But first I had to get to Tamara's rehearsal dinner. I wasn't late yet, but I would be soon, and I definitely didn't want to chance passing through the door to Faerie again. I might miss the wedding entirely if it decided to act up and spit me out in the middle of next week. Maybe I'd go back to Faerie to search and ask some questions after the wedding. If I couldn't find any other solution to my court problem, I might have no other choice.

"I'll consider it. But not tonight," I said, and the queen's smile faltered.

"Fine." The heel of her shoe clicked on the ground, accenting the word. Then she turned to Falin. "Accompany her. If she gets too weak, carry her back to Faerie if you have to. If my planeweaver fades, I'll be very disappointed. The rest of you, let's go."

Falin nodded without a word and passed the knapsack of bones to Ryese. He grimaced, taking the straps with two fingers and holding the bag away at arm's distance, but he followed his aunt. The rest of the council fell in step behind them. The queen cast one more appraising gaze my way, then turned on her heel and bustled out of the garage. Maybe it was a display of power, or maybe it was just her irritation getting the better of her, but a trail of snow flurries followed in her wake. Despite the warm autumn night, they clung to the cement several seconds before finally giving up and melting into wet dots.

The small procession had already turned the corner before I looked away. Falin said nothing, but walked back to his car, slid in, and then popped the passenger door open for me. I stared at it.

Guess I have an uninvited houseguest a little while longer.

Roy, my self-appointed ghostly sidekick, was in my apartment when we arrived home. He'd apparently been pushing Scrabble pieces around on the counter for quite some time because he had several completed words. That might not sound like such a feat, but when you don't exist on the mortal plane, manipulating objects that do takes quite a bit of energy and concentration. He looked up when I entered, his thick-framed glasses sliding down his shimmering nose.

"I was in the office this afternoon but nobody was—" He cut off, his mouth dropping open and a Scrabble tile falling from his fingers. I didn't have to guess too hard on why.

Icelynne had followed me home.

I would have rather she hadn't, but hey, I already had one ghost hanging around, why not two? Also, I felt bad for her. She had spent most of the drive to my house crying in the backseat.

"Alex, who and what is that?" Roy asked, shoving his fists into his faded jeans and backing up several steps. As a whole, ghosts tend toward a solitary existence. They are remanent traces of their own will, empowered by energy. When that energy runs low, some ghosts have a bad habit of cannibalizing their fellow spirits.

"Roy meet Icelynne, and vice versa," I said as explanation of who. I pointedly ignored the "what" part of his question.

"Uh, hello," Icelynne said. She wasn't exactly hiding behind me, but it was a near thing.

Roy didn't reply. He just stared. He usually had perpetually bad posture, moping around with slumped shoulders, but he was standing at his full height now, his dingy flannel shirt swaying in an unfelt breeze rolling through the land of the dead. I wasn't sure if he was getting ready to run or rush her.

I shook my head. *Ghosts.*

"Play nice," I said, and then walked across the room and sank onto the bed. I was so tired. If I blinked too long I'd probably be out for the night. But I couldn't do that. I had to get out of this ridiculous ball gown and get to Tamara's dinner. I bent to unzip my boots, and PC jumped in my lap. He licked my chin twice, and then hopped down and paced in front of the door. Damn, he needed a walk. I'd totally been slacking in my job as a puppy-momma today.

"I'll take him out, if you want," Falin said, grabbing PC's leash. The little dog lifted on his back legs, pawing the air in front of Falin.

"Would you? That would be great."

He gave me a smile that probably would have been dazzling if I hadn't been so bone-dragging tired. Once the door shut behind him, I changed as quickly as my aching body would allow, but I'd only barely finished when the door opened again and PC rushed back inside.

I was officially running late now. Holly hadn't waited for me. I couldn't blame her. After all, I'd told her not to when I'd texted on the way to Faerie. But that meant I didn't have a ride, and with dark having officially fallen, I couldn't drive myself. I considered asking Falin along as my date, but that seemed way too weird, especially since I'd be doing so just for his car. So, I called a cab and hoped the restaurant served energy drinks, or at least espresso. It was going to be a long night.

Chapter 11

I woke the next morning to the sound of my phone blaring R.E.M.'s "It's the End of the World as We Know It," which wasn't what I'd left my ringtone set as. *Roy.* I needed to have a serious talk with that ghost. Neither he nor Icelynne had been in my apartment when I'd gotten home, but clearly he'd visited during the night. *And his outlook on my current situation leaves something to be desired.* Or maybe it was on his own situation. I didn't have time to puzzle over the meaning of the ringtone. Fumbling for my purse, I dug out the phone and stared with blurry eyes at the display. The number didn't look familiar.

"Hello," I mumbled, trying, and failing, to keep the sleep from my voice.

"Craft, Jenson here. We've got another one."

I blinked at the daylight playing over my ceiling. *Another one?* "A murder?"

"Yeah. Another locked room mystery—literally. And a jurisdictional nightmare. Your boyfriend's already down here."

"Uh . . ." I frowned. I was barely following this conversation. Maybe it was the groggy haze of being half asleep.

No way could Jenson see Death, though as Jenson was a homicide detective, a collector's presence at a crime scene wouldn't be completely unheard-of. Still, that couldn't be what he meant.

I glanced to where Falin had been sleeping last night. The bedding was neatly folded in a pile. I looked around. The apartment was empty, the bathroom door open, and the room beyond dark. *I must have been sleeping hard.* But Jenson had to mean Falin was there. He certainly wasn't here.

"The FIB is on the scene?" I asked, feeling a little slow on the uptake. I shook my head to clear it and sat up. The move made me dizzy and I had to pause a moment before asking, "Did you want me to meet you at the morgue when they release the body?"

"Bodies, plural. And no. I'll give you the address. We need you to get down here pronto."

"Here as in the crime scene?" I never went to active crime scenes. Well, maybe "never" was an exaggeration, but usually I didn't get invited officially.

"Yes, the crime scene. My boss and your boyfriend already—"

"Falin isn't my boyfriend."

Jenson paused, when he spoke again, I could hear the familiar sneer in his voice. "Fine. My boss and the FIB *agent in charge* already cleared you doing the ritual on-site. The coroner will clear the bodies in a minute so get your ass down here. Do you have something to write with?"

I scrambled for a pen and grabbed a piece of junk mail off the counter. Jenson gave me the address and I wrapped up the call. Then I stared at the address. I didn't get called to crime scenes. I just didn't. But I didn't have time to wonder about it. I needed to get dressed and on the road.

*   *   *

The address Jenson had given me was a high-end hotel in one of the ritzy areas of town. Roy and Icelynne had walked through—literally—my front door right before I'd left, so they'd decided to accompany me to the scene. Roy because he fancied himself a PI and Icelynne, well, I think she just didn't know what else to do with herself. At least she wasn't crying today. Of course, with her recent trauma, taking her to a crime scene probably wasn't the best thing, but she was an adult and it wasn't as if I could stop her. So, the two ghosts sat in the backseat of my car, making me feel like a chauffeur to the dead.

It took me exactly forty-two minutes from the time I disconnected with Jenson to reach the hotel. I anticipated a chaotic scene; after all, Jenson had said more than one division of law enforcement was on the scene and that never led to happy times. What I didn't expect was for both agencies to be milling about the parking lot. The officers in their blue uniforms were easy to identify, but even the plainclothes detectives were easy to distinguish from the FIB agents—most of the agents looked a little too pressed and polished. Likely because little things like weather and environment didn't affect their perfect glamour while the wind heralding an oncoming storm whipped at the detectives' hair and clothing.

The two groups didn't mingle.

Parking the car in the back of the lot, I walked toward the gathered detectives. Three men broke off from the others. The wind-bedraggled shapes of John and Jenson headed over from among the sea of officer blue and Falin walked toward me from the FIB side. We met just beyond the farthest cop car.

"Hiya," I said, because I didn't know the protocol. I assumed since Jenson had mentioned the coroner was ready to release the body that they would roll the gurneys out to the parking lot. It was a little public for my comfort, but that wouldn't affect my ability to perform the ritual. If an ambulance had been on scene that would have been preferable than out in the open, but I didn't spot one.

"Alex." John nodded in greeting. It was far from cold, but considering he'd been a father figure for most of my adult life, the recent distance between us stung. I nodded back, trying not to frown. If John was on the scene, why had Jenson called me. *Because John didn't approve of hiring me?*

It was a real possibility. Someone higher up than John must have ordered me to be brought in, and he didn't look happy about it. Or maybe the scene had been that bad. Whichever the case, his mustache was pulled down hard in a frown.

"You ready to go up?" he asked, nodding to the hotel.

I blinked. "You mean, to the murder scene? You're not bringing the bodies down here?"

"What's wrong, Craft? Can't handle getting your hands dirty?" Jenson's voice was all sneer, ugly and mean. I frowned at him. His eyes were pinched tight and there was a little something at the corner of his mouth. Jenson didn't handle crime scenes well, and I was guessing he'd puked, which explained why he was being extra nasty today. He got like that sometimes. It also meant this was going to be bad, very bad.

"So what's the story?" I asked as John led us toward the building. Falin fell in at my side, but Jenson trailed behind. I guessed he didn't want to go back to the scene. Roy and Icelynne brought up the rear, mostly because the ghost-fae dragged behind. Otherwise, Roy likely would have been the first in the building.

"It's a proper mystery. Two local high school students checked in after a fall dance," John said, and then paused as I signed in with the officer maintaining the perimeter. Once the officer had recorded my name and verified my ID, John continued. "The doors are operated with a swipe card, so we have a record of every time the door opened. The kids swiped in at eleven twenty-three last night.

Door wasn't opened again until housekeeping came by at nine seventeen this morning. What she found . . . Well, you'll see. The important thing is that she saw no one else in the room when she walked in. Video of the hall confirms that no one entered or exited the room between the kids entering and the maid's arrival." He stopped in front of a door and pulled out a swipe key. "I should warn you—it's bad."

I nodded but put up a hand before John could use the key card on the door. "Who exactly is hiring me here?" I asked, looking from first John and then to Falin.

The two men looked at each other. Falin cocked an eyebrow, it was a jaunty expression, and more than a little challenging. John scowled.

"Currently, NCPD is picking up the tab." He pulled a folded stack of papers from his jacket pocket and passed them to me. Then his gaze cut to Falin again, his next words directed at him instead of me. "We will, of course, bill half of the ritual to the FIB if we hand over the case."

Falin shrugged. A slightly pink tinge crept over John's expanding bald spot, and he turned back to the door. He shoved the key card into the lock a little too hard, jerking it back fast. The light flashed red. It didn't unlock. He cursed under his breath and tried twice more before the door beeped, flashed green, and unlocked.

As he fought with the lock, I gave the paperwork a cursory scan. I'd been on retainer for the police for years, so most of the paperwork was the boilerplate form we'd established when we'd initially worked out the terms of my retainership. The finer details had been hastily added with a ballpoint pen, but considering the circumstance, that didn't surprise me. Everything looked to be in order, so I signed both copies and handed one back to John.

He took it without comment, waiting in the open doorway.

Falin leaned down, his words a whisper meant only for me. "You up for this?"

I wasn't sure if he meant the scene or if I was strong enough for the ritual. Maybe both. I nodded again and hoped I was right.

I started forward but John held up a hand before digging out gloves and covers for my boots. I accepted them and pulled them on, the three men doing the same. Yeah, this was going to be a bad.

"You know I'm going to have to disturb the scene to draw a circle, right?"

"It's already been photographed," Falin said, sliding on a bootie over his dress shoes. "That doesn't mean we should track in unnecessary trace."

Okay, he had a point.

"So why aren't we doing this back at the morgue?"

"Because we're in a disagreement over who has jurisdiction and it was agreed you would be the fastest way to settle it. Besides, in all likelihood you'd end up on the case anyway. This expedites things." John didn't sound happy about it. *Nice to be wanted.* But I guess I couldn't really blame him. The FIB and NCPD didn't have a great track record of working well together.

Roy and Icelynnc floated ahead of us into the room. I still couldn't see what was beyond the door, but Icelynne made a sound somewhere between a scream and a gasp. I couldn't quite make out what Roy said in response, but the rhythmic sound of his murmuring made me think he was comforting her. Apparently they'd become fast friends.

John motioned me forward, but I hesitated, thinking about what he'd said about the scene being up for debate on who had jurisdiction. If the victims were fae, it would be clear-cut, so it must have been the killer the police were uncertain about. Okay, maybe I was stalling stepping into the room, but from what I already knew by Jenson describing the scene as a locked room mystery and John's explanation, it appeared we had a murder with no apparent means of unmonitored egress. Unless, of course, the killer slipped out when the maid entered or while the police were there.

"You think it's possible the killer was using an invisibility charm?" I asked.

John nodded. "We scanned the room once we arrived, but personal charms don't leave a trace once the witch has left the premises."

The other option was glamour. That didn't even need to be said. So it would come down to what the kids' shades said to determine if the FIB or NCPD would be taking lead here.

"Ready?" Falin asked, his hand moving to the small of my back. The touch surprised me. I tried to believe it was just a friendly urge to get this over with, but the heat that lifted in my cheeks betrayed me. I hurried forward, almost stepping on John's heels as I followed him into the room.

The curtain covering the wall-length window in the far corner of the room had been drawn aside, letting in the late-morning light. All the lamps were on and a few extra work lights had been brought to the scene, but despite the fact there was adequate light in the room, my eyes refused to make sense of what I was seeing. At least when trying to take in the room as a whole. I frowned, trying to focus on one piece of the room at a time.

There, closest to the door, was an armchair toppled over, stuffing exploding from it in long vertical slits. Beyond that was a desk, the wood scarred by a gash that nearly bisected it. My eyes moved farther over the wall, where it looked like someone had pressed their hands in red paint before running them over the otherwise neutral wallpaper. I knew it wasn't actually paint, but I didn't stop to dwell on it, instead letting my gaze move on to the bed, only slightly disheveled and still covered with a teal comforter. A figure knelt at the end of the bed, leaning against it heavily. It was a male, as soon as I saw him my grave magic told me that much. Young, maybe eighteen. Blood had dried in a dark stain where it soaked the carpet around his legs, almost blending in with his black tuxedo slacks. At first I couldn't tell if he still wore a shirt or not, there was too much blood, but I decided he didn't and the flayed material hanging from his back was flesh.

I tore my gaze away, forcing myself to keep inspecting the room when what I really wanted to do was squeeze my eyes shut and back into the hallway. But I had to look. I could already feel the second body, the grave essence pulling at me.

The girl was a few feet from the boy, between the base-board of the bed and the large-screen television. She wore only a slip that must have been tan or white when she put it on the night before. It was a dark brownish-red now. Lacerations covered her arms, her torso, even her face. Congealed blood matted her blond hair and had dried in flaking rivulets on her arms and bare legs.

I moved on. The way the girl had been facing, I couldn't tell if she'd been running toward the door or the bathroom when she'd been . . . stabbed? That made the most sense, but I'd know for sure soon. Sprays of blood trailed across the TV screen, the walls, even the ceiling sported blood. The bathroom door hung open, but I couldn't reach it without stepping over the couple. Whatever evidence might or might not be in that room wasn't my concern—I was here only to raise the shades—so I didn't bother trying to navigate to the bathroom. The carnage ended before it reached the back of the room anyway. From my vantage point just inside the main door, I could see an emerald green dress hanging in the open closet. She must have undressed before whatever happened began. I didn't know anything about the girl, not yet at least, but I was guessing she and her boyfriend hadn't been receiving visitors while she was wearing only a slip.

After taking in as much of the room as I could stomach, I averted my eyes. I'd missed details—I knew that—

but I'd seen enough, more than I wanted, and for what they needed, only the bodies were important. Unfortunately, I'd have to move the couple to draw my circle. With their positions and relation to the furniture, there was no other way.

Unless I work without a circle.

Just the idea made my skin crawl. It was dangerous, but we were actually fairly far away from any cemeteries and the only two bodies I felt in the immediate area were the couple. Of course, I'd light up like a beacon as soon as I straddled the chasm between the living and the dead. And nasty things lived in that wasteland. I really didn't want to encounter one of them.

"We're going to have to move them," I said, nodding at the couple while keeping my eyes averted.

"Is it possible to perform the ritual without disturbing them?" Falin asked.

"I can't draw my circle. The bed is in the way."

The three men conferred quietly. I meant to listen, but the two ghosts poking around the scene distracted me. Roy kept kneeling and pointing at this or that while Icelynne followed him, her dark eyes a little too wide. I couldn't catch everything he said, but I clearly made out the words "arterial spray" and "signs of struggle." Roy had been a computer programmer in life, and Tongues for the Dead didn't typically work active scenes, so he had to be guessing, most likely based on crime shows, but Icelynne hung on every word he said, clearly impressed with his prowess as an investigator. I left them to it.

While I'd watched the ghosts, Jenson must have left the room, because he walked back into the door as I turned, two morgue techs behind him.

"Where do you need the bodies moved?" a young tech with a flush of pimples on his cheek asked.

I glanced around the room. I wanted to disturb the scene as little as possible, which meant I didn't want to walk—or draw my circle through—any of the blood. I probably shouldn't move the furniture either if I could help it. It was going to have to be a very small circle. Fine by me, but I still needed enough clear space to do it. It was a nice hotel, but the room was far from large.

I pointed to the largest clear spot in the room. One of the techs spread a drop cloth—which I hadn't even considered before—and then the techs moved first the boy and then the girl side by side on the cloth. They were both in full rigor mortis, so while the techs tried to lay the boy on his side, the position was unnatural, his knees bent and arms and head curled forward like the overanimated pose of someone pretending to be scary for the benefit of a child. The girl was just as stiff, her legs twisted at awkward angles and one arm up as if she'd been shielding her face, but at least she lay flat.

Once the bodies were moved, I pulled out my wax chalk and drew my circle tight around the couple, being sure to keep to the drop cloth. I actually stood on the outside to draw it, because inside the circle the open spaces were too narrow and awkward for me to squat while ensuring I didn't accidentally brush against the bodies.

With my circle drawn, I glanced at Falin, John, and Jenson. "Ready?"

John nodded and pulled out a camera that I guessed shot still and video based on the small red light that began blinking when he hit a silver button on top. I doubted the video would be as good as what was shot at the morgue, but it would do to document the ritual.

Falin glanced at the camera. "You know I'll have to confiscate that if this officially becomes a FIB case."

"Yeah, you can file for it with the main office. Alex, go on."

I didn't wait to see if the argument would continue, but activated my circle, dropped my shields, and embraced the grave. The chill rushed into me, the unearthly wind tossing my curls around my face. The boy was closest to me, so I reached for him with my magic, my power sliding into the corpse.

The shade I found was weak. Not impossible to raise, and not as weak as the male victim Jenson had me raise days before had been, but noticeably weaker than a fresh body should have been. I paused. Raising a weak shade would take a lot more energy than raising a normal one. And I didn't have a lot of energy to spare. Time to check the girl. Hopefully, she could give us all the information we needed and I wouldn't have to expend energy into the weak shade.

I drew my magic back from the boy and reached out to the girl. Sometimes, when I hadn't performed a ritual in a while, my power all but hemorrhaged out of me, rushing toward any corpse in my vicinity. But I'd used my grave magic a lot recently, and I wasn't at my strongest, so it reacted placidly as I guided it into the girl.

I frowned. Her shade was even weaker than the boy's.

"Something has damaged them," I said, opening my eyes to look at the men in the room with me.

Jenson huffed out a breath between his lips. "Well, I'd say that is stating the obvious."

I turned a glare toward him. "No, I mean their shades. What was done to their bodies shouldn't have weakened their shades. But . . . *something* did."

"You can't tell what?" Falin asked.

I shook my head. I'd felt shades that had been shredded by a soul-eating spell before—this wasn't like that. It was more as if they'd burned out, like a candle that had run out of wick. "Something *used* them up. Wore them out."

"What can do that?" John asked, stepping to the very edge of my circle. I tensed—John was a null with absolutely no magical sensitivity. He had a bad habit of walking through my circles.

I shook my head. "I don't know. Some sort of massive

energy drain before death?" I'd read a study once that explained how a death due to magical depletion damaged a body down to its DNA. Maybe it could damage the shade as well. It was so rare, I doubted it had ever been studied. "Do we know if either of these victims was a witch?"

John pressed his lips together and then shrugged. "They attended public high school, but that's not always a good indicator. As high school students, of course, neither had achieved any OMIH certifications, so they aren't card carriers. Without questioning them or their friends and family, or running a Relative Magic Compatibility test, it's hard to say. What are you thinking?"

What *was* I thinking? Magic couldn't cause knife wounds. Sure, there were offensive spells that could rend flesh, but I doubted that was what we were dealing with in this situation. For one thing, that would still require an outside caster to have delivered fatal blows to both kids, which meant they hadn't been the ones performing a ritual that had gone out of control and drained their life essence. And if the wounds were magical backlash, they should have been inflicted from the inside out, and while I was no medical examiner, even I could tell the wounds started at the flesh and not vice versa.

I turned back toward the bodies. "I'm going to raise the boy now."

No one said anything as I pushed my magic into the boy's body again. It took a lot of magic, and I felt the strain before my heat even rushed out of me, but the shade sat up, solidifying. While the corpse was a mess of lacerations, the killing blow must have come pretty quickly because the shade looked fairly normal, at least from the front. I could have walked around and seen how much damage he'd taken premortem, but I wasn't that curious.

"What is your name?"

The shade turned his head toward me, his eyes dull, unfocused. Not surprising. "Bruce Martain."

I nodded in acknowledgment—not that the shade noticed, but even if they weren't sentient, they looked like people and I tried to be polite. Then I turned toward John. I could have questioned Bruce without guidance—I'd done this dance before—but he'd hired me, so I'd take his lead. Besides, he was recording this. It was better if the cop directed the questions.

"How did you die?" John asked, and I repeated the question for the shade.

"The clown crawled out of the TV. It had a knife."

The room went utterly silent, as if everyone present had drawn in a breath and then held it. Even Roy's constant whispered prattling paused. All eyes stared at the placid shade.

If I'd been asked to make a list of the top one hundred possible explanations for what happened to these kids, going from most to least likely scenarios, "a clown crawled out of the TV" wouldn't have made said list. I blinked at the shade. It couldn't lie. I knew that. It could only repeat what he had seen or thought while alive.

"A clown?" I asked, hearing the uncertainty in my own voice. "Bruce, did you take any drugs recently?"

Okay, I should have waited for John to ask that, but it was too obvious a question to not follow up "a clown crawled out of the TV" with drugs.

"Yes, and not *a* clown. *The* clown," Bruce clarified, as if that actually helped. "We were watching a movie. I picked a scary one because when Shannon is scared she all but climbs in my lap, and I'd already talked her into her slip so she didn't wrinkle her dress." The shade said all this with no shame, and I groaned under my breath for all teenagers everywhere. "We'd just watched the scene where the killer dressed up as a clown at a frat party and started hunting down co-eds. Then he turned and called us out by name. He said he was coming after us next. And he did. He crawled right out of the TV. I thought it was the drugs taking effect at first, until Shannon started screaming and I realized she was seeing the same thing."

"What drugs did you take?" I already had an idea. I wanted to be wrong but . . .

"A guy was giving out samples in the parking lot outside the dance. He said it was like a magical hit of ecstasy. Everything would feel more intense for a few hours, and he suggested it would really get Shannon in the mood. He called it Glitter."

Shit. I turned to Jenson, my eyes wide. The detective looked away from me. Actually, from everyone. Had he told anyone about the shades I'd raised for him? I'd thought that was why the FIB was here now, but maybe not. Actually, by his response, I was sure not. Damn. That would make things more difficult.

John opened his little flip notebook, trying to write notes while simultaneously holding the camera steady on the shade. It wasn't working out well for him, but with him distracted by the task, I couldn't read from his expression if he was familiar with the drug or not. I looked at Falin.

"Have you heard of Glitter before? Did you guys find any drug paraphernalia?" I knew they hadn't at Jeremy and Emma's crime scene, but then, they hadn't been looking. Whatever Glitter was, it didn't pop on a drug screen. Not the normal ones the ME usually ran, at least.

Falin's face gave away nothing. "Some personal items were bagged in the bathroom, but no syringes, pipes, or pills."

I'll take that as a no.

"Ask how the drug was ingested," John said. He'd pressed the notepad against the back of the camera and was writing at a vertical angle. Every move of his pen caused the camera to bob, and I hoped whoever reviewed the footage wasn't prone to motion sickness.

I repeated his question to the shade.

"We drank it. The drug came in little glass vials. The kind cologne samples sometimes come in."

I glanced at Falin, who nodded to indicate something that met that description had been bagged as evidence. From the corner of my eye, I saw the two ghosts float toward the bathroom. Roy clearly wasn't done playing detective for Icelynne yet.

"We need to establish a timeline," John said, looking up from his notebook.

I nodded and turned to ask the shade to recount the order of events, but froze when Roy burst back out of the bathroom.

"Alex," he yelled. "Alex, we need you."

I make it a rule not to talk to people no one else in the room can see. It was easier before my planeweaving went into full gear and I heard ghosts only when I tried. These days I actually had to work at ignoring ghosts. But the pitch to Roy's voice was equal parts excitement and concern, not the type of thing I should ignore. He'd found something. Or at least he thought he had.

But I couldn't just stop questioning a shade midritual and mosey to the bathroom. I turned toward him, hoping my expression was enough of a question for him to tell me what he'd found.

"The vials? The ones the shade said the drug was in?" he said, and I nodded for him to continue. "Icelynne recognizes them. She said they are what the alchemist used to store the glamour he stole."

Chapter 12

I stared at Roy. The killer in Faerie kidnapping fae and draining their blood to distill their glamour was then creating a drug with it that was somehow making it to mortal hands? *Why?*

I glanced at the bodies at my feet. Both teens had imbibed Glitter and now their shades were weak, exhausted. The first victim we knew of, Jeremy, had also taken the drug and had a weak shade. There had to be a connection. The drug somehow burned them out to their core. And it had something to do with pure glamour. And snakes, which Jeremy was terrified of, and a clown from a horror movie. But again, why?

How did murder of kidnapped fae and seemingly randomly chosen mortals relate? What could a fae gain out of the deaths? Fae who lived in Faerie rarely cared about mortal currency, and besides, with both cases involving Glitter, the shades claimed the drug had been given to them, not sold. So what did the alchemist want? *And how can we find and stop him?* I did not want to see any more horrific scenes like this or like the grotesque display of Icelynne's body.

I turned to Falin. I guess I expected him to be thinking

the same thing, but all that was written across his face was cautious concern. John was similar. Jenson just looked impatient. Of course, they couldn't hear Roy. As far as they knew, John had asked me to question the shade. I'd turned, and then stared off into space.

I opened my mouth to tell them what I'd learned and then stopped. It was fae business. Falin needed to know, obviously. Jenson was debatable. He was feykin, and a cop, but he was independent. Once the FIB knew the connection, he'd likely be off the case. John was plain vanilla human. The queen might be annoyed if I told a mortal cop someone in Faerie was releasing a drug made from glamour to humans. Still, he was a friend, and a cop on this case. Didn't he deserve to know?

"The drug is from Faerie," I said, and the expressions around me went from concern, to confusion, and then the two faes' features turned toward dismayed anger. I decided it was best not to add any specifics.

Falin's features returned to neutral annoyance in the blink of an eye, and he turned toward John. "This is now officially an FIB matter. Clear out your men."

John huffed and stood straighter. John was by no means a small man. In fact, I've used the phrase "grizzly bear" to describe him before. But Falin was the freaking assassin and knight of the winter court. Even if John didn't know those particular facts, Falin had a badass aura to him. When you met his gaze, something inside you knew that he wasn't someone you wanted to meet in a dark alley. It didn't hurt that he was taller as well so he literally stared down at John, making the detective look up at him.

"Unless Alex has some proof for that statement, I intend to finish the interview with this shade," John said, and then looked at me.

I looked to Falin. He scowled. The queen would be royally pissed if I discussed Icelynne and what was happening inside the winter court—she'd been trying pretty hard to conceal it. Continuing the interview seemed the better plan. When Falin didn't stop me from turning to the waiting shade, I assumed he agreed.

I asked the shade John's timeline question, and he laid out the events of his evening. Most of the events we already knew or guessed, but confirmation was always good. The couple had arrived at the hotel and checked in just after eleven. Bruce had shared the Glitter with Shannon soon after they arrived. They'd gotten comfortable aka clothes had been removed—and then Bruce had cued up the horror movie. The movie was less than halfway through when the clown had climbed out of the screen.

His description of the nightmare clown chasing them around the room was delivered clinically, the shade detached from the story, even as he described the first stab to his back. How he'd stumbled into the bed. I shivered and wondered why no one had called the police, or at least the front desk. Surely the teenagers were screaming? The story wrapped up soon after that, Bruce's death not far behind the stab to his back. Shannon was still alive in his last memory, but she clearly hadn't been for much longer.

John then sent for a sketch artist to question the shade on the appearance of the man who'd given him the drug. The artist took notes without starting his sketch. He'd worked with me before, and he knew that as the shade couldn't provide feedback about the drawing, his time was better spent asking detailed questions about the dealer's physical description. I knew he'd review the audio back at the station where he would put pencil to paper.

Finally, the sketch artist nodded, his questions finished. I sighed in relief, a sigh that came out jagged as I trembled. I looked around, asking with my expression if anyone had other questions. Exhaustion clutched at me and the icy chill of the grave sliced at my skin. Being so cold while still in touch with the grave was a bad sign. No one ventured another question, and I sighed with relief.

"Rest now," I told the shade, releasing Bruce back into his body. Some of my life-affirming heat followed the well-worn path through my psyche back into my body, but it did little to warm me.

"Did you need to question Shannon as well?" I asked, trying to keep my teeth from chattering.

John glanced at his notebook, then at the bodies in my circle, and then finally at me. For one excruciating second I thought he'd say yes, but finally he shook his head. *Thank goodness.* As tired as I felt, I wasn't sure I had the energy to put the eroded shade back together. It couldn't have been much after noon, but I was ready for bed, or at least a long nap. Yeah, that sounded divine.

Wrapping up my ritual, I released my hold on the grave, not the least bit surprised when unbroken darkness covered my eyes. I'd used a lot of magic. I'd be blind for a while. I broke the circle, but then just stood there. Not being able to see while standing in the middle of a crime scene beside a pair of murder victims was *not* a good thing. With my luck, I'd end up tripping and sprawled on top of the bodies.

I had a moment of indecision as I debated opening my shields so I could at least navigate out of the hotel. Then a hand cupped my elbow.

"Let's get you out of here," Falin said, his hand on my arm guiding me gently.

I let him. The AC of the hotel gave way to the midday heat, the sun only slightly warm against my chilled skin.

"Do you need a ride?" he asked, and I heard the unmistakable sound of a car door opening. As I was pretty sure I'd locked my car and he hadn't pickpocketed the keys, I assumed it was his car.

"Yeah, otherwise I have to hang around here for a while."

"Unavoidable either way, I'm afraid. That is, unless you want me to arrange for someone else to drive you home."

Not really. A yawn caught me by surprise and my jaw cracked with the movement. I covered it the best I could with the back of my hand before shrugging to Falin.

"If you don't mind me catching a nap in the passenger seat, I'll be fine here for a while."

I couldn't see it, but I swear I could feel his frown. I was weak and I'd just used a lot of energy while I didn't have a lot to spare. At least we'd learned something useful.

"About the vials of Glitter . . ." I told him what Icelynne had told Roy about the alchemist and the direction of my current thoughts on the case. He made a couple of noncommittal noises as I spoke, but didn't interrupt or add his own opinions. He was silent for a long time after I finished.

"You should get some rest," he finally said, and while it was true enough, I couldn't help feeling disappointed that he'd brushed me off without word one on the case. He knew finding the alchemist and associates was the only way I was going to get my independent status. Of course, he was the queen's man, and she'd rather add me to her court than let me have relatively free rein.

I yawned again, the movement turning into a full-on sway. I needed to sit down. Without another word, I climbed into the car and reclined the seat. I barely even heard the door shut as I closed my eyes and drifted off.

Chapter 13

Later that afternoon I sat in the middle of my bed, PC sprawled across my lap, and my laptop propped on one knee. Falin had dropped me off hours ago, saying he had to go to court and he'd be back tonight. He'd promised we'd discuss the case when he got back, but he'd given me no new information on the car ride home.

Icelynne flitted about my room. I'd spent the last hour grilling her on absolutely everything she could remember about her confinement. When she'd called me a bully Sleagh Maith and broke out in tears, I let it go—she hadn't been able to tell me anything she hadn't already said when the queen and Falin had questioned her. Now I was writing up all the details she had given me in a document, along with everything I could remember from questioning Jeremy's and Bruce's shades. I was hoping organizing what I knew about the case would shine a new light on it, but I was running in circles.

I knew fae were being kidnapped, held, and drained in the winter court by an unknown fae who was making a drug from their blood. That drug was being distributed to mortals, but I wasn't sure how. Jeremy had said he picked it up at a club. Bruce had gotten it in the parking lot outside his high school dance. And why was the drug being distributed? Money would be the normal guess, but most fae didn't care much about mortal money. And if it was just about money, why go with an exotic drug that used fae glamour? Why not something more mundane?

And what about the deaths? What was the drug supposed to do? Were these deaths abnormalities and there were lots of people using Glitter with no consequence? Or was it a death sentence? Did nightmares always come to life on the drug?

I stared at the screen, and then highlighted the word "nightmares." Faerie had nightmares. An entire realm of them that fed on the bad dreams of mortals. To my knowledge they didn't kill anyone, but I was far from an expert.

The cursor blinked at me, taunting me with my lack of information.

I shut the laptop a little harder than I needed. Then I looked up. Lusa Duncan, the star reporter for Witch Watch lacked her camera-worthy smile, which never happened. Either she didn't like what she was reporting on, or she was trying to give the piece a serious tone. It was always weird when reporters delivered bad news with a brilliant smile. I grabbed the remote and turned up the volume.

"—a new drug called Glitter. Officials are warning that reports of this particular drug just appeared on the street but is already responsible for several deaths. Citizens are warned to avoid this drug at all costs and report anyone who approaches trying to sell or give it away. While authorities won't release any information on the alleged deaths, they say the drug is classified as extremely dangerous." Then she did smile. "But aren't all illegal drugs, Todd?"

The camera panned to another anchorman. "That they are, Lusa. The number at the bottom of the screen is a toll-free crime stoppers line. If you spot suspicious activities—"

I muted it again. So John, or most likely someone higher up in the NCPD, had given a press release about Glitter. That was fast. I guessed it had to be the police though—I doubted the courts wanted the name of a drug with ties back to Faerie announced on television. I hoped the announcement would prevent some deaths, but I doubted it. From my experience, people who wanted to try a drug did so. I'd raised more than a few shades of addicts. The families always wanted to know why they had to take that one last hit, go for that last high. The shades never had a satisfying answer.

My brain centered around the word *addict*. What was the point of a drug that killed the user? You never got repeat business. Definitely not a profitable way to do business, though I already doubted profit was a motivation. Still, what was the benefit of a killer recreational drug? Maybe it wasn't supposed to be deadly?

Or mortals weren't the intended users. But then why distribute it in the mortal realm?

If it wasn't aimed at mortals, the human element of this was likely the weak point of the operation. I knew the drug was made in Faerie, but it was making its way to the mortal realm, which meant it was likely passing through the Bloom. The door was on the VIP side, but the mortals were on the tourist side. Maybe I could learn something there. *Unless, of course, it is passing through some other door and being shipped into Nekros.* But Icelynne was sure she'd been held in the winter court, and the winter court just happened to be the court currently tied to the door in Nekros. The simplest solution was often the correct one, so while I couldn't discount the drug being shipped in, it was fairly safe to assume that it was passing through the Bloom.

I glanced at my clock. It was nearly four and Falin wasn't back yet. It would be dark in a few hours, so I couldn't legally drive if I'd be out long—I had a restricted license. For some reason people weren't keen on drivers with deteriorating vision operating a vehicle while completely night-blind. Go figure. Besides, I'd been more or less blind when Falin had dropped me off, so my car was still parked at the hotel.

It was a little early for dinner, but I was betting Holly wouldn't object to heading to the Bloom early today. As a mortal addicted to Faerie food, it was the only place in town she could eat, so she and Caleb ate there daily—usually multiple times a day. I'd just catch a ride with them. Decision made, I refilled PC's bowl with kibble, and then grabbed my purse and headed downstairs to track down my housemates.

I leaned against the polished oak counter. I'd broken off from my roommates and headed for the tourist side of the bar. The drug was being distributed to mortals, so I hoped I'd have better luck on this side. Besides, the patrons were less intimidating.

The bartender was an unglamoured satyr, his top that of a man, his bottom half furry with cloven hooves. As far as I could tell, he was one of only three fae in the bar, well, other than me. While part of the reason I'd decided to hit up this side of the bar was the fact it boasted less fae, the bartender was still the most likely to know what happened inside the bar. Or at least, that was my hope.

So, I waited as he served mortals overpriced beer and the occasional basket of pretzels. He was here to be seen, and he was doing that. He kicked up his hooves as he walked, exaggerating the movement so no one could miss the goat half of him. It was probably great for his tips.

"What's your poison, darling?" he asked as he stopped in front of me. He tossed his head, making his curly hair slide back to show off stubby spiraled horns.

I wasn't impressed—I'd seen much larger horns before—but he was working it for tourists, so I smiled politely. Leaning conspiratorially close, I said, "Actually, maybe you can point me in the right direction. I'm look-ing for Glitter."

The satyr's eyes rounded slightly, the smile faltering, but if I hadn't been watching for a reaction, I wouldn't have noticed. "Should I know what you're talking about? What can I get you to drink?"

He hadn't said he didn't know what I was talking about. Only asked if he *should.* Which probably meant he knew something. Of course, it was possible he was hedg-ing for no reason. The fact fae couldn't lie meant many were naturally ambiguous in all their answers, regardless if they had something to hide or not. It was a defense mechanism of sorts. I didn't know anything about this satyr, so I had no idea where he fell, but I was sure he'd recognized the drug's name.

How did one establish a buy with a drug dealer any-way? Geez, who knew I'd ever need that type of knowl-edge? I didn't even know how to pull off acting like a junkie who needed a hit. The movies sometimes showed rich kids heading down to the wrong side of the tracks to score drugs, but I didn't have the spare cash to throw around on a bribe—unless the seven bucks I had in my purse would buy me information. I really doubted that.

I fingered the charm around my neck. There was one thing I had, though I had no idea if it would help me. Pulling the chain over my head, I dropped the charm in my purse. As soon as it lost contact with my skin, my flesh began to shimmer. The glow was subtle, but in the dim bar, more than a little noticeable.

Someone *ooh*ed behind me, heads turned. The satyr backed up, then he dipped in the smallest bow.

"My lady, I didn't recognize you."

I frowned at him. He didn't *know* me, but he meant recognize me as Sleagh Maith. It didn't matter who I was or what court I was in, the assumption was that all Sleagh Maith were nobles. It earned my table the best spreads of food on the other side of the Bloom, so I knew it had some sway, but I hadn't expected quite such a reaction from the satyr. Of course, from what Caleb had told me, the fae working on the tourist side of the bar were all independents required to flaunt their otherness whether they wanted to or not if they wished to remain in this territory. Most had very few encounters with court fae, especially the court nobles.

"Glitter?" I asked. I figured short sentences were best—I was less likely to spoil the royal air.

"I don't know much. There is a hobgoblin . . ." His gaze darted around the bar, but apparently didn't find what he was looking for because it landed back on me quickly. "He doesn't come in often, but I've heard him talk about the stuff. He meets people here sometimes."

Perfect. Well, okay, maybe not perfect, but it was more than I knew before. I smiled at the satyr and passed him my business card. "Give me a call the next time he's in."

He frowned at the card, staring at the Tongues for the Dead logo. "Yes, yes, of course," he said, and tucked the card into his smock. "I'll return to my customers now?" He said it as a question, so I nodded and he scampered off, looking relieved to get away.

I turned and scanned the bar. Several of the tourists openly stared at me, which wasn't surprising. This was a "safe" place to gawk at fae. According to Caleb, places like this existed specifically so mortals could stare at fae—it helped cement the belief magic so necessary for Faerie's survival. Which likely explained why the other three fae currently present were all employees. Aside from the bartending satyr, there was a dryad cocktail waitress who passed between the tables all smiles and rustling leaves—which were changing to brilliant reds and oranges with the progressing fall weather. A small platform that acted as a stage stood in the far corner of the room and held the final fae employee. She sang, her voice low and haunting as it slid over those watching her. She was beautiful in a dangerous way, like the lithe and dark beauty of a black widow spider.

I didn't know when the singer would take a break, and while I'd have liked to question her about Glitter or the hobgoblin the satyr had mentioned, interrupting her set didn't seem like a good idea. I was on a restricted time frame. If she finished before I had to leave, I'd ask, but for now I focused on the cocktail waitress. Unfortunately, while she didn't make it blatantly obvious she was ignoring me, she seemed to very intentionally never look in my direction, and some other patron always seemed to need her immediate assistance. There were no empty tables, and I wasn't about to chase her around. After trying to flag her down unsuccessfully, I finally resorted to cornering her when she approached the bar for drinks.

The vines of her hair twitched as I neared, making the leaves rustle louder. The smile she'd been wearing fell as she faced me. "I have a lot of customers," she said, gesturing to the full room with the pint in her hand.

"I just need a moment of your time. Do you know anything about a drug called Glitter?"

She shook her head and lifted her now-full tray of drinks. I didn't move out of her way and the vines lifted slightly, like a mass of angry snakes.

"How about any hobgoblins who frequent this side of the bar?"

"Mortals, hobgoblins, or other minor fae, they are all the same to me. I simply wish to finish my shift and return to my trees."

Right. I let her go. I couldn't force her to talk to me. Her smile reappeared as she approached the tables. She never so much as glanced back my way.

I watched the bar a little longer, but no one suspicious entered. People laughed and drank. One couple was clearly arguing, her body language closed off and his face flushed with anger. Another couple was obviously on the opposite end of their relationship, just starting to feel each other out, maybe they'd even met tonight in the bar. It all looked so normal. Like any other bar in Nekros, except with a few more souvenir shirts. I had no idea what I was doing or should be looking for. Maybe Falin would have info for me by the time I got home? Or I'd call up John tomorrow. Either way, I wasn't accomplishing much here.

I checked the time on my phone. Holly and Caleb would be looking for me. It was time to go. I'd learned all I could. I dug out my charm, though it likely wouldn't work on the dryad, satyr, or anyone else who'd seen me in the bar—it showed people what they expected and now they'd all seen me glow. But it would disguise my nature from those who didn't yet know better, so I slipped it over my head.

I had a potential lead if the satyr followed through and called when the hobgoblin made his next appearance. It was the best I could do on the mortal side of the bar. On the VIP side? Asking questions would likely be a lot more dangerous. For today I'd just send Rianna a message letting her know about the fading and have some dinner with my housemates. I was starving.

Chapter 14

Falin didn't return that night. I should have been happier about that fact; after all, that meant I had my small overhouse apartment all to myself for the first time in nearly a month, but really it just made me anxious as I kept expecting the door to open. It also meant I didn't get any answers about what else he may have discovered at the crime scene.

I considered checking in at the office the next morning, but it was Sunday so we had no posted hours for the day, plus Ms. B and Rianna were holding up in Faerie to conserve energy. The response Rianna had sent me last night hadn't been encouraging, mostly because it had consisted of only one word. *Hurry.* I had to get my link to Faerie, and fast.

I had other reasons to find the alchemist as well. If he was really behind the creation and distribution of Glitter, he had to be stopped before more vials of the drug hit the streets or more fae died under his phlebotomy tools. I had only a handful of hours before I needed to meet Holly and start getting ready for Tamara's wedding, but I couldn't waste them. It would help if I could track down the distributors in the mortal realm and then follow that line back to the alchemist. But I couldn't just sit around hoping the satyr from the Bloom called. The hobgoblin he'd mentioned was my only lead, but it was also possible he wasn't involved. Even if he was, who knew when he'd show up at the bar next, especially with Glitter being all over the news. How much time did I have before I faded so far I wouldn't be able to stay in the mortal realm? I needed to be proactive. The problem was, I had no idea how to investigate a drug ring. But I knew someone who did.

Grabbing my phone, I called the front desk at Central Precinct. I confirmed John was in today, but declined to be transferred to his private line. He probably wasn't too happy with me right now, and hanging up a phone was easy. I'd be way harder to dismiss in person.

John frowned at me from across his desk. I hadn't even said anything yet—just sat down.

"Alex, if you're here about yesterday's murder scene, there isn't anything I can tell you. We handed over everything we had on it to the FIB already."

I smiled, trying to look innocent and disarming. John's expression didn't change and he closed the file he'd been scanning when I walked in.

"It's connected, but not directly. I need guidance. You worked narcotics before homicide, right?"

John cocked one bushy eyebrow before giving me a single curt nod. That was apparently as good as I was getting from him. I rushed on.

"Well, I need to track down who is making Glitter, but I'm not sure where to start. I know the kids from yesterday got their hands on it, and I know it's being manufactured in Faerie—"

"So you said. I'd like to know how you know that."

Now it was my turn to frown. I hadn't actually been oath bound to refrain from talking about Icelynne and the circumstances of her death, but that didn't mean I wanted to recklessly piss off the queen by discussing court business. The drug, while connected, was tertiary to that case. Still . . . "I was hired by the winter court to look into a case that involved the drug," I said after what was probably too long of a pause.

"And now you're looking for the manufacturer? No offense, but that not only doesn't sound like your kind of case, but you're in way over your head. You're excellent at raising shades. Stick to that."

He'd given me that particular *advice* before. It hurt no less this time. If my actual father had said as much, I wouldn't have cared. But coming from John, the man who'd encouraged me to go through with getting my PI license in the first place, who'd encouraged me to open Tongues for the Dead, and who'd connected me with my retainer position with the NCPD—yeah, it stung. A lot.

But it wasn't like I had time to cross my arms over my chest and pout. John didn't know I was fae, and with the current strife in our relationship, I wasn't feeling particularly willing to share. That also meant he didn't know my precarious position of lacking any tie to Faerie or the urgent reason I had to solve this case and find the alchemist.

I didn't bother forcing a smile, but I did lean back slightly in my chair, trying to look relaxed. And as if I wasn't going anywhere. "So have the narcotics guys interviewed any of the other kids from the dance? Did they find anyone else who saw the dealer?"

"I told you. That case was handed off to the FIB," he said, but his eyes darted to his half-full coffee cup as he spoke.

"Yeah, you guys handed off the murder case," I said, putting my hands on the arms of the chair and leaning in toward him. "But you can't tell me you guys aren't look-ing into the drug connection."

He huffed, still not meeting my eyes. Which was pretty much a yes.

"So the kids? Surely Bruce wasn't the only one ap-proached with the drug." Though I hoped that if anyone else had accepted, that they hadn't used it and had heeded the warnings about the danger. "Did you get more infor-mation on the dealer?"

John finally looked up, his blue eyes were tired, the wrinkles around them deeper than I remembered. I'd never thought about it before, but John was probably get-ting close to retirement age, and it was starting to show. He ran a hand over his bald spot before letting his fist fall limply to the top of his desk.

"Narcotics investigations aren't as . . . straightforward as murder investigations. In murder you examine the body, the scene, and gather what information you can. Then you talk to the friends, the family. You find out who wanted to kill the person, who had motive and oppor-tunity. And hopefully, at the end of the day, you get a confession or have enough evidence to nail the suspect in a trial."

He picked up the file he'd been studying before I en-tered. He tapped the edge of it against his desk, not open-ing it. "Narcotics tends toward long-term investigations. You bust someone low on the pole, usually a user. You get them to give you information on their dealer. Maybe you turn them, or maybe you use an undercover to do some buys and then you bust the street dealer, but these are still the little guys. They might be carrying three hundred dollars' worth of product on them at any time. You try to work them back to their source. This guy's the real dealer. If you're lucky, he's the one cooking the drugs, but usually, he's still a middle man. Oh, he might be the local 'drug lord' but he's getting the drugs shipped in from somewhere else—especially if it's being run by a gang. Anyway, getting to him isn't easy. You need probable cause for a warrant and you want to bust him when he has a large stash you can put him away with. It takes surveillance, maybe even getting a man inside, and once you do have the warrant, a raid. You're talking weeks, months, sometimes even years of police work to get that far, and even then, you don't necessarily know where the drugs are coming from." He frowned at the file.

I chewed at my bottom lip. I didn't doubt anything he was telling me, but I didn't have that kind of time to wait on the cops, and I certainly didn't have the resources or knowledge to do it on my own. "So how far have your guys gotten?"

"Alex, we found out about all this yesterday. We haven't scratched the surface. We've got a rough sketch of the dealer based on the shade's description, and we've tracked down and questioned a couple of kids who were at the dance, but no one is saying anything."

I sighed and pushed out of the chair. "I suppose if I ask if there is anything I can do to help . . . ?"

"That I'll tell you to go home." He gave me a look that said it wasn't a hypothetical suggestion.

I nodded and grabbed my purse, but I paused at the door. "John, it's important I find this guy. Like life-and-death important. Just . . . just give me a call if you can."

I didn't stay and press him. It wouldn't help, I knew that. Without waiting for him to sputter something about police business or ongoing cases, I left.

By the time I reached my house, I was more than a little discouraged. I'd heard nothing from the satyr at the Bloom, which, as it was fairly early in the day, was not surprising, but I realized I didn't even know when he'd be bartending next. For all I knew he was required to work only once or twice a week. I hadn't heard from Falin ei-

ther. I'd taken a taxi back to yesterday's crime scene to
retrieve my car, and I was sure he'd be at my place by the
time I drove home, but when I pulled up to the house, the
driveway was empty.

But my porch wasn't empty.

I stopped, my foot frozen above the bottom step leading to my rented room. A tall figure stooped in front of
my door, something long and wrapped in black paper in
his arms. Whatever the object was, I couldn't tell if he'd
been in the process of picking it up or putting it down
when I'd mounted the steps, but he straightened when he
heard me, turning to face the stairs.

Ryese grinned down at me from the landing in front of
my door. The bright sunlight caught in his hair, making it
glisten like crystal refracting light and spilling prisms of
color around his face. The effect was blinding. I frowned
at him and briefly considered turning and getting back in
my car, but I wasn't going to be driven away from my own
home. Not more than I already had been, anyway.

I took the stairs at a slow, but deliberate pace. While I
didn't relish seeing the fae, and I was more than a little
unsure about what his presence at my home meant, I didn't
want him to see me frightened. Still, it took everything I
had not to draw my dagger as I climbed the last few steps.

"Lexi, dearest," he said, opening his arms as if he'd
sweep me into an embrace.

I stopped, out of arm's reach, and glanced at what he
carried. The long, paper-wrapped object turned out to be
the largest bouquet of roses I'd ever seen. Black roses at
that, mixed with sprigs of delicate baby's breath. It was a
striking contrast.

"What's that?" I nodded at the roses.

Ryese glanced down as if he'd forgotten about the
flowers. Then he shot me a sheepish smile. No, not sheepish, guilty.

"This? Nothing. I—" He swung the bouquet over the
porch rail as if he intended to drop it.

I stepped forward and grabbed the paper-wrapped roses. Something about the whole situation was off. Not like a trap, though if that thought had entered my mind a moment earlier I probably would have hesitated long enough for him to toss the bundle, but the resounding thought in my head was that black really wasn't Ryese's color. He tended to deck himself out in so much white it was blinding. And the queen favored things dusted in ice or snow.

Ryese scowled as I rescued the roses, but quickly covered the expression with a blatantly insincere smile. "Shall we linger in doorways like a couple of peasants?" he asked, gesturing toward my door.

I ignored him and fished the card from among the roses.

FOR MY LOVELY BETROTHED.

There was no signature, but with that message, it didn't really need one. Dugan had been here.

I tucked the card back into the bouquet, careful to keep my expression schooled to neutral. Now that I knew for certain where it had come from, I couldn't care less if the roses ended up tossed in the trash—or over the rail—but Ryese was watching, his expression dark, and I didn't want to show my hand. I had no doubt he'd report back to the Winter Queen on whatever I did. He may or may not know who had sent the roses, but I doubted he'd missed the word "betrothed" on the card.

So, I kept my features neutral as I unlocked the door and stepped inside. Then I had a moment of uncertainty. Theoretically I should put the roses in a vase of water or something. But I didn't own a vase. I wasn't really a flowers kind of girl. I settled for placing the still-wrapped bouquet on the counter before turning back to Ryese, who, no real surprise, had followed me in.

"What do you want?"

"Lexi, Lexi, Lexi, is that any way to treat your beloved?"

I cocked an eyebrow—I'd been practicing and I was damn good at it now. He was most certainly not my beloved. Hell, he wasn't even my "be*liked*."

When I just crossed my arms over my chest and stared at him, he coughed quietly and turned away. His attention settled on PC, who normally greeted my guests, but was standing a careful distance away from Ryese, sniffing. *Smart dog.*

"That is one ugly mutt," Ryese said, shaking his head.

My fists clenched, heat lifting to my face. "You're not endearing yourself here."

He glanced up and shot me a quick smile. I never realized a smile could look quite so hateful.

"Dearest Lexi, I am simply here to see how you are doing on your little case. I thought you might need some help, especially since the knight is otherwise engaged."

I opened my mouth to turn him away and then closed it. I did need help. But could I trust anything that came from him? Well, I guess he wasn't really any *less* trustworthy than Falin: both would be reporting back to the queen. But it was certainly a less appealing offer.

And speaking of Falin . . . "What do you mean 'otherwise engaged'?"

His smile spread, lips parting in a gleefully malicious grin. "Oh, I suppose you wouldn't know. He's been dueling."

He said it casually, turning as he spoke and wandering around my small space.

"Dueling?"

He stopped in front of my dresser, leaning in to examine the pictures surrounding the edges of my mirror.

"Oh yes. Between the recent, high-profile fae-related crimes in winter court territory and the . . . rumors. Well, let's just say some aren't terribly confident in my aunt currently. Which means she's received several challenges for her throne. Of course, all challengers have to duel her knight first, so he's rather busy."

The blood drained from my face. While I wasn't a fan of the queen and didn't care if she lost her throne, Falin fighting everyone lining up to challenge her didn't sound good. He was a spectacular fighter, but he wasn't invincible and each challenger would be coming to him fresh while he'd still be recovering from the previous.

Ryese turned, his eyes twinkling as he took in my expression. "So, you see, there is a lot of interest in your progress. What have you learned?"

If I'd had something—anything—I'd have told him then. But I didn't know anything. I was floundering.

I moved like a sleepwalker across my room and sank onto the edge of my bed. Damn this alchemist. How the hell was I going to find him? And now Falin was in the winter court fighting the queen's duels.

"Going that well?" Ryese asked as he leaned against the dresser. Why the hell did he always smile so much? He didn't mean the smiles. Wasn't that a kind of lie?

I didn't stand, but I forced myself straighter, trying not to look like I was shrinking in on myself, even though that was how I felt. "The alchemist is making a drug. I don't know why. It's killing mortals with nightmares or hallucinations. I'm working on a lead tracking down a hobgoblin who might be involved."

Ryese tapped his chin with one long finger. "A hobgoblin you say? Anything else?"

I cast around for any other strands I had to follow, but it was too early in the investigation. I just didn't have anything.

After my silence stretched, Ryese nodded. "Well, then, I think I will return to court to pass on this rather distressing news. You are, of course, welcome to join me."

I shook my head. I had even less idea of how to go about tracking down the alchemist in Faerie than I did here in a realm where I at least understood the rules. I'd likely have to take my investigation there eventually, but right now I'd likely just end up dead or trapped if I started blindly poking about Faerie. For now I'd keep looking for the Glitter connection here.

Ryese shrugged, taking my silence for refusal. "If you change your mind . . ."

My phone rang, cutting him off as Annabella Lwin proclaimed her want for candy. Holly's ringtone.

I shooed Ryese toward the door as I dug the phone out of my purse and answered. From the background roar of wind it was obvious wherever Holly was calling from, she was driving.

"You going to be ready in about an hour?"

Ready? I glanced at the clock. More time had passed than I thought. I had to get ready for the wedding. Hair and makeup we'd all work on together, but— "Shoes. I don't have shoes for the wedding yet."

"Seriously? Alex, okay, I'm turning around. I'll be there in twenty."

I hastily agreed before hanging up. I started toward the closet before realizing Ryese still hovered by my front door.

"Out," I said, pointing at the door.

He lifted his hands as if surrendering, but made no move to leave. "Big day?"

I considered saying yes and leaving it at that, but if he'd read Dugan's card he would already be reporting back that I was *theoretically* betrothed. He likely guessed it was to someone in another court. If the queen thought my marriage into a rival court was imminent . . . who knew what she might do.

"I'm a bridesmaid. Now leave so I can get ready."

Ryese pursed his lips, and for a moment I thought he was going to refuse to get out of my house. Then he gave me an elaborate—and dare I say, mocking—bow complete with intricate hand flourish, before ducking out the door.

There'd been no other car in the driveway, so I wasn't sure how he'd get back to the court, but I hoped he'd be off my porch and out of my yard before Holly arrived. In the meantime, I gathered the pathetic collection of makeup I owned, the hairpiece Tamara had given me as a bridesmaid gift, and the dress. Then I went on a mad search for panty hose.

Chapter 15

I channeled a small string of magic into the flower arrangement in front of me, activating the charm held within. The spray of chrysanthemums glimmered faintly, like a small ember had taken hold of each scarlet petal. Then I stepped back, glancing around the gazebo.

"I think that's all of them," I said as Holly straightened, moving away from a similar display of shimmering orange mums.

She nodded and glanced around, checking our work. Every flower in the quaint wooden structure glimmered from within. The effect was faint now with the sun still a deep orange hanging low in the sky, but once dusk hit, the glow would give the gazebo a romantically dreamy look as Tamara and Ethan exchanged their vows. Which was, of course, the point, and why Tamara had spent the last two days charming all the flowers. We may have planned this wedding in a month, but that didn't mean she was willing to skimp on her fairy tale.

"Looks like we finished just in time," Holly said, nodding toward the front of the gazebo.

A long red carpet ran down the wooden steps into the grass beyond. White folding chairs were set up on either side of the carpet in rows of five across. A small cluster of people were gathered behind the last row—the first wedding guests. I didn't recognize them, so I guessed they must have been Ethan's family or friends.

Tamara's younger brother, who was acting as an usher for the wedding, was already striding across the grass so I felt no pressure to go greet them. I gave the decorations one last glance. Everything looked fabulous. I'd have liked to take credit for that, but Holly and I had mostly just activated the charms. Tamara, her sister, and her mom had done all the actual arranging.

"We should get back to the tent," I said, heading down the short stairs, but neither Holly nor I hurried.

Both the bride and the groom had small pagoda-style tents so that the bridal party could get ready on-site. The tents were on opposite sides of the park so Ethan wouldn't accidentally see his bride before her procession, and all the bridesmaids were supposed to be in the tent helping the bride. Tamara was one of my best friends, but I was seriously considering stealing off to the groom's tent. After all, while us girls had hair and makeup, what could the groomsmen be doing? Probably talking about football and tossing back a beer while they waited. Okay, maybe not, but at least they didn't have—

"What took you two so long?" a shrill voice asked as Holly pulled open the tent flap.

—The Mother of the Bride.

I sighed, but forced my expression to pleasant as I stepped inside. While I'd met Mrs. Greene on only a few occasions, I'd liked her in the past. Today? Not so much. *Isn't it the person actually getting married who gets the free pass to be a bridezilla? Not her mother?* Granted, while Tamara's little brother was married, she was the first girl in the family to get married. Still, the woman had been a hovering micromanager since Holly and I arrived—late, which hadn't helped.

Mrs. Greene had curled her lips at the shoes I'd picked

out, berated every color I chose for my makeup, and had finally forced me in a chair so Tamara's sister could redo my hair. When it had been mentioned that the charms needed to be activated in the flowers, Holly and I had jumped at the opportunity to escape the tent. But now we were back.

"How's it going?" I asked, hovering near the tent exit. That was apparently the wrong thing to say, as it opened the door for Mrs. Greene to go into a spiel about everything from the bouquets to the fit of Tamara's dress.

For her part, Tamara sat serenely in front of the large vanity mirror, apparently unfazed by her mother's incessant commentary or meticulous administrations with the curling iron. Personally, I would have been cowed, or at least annoyed. But Tamara only sat there, beaming at the room as a whole. A month ago she'd nearly deteriorated into a ghoul as her life force had been drained away. We'd stopped the process, but the experience had turned her normally full-figured, curvy form to one that was skeletally thin. A month's time to recover had helped, but she was just now barely out of her first trimester of pregnancy, and the unending morning sickness had made it hard for her to regain the weight. But while she was still a little too thin, her honey-colored skin had a glow to it that said she was much healthier.

Her mother had created a gorgeous maze of corn rows along her scalp, leading to a high ponytail, her hair spilling out in dark ringlets from around a thick wall of pearls. She wore a matching necklace of pearls, and even more accented her dress, hanging like opaque teardrops from the gauzy material over a white satin sheath. In a word, she was stunning.

"You look awesome," I said, walking up to squeeze her hand. Her smile brightened a shade more, her eyes sparkling.

"Knock, knock; everyone decent?" a male voice asked from outside the tent flap. "I'm finished with the groomsmen and groom photos. Are the bridesmaids and bride ready?"

"The photographer," Mrs. Greene said, a hint of panic in her voice. She tossed the curling iron onto the vanity top and grabbed Tamara's veil, looking frantic.

Tamara took it calmly from her trembling hands and attached it to her hair. Her mother and sister fussed over the veil and the hang of her dress as she stood, even Holly moved forward to help. Me? I stayed out of the way. I thought she looked great, but they tugged at what seemed to me to be imagined misalignments. Finally everyone stood back. Even Mrs. Greene smiled.

We were ready.

By the time I took my place at the end of the line of bridesmaids at the steps of the gazebo, my feet ached from standing in the new heels, my head hurt from all the pins taming my blond curls, and I was tired of carrying the bouquet of faintly glowing orange mums. But, at least I hadn't tripped and fallen as I walked up the aisle.

The music changed to the obligatory rendition of "Here Comes the Bride," and everyone turned. Tamara appeared between the arch at the end of the carpeted aisle, her arm hooked around her father's. He was a tall man, age just beginning to bend him. He carried a cane, but today, for this walk, he seemed determined to use it as little as possible. The sun was steadily sinking, casting a warm glow over everything. Tamara's white dress practically blazed as she all but floated down the aisle. Under her veil, I could see her smile trembling.

Did she still have second thoughts? I hadn't seen any indication of the panic she'd called me in a few days ago when we had all been in the tent. No, likely her lips trembled from her attempt not to cry from joy—I've heard brides do that sometimes. I tried to imagine how I'd feel, but I couldn't picture myself a bride. Though Death would look good in a tux. . . and so would Falin.

I frowned, and then forced the expression off my face. This was Tamara's wedding. I focused once again on her slow glide up the aisle.

By the time she reached the front, her father's eyes twinkled with unshed tears. He lifted her veil and kissed both of her cheeks before formally handing her off to her soon-to-be husband. For his part, Ethan beamed, his smile wide as he watched Tamara. His hands were steady as he engulfed her smaller, trembling ones and they both took the squat two steps up into the gazebo.

Then all hell broke loose.

We were all focused on the bride and groom, so no one noticed the two wedding crashers slink into the back. At least, not until the child screamed.

I think, at first, everyone tried to politely ignore the child. But the louder she screamed, the more eyes slid in her direction and discreet glances were tossed over shoulders. Finally even the bride and groom turned.

The mother, a young woman on Ethan's side, looked more than a little embarrassed as she tried to calm her young daughter, who was maybe three years old. Someone muttered that she should take the girl to the car, and the woman ducked her head, uttering both agreement and apologies. The woman scooped up the small child, but the girl twisted in her arms, crying and pointing at a couple who seemed to be trying their best to ignore the girl's attention. But now she wasn't the only one.

Tamara's nephew, who was just shy of two, lifted his voice to join the young girl's. At first I thought he was crying because she was, but though he buried his face against his father's leg, he kept peeking at the back row. At that same couple.

I frowned. The couple looked inconspicuous enough, she in an ankle-length navy dress and him in dark slacks and a polo shirt. I didn't recognize them, but they were sitting on the groom's side, and I didn't know most of Ethan's friends or family. Still, more than one young child being terrified was odd.

Before the magical awakening, some normal-looking—at least to adults—people scared children for reasons no one understood. Now we knew that there were certain fae whose glamour worked only on older adolescents and adults. Young children saw right through it. In particular, Bogies couldn't hide what they were. That is, the traditional bogeymen who hid in closets and under beds but were never there when mom or dad looked, and of course, all the folk that mothers once warned naughty children would gobble them up if they played by lakes or under bridges.

I lowered my shields, just a crack. Around me, all the glowing flowers appeared to decay despite the swirls of purple and blue magic fixed inside them. Clothes on the party guests lost their splendor, instead appearing to fray and deteriorate.

And the otherwise inconspicuous couple in the back? Their rather normal appearance morphed into a nightmare as my innate ability to pierce glamour through the veils of reality revealed what hid beneath.

The man, who'd appeared to be a robust but normally sized and proportioned human male, was truly a good two feet shorter, so that he stood at four two tops. While not fat, he was wide, thick. His arms had to be larger around than my thighs, his meaty hands the size of bowling balls with red-tipped talons on each large finger. His features were spread across a leathery face, thick lips chapped and callused below a bulbous nose. Above oversized ears he wore a sagging red cap, which dripped viscous red liquid down the edges of his head, like a slow stream of blood. It was a horrific visage, the very thing to inspire night terrors in children and I had no doubt the fae was indeed of the bogeyman variety.

The woman was perhaps less physically frightening, at least compared to her companion, but she had an air of maliciousness about her. Where the man was squat and wide, she looked almost overstretched, with long, thin limbs that reminded me of naked tree limbs reaching for unsuspecting travelers in dark woods. Her skin had a green tinge to it—not unusual in many of the nature spirit fae, but while the green men, like Caleb, had a coloration that reminded one of spring and new growing things, her skin was more reminiscent of murky slime growing in stagnant water. Her dank green hair hung tangled about her shoulders, rotting plants and the bones of fish caught in the muck-covered strands. When she smiled, her teeth were small and pointed, like the grin of a piranha.

It wasn't a huge mystery why the children had screamed. The real question was, had the couple been invited as guests or not? Being the subject of childhood tales didn't automatically disqualify one from having friends. Many independent fae lived alongside their human neighbors without revealing their true nature. Others, like Caleb, my friend and landlord, didn't exactly hide they were fae but didn't advertise it either.

Thinking of Caleb, my eyes slid to where he sat on Tamara's side of the aisle. With my shields down, I could see through the boy-next-door glamour he wore in public to his green man coloration and vaguely *other* features. *He* didn't look scary, but then I knew him well and he was descended from rather harmless nature spirits, not bogeymen. The couple, Caleb, and well, me, were the only fae currently in attendance, at least that I could spot from a quick glance around the crowd. Caleb and I were obviously invited guests, but was there any reason to believe the couple weren't guests? Ethan taught a course on the ethics of magic at the university. The couple could be colleagues or family friends.

I glanced at the couple again. The red liquid trickling from the man's cap really did look like blood. I had a book at home detailing different fae from folklore, which, as most were oral stories written down in the Victorian era, wasn't always a reliable source of information on the fae, but it was the best I could do. I'd been studying the book since I'd learned my own heritage, and I vaguely remembered a couple of stories about a classification of fae called *Red Caps*. If I remembered correctly, they were a type of goblin . . . Maybe even hobgoblin?

The two kids were being carried out now, the crowd murmuring softly. The couple exchanged a glance and then both looked directly at me. The way their gazes bore into me, I got the distinct impression they could tell I was looking across the planes. My charm hid my own *otherness* only if what you expected to see was human. If they could see through my illusion, they knew exactly who and what I was. I knocked a couple of points off the probability of them being just another pair of guests.

They stood as a unit and began making their way out of their row. Tamara and Ethan had turned back around, the wedding proceeding, but as the two fae slipped onto the red carpet, the crowd began to shift nervously again.

Holly noticed the couple and shot a glance back at me, her face a question. I had no answers, but a bad feeling slid along my spine. I clenched my fists around my bouquet. My dagger was in my purse, which was in the bridesmaid tent. My instincts urged me to move, to stop standing like an attending statue, but I really, really didn't want to be the one to ruin Tamara's wedding just because a creepy pair of fae were moving to a better seat. *Unless their plan is more sinister.* Trying to maintain my already feeble smile, I watched the couple's slow progress.

Mrs. Greene finally noticed the shifting and backward stares around her and tore her gaze from her daughter. I could see only the edge of the dirty glare she shot at them, but I was glad I wasn't the one on the receiving end. She stood without a word, the picture of poise as she silently but purposefully moved to the aisle and intercepted the fae. I could catch only the hiss of her voice, not her words, but while her gestures were contained to a tight box in front of her body, they were sharp, betraying not so hidden anger.

The fae ignored her. The hobgoblin pulled something from inside his jacket pocket. I still had my shields cracked, so I had to squint to figure out that the crumbling object was some manner of reed pipe. He lifted it to his thick lips like it was some sort of instrument. I seriously doubted music would be what emerged.

"Get down," I yelled, grabbing Holly's arm and dragging her to the ground with me as I took my own advice.

A moment later a small dart flew silently through the spot I'd been standing seconds before.

Someone in the crowd screamed and wooden chairs creaked and toppled, as people rushed out of their seats. Tamara moved as though she would run to Holly and me, but Ethan grabbed her arm and rushed up into the relative safety of the gazebo. I was thankful for that. Goodness knew there was no cover where Holly and I crouched in the grass.

"We've got to move," I said, but other than the gazebo, there was no cover anywhere near us.

Holly seemed to realize the same thing, because without a word, she turned and crawled toward the wooden structure. I followed, the grass damp through the thin material covering my knees. With Holly in the lead, I needed only to pay marginal attention to where I was going, leaving most of my attention free to watch the two fae.

The hobgoblin reloaded his blowgun, his large fingers fumbling with the small dart. The woman was otherwise engaged, primarily with Mrs. Greene. Now that her daughter's wedding was well and truly interrupted, she'd lost any pretense of civility toward the two fae and was now cursing, loudly. Not bad words mind you, but a true curse. The kind that made the Aetheric swirl around her, giving her curse power.

I was still a foot away from the gazebo when the hobgoblin lifted the blowgun to his lips. I cringed, an instinct that did nothing to help me get to cover sooner. Thankfully, while I may not have thought it necessary to wear my dagger under my bridesmaid dress, many of Tamara's guests were on the police force, and they'd had no such compunction against carrying their service weapons.

The hobgoblin's small red eyes flickered to the crowd of off-duty cops as a half dozen officers drew on him. It wasn't much of a distraction, but it was enough for me to dive behind the gazebo.

"You okay?" Holly asked, leaning down to help me to my feet.

I nodded, turning to peer back around the edge of the gazebo while staying as covered by the structure and glowing flowers as possible. I'd missed only a moment, but in that time the scene had changed. The two fae were running from the wedding now. I could see them clearly, but then I was still peering across planes of existence. Judging by the fact the cops had lowered their weapons and were looking around in all directions, I guessed the fae had glamoured themselves invisible.

Once the two fae vanished through the arch and across the park, I stepped out from behind the gazebo. Chairs had been knocked over on both sides of the aisle, and nearly half the wedding guests had fled. Holly and I both had grass stains on our knees, and Tamara's bouquet looked the worse for wear where it lay forgotten at the steps of the gazebo. Mrs. Greene fluttered around, trying to put things back in order, but even if most of the guests returned, I seriously doubted this wedding would continue.

I surveyed the chaos and guilt clawed at me like daggers sinking into my guts. Was this my fault? Had the bogeymen been targeting me? It seemed likely. They had appeared to be able to *see* me. And whatever the man had shot from his blowgun had been aimed at the bridal party, of which I was a part. But I wasn't the only bridesmaid. Still, who else here had recently taken a trip to Faerie, questioned shades who'd died from drugs distributed by fae, or left her card at the Bloom after asking questions? I wasn't sure which action had gotten me noticed, but it certainly seemed I'd gotten someone's attention.

Chapter 16

Two hours later I sat in the reception tent with a huge slice of wedding cake in front of me. The dance floor was empty, as were most of the tables. Tamara sat beside me, what looked to be an entire half a tier of wedding cake crammed onto her plate. Since the wedding had never resumed, there really weren't any guests to eat the cake, so Tamara had stated that she'd be damned if we didn't eat and enjoy it. It wasn't like she could return it. Despite her words, she was only poking at her ginormous slice with her fork. Holly just watched.

Several cops still milled around—some guests but others on duty finishing up their reports on the "interruption." Crime scene techs combed the area around the gazebo, searching for the dart the hobgoblin had shot from his blowgun. It had yet to be found. One FIB officer had responded to the scene. Aside from the children, I was the only person who'd seen the true faces of the two bogeymen, but everyone had seen them vanish without a trace and there were more than a few sensitives who hadn't felt an invisibility charm trigger. Despite all that, since no one had been hurt and there was no proof fae had been involved, the FIB agent who'd responded seemed less than interested in what he labeled "a disturbance of the peace." When I'd ask about Falin, the agent had only scowled at me and refrained from answering.

So, cake.

But I wasn't eating much more of it than Tamara was. I shoved it around my plate, staring at the fluffy white frosting. It was good cake. I knew that. I'd been part of the sample group who'd tasted all the options and helped Tamara decide which to order for tonight. But the sugary concoction no longer tasted good.

It tasted a lot like guilt.

"This is not what I imagined," Tamara said, stabbing her cake. She'd said that exact phrase a dozen times over the last hour, and I still didn't know how to respond. I wasn't even sure she was aware she'd spoken. At least she wasn't crying anymore.

Holly put her arm around Tamara's shoulder, but she seemed just as lost for an appropriate response. I mean, this was not a "sometimes these things happen" kind of situation. People did not prepare for the possibility of bogeymen crashing their big day. There were no Hallmark condolence cards with sympathetic phrases for when your wedding turned into a crime scene.

"It could have been worse," Tamara's sister, Donella, replied. She'd floated between Tamara and their mother, so it was quite possible she hadn't heard the earlier reiteration of the statement.

Tamara set down her fork. "Oh yeah? How, exactly, could it have gone any worse?"

Donella paused, her bite of cake hovering in front her mouth, and then she smiled. "Ethan could have been turned into a toad."

Tamara's lips parted, and for one lingering moment, I thought she'd laugh at that. Then her bottom lip stretched as the edges of her mouth turned down and she gave out a loud, stuttering sob. Her arms curved around her stomach, and she collapsed into herself.

Donella looked mortified, and far too stunned to move. I slid my seat closer to Tamara's. I'm not what one would call a hugger, but I put my hand on her shoulder and squeezed lightly, offering what silent support I could. She shook, her entire body trembling with her tears.

"Maybe it's a sign," Tamara said, between gasps for air. "Maybe we should wait until the tests next month." This she directed toward her still-flat stomach, her palm rubbing the space under her belly button.

I was about to tell her my theory on the two bogeymen. To apologize for my part in them coming here, to her wedding, and take any amount of debt that apology might require, when a deep masculine voice spoke from directly behind me, making everyone at the table jump.

"Are you saying there is anything those tests could tell us that would make you not want to marry me?"

Tamara twisted to stare at Ethan with rounded, red-rimmed eyes. "What if they tell us . . ." She trailed off, her hand once again pressing protectively against her stomach.

"We will deal with whatever happens, together." He knelt in front of her, cupping both her hands in his. "Tamara Amelia Greene, I love you. Marry me. Right here. Right now."

Tamara looked around at the disheveled group, at the disarray of the trampled scene, at the half-eaten cake, and then down at her white gloves that were stained with the makeup her tears had washed away. "This is not how I imagined it."

"Oh, but think of the stories we'll have," Ethan said, and gave her a beaming smile before climbing to his feet and pulling her up after him. "The most important people are still here. Marry me, Tam."

She finally smiled. "Yes." She kissed him. "Yes, yes, yes."

I slipped out of my seat silently and backed away. It

would take them a minute to gather the necessary people and work out the details. If they had a quick ceremony, I'd stand with Tamara as one of her bridesmaids—if she'd still have me after all this—but for now I let them have their moment without a crowd.

John, who'd attended the wedding as a guest but had been hanging out with the cops investigating the case since the disturbance, met my eye and waved me over to join him. My legs were numb from sitting in the folding seat too long, and between that and the heels, they wobbled under me as I walked. Or at least that was what I told myself. I really didn't want to think I was simply that weak from the fading already.

I smoothed my dress as I crossed the empty dance floor—which was pretty pointless as the dress was well and truly ruined. Between throwing myself to the ground and then crawling to the gazebo, the dress had more than one grass stain on the maroon fabric. Fussing with the fabric did give me something to focus on besides the questions John would inevitably ask. But all too soon I'd crossed the garden and reached the friend I feared I was losing.

He led me to a table and gestured for me to take a seat. I did, but immediately regretted doing so when John didn't sit but instead loomed over me, his arms crossed over his chest.

"So what exactly happened? Was this about a case you're working?"

No one had actually questioned me yet. There were a lot of witnesses, many of them cops, and I'd been with the group comforting the bride, so I hadn't been singled out to report on what I'd seen. John knew a little bit more about me than most though. He didn't know I was fae, but he knew my propensity for attracting trouble. Particularly fae-related trouble.

"You're assuming they were targeting me."

He lifted one bushy eyebrow that used to be red but was now salted with white. Yeah, he was making that assumption. And so was I.

I sighed, debating what to tell him. He was a homicide detective, so this wasn't his case. Even if it was, the suspects were fae and he wasn't equipped to trace and arrest them. Still, while I might have preferred to hash out the details with Falin—he was a resource even if things were awkward between us—I could use any help I could get.

"The two wedding crashers were bogeymen. That's what set off the screaming fits—they can't hide their nature from kids. I think one of them might have been a hobgoblin, which can't be a coincidence as yesterday I got a tip that a hobgoblin might be dealing Glitter."

I expected some sort of response, even if it was a grunt approving my supposition or maybe a skeptical crinkle of his brows, but John gave me nothing. His expression froze as he thought, sharing nothing. After an agonizing stretch of seconds, he pulled out the chair beside me and sat.

"Tell me what you know."

I didn't know much, and some of what I did know I couldn't share, but I described both my short exchange with the bartender at the Bloom as well as what I'd observed today at the wedding. John didn't question how I'd seen through the faes' glamour and I didn't offer any explanation.

"Why can't you stay out of these kinds of cases, Alex?"

My shoulders fell, heavy with the weight of his disapproval. "I don't go out looking for them, but I can't drop this case, John. I can't." Not if I wanted to track down the alchemist. He had to be stopped, and not just so I could retain a semblance of freedom. He had a lot of deaths on his hands. Plus he had to be held accountable for wrecking my best friend's wedding.

John ran a hand down his face, his thumb and forefinger pulling the skin around his eyes taut for a moment before dropping to the tabletop. "Why the hell not, Alex? Until the dart they shot at you can be found, we have no idea if they intended to kill you or capture you, but this looked a little more serious than just a warning. I mean, where do bogeymen even come from? Did they crawl out of a nightmare?"

I opened my mouth, but then snapped it shut with a click. Where had the bogeymen come from? I'd assumed they had to be winter court or maybe independent. But what if they weren't? Checking probably wouldn't be too hard—the queen's people had to have some sort of census list of everyone in her territory. Again, I needed to talk to Falin. Hopefully he was all right. Anyone at the FIB probably had access to a list of the independents at the very least, but I doubted any agent beside Falin would give me access to search for the bogeymen.

But what if they weren't independents or winter court? I'd made the assumption they were because this was winter's territory, but bad guys didn't follow the rules, that sort of went along with being a bad guy. But if not winter, what court did they belong to? Fae took oaths to their courts, but it wasn't impossible to change allegiances. A frost pixie like Icelynne was likely to belong to the winter court, but while it would be uncomfortable, it wouldn't be impossible for her to join, say, the summer court. Bogeymen were creatures that thrived in darkness, and like John had said, the subject of nightmares.

I knew neither fae was an actual nightmare—I'd seen nightmares before in the realm of dreams—but that didn't mean they didn't belong in that creepy landscape. Or possibly in the shadow court. There was no guarantee, but I could make some inquiries. I even had contacts, of sorts, in both places.

"You've thought of something," John said, his expression caught between a scowl and concern.

I shrugged, trying to make the movement look unconcerned. Judging by John's deepening frown, I didn't succeed.

"I suppose nothing I say will convince you to drop this case?"

"I would if I could, John. If I only could."

Chapter 17

"Are you sure this is the best idea?" Caleb asked after he, Holly, and I signed in on both sides of the door in the VIP room of the Bloom.

"Unless you have contacts that can help identify the bogeymen who crashed the wedding, yeah, it's the best plan I can come up with."

Caleb and Holly exchanged frowns. In truth, Caleb's concern worried me. He was my go-to resource for all things fae. I didn't know how old he was—it was impolite to ask—but he'd been around a while and he understood fae politics a whole lot better than I did.

"If you could give me a couple weeks, I'm sure we could track down someone who knows," he said, but followed the comment with a sigh. "I know, you don't have weeks. Damn, Al, I wished we'd realized earlier that you are fae enough to fade."

So did I. But we hadn't, and now time was of the essence. "You two go find a table, I'll be there in a minute."

Again, a concerned glance passed between them, but Holly nodded. "We'll keep an eye on you," she said, offering what I'm sure was supposed to be an encouraging smile, but it came out too feeble to be very reassuring.

Still, I nodded and headed for the long bar at the far side of the room.

Today's bartender was an enormous cyclops. The pint glass he was wiping as I approached looked like a thimble in his huge hands. He had a row of horns running down his bare scalp, like a boney Mohawk.

"Uh, hi. I need to send a couple messages," I said, trying to meet his gaze, but it was hard to figure out how to properly focus on his single red-irised eye.

The cyclops grunted and grabbed something from under the bar. The meaty hand swung out in front of me and I fought the urge to cringe away. He opened his hand and an honest-to-goodness quill floated onto the bar top, followed by a handful of dried leaves.

I nodded my appreciation and scooped up the items. Then I scurried to the other side of the bar, farther from the silent mountain of a bartender.

The first message I scratched on one of the leaves was to Rianna. It said simply that I had a lead to follow and for her and Ms. B to remain in Faerie and contact me if things got too bad. It was a simple message, but scratching it out with the quill still took a while. Once I was finished, I crumbled the leaf. It was so dry, it turned into powder in my hand. I didn't know how the messages worked, but I'd sent Rianna several over the last few months and the magic always ensured the messages made it to the intended party in Faerie.

Faerie magic—maybe one day I'd understand it.

The next leaf I addressed to Dugan, the prince of the shadow court. I hesitated, quill poised over the leaf. I'd been debating how to word this missive since I got the idea while talking to John, but the exact wording was elusive. Dugan believed he was my betrothed, so asking to meet with him shouldn't be that hard, theoretically, but he was also heir to the shadow throne. The whole Faerie royalty thing was daunting.

Finally I just scratched down a quick message stating that I was at the Bloom and asking him to meet me. I was about to crumble the leaf when it occurred to me that it would probably be polite to mention something about the bouquet he'd sent. I scratched out *I got the roses. They are* but then I paused, tapping the leaf with the quill. Finally I finished with *pretty*, which sounded rather pathetic, but I'd already written it. Signing the letter, I crumbled it to dust and let the particles float away.

Just one letter left, but it was arguably the hardest. The last leaf I addressed to Kyran, usurper kingling of the nightmare realm. I'd met him only once, months ago, and he was . . . different. I had no real tie to him, and there was no reason beyond his own curiosity that he would agree to meet with me. Hopefully that was enough. As with my letter to Dugan, I wrote that I would be having dinner at the Bloom and asked him to meet me. Then I signed and crumbled the leaf. That done, I returned the quill and extra leaves to the cyclops before making a hasty retreat to the table where Holly and Caleb sat.

The table had already been laid, full of golden loaves of corn bread, pitchers of what I could only guess was ale, and bowls of stew brimming with large chunks of meat, potatoes, and veggies. It wasn't quite as grand a meal as I was accustomed to at the Bloom, but meals were served based on perceived rank, and neither Caleb nor Holly had much in the way of rank in Faerie. The waiters always laid out a feast when I was the first to the table. Honestly, it was awkward, and I was happy for the hearty stew.

I sat down, helping myself to a generous portion of corn bread. Today's waiter, a fae I couldn't name the family of with an iridescent purplish tinge to his skin, hurried over with another bowl of soup and a tankard in his hands, but stopped short a few paces away.

"I'll bring something more suitable," he said, starting to turn.

I held up a hand. "The stew looks great."

The fae waiter looked down at the bowl on his tray before pointing his three-fingered hand back over his shoulder. "It would only take me a moment to—"

"I'd like the stew," I said, cutting him off before he could scurry away. Holly pressed a hand over her mouth, and I got the distinct impression she was hiding a smile under her fingers.

The waiter wavered, glancing toward the kitchen—or whatever they called the area where food was prepared. It certainly wasn't cooked, and actually, it was a little questionable if it was food or not. Faerie food was both real and not real. I wasn't completely sure what it started out as, but if you tried to remove it from Faerie, it turned into toadstools, which quickly rotted away. But inside Faerie it was tasty and filling.

For a moment I thought I was going to have to either let the waiter retrieve a feast or cause a scene by demanding he leave the stew, but after one more uncertain look over his shoulder, he conceded to setting the bowl on the table. He bowed as he did so, placing the tankard of ale beside the bowl.

I had the urge to groan, but restrained myself, instead giving him a tight-lipped smile. Still bent in half, he backed away three steps before turning and hightailing it away.

Now Holly did laugh. "Perhaps we should call you 'Your highness.'"

I tossed a piece of corn bread at her, which only made her giggle harder. I turned to Caleb. "Any way to make the fae here not react that way again? What gives; it didn't seem this bad the last time I was here."

Caleb just shrugged. "Your fae mien is more obvious these days, and your glamour leaves something to be desired."

As in I didn't have any glamour—not any I knew how to use properly at least. I had to work on that.

"Sleagh Maith don't socialize with us lowly independents much," Caleb said, scooping a large chunk of meat onto his spoon.

"So I'm descended from pretentious assholes, gotcha." I sighed again, and then forced myself to focus on the stew, which was delicious but I was eating mindlessly. I might as well enjoy it. I didn't eat Faerie food that often. Until recently I hadn't realized I could. But it posed no threat to me.

I'd polished off half my bowl when the waiter scurried over. I was honestly worried that he might try to whisk away the remainder of my soup and insist I let him lay out a banquet or something, but he just bowed and held out two large leaves.

I accepted them gingerly, so I didn't crush them, and almost thanked the waiter—some habits die hard. I stopped myself at the last moment, nodding at him instead. He hurried away, looking relieved to escape our table.

"What's that?" Holly asked, leaning forward to peer at the leaves.

"Replies, I guess."

I read the first leaf. It was from Rianna, and the message was the same as her last. It read only *Hurry*.

"I'm trying," I mumbled under my breath, crumbling the leaf.

The second reply was from Dugan. It was considerably longer.

While I would grant my betrothed any wish her heart desires, the location you have chosen is problematic. I do not have leave to pass freely through winter's court. Meet me instead in the pocket space where we saw each other before. I will await you with great anticipation.

—Dugan

The pocket space from before? Great. Now I was going to have to see my father.

As the time spent inside the Bloom had little effect on the amount of time that passed in mortal reality, I put off leaving as long as possible, nursing my soup until Holly and Caleb threatened to leave without me. As I hadn't driven, and it was after dark, that wasn't an option I relished. Still, I was also waiting for one more reply, but if Kyran received my message, he didn't write me back or meet me in the Bloom. The other issue was with the leaving of the Bloom in general. I felt pretty good during dinner, but I knew the effects of fading would crash back down on me the moment I stepped out the door.

At least I was prepared for it this time, though I should have warned Caleb and Holly. I'd mentioned I was fading, but their concern as I all but stumbled down the front stairs of the Bloom made me feel even worse. I really needed to cement my tie to Faerie.

I could join a court, a little voice said in the back of my mind. I *was* going to see the prince of the shadow court, after all. He'd surely have no qualms against taking me home to his court. But then who knew when I'd see my friends, my life, or hell, even the mortal realm, again. The shadow court had no natural doors to mortal reality. I'd be stuck in Faerie—and I was damn near powerless in Faerie.

The idea did not appeal to me. Besides, with Falin busy fighting the queen's duels, I was the only one with ties to both Faerie and the mortal realm searching for the alchemist, and he had to be found before more Glitter hit the street.

I called my father while Caleb drove. He answered on the second ring.

"Alexis, since you've deigned to call me, should I assume this is an emergency?" His voice was flat, bored sounding, so I wasn't sure if he was trying to make me feel guilty—hey, he cut me out of his life first—or if he honestly didn't care one way or another.

"No emergency, but I need a ride to your house."

As I spoke, I caught Caleb's eyes flicker toward me in the rearview mirror. The look seemed to question why I hadn't asked him for a ride. We *were* in the car already. I shot him an apologetic smile, but I didn't explain. In truth, I'd considered having Caleb drop me off, but that came with its own slew of problems, the least of which was that I'd eventually need a ride back home, and closer to the top of the list: the fact that my father was currently the acting governor of Nekros whom no one knew I was related to. Oh yeah, and he was pretty much considered the biggest public enemy in Nekros to witches and fae. My life was complicated.

My father said nothing for several moments. I imagined him sitting on the other side of the phone, fingers steepled as he waited for me to say more. I didn't, not yet.

"Alexis, you do realize the hour, do you not?"

I hadn't checked. It was after nine when we'd tossed rice at the newlyweds and Tamara and Ethan had driven away in a car Holly and I had decked out with the tackiest JUST MARRIED signs we could come up with. Caleb, Holly, and I had headed directly to the Bloom after that, as Holly hadn't eaten at all today to ensure a tricky door didn't cause her to miss Tamara's wedding. Typically no time at all passed while inside the Bloom, but occasionally hours or even days slipped away. The latter had only happened to me once, thankfully, and that was before I'd known the importance of signing the ledger. Still, I was guessing at best it was about ten, and at worst sometime after midnight. Yeah, probably a little late for a visit, but it was what it was.

So, I played the one card I had that I was sure would work. "I'm scheduled to meet Dugan."

"And you didn't lead with that because . . . ?"

Because it was my business and I didn't want him to get any ideas about his whole breeding program plan for me. Not that I'd had any illusion that I'd have been able to get to the pocket of Faerie and meet with Dugan without him finding out.

When I didn't answer, my father said, "I can pick you up in thirty minutes." Then he disconnected without saying good-bye.

It took my father only twenty minutes to reach the house. I had enough time to change out of the bridesmaid dress, but I was still walking PC when he arrived, his fancy Lamborghini glamoured to look like a much more mundane sedan. Good move—the sports car would have stood out in our neighborhood. I mean, the Glen, or Witch's Glen as it was often called, was a nice area, but it wasn't *that* nice.

He idled as he pulled up to the curb, and then leaned over and popped open the door. "Get in."

I glanced from the open door to my little six-pound Chinese Crested. PC had visited Faerie with me once because I hadn't had any other choice at the time. Neither the dog nor I wanted him to go on a repeat adventure, so I took him back upstairs first.

Forty minutes later, I was standing outside the invisible line where Casey's circle had once stood that now marked the boundary between normal, mortal reality and the chaotic space where I'd lost control of my magic and permanently woven Faerie into this small fold of space. My father watched me, his glamour down so the fae face that looked not too much older than me studied me.

"Did you need a chaperone?"

I frowned, but then, I guess I was lingering in doorways. "No. I'd prefer to go alone." Or, at least I thought I would. I was off to see a Faerie prince—the prince of shadows and secrets at that. Was it safe to go alone?

Was it any safer to take my father?

Without another glance at him, I stepped through the doorway and across the circle line. The change was immediate. My eyesight sharpened, the air turned sweeter, as if perfumed by unseen flowers, and distant music played just at the edge of my hearing. It was annoyingly comforting. Faerie, as scary as it was, felt like home.

It scared me because I enjoyed it.

Shrugging off the feeling, I walked across the room, dodging the dead zones that looked washed out and decayed. Those were the places my magic had dragged the land of the dead into this reality. If I stepped through one, my very clothing would rot off. This meeting was going to be awkward enough without me showing up in tatters.

A lone figure stood by the stone bench in the center of the room, his back toward me. He cut an impressive figure, and really did look like a prince out of an old tale. His dark hair was pulled back at the nape of his neck so it fell in a straight line down the center of his back. He wore a red cape over his black oiled armor, the material swishing around his calves as he turned to face me.

He smiled, and it was a handsome smile, but there was no warmth to it, no sincerity. "I brought you these." He held out yet another bouquet of roses, this time the black intermixed with deep red.

"Uh . . ." I accepted the roses, feeling more than a little awkward. How did fae manage to interact without insincere thank-yous? Finally I said, "They're lovely."

Then I had to figure out what to do with the enormous bouquet. I had no interest in holding it the entire conversation. I settled for setting it down on the bench.

Dugan looked from me to the flowers and back. The fake smile slipped, ever so slightly, but he stepped forward, capturing my hand in his. I think, perhaps, he'd meant to lock our fingers, but he paused as he caught sight of my palm.

I jerked my hand away, but not fast enough. I always

remembered to put my gloves on before I entered the Bloom, but I'd been so preoccupied, I hadn't even thought about it before entering this small pocket of Faerie.

"You wear the blood of your enemies," he said, his voice betraying what sounded a lot like impressed amazement. Which wasn't what I was expecting. Faerie took the phrase *their blood on your hands* very seriously and most fae reacted with fear or revulsion. His gaze moved to where I'd pulled gloves from my purse and he frowned. "Why do you try to hide it?" He reached out and took the gloves. "That is not the way of the shadow court. We wear our blood with honor."

"Yeah, well, I'm not exactly proud of it." And I wasn't a member of the shadow court. Not yet at least. Hopefully not ever.

Dugan didn't give me back my gloves. "Was the kill disgraceful or unrighteous?"

I thought back to the fight that had earned me the blood on my hands, or at least, the first blood on my hands. It had happened in this very room, on the night I'd learned I was a planeweaver and I'd first merged the planes. But I'd more than just killed the body of my enemy that night. I'd consumed his very soul in my attempt to stop him. I shivered.

"This isn't what I asked you here to discuss," I said, trying not to look at the spot where Casey's bed had been. Where I'd almost died under the Blood Moon.

"Of course. The planebender awaits us whenever you'd like to travel to our court." He pointed to a far corner. I hadn't even noticed the small cloaked figure at the back of the room. Good thing he hadn't been an enemy intending me harm. "I thought you'd bring more with you. It will be . . . complicated to return."

"Wait. You thought I—" I cut myself off. Had he really thought a bouquet or two of flowers would convince me to marry him? To run off and join his court? Yeah, no. Not happening. I shook my head. "I'm not going to Faerie," I said, but when his frown deepened I added, "Today, at least. I just wanted to ask you some questions about the shadow court."

He studied me for a long moment before nodding. "That is a reasonable request. You did not grow up in our lands. You likely have many questions."

He motioned me to sit on the bench, and then joined me. While his smile might look less than genuine, his expression was earnest. He wanted to convince me to join his court—and take his hand in marriage—and he'd answer my questions if that would help. I got the distinct impression that his betrothal to me was the only reason he was the named heir and prince to the shadow throne. If I reneged on the agreement my father had made, what would happen to him? It didn't matter. Even if he was a decent guy, I wasn't marrying him just because my father approved of his bloodline. Hell, I wasn't sure I'd ever marry anyone. That fact wouldn't stop me from pumping as much information out of Dugan as possible though.

Now to find a way to word my questions that wouldn't offend him or cause him to cut me off. "What types of fae are members of the shadow court?"

His brow crinkled. Not confusion, more like bafflement that I'd ask such a stupid question. "Like any court, all types of fae make up our kingdom. The nobles are of course Sleagh Maith, though admittedly, we have fewer than we once did . . ."

"Because you lost some power when the realm of nightmares was severed from the court?"

Again, I'd surprised him, but he didn't look displeased that I knew this fact. "Quite so. With no physical doors like the seasonal courts, the shadow court and the light court rely directly on mortal imaginations. The shadow primarily through mortal's dreams and nightmares and light primarily through mortal creativity and flights of fancy, daydreams. Without the realm of dreams we are . . . weaker than we should be."

It sounded more like they'd been forcibly crippled, but I didn't point that out.

"Hopefully that will be repaired soon and we will be returned to our former glory."

Interesting. I wanted to ask how, but we were getting off topic. Faeries were notoriously secretive. While I had him talking, I needed to keep this conversation on point.

"Are there many bogeymen in the shadow court?"

He nodded. "We tend to be an ideal court for those who like to lurk in darkness."

Which was exactly what I'd been expecting. Now for the tricky part. "If I described two bogeymen to you, do you think you'd be able to tell me if they are part of your court?"

"Perhaps," Dugan said, but the suspicion was clear in the tightness of his eyes, the thinning line of his mouth. "Why?"

Moment of truth. If I refused to tell him why I wanted to know, he'd likely end this conversation here and now. But if I told him too much? I didn't know. The Winter Queen was more than willing to drag me to Faerie against my will if she could claim it was for my own protection. I had some value to the shadow court and clearly to Dugan in particular. If he knew two fae had tried to kill or capture me, would he summon the planebender and haul me off to the dark halls of his court?

"I . . . had an encounter today with what I believe were two bogeymen. One was a hobgoblin. The other, well, I'm not sure what type of fae she was. She looked like a much scarier version of a nature spirit."

Dugan's eyes widened, his gaze searching my face. I worked hard at keeping my face neutrally pleasant, studying him right back, looking for some sign he might grab me and try to force me to his court. An array of small micro expressions swarmed over his face, but I didn't know him well enough to read them. Finally he seemed to come to some conclusion and held up his hand, palm toward me so I could see the blood gathered there.

"My oath, neither your uncle nor I sent any of our people to harm or threaten you. I know nothing of this encounter."

Great, he'd jumped to defensive. "I never said you did. I'm just trying to identify them. If I describe them, do you think you'll recognize them?"

He frowned at me. "Perhaps, but I make no promises. I may only be able to guess what manner of fae they are and not be able to name the individuals themselves."

That was better than nothing. Certainly more than I had now.

I described the woman first, detailing everything I could remember from her height to her strange sludge-and-algae-filled hair to her green pointed teeth. By the time I finished, Dugan's features had darkened, his jaw clenched, but he motioned for me to continue. I described the hobgoblin next with his peculiar dripping hat and overwide features, and even the blowpipe he'd used that had resembled a hollowed bone.

Dugan stood and paced before the stone bench, one hand clasped on the sword hilt at his side. "What manner of encounter did you have with these two?"

"They crashed my friend's wedding." I left out the fact they'd taken a shot at me.

"I must speak to the king about this," he said, turning to where the planeweaver waited.

I jumped to my feet. "Do you know them? Do you know their court? Their names?"

"Names do not have the power told of in the old legends, little planeweaver."

No, maybe not, but a name would at least give me more information for my investigation. It would make researching the pair easier and questioning people more targeted. I stood there, my arms crossed, my expression expectant. I wasn't going to say please and indebt myself to him—I doubted I could afford whatever favor he would claim if I did—but I needed this information.

He pursed his lips, one hand still on his weapon, but after a moment he said, "I cannot be certain, but most of the bogeymen are rather unique. The belief in the tales told of them reshapes them until they are unlike others of their kind. So, my guesses are likely good. It sounds like the woman is a hag known as Jenny Greenteeth, who once gobbled up small children who ventured where they shouldn't. The other a hobgoblin name Tommy Rawhead who hid under stairways and ate naughty children. They were both once part of our court, but left after our influence began to wane. I do not know who holds their allegiance now. If you 'encounter' them again, I suggest you stay away. They are of a nasty sort and I do not wish to see you harmed. Now, I must return to my court. I hope that you will meet me here again." He gave me a small bow, and with a twirl of his cape strode across the room toward the planebender, who'd already opened a darkened hole of a doorway. Both vanished a moment later.

Well, at least I had names to work with. Now to track down a couple of bogeymen who liked to eat kids. Yikes.

Chapter 18

Of course, having a couple of names didn't mean I could accomplish much tonight. By the time my father dropped me off back at home it was nearly three a.m. I all but stumbled up the stairs, my exhausted legs protesting the climb. Even PC didn't bother to greet me at the door, just lifted his head from where he was curled up on one of my pillows, gave me a look like "what took you so long?" and then closed his eyes, going back to sleep.

"You're a very loyal dog," I told him as I took off my boots.

He snored in response.

Right. I stripped off my pants and left them in a pile by the boots, and then, in just my shirt and underwear, collapsed into bed.

I woke standing in a plane of endless sand and darkness.

"A most interesting outfit, planeweaver," a voice said behind me.

I whirled around. Where there had been unbroken sand before, there was now an enormous obsidian throne. A fae lounged across it, one black-leather-clad leg kicked up over one armrest and his elbow on the other, his head balanced on his knuckles.

"Kyran," I said, recognizing the nightmare kingling.

"At your service, my dear." He gave one of those elaborate hand gestures where he rolled his wrist, pantomiming a bow, even though the rest of his body didn't move. He leered, a small secret smile at the edges of his mouth.

The first thing he'd said, about my outfit, finally registered and I looked down. I was wearing only the shirt and panties I'd crawled in bed wearing. No boots. No pants. No dagger.

"Shit." I pulled at the edges of the shirt, trying to tug it down, but it was a fitted top, hitting right at my hipbones, and there wasn't any stretch in it.

Kyran laughed, a boisterous full-bellied sound of mirth. I glared, which didn't quiet his laugh at all. Well, glad I could amuse him.

"So I guess you can chalk this up to being one of those awkward dreams when you show up to work naked?"

"Why am I here?" I asked, trying to decide which was worse, trying and failing to cover myself better, or just saying screw it and pretending I didn't care I was in my underwear. Tugging at the shirt was gaining me nothing, so I went for the latter, crossing my arms over my chest and ignoring the heat in my cheeks—the ones on my face, that was. The other cheeks were a little chilly.

"You're the one who asked to see me, my dear."

True. But . . . "I asked you to meet me at the Eternal Bloom—not drag me off to this creepy nightmare realm." And speaking of the nightmares, where were they? The darkness around me was unending, but nothing seemed to be moving inside it. That was good, but how long would that last?

Kyran made a dismissive sound and lifted one shoulder in a half shrug. "Why fuss with all that political red tape when you come here nightly?"

Nightly? The first time I visited the realm of dreams

and nightmares I'd been having trouble maintaining my shields during sleep, and as I'd already been in Faerie, my planeweaving had caused me to literally fall into a recurring nightmare, landing me physically in this realm. But, the way he'd worded his sentence . . .

"Do you mean this is a dream?"

"Of course. I simply pulled you out of the mundane imagery your exhausted mind typically conjures."

I looked around at the endless, empty landscape. "If this is a dream, that means I can direct it, doesn't it?"

"What, like lucid dreaming? Don't do that. It's annoying. You know that actually steals magic back from this place. Plain frustrating."

Which didn't mean I *couldn't* do it. And that meant I didn't have to stand here half naked. I imagined the black pants I'd been wearing before I'd gone to bed, the way they looked, the softness of the leather. The sand crawled up my legs, which was a totally weird sensation, but between one blink and the next I went from half naked to wearing pants. Well, mostly. Something was wrong with the pants that I couldn't quite put my finger on. The way things are sometimes just *off* in a dream. Like I was looking at them through distorted glass. Still, at least I wasn't half naked anymore.

I looked up to find Kyran frowning at me. He'd taken his legs off the arm of the chair and rotated forward, focused. "Didn't I say not to do that."

"What? You do. Or are you going to say that intimidating throne that follows you around isn't made completely out of dream sand?"

"Yeah, but I live here."

Point. I bowed my head, acknowledging that I was in the wrong, but I didn't apologize. I'd needed the pants, damn it.

"You asked for this meeting. Surely it wasn't simply to leach away magic from my land," he said, propping both elbows on his knees and managing to sound both annoyed and bored. I wasn't sure if he was agitated that I'd manipulated his realm or just that I knew I could.

But he was right—I had asked to meet. Not in these circumstances and I sure as hell would have preferred a more neutral ground, but I was here now. I looked around for a place to sit. There was, of course, nothing besides the throne where Kyran perched and the sand. I briefly considered dreaming up a chair, but I didn't want to piss off the kingling right before asking for information. That likely wouldn't go over well.

So, I shoved my hands in the back pockets of my dream pants and stood.

"The nightmares are stuck here without a door, right? They can't be conjured up in the mortal realm?"

Kyran's brow pinched, and he studied my face, clearly wondering where this line of questioning was headed. "You mean waking dreams? The kind where the dreamer drags his nightmares home to haunt him long after he leaves his bed? That was one of the High King's fears. Nightmares growing too strong and walking out into the waking world in the mortal realm. It was why he severed this realm from the rest of Faerie. In its current state, nothing escapes without a door."

I started to nod, and then stopped. I'd opened a door to the mortal realm the last time I'd been here. I'd had no other choice. The citizens of Nekros had rather vivid nightmares that night, but no unusual deaths had been reported. I was pretty sure he was implying that without a door like I'd opened, the nightmares were stuck. But implication left a lot of wiggle room.

Were there other ways to open a door? I knew Glitter was made from distilled glamour and that somehow fears were manifesting. Could the users become doorways?

"A penny for your thoughts, planeweaver."

I'd been quiet too long, Kyran studying me intensely. I picked my words carefully. "Do you know if any of the nightmares left in the last few days? Or maybe . . .

projected into the mortal realm, somehow?" Because that could be a possible explanation, couldn't it?

Kyran tapped his steepled fingers together. "There are no days here. Only dreams." He smiled his Cheshire Cat grin.

That so didn't answer my question. Of course, he was under no obligation to answer my questions, and I'd asked him several without him asking me anything in return. I had to be careful or he might try to open a bargain in retrospect. They weren't very binding, but I'd nearly been caught in one once before. Which meant I'd better start offering up information if I didn't want to stumble into a debt. Not that Kyran was being horribly helpful.

Something caught at the edge of my attention, and I turned, searching the darkness. Nothing. I focused on Kyran once more, but tried to keep an eye on my peripheral vision.

"There is a new drug in Nekros. The people who take it, their fears come alive. Hallucinations given form." I hesitated before continuing, though I was sure he guessed what I was getting at. "Maybe, their nightmares coming to life."

"*Alex.*"

I froze. I'd definitely heard my name. And it wasn't Kyran who'd said it. I twisted, glancing at the unending darkness and sand all around us. There was only the two of us.

Kyran leaned back in his throne, tapping one long finger against his jaw. "I think someone is trying to wake you. We are running out of time."

And he hadn't answered any of my questions.

"*Alex.*"

The darkness was starting to gray out. The sand under my feet fading away. Desperate, I blurted out, "Is it possible? With the help of a Faerie drug, could the nightmares cross over? Could they harm mortals if given form by glamour?"

Kyran's form was hazy by the time he smiled, once again lifting a single shoulder in an indifferent shrug. "I think you're looking in the wrong realm, planeweaver. Only those who are sleeping journey here. If your mortals are awake when their fears take form, you should be talking to the light court about their realm of daydreams."

Then the gray fog thickened, becoming heavy and obscuring everything, as my consciousness returned to mortal reality.

I gasped, going from deep sleep to wide awake as I sat up. The covers spilled off me, and I felt the comforter against my bare thighs, the dream pants I'd conjured in the realm of nightmares having not followed me back to the waking world.

I blinked in the darkness of my room. The smallest trace of gray light peeked through my shuttered windows. Dawn was close, but it didn't provide near enough light for my bad eyes. That didn't matter though. I didn't need my normal sight to make out the familiar form in my room.

Death.

"That's an awful big frown, Al. A man might think you're not happy to see him."

"No, it's not that. I— " I stopped and focused on changing my expression. And then reached out, wrapping my arms around his shoulders, and kissing him lightly in greeting. Because that's what girlfriends did, right? Man, I sucked at this.

"Hi," I said, which caused him to smile. An expression I felt against my lips rather than saw.

"Hi," he said in return before kissing me again. A much deeper kiss than I'd greeted him with.

I tried to abandon myself to the kiss because he was Death and he was here. But the conversation I'd had with Kyran had occurred in a dream, and like most dreams, now that I was awake, it was slipping away, becoming elusive. Kyran had said something significant, right as I was waking. I had the feeling it was the most important thing he'd said—maybe the only important thing—during the entire conversation. What had it been?

"You seem distracted," Death said, pulling back. He kept hold of one of my hands so he could sit on the bed without the mattress becoming intangible to him.

I opened my mouth to apologize but stopped. I was too fae to incur a debt for such a small thing. I couldn't do it, even to make Death feel better. That realization hurt. And probably would have stung him as well. After all, he was the least likely person to abuse a debt between us. I covered by saying, "I was having a dream. Well, more like a meeting in a dream. I'm trying to remember what was said."

He nodded, not saying anything, presumably giving me time to work it out. I racked my brain. What had Kyran said? Something about sleepers traveling to his realm.

But that visions seen when awake were daydreams.

The court of light.

"You thought of something?" Death asked, his thumb rubbing over my knuckles.

I nodded, but my shoulders slumped. "I apparently need to talk to someone in the light court." And I knew absolutely nothing about that court, aside from the fact that their members glowed with an ephemeral beauty. Much more so than just the ethereal glow of the Sleagh Maith, and from what I'd seen at the Fall Equinox, the entire court held that delicate, awe-inspiring glow. They were the muses of Faerie.

Death looked around my small room. "You got rid of your houseguest?"

I nodded absently. "He's off fighting the Winter Queen's duels." I frowned. "Could the light fae be involved in a drug that results in grisly murders? I mean, they thrive on daydreams. On inspiring creativity in mortals."

"Darkness often takes creativity. I've collected many victims of those who considered themselves 'artists.'"

I snapped my attention back to him. "I—You're here, we shouldn't be discussing such morbid topics."

Death shrugged. "I am a soul collector."

True. Still, I'd barely seen him over the last few weeks. He was my closest and oldest friend. My lover. He knew my secrets. I could tell him anything. We should talk about something happy. Something couples would discuss.

But the only thing I could think about was the case. And I was exhausted. Either my dream meeting with Kyran hadn't corresponded with refreshing sleep, or I was running out of time. I needed a tie to Faerie. It occurred to me that Death didn't know about the fading, though I was sure he could see something was wrong.

So I filled him in on everything that had happened recently. He listened, his hazel eyes growing increasingly concerned as I related my father's revelation both of my ailing condition and of my theoretical betrothal, of my meeting with the queen and my need to find the alchemist, and of the two wedding crashing bogeymen. He asked a few clarifying questions, but he didn't interrupt or redirect, he just listened, because that was what he'd done all of my life. It was one of the reasons I loved him.

That thought made me pause. And not just because of the panic that swelled up inside me at the word. *I loved him.* I did. Despite the fact I knew almost nothing about him. I'd learned more in the last few months than ever before, but I still knew very little about him or the man he'd been before he died and became a collector. I didn't even know his name.

"What is it?" he asked, and I realized I'd fallen silent. I couldn't remember where I was in my recap, and I had no idea where to pick back up.

I looked into those heavily hooded eyes, studied that strong jaw and full lips I knew so very well, and I thought about telling him. Just blurting out that I loved him. I knew he loved me, he'd told me so, but the words wouldn't form. Instead I scooted closer to him, my arms sliding around his waist so I could lean on his shoulder.

I'd wanted to enjoy touching him without feeling the burning chill of the grave for so very long, and now I could, and it was thrilling, and comforting, but also wrong somehow. That thought made me frown, and I pushed it away, bringing my thoughts back around to safe topics. Like the case.

"So, like I said, it's possible the light court is involved. Or maybe this is a wild-goose chase. I know you mentioned that creativity can be twisted and turned dark, but these people died from manifestations of their fears and nightmares. Maybe it's not connected at all."

Death didn't say anything for a long moment, the silence stretching long enough for his lack of response to be noticeable. Finally he said, "Are you sure all the deaths have been from malicious manifestations?"

I straightened, meeting his gaze. "You know something."

His eyes darted away, refusing to hold mine. He did know something. The secrets of soul collectors were well guarded and they were forbidden from speaking about those secrets. The souls he collected and their manner of death fell into that category. Still, he was also forbidden to see me, and for better or worse, he was breaking that rule, so I waited. If he decided he could tell me, he would. But I wouldn't press him. Our relationship was already dangerous for him. Which made me feel guilty as hell, like I should send him away for his own safety. So I'd wait, let him set the pace.

Finally he looked at me again, and ran a hand through his dark, chin-length hair. "What have you found when you interacted with the bodies?"

"Weak shades." I'd told him that already. I stopped. "Almost completely depleted shades. Like all the life energy of their being had been drawn out." If the victims were unintentionally using the glamour in the drug to make their hallucinations real, they had to fuel that glamour somehow. Fae were born with the power to manipulate glamour, or maybe it was fueled through their tie to Faerie. But what happened when a mortal, especially a nonmagical mortal, used an artificial infusion of glamour? It still had to draw power from somewhere. I'd theorized that already. The victims felt like they'd been through some life-threatening magic burnout. But that wasn't what had killed them. The hallucinations turned real had.

As if he could read the course of my thoughts, Death prompted me further. "And what if those children hadn't manifested a nightmare, but something harmless?"

I thought about it. About how weak their shades were. About how much life force it must have taken to make that clown real. "They probably would have burned out completely and died anyway," I said. Both sets of victims we'd found had died from violence, likely before they could get to a critical stage. But what if their hallucinations hadn't been violent? "Are you saying there have been good manifestations?"

Death didn't answer, not verbally at least, but he gave me the smallest incline of his head. My thoughts tumbled around my brain, a jumble of different half-realized ideas, until a memory rose to the surface. *The homeless man on the unicorn.* He'd been found dead several hours after I'd seen him, and from what I'd heard, the cause of death was unknown. I'd forgotten all about him with everything else that had happened, but I'd gotten a good look at that unicorn. It had definitely been glamour.

And nothing but glamour.

In the past I had seen constructs made from a mix of magic and glamour. And, of course, I'd seen fae disguising themselves with glamour. The unicorn hadn't been either of those. If it had been something else, something with a soul or even something nonliving but with real components, I would have seen that when I opened my shields. But it hadn't been. It had just been glamour. No more alive than a glamour-conjured chair and even less real than the cars my father transformed with his glamour.

I had been making assumptions about the hallucinations that had killed the victims. I'd assumed something that chased down and killed had to be sentient, cognizant. But if all of the nightmare-like images—and their actions—had come straight from the victim's own minds? Maybe I wasn't looking for any fae creatures, light or dark, that were possessing the glamours. Maybe it was all from the victim's drug-addled mind. And of course, the dose of glamour in the drug itself.

Jeremy and the two high schoolers had had a bad drug trip. Their hallucinations had been frightening, deadly. How many users had partaken of Glitter and had a "good" trip? How many had gotten sucked into a fantasy until the glamour burned out their life force?

I repeated the question to Death, but I wasn't surprised when he didn't answer. He'd already given away more than he should have. Of course, technically he shouldn't have been here at all.

I glanced at the window. I needed to go to the morgue, confirm my theory that our unicorn rider had died from burnout, and if I could, see if there were any other bodies with the same COD. Had the police found a way to test for Glitter use yet? I'd know just by feeling the shades, but the ones I'd raised already had been so drained I'd barely managed it. Would I even be able to raise a victim who'd died of magical burnout? It was worth a shot. I knew the probable identities of our bogeymen, but I had no idea how to track them down. Not yet at least. I didn't have any proof that they were involved with Glitter, but it would be pretty damn coincidental that they'd attacked me in the middle of the investigation. Usually when bad guys started wanting me dead or captured, it was because I was getting close. If I could question the victims, maybe find a common link to how or where they acquired the Glitter . . .

The dull gray light of predawn still claimed the world. I couldn't safely drive in the dimness, and the buses this far into the Glen wouldn't be running yet. Unless I was going to wake someone for a ride, or call a cab, I'd have to wait a while. The graveyard shift at the morgue was also likely not the best time to show up.

A yawn caught me off guard, feeling like it all but cracked my face as I sucked down a huge lungful of air.

"Let me hold you, before I'm called away," Death said, reaching out to tuck a curl behind my ear.

I couldn't go anywhere for a while anyway, so in answer, I pulled the cover back and scooted over on the bed. He crawled in beside me, tucking us both in. And it did start with him holding me. But his warm hands on my waist, the familiar dew-like smell of him in my bed, the hard planes of his chest under my fingers—it didn't stay just holding very long.

Much later, when the morning light streamed into my windows and we were both exhausted, but exhilarated, I fell asleep in his strong arms.

By the time I woke again. He was gone.

Chapter 19

For the second start of my day, I showered, dressed, and walked PC. Caleb was on the back porch, and I stopped long enough to ask him about the two bogeymen. He had a few vague recollections of old folklore about both Tommy Rawhead and Jenny Greenteeth, which amounted to about the same information as Dugan had given me—basically, both bogeymen had a predilection for eating children who disobeyed their parents—but he hadn't heard anything about either bogeyman taking up residence in Nekros. Caleb was fairly well connected to the independents' society so if they were here, they were new additions.

"I can ask around," he said after taking a sip of coffee far too diluted with cream to look tempting. "But I can't say anyone will pass on the information. Independents are just that because they prefer to avoid getting tied up with the affairs that concern Faerie, so most keep to themselves and expect others to do the same. You've helped the local independents before, but not all of them see it that way, and the courts are a little too interested in you for most of the more solitary faes' tastes."

"But you will ask?"

He nodded, and as I couldn't thank him, PC and I headed back upstairs.

I poured myself a bowl of cereal as I made some phone calls. My first call was to John, but he wasn't in. My next was to the morgue. I didn't know the tech who answered, and unfortunately, I didn't have anyone to ask for. Tamara was on her honeymoon by now and she was my only real contact in the morgue. Typically the head ME is enough. But without anyone who might help me out just because they knew me, the only thing I could do without an official job from the police or a release from the family was inquire about the body.

I should have done some research before I made the call. I'd seen news clips on the homeless man, but I couldn't remember his name and the tech wasn't very impressed with my description of "homeless man who rode the unicorn." Go figure. Thankfully my laptop was close at hand. I set down my spoon, pulled up a search, and scanned the plethora of hits that popped up on my screen.

"His name was Gavin Murphy," I said, after clicking the first article I found. "He died about five days ago. Is he still at the morgue?"

The tech grumbled under his breath, but I heard keys tapping in the background as he looked up the status of the body.

"Huh, well, looks like Mr. Murphy is still here," he said, and more keys clacked. "Sad case. Looks like he has an estranged sister who declined to claim his body or make arrangements. No other family can be found. If he's not claimed in another week, he's doomed for potter's field."

A week. If I couldn't find a legitimate case to grant me access to his body, I'd have to wait a week before he was released and buried. "Where is potter's field?" I asked, because I thought I knew all the cemeteries in Nekros. It was sort of a professional eventuality.

"It's just an old expression. He'll most likely be cremated at the expense of the state."

Well, crap. Cremation destroyed pretty much everything down to the DNA, which included all the memories stored in the cells of the body. If my suspicions were correct, raising a shade from anyone who'd used Glitter would be difficult with a fresh body, let alone a cremated one. Hell, normal, strong shades were almost impossible to raise from cremation ash.

"Do you have to be family to claim a body?" I asked, casting about for ways I could get access to the body.

The tech was quiet for a long moment. "You could likely donate a burial plot," he finally said.

And that sounded expensive. The business was barely paying out enough to cover expenses and a very small salary to Rianna and me. Most of mine went to bills. I'd started putting aside a savings, but it was a piddly amount and blowing all of it on burying a stranger whose shade I might not even be able to raise and who, if I could raise, might or might not help probably wasn't the best option. I wasn't going to take the possibility completely off the table, but I'd definitely hold off for now.

"You've been helpful," I told the tech as way of thanks before disconnecting.

I needed to talk to John. Or find Falin. Any case connecting to Glitter the FIB could likely claim, so he could probably get me access to the bodies. But he was still in Faerie and I had no idea when he'd return. No other FIB agent would assist me. If I hadn't already figured that out after previous encounters with them, the agent who'd shown up after Tamara's wedding had made that fact perfectly clear.

No, I needed Falin. Not just for access to the bodies, but to find out any information the FIB and winter court had on Tommy Rawhead and Jenny Greenteeth. If Tommy Rawhead was the hobgoblin the satyr saw distributing Glitter at the Bloom, finding out as much as I could about the two bogeymen was my best lead on the alchemist. That was a big if, but the coincidence of the bartender mentioning a hobgoblin and then getting attacked by one was just too great otherwise.

Now I just had to figure out how to contact the queen's bloody hands.

It was nearly noon when I arrived at the Eternal Bloom. I headed into the tourist side of the Bloom first. The satyr I'd spoken to at my first visit wasn't working. I asked both the current bartender and the cocktail waitress about the two bogeymen, but neither had seen them. I left my card and headed to the VIP room.

I scratched out a note to Falin the same way I'd sent notes to Rianna, Kyran, and Dugan. I didn't exactly know where Falin was, aside from somewhere in the winter court, but that didn't matter to the magic. It would find him. I wrote simply that I needed to see him ASAP about the case, and then I headed for a table in the corner. I hadn't even pulled the chair out yet when a pixie, no larger than my forearm, fluttered over, trailing colorful sparkles and carrying a large dried leaf.

That was a fast reply.

I accepted it and nodded my appreciation, but once I flipped it over to read it, my stomach clenched as if a pound of ice had dropped into it.

The leaf had only one sentence written across it: *Attend me now, planeweaver.*

Instead of a signature, the queen's official seal looked as if it had been scorched into the leaf. I stared at it, willing it to say something else—just about anything else.

Then I glanced at the giant tree sprouting through the floorboards in the center of the Bloom. Damn, I'd been summoned to an audience with the queen.

I'd never entered Faerie alone before. Hell, I could count on one hand how many times I'd passed through the door to the winter court. Not one trip had been entirely voluntary, so I guess it wasn't a huge surprise that I'd always had an escort. This time, I had to go it alone.

I stood to one side of the massive tree, staring at the innocuous-looking bit of space that appeared to be just another part of the bar wrapping around the tree, but I knew better. As soon as I stepped around it, this pocket of Faerie would melt away and I'd be at one of the entrances to the winter court. I didn't want to do it.

But I had to.

I took a deep breath, nodded my head, and had almost psyched myself up to stepping forward when someone cleared their throat behind me.

"My dear, it works better if you walk into it," a dry, raspy voice said, and I spun around.

An old woman, bent with age, stood there. She smiled, making the wrinkles in her face rearrange as she flashed her toothless gums.

"Of course," she said, "if you have the will and magic, you can make it move around you." She clicked her tongue and patted my arm with twig-thin fingers that felt rough and brittle. "But walking is much easier."

This sage advice imparted, she turned and shuffled away, her wooden clogs loud on the hardwood floor. I stared after her and shook my head. This place always had interesting characters. I didn't know what type of fae she was, or if she was fae, though it could be assumed she was, but I had no doubt that somewhere lost in time there was a tale about her.

I turned back toward the tree. "Might as well," I muttered, and as the old woman had suggested, I walked through the "door." The bar blurred, melted, and the halls of the winter court snapped into cold relief around me.

"Lady Planeweaver," a snowy-cloaked guard said, stepping from who-knew-where and into my path. He gave me a small bow. "The queen awaits you."

Under his cloak, I could see the edges of his ice armor

and the hilt of a huge sword at this waist, but with his hood pulled down and his head toward the floor in his bow, I could see nothing of his face. I waited for him to straighten, but the seconds stretched.

"Uh, lead on," I said, awkwardly shifting from foot to foot.

Thankfully, the guard straightened, turned on his heel and started down the corridor. I followed, knowing it was likely futile to try to memorize which turns we took, but that didn't stop me from trying. Of course, I suspected they changed and rearranged themselves after we passed. I was never going to learn to navigate Faerie.

My guiding guard stopped in front of a threshold and stepped aside without a word. Like any door in Faerie, it appeared to lead nowhere so could go anywhere. I assumed it led to the queen. Well, looked like this was it. I took a deep breath and stepped through the threshold.

The space beyond the threshold was smaller than I anticipated. Most of the rooms I'd seen in the winter court had been large and dauntingly impressive. This one was no larger than the reception room at Tongues for the Dead. The walls were the same ice-crusted architecture I'd seen elsewhere, the ceiling lost in swirls of snowflakes that never touched the floor, but this room was much more intimate. Two plush couches sat facing each other in the center of the room, a coffee table carved of ice between them.

The queen paced in front of these couches. She looked up as I entered. Her normally perfect curls were slightly frizzed today and the icicles on her gown appeared to be melting, which I hadn't even known was possible. Her gaze fell on me, her blue eyes feverish. Was she unwell?

Beyond the queen, his posture rigid, sat Falin. A nasty-looking gash bisected his cheek from the corner of his eye to the edge of his mouth, and a bloody bandage showed under the sleeve of his shirt, just above his elbow. From his slightly pained posture, those weren't the only wounds he sported. My first instinct was to rush to him and see how badly he was hurt, but I ground my heels to the spot. Ignoring the queen to rush to her knight's side sounded like a dangerous choice. Particularly now. There was something off about her.

Falin was alone on his couch. Lyell and Maeve sat on the opposite one. Ryese leaned against the arm of the couch. He was staring at nothing, and didn't look up as I entered. I wasn't even sure he'd noticed my arrival. The fourth council member, Blayne, was missing.

"About time," the queen said, tossing her disheveled curls. "I want a full update. Your missive said you had information on the case for my knight. Where are you on finding this menace in my court?"

Actually, the letter had said I needed to discuss the case with Falin. It didn't say I had any new information. And it hadn't been sent to her.

Not that I was going to point out any of those things. It was only yesterday she'd sent Ryese for a progress report. I was working as fast as I could. I had actually learned something new, but I wasn't sure how much closer that information put me to the alchemist. I let my gaze slide past her again until it snagged on Falin. He was watching me, his expression grave, intent. Then his eyes flickered to the queen as she began pacing again, her movements jerky, her stride graceless.

"Are you well, your majesty?" I asked, and then immediately regretted the question as she rounded on me, those feverish eyes slamming into me like a physical weight.

"What I am, Lexi, is under attack in my own court and betrayed by those I trusted. You were supposed to be looking into it. Or, perhaps, you are in on it?"

A shock of panic ran through me, a sour jolt of fear. I tried to keep my too wide eyes from moving to Falin. He couldn't help me, and looking away would make me look guilty. Not what I wanted. Ryese had mentioned there were questions as to the queen's fitness to rule, between the pressure of challengers to her throne and Icelynne's bones displayed in clear threat, the queen was feeling the stress. I didn't want to get ripped to shreds in her wake. I tried to calm the panic, or at least hide it, and school my face to something more placating.

"I meant no disrespect," I said, dropping my gaze to the icy floor. "I have a lead I'm following. Two bogeymen. A hobgoblin named Tommy Rawhead and a hag named Jenny Greenteeth. I believe they are connected to the case." I paused and chanced a glance up. The queen had gone still, her mouth twisting downward. "Are you familiar with them, your majesty?"

Her lips pursed, buckling in an expression that made her pretty face much less so. "No. Knight? Council?"

Maeve and Lyell glanced at each other, too much of the whites of their eyes flashing before both shook their heads. Falin rose, the motion slow, clearly painful. He walked to the queen's side. He didn't limp, or hold himself, but his stride lacked the predatory grace I was accustomed to from him. How badly had he been hurt? I couldn't ask. Not yet at least.

"They are not members of your court, my queen. I would have to check the records to determine if they are independents in your territory."

The queen flicked her wrist, and I couldn't tell if she was acknowledging his words, brushing them aside, or if it was just a twitch. She seemed more than a little twitchy.

I chewed at my cheek, weighing my words before I spoke. Finally I let out a breath I'd barely been aware I'd been holding before saying, "Falin's assistance would be useful to me on this case." After all, he had access to a lot of information I didn't, and he could cut some red tape for me when it came to interviewing potential victims. Well, the dead ones at least.

"Oh, you would love taking my knight away from me, wouldn't you, planeweaver?"

"No, I—" I floundered and glanced toward Falin, hoping he could offer me some guidance before I put my foot so far in my mouth the queen decided it needed to be cut off. Along with my tongue. And maybe my head.

I swallowed and cleared my throat.

Falin stared back at me for a moment, then, slowly, he lifted one hand to his side, pressing his ribs ever so slowly. *What the hell did that mean?* His hand moved to the nasty-looking gash on his face next.

Oh. I could guess his shirt hid a wound on his side as well. I turned back toward the queen.

"Your majesty, if he is to continue to win duels, he needs time to heal. Wouldn't he be best utilized investigating the alchemist while he recovers?"

She lifted one dark eyebrow, studying me. Then a smile crawled across her face, making her red lips spread wide. "Yes, a tool must be used to keep its edge. But duels can only be postponed so long." She turned to Falin. "You have forty-eight hours, Knight. Then you must return to my side. I expect you to return with this menace's head." She turned, her gown swishing and flinging melted drops of water. "You're both dismissed."

She didn't have to tell me twice. I glanced at Falin, and then turned and hurried out of the room.

Chapter 20

***

"The queen seemed . . . different," I said as Falin rummaged through the first-aid kit in his glove box.

He grunted, the sound noncommittal, before pressing a large gauze pad enchanted with a healing spell against the vicious-looking gash across his ribs. I winced. The first-aid kit seemed painfully inadequate for how hurt he appeared to be, and while I could attest to the fact he healed faster than normal, it still seemed as if he should be getting medical help. But I couldn't make him see a healer or doctor, so I didn't bother arguing.

"She mentioned she'd been turned on by her own court. Betrayed. I'm assuming she didn't mean the alchemist. Blayne?" I asked, guessing.

Now it was Falin's turn to wince, and I didn't think it had anything to do with the wound he was cleaning.

"Dead," he finally said, shutting the first-aid kit.

I was not expecting that response. "A duel? He challenged the queen for her throne?"

Falin sighed. "He did not intend to. But the queen is, as you said, not herself. By the time she'd twisted everything, he had little choice but to challenge her."

"And he lost." I wondered if he'd been the one to de-
liver the worst of Falin's wounds. "I don't suppose he was
the alchemist by any chance?"

"No." Falin closed the glove box and slid stiffly into
the driver's seat. "He did not die in the dueling ring, but
after his defeat was treated to the queen's hospitality in
Rath. He knew nothing of the alchemist."

I shivered. Rath was the name of the queen's dungeons. I doubted Blaync had a pleasant death. Or after-
life. Whatever she'd done to him, if his body was still in
Faerie, his soul was trapped.

Falin stared straight ahead as he drove, his lips pressed
into a tight line and the muscle over his jaw bulging.

"You liked him?" And he'd had to duel him, and
whether he struck the final blow or not, he likely now
wore the stain of Blayne's blood on his hands.

Falin nodded. "I respected him. But I think when the
queen considers her actions later, she will regret them.
He'd been with her a long time." He paused. "He was also
Ryese's father."

Well, that explained why Ryese hadn't been his normal, leering self during my visit. The queen had tortured
her own brother-in-law to death? Of course, as marriages
expired among fae, maybe he wasn't her in-law anymore,
but still. That was harsh. And very scary.

If Ryese and his father were both on the queen's council, was his mother as well? "Is Maeve the queen's sister?"

"No. Maeve was the consort of the last Winter King."

I twisted in the seat and stared at him. "You mean
Maeve was queen until the current Winter Queen challenged and killed the king?"

Falin shook his head. "She was never powerful enough
to be queen. She was the king's wife at the time of his fall,
and from the whispers I've heard, she'd been close to losing that position to our queen as well, even if the throne
hadn't been usurped."

So the Winter Queen had challenged and killed her own lover? Somehow that didn't shock me. "And the queen keeps Maeve on her council? Why? Hell, for that matter, why did Maeve stay in the winter court?"

He gave a tight half shrug. "I believe the queen is of the mind to keep her potential enemies where she can keep an eye on them."

And here I thought she simply eliminated potential threats.

"Besides," he said as he pulled into the parking lot in front of a nondescript gray building, "all of that happened hundreds of years ago. Most of the nobles have messy, intertwined pasts."

Not a surprising complication with being near-immortals. Live long enough and I suppose you'd have a lot of complicated history. But I didn't have time to dwell on that because we'd arrived at our destination: FIB headquarters.

The building squatted on the very edge of the Magic Quarter, nearly backing up to the river that separated the main part of the city from the more witchy and fae districts. The building had a sign, but it was a small one, easily missed if you weren't looking for it. Clearly it wasn't a place the public was welcome to stop by and file reports or check up on a case.

Falin parked behind the building and turned off the engine. Then he sat there, frowning at his steering wheel. I paused, my hand on the door.

"If you say you don't want me to come in, I might strangle you," I warned him.

His gaze tore away from the steering wheel slowly, the frown not moving as his eyes refocused.

Crap. Judging by his expression, that had been exactly what he'd been thinking.

"No." I crossed my arms over my chest. "I have everything at stake here. I don't care what secrets the FIB might have in there—in fact I promise to try to forget anything not relevant for this case—but I need all the intel I can get right now, and I need it sooner rather than later."

For a long moment he just stared at me. I swear, he didn't even blink. His gaze moved over my face, no doubt taking in the bruiselike circles I'd noticed under my eyes or the fact the mirror had reflected back a face slightly paler and gaunter than I'd worn a few days earlier. His frown tightened, and then he nodded, pocketed his keys, and climbed out of the car.

I'd been expecting an argument, been sure I'd get a lecture on fae secrets—or hell, the FIB were technically classified as a government agency, so admonishment that we were dealing with state secrets and classified information not meant for a civilian wouldn't have been unwarranted. The lack of argument was actually more frightening. It highlighted exactly how little time I might have left.

Please let us find something. I needed a break in this case. A map with a big red X on it was unlikely, but hopefully the FIB database would have *something*.

Falin used a glyph to unlock the back door of the building and led me through a bland gray hallway. A couple of doors lined the hall, most closed, but the few open ones were rather disappointing. I'm not sure what I was expecting from the FIB offices, but they were run by fae, so something more interesting than a shoebox-sized break room complete with a crappy folding table and a mostly empty vending machine. Falin stopped in front of an office with his name on the placard by the door. Again, no key, just a few glyphs by the lock and the door popped open.

His office was as dull as what I'd seen of the rest of the building. It had depressing gray walls, a pressboard desk with a computer, and a window covered by dusty blinds. *Wow, the Tongues for the Dead offices are actually nicer.* Of course, that was because of one decorating-savvy brownie who'd had access to a vault of gold I hadn't known existed until she'd spent all of it, but still. This was the court's official representation in Nekros, and it was depressingly boring. After the terrible beauty of Faerie, I'd expected more.

I started to say something, but Falin crossed directly to his computer, his face still grave. Yeah, probably not the time to discuss decor. I watched over his shoulder as he pulled up an official-looking program and logged in.

He glanced back, and for a moment I thought he was going to comment on my hovering, but after a brief pause he said, "About twelve years ago the winter court began keeping an electronic database of all the fae in our court and all the independents in our territories. Before that, censuses were conducted when the doorways changed and recorded only on paper."

"And how many times have the doors changed since the electronic database was created?"

Falin's shoulders sagged. "We are still in the same territories."

My lips formed a silent O as Falin keyed JENNY GREEN-TEETH into the program. I knew that the doorways to Faerie moved, and that they may stay put only a single season or might take decades to move again, but I hadn't realized the Winter Queen had counted Nekros as part of her territory for quite so long. I doubted many mortals knew who ruled the area where they resided—it didn't affect their lives much. Fae were another story.

"I'm guessing the fae in other courts' territories aren't in your database? Is there some sort of shared database?" The look on his face was a clear *no*. Humans might believe the FIB was a large unified agency, but each court governed their own territories with totalitarian control. And apparently they didn't share information.

Falin hit ENTER and a pixilated SEARCHING popped up on the screen. This wasn't exactly cutting-edge technology, but considering most fae were hundreds, if not thousands, of years old, it probably seemed pretty new and advanced to them. Falin was fairly young for a fae—how young, I didn't know, just that he'd been born after the Magical Awakening, so no more than seventy mortal years. He was also more technologically savvy than many of his contemporaries and he thrummed his fingers against the desk in a staccato of impatience as he waited for the sluggish program to search for our query.

Finally the computer beeped. I scowled at the NO RESULTS message flashing in the center of a pop-up box. Falin tried TOMMY RAWHEAD next, with the same results.

Falin collapsed backward in his chair, a loud sigh escaping between his lips. I felt equally defeated.

"Now what?"

He pushed out of the chair. "Now we know these two aren't members of the court or independents in the winter territories, which means they must have sworn themselves to a court member."

"They couldn't have refrained from showing up on census day?"

Falin shook his head. "Each time the doors change or an independent relocates to a new territory, he or she has to present himself to the new court or his tie to Faerie erodes and . . ." He made a vague gesture in my direction.

Yeah, I knew exactly what happened to a fae without a tie to Faerie. The two bogeymen hadn't looked like they were fading. "So if they've sworn themselves to another fae . . . ?"

"They'll be hard to find." Falin stood, heading for the door. "Fae are supposed to inform the court if they take on sworn fae or changelings. The master provides the tie to Faerie, and while it breaks our laws to hide a sworn fae, being unreported doesn't affect their tie to Faerie through their master. Fear of the queen's wrath if discovered is usually enough of a deterrent—"

"But the alchemist has already proven himself to be a less than law-abiding courtier, so it is not terribly surprising that he didn't declare his sworn fae." I sighed and shot a longing glance at Falin's abandoned chair. I was so tired. "If they aren't registered, how do we find out more about them?"

Falin motioned me to follow him, and I trudged behind him into the hall. "We can check the records and see if we can find out if they were in a territory we once held. That might give us more information on how the alchemist met them." He paused in front of a door. Drawing a few glyphs on the door caused it to pop open, revealing a huge storage room filled with rows of book shelves, most crammed to the point of bursting with old, leather-bound books. The few shelves not filled with books were stuffed with stacks of ancient-looking scrolls.

"The censuses?" I guessed.

He nodded.

I stared at the rows of shelves. "Both used to be members of the shadow court. When they left, wouldn't it be most likely they would become independents under shadow?"

"You can't assume that being bogeymen makes them shadow."

"It's not an assumption. I had a reputable source. But I don't know when they left or where they went."

He turned to study me, but he didn't ask about my source. He knew my great-granduncle was the king. I wasn't about to reveal that I was *theoretically* betrothed to the prince.

"The shadow and light courts have no direct doors to the mortal realm—only the seasons do, so only the seasons have independent fae."

Well, crap. That made sense. Shadow and light touched all of mortal reality indirectly, gaining belief magic through shadows, secrets, and nightmares for one court, and daydreams and creativity for the other. Light and shadow balanced each other the same way the seasons all balanced one another, but no direct doors meant no distinct territory, so no independents.

Where would the bogeymen have gone when they left the shadow court? Had they pledged to a season? Had they been granted the right to declare independent? Or had they immediately sworn themselves to the alchemist?

I glanced over the rows of books. It would take forever to go through even just the most recent ones.

"There is one more thing," Falin said, crossing the room to a small nook I hadn't noticed. A dark wood cabinet stood in the nook, and Falin had to use twice as much magic to open it as it had taken to enter the building. I peered around his shoulder as he opened the cabinet, but all it contained was yet another book—granted, a massive one—on a pedestal.

"Another census?"

"No," Falin said, hefting the book out of its nook. "This is a collection of lore. Actually, all lore. If enough mortals to shape belief magic have ever believed in something fae related, it is in this book."

I eyed the book. While it was the thickest book I'd ever seen, it didn't look big enough to back up that claim. And anyway, how would one collect *every* bit of folklore that mortals believed? Well, there was one way.

"Magical artifact?" I asked, and Falin nodded. "Okay, I'll take the folklore," I said as Falin placed the book on a small desk tucked away in the corner. "You take the census."

Falin looked less than thrilled at the idea, but he didn't object. Then we both settled down for some research.

A spell in the book's binding brushed my mind the moment I touched the cover. I jerked back at the mental touch. The artifact automatically recorded folklore, I knew that, but what else did it do? I mentally poked at the book with my ability to sense magic, but this was fae magic, not witch, and I was still only beginning to sense that. I let my hand hover over the binding again. While the brush of the spell was a very *other* sensation, it felt similar to the enchantments worked into my dagger. After hesitating a moment more, I flipped open the book.

The pages immediately began to turn, flipping rapidly as if caught in a breeze I couldn't feel. Then they stopped. The book going still. Without touching the book again, I glanced at the page. Two words jumped out at me: *Jenny Greenteeth.*

I grinned. The book was apparently enchanted to help the reader find what they were looking for. *Finally, something helpful.* I scanned over the page and the grin slipped away. The book was written in Old English.

This was going to take a while.

Several hours passed. My back ached from poring over the book, but I pressed on. I had to read most of the passages aloud. While my eyes couldn't make much sense of the Old English spellings, when I read aloud and heard myself pronounce the words, I could decipher at least seventy percent of the text. It wasn't perfect, but it was better than nothing.

I'd read a dozen tales about Jenny Greenteeth and had found three aliases she'd been known by over time or that had been associated with her. Tommy Rawhead had only one other alias that I'd found: "Rawhead and Bloody-bones." Yeah, he sounded like a pleasant guy. I'd passed the aliases on to Falin, in case they were listed under those names in the census, but so far he hadn't come up with anything.

I wasn't sure I was doing much better. I was jotting notes in my phone, but most of the stories illustrated what we already knew: they were both bogeymen who ate naughty children.

I leaned back, trying to stretch the kink out of my back. Somewhere down the hall a door slammed open hard enough to bounce off the wall, the loud boom followed by the sound of running feet. A shrill voice called out, "Is anyone here? We need all hands, pronto."

Then the owner of the feet and voice passed in front of the records room door and ground to an abrupt halt. "Sir, I—I didn't know you were here," the agent said, her voice thin as she gasped for breath.

She was glamoured to look human, and with my shields up I couldn't see what she looked like beneath that glamour, but she didn't quite pull off human. She was too small, too thin, and her features too wide on an angular face.

"What is it, agent?" Falin asked, looking down at the smaller fae.

"We just got a call. There's a fire."

"What does that have to do with the FIB?"

She swallowed, her full lips pressing into a thin line as she gulped. "Well, um, early reports say the fire isn't natural and, um, something about daemons dancing in the flames."

Chapter 21

Dark had fallen by the time Falin pulled onto Cardinal Avenue. If I'd been afraid my night blindness would be an impediment, I needn't have worried—the scene was ablaze with light. Literally.

"They haven't gotten the fire out?" I said, staring through the front windshield. An effort had been made to clear the narrow suburban street, but official vehicles, from ambulances to cop cars with their lights flashing and, of course, fire trucks, clogged the way forward. We were nearly a block away, which was about as close as we'd get in the car, so I couldn't make out any details, but from what I could see, the fire had to be huge. And raging out of control.

Falin made a noncommittal noise as he pulled off the side of the road, his tires brushing the sidewalk, but he said nothing. He popped the trunk, and I followed him to the back of the car, where he grabbed his gun with holster and his badge from a bolted-down lockbox. Shrugging into the shoulder holster, he nodded toward the mess of lights and flame before striding down the sidewalk.

Oh, please let this be a normal fire. But I knew it wasn't. Even before I saw it, I knew it wasn't just a fire. After all, the other agent had said there were figures dancing in the flames.

Falin had to badge his way through the crowd of on-lookers that had gathered at the edge of the police barricades. People muttered as they shuffled aside, barely opening a path. I stuck close to Falin's heels. I had no official reason to be here, so if we got separated there was little chance I'd make it past the police line.

"This is your kind's fault," a man said behind me.

I didn't realize the comment was directed at us until I heard someone spit. Falin stopped, looked at the wet spot on the leg of his pants, and then turned. His face was carefully blank, but I knew him well enough to see the icy anger in his eyes.

"Is there something I can help you with?" There was nothing menacing about the words, and Falin's tone, while low, was polite enough, and yet the man stumbled back as if threatened. Hell, I felt like taking a step back myself.

"No, I—" The man's Adam's apple bobbed. "I'm just saying they were a nice family. Never did nothing to the fae."

Family? I glanced toward the scene ahead of us. I still couldn't make out more than the general shape of the fire, but judging by what I could see of the houses on either side of us, it looked like a nice neighborhood. A family neighborhood.

"Little Sam was only three," a woman's voice said, but I wasn't sure where in the crowd she'd spoken from. "And Molly was a sweet girl, for a teenager."

Dread clawed at my stomach. We hadn't seen the scene yet. It could be anything. Hell, it could still be a natural house fire. But if the fire had been caused by Glitter . . .

I touched Falin's shoulder. "Let's go."

He didn't need a second prompting. He grabbed my elbow and marched us through the crowd. He still held up his badge, but he was less polite to those who didn't move fast enough, bodily moving them aside with his arm and shoulders as he cleared a path. A grumble of mutters followed in our wake, most antifae sentiments.

The cop manning the barricade looked frazzled when we reached him, which wasn't terribly surprising as it was his job to control access to the scene, but with as many different agencies as appeared to have responded, figuring out who was authorized to enter wasn't an easy task. From what I could make out in the flame-lit darkness, the full alphabet soup of law enforcement and emergency services had made an appearance. The perimeter cop stepped aside when Falin flashed his badge, and then, after writing down Falin's information for the log, glanced at me.

"Craft is with me," Falin said, giving my arm a tug so I had no choice but follow him past the barrier.

The cop didn't try to argue. He'd clearly given up on controlling access and was simply acting as a record keeper. I handed him my card for his log and kept moving.

Falin paused to scan the scene ahead of us. We were across the street from the blaze, numerous official vehicles between us and the burning house. Groups of officials congregated in small clusters on the opposite sidewalk, but I couldn't make out any features to differentiate the groups. Between the fire and the strobes from police, fire, and ambulances, the light was too chaotic for my poor night vision to process details, at least at this distance. Falin clearly didn't share my difficulty, but tugged me toward one group hovering around the back of several open ambulances. With each step, the air pushed heat against us, like a tide rushing out from a fire I could still only see raging somewhere beyond the vehicles.

I was expecting paramedics, but as we got closer, I realized most of the figures were too bulky with protective suits, helmets, and air tanks. *Firemen.* And not all of them were outside the ambulances—several sat in the backs of the vehicles or on the gurneys, oxygen strapped over soot-darkened faces, paramedics tending to blistering burns and . . . *other* wounds.

"Bring me up to speed," Falin said, flashing his badge to one group of men.

They glanced at his badge, then at Falin and me. More than one man shuffled, as if uncomfortable, but after a moment a large man in his early forties stepped forward.

He pursed thick lips, studying Falin's badge. "FIB, huh? You think this is fae related?"

"I don't know yet. Tell me what you know." Falin paused, and then added, "Chief."

The man nodded, indicating Falin had been correct that he was, indeed, the fire chief. He gave a brief summation of the callout and the time the first trucks arrived. "The house was already engulfed, so my men got hoses on it immediately. As more trucks arrived, we got hoses on the surrounding houses to keep the fire from spreading, but focused on getting as much water as we could on the Wilson residence. The fire didn't respond to mundane or magical intervention, and the neighbors were convinced the family was still inside. A couple of my men decided to play hero and rush in, but they didn't make it far." He jerked his head to the men being treated by the medics. "They found the two adult residents, both unconscious. After bringing them out, we realized many of their wounds had nothing to do with the fire. Both were rushed to the hospital and they're stable. About then was when my early teams rushed back out of the house. That's when we started seeing forms in the flame. At first we thought it was the kids trying to escape, but the shapes were twisted, evil." He shivered, the movement making his jowls quiver. "And the men who went in and made it back out? Well, they might as well have gone in wearing only their skivvies for all the protection their suits provided. They also suffered wounds that weren't caused by fire. I don't know what's in there or what caused the fire, but we can't put it out and we can't enter. The best we can do is try to contain it until it burns itself out." He stopped, his hard gaze locking on Falin. "That is, of course, unless the FIB know how to stop it."

The dread that had been clawing at me since we first heard about the fire turned icy and sank low in my belly.

Falin said nothing, just gave a vague gesture to acknowledge the chief's words and then started making his way around the vehicles. I followed, my steps heavy as if the dread had sunk all the way to my heels and weighed them down.

We stepped around the last fire truck, and I finally got my first unobstructed view of the scene. Firemen rushed about on the sidewalk and lawn. Most of the trucks had already run out of water, but there was a hydrant one house down, and several men braced the hose, controlling its jet of water. Fire witches chanted at the edge of the lawn, though I wasn't sure if they were trying to diminish the flame or, as the chief said, just trying to contain it to the one house.

And beyond them, the fire raged, uncontrolled.

I couldn't make out anything that made me think of a house. It looked like the earth had opened and bellowed out a ball of fire, the flame reaching for the sky. The heat of it beat against my bare face, my arms. Sweat broke out on the back of my neck, trickled down my spine. I couldn't breathe, the air was too hot, almost thick with the heat. I coughed, unable to look away from the flames. Then I saw the shapes the chief had mentioned.

The figures were nothing distinctive, just shadows among the flames. If someone had said it was nothing more than an illusion from the flickering firelight, I might have believed it, but the more I stared, the more I thought I saw stretching hands with curved talons and gaping mouths with jagged fangs. I tore my gaze away.

And found Falin staring at me, not the fire.

"What do you see?" he asked in a voice barely above a whisper, and I realized why he hadn't objected, even once, to me following him all the way to the front of a potential crime scene. I could see through glamour, and he was one of the few people who knew that fact.

Taking an overheated gulp of air, I braced myself for lowering my shields in a location with a possibility of fresh corpses nearby. Releasing the breath, I pried apart the vines enclosing my psyche.

As if the wind blowing across from the land of the dead had snuffed it out, the fire vanished, the heat disappearing between one heartbeat and the next, and, in my eyesight at least, the street turned significantly darker. The sweat forming on my skin chilled, and I shivered.

"Glamour. It's all glamour."

I let my senses stretch. The fire chief had indicated that the two children were still inside, but no grave essence clawed at me. If they were in there, they were alive. *Thank goodness.* But how much longer could they last in that inferno?

I searched the house with both my senses and my sight that currently reached across planes and pierced glamour. Unless a fae had, for unknown reasons, decided to summon a glamoured fire on this family, this had to be the result of a Glitter user's fears. I'd seen one other Glitter crime scene, and I'd heard accounts of two Glitter-glamour attacks, but I would never have guessed glamour could do so much damage. In my gravesight, the houses on either side of the Wilson residence were dilapidated, decayed, but the Wilson house was devastated. The glamoured fire appeared to have reduced the house to little more than rubble and ash. A few walls still stood, but most had crumbled. It was worse, I knew, seeing it across the planes, but still, the damage was beyond repair.

I shook my head, and my eyes skittered over a soft yellow glow emanating from somewhere in the center of the ruins, behind a wall that looked far more solid than the ones around it. I stopped, trying to focus on the glow. I could catch only small glimpses, but it looked like a . . .

"Soul. Falin, someone is still alive in there." I squinted. "Maybe two someones. The kids." I stepped toward the house.

Falin caught my arm, stopping me.

"What are you doing? They're still alive in there, but who knows for how much longer." I tried to jerk my arm away, but he held on tight.

He pulled me closer to him and dropped his voice to a harsh whisper. "You can't just walk into a burning building."

"But it *isn't* burning. The fire is glamour." And I couldn't see it anymore. Couldn't feel the heat or smell the smoke. It no longer existed for me, or at least, it didn't as long as I gazed across planes.

"Okay, so you can break the glamour, but did it do real damage to the building?" He pointed to the crumbling rubble pile that had once been a house. "What if the ceiling collapses on you?"

I hadn't considered that.

I stopped trying to jerk my arm away and turned back to try to study the glints of soul light. How much longer could the kids survive in there? How had they survived this long? I had to find out what was happening.

I let more of my psyche cross over to the land of the dead. Cold wind whipped around me, tousling my hair and ripping at my clothes. Now that I wasn't struggling, Falin dropped my arm and stepped back, flexing his hand as if I'd burned him. As open as my psyche was, it was more likely I'd chilled him.

"Roy," I said, not caring if my voice carried to those watching. Then I waited.

Roy had once told me that normally I looked much like any other living mortal to ghosts, until I straddled the chasm between the living and the dead. Then I lit up like a beacon. I only hoped he was paying attention.

I'd almost given up on him responding when I saw a pale shadow begin to materialize beside me. I'd never been straddling the chasm when a ghost appeared before—usually they either suddenly appeared or they walked into the area where I was. I knew there were multiple layers to the land of the dead. On one notable, and nearly deadly, occasion, I'd traveled down to the place where the living world was nothing but gray ash. But usually my psyche only brushed the uppermost layer where the living world was reflected as a slightly decaying version of mortal reality. Now I saw Roy push up from the deeper layers, becoming more solid and *real* as he emerged. Icelynne followed close behind.

"Heya, Al. What's happen—?" He cut off abruptly as he caught sight of the scene around me.

I wasn't sure if he could see the fire or not, but as it didn't exist in the land of the dead, I knew it couldn't hurt him. I pointed toward the house. "There are two kids in there. Can you go check on their condition, and as you go, see if you can find the safest route I could travel?"

Roy glanced from me to the house, and then shrugged. "Sure thing, boss," he said, and then trudged toward the rubble.

Falin grunted behind me, and I turned to find him giving me a dubious look. "Did you just send your ghost to check the integrity of the structure?"

"Maybe." I knew Falin couldn't see Roy—I hadn't expended the energy to manifest him—but he knew about the ghost. And it seemed like a good idea to me. If I couldn't enter the house, why not send someone who couldn't be hurt by the house falling down on him to check on the kids?

"How can someone who can walk through walls tell if the house is safe?" Falin asked, and I sighed.

"Ghosts don't actually walk through solid objects. They just *look* like they do. In reality, if they pass through what we see as a closed door or wall on our plane of existence, that object doesn't exist on their plane," I said, turning back to the house. Then I frowned as Roy sprinted across the yard toward me. "That was fast." Which was either good news, or very, very bad news.

"You failed to mention the reaper in there," Roy sputtered as soon as he was in yelling range. "I'm not going to go advertise I exist and get sent on to the hereafter."

Crap. Roy called all soul collectors reapers, as in Grim Reaper. And if a collector was there, the kids were about to die.

I took off at a run. As Falin couldn't hear Roy, he hadn't been anticipating my sudden dash and his surprise bought me a several-yard head start. Add in the fact he had to contend with the heat from the glamoured fire, and he didn't have a chance of stopping me. Nor did the firemen and cops yelling behind me.

I passed the charred wound that had once been the front door and then slowed. Ahead I could see hints of yellow glinting through chinks in the wall, but I couldn't see the collector—the wall was still too intact. *Let it be Death.* If the collector was Death, he would listen to me. Let me try to save the kids. One of the other collectors? I was far less confident.

I needed to hurry. That said, I really didn't want to get buried alive if the house collapsed. After all, the fire was still raging, even if I couldn't see it.

Maybe if I could get the collector's attention? I opened my mouth to call out, but then stopped. I didn't have a single name to call out with—not even for Death. And the collectors were unlikely to respond to the monikers I'd given them. No, I'd have to make it to that room.

I glanced around. Sooty ash drifted from the ceiling above me and crumbled down the walls. The question was, how much of what I could see reflected mortal reality. Walking into a wall that was decayed in the land of the dead but still solid in reality would not only hurt, it could cause a deadly collapse. But if I sealed my shields so I saw only the mortal plane, I'd also see—and more important, *feel*—the fire. And that was assuming I'd be able to see anything at all with my shields closed.

I chewed at my bottom lip. I had an extra shield I'd spent the last few months erecting. In my mind's eye, I saw it as a bubble around my psyche, as clear as glass but nearly impenetrable. It helped me gaze across planes without touching and merging them. But if I dropped that shield . . . I might cut a swath across reality, leaving a trail of other planes in my wake, but I'd be able to move through the house trusting my eyes—if I stumbled into something that reality disagreed with, my power would weave the planes so what I saw existed.

Probably.

I'd never actually tested that theory. Usually if I merged planes, I did it accidentally.

"I hope this works," I muttered, popping the dome shield.

The wind from the other side of the chasm picked up, stirring the ash around me in a small whirlwind. The house creaked. I tensed. *Maybe this wasn't such a good idea.*

When the house didn't topple down onto my head, I took a tentative step forward. Nothing changed, and I let out the breath I'd been holding. *Just get to the kids, Alex.*

With that less than stellar mental pep talk, I began picking my way through the rubble, moving as quickly as I dared. The shields in my charm bracelet still held, buffering me from some of the torrent of realities around me, but with my main shield cracked and my dome popped, the grave pricked at me, distant corpses calling to my wyrd magic. Color also washed over the world, the Aetheric plane attempting to push into reality. I pointedly ignored both as hard as possible, focusing on the building.

I stumbled twice. The house quaked as reality shifted and the wall I tumbled into crumbled down to what I saw in the land of the dead. *Maybe this wasn't the best plan.* But, if the ceiling did fall, it would disintegrate around me—hopefully before crushing me.

I finally reached the oddly intact wall. It wasn't just one wall, but an entire room, complete with door. I paused before reaching for the handle. The door looked ready to fall off its hinges in my sight, but something had preserved this section of house, and I was guessing it was in a lot better shape than my gravesight indicated. If I pulled this small intact section into contact with what I saw across the chasm, I might destabilize the whole house. While I had a decent chance of surviving a small collapse, the structure would not crumble harmlessly around the kids.

Which meant I needed my shield back.

It took precious seconds to erect the shield. Through the rotted door, I could see one of the yellow glows dimming—I didn't have much time. As soon as the bubble formed around my psyche, I grabbed the doorknob and twisted, throwing open the door.

The room beyond was a small bathroom, and while it was hard to be sure in my gravesight, it appeared that it hadn't taken so much as smoke damage. A teenage girl huddled in the large claw-foot tub in the corner of the room. *Molly.* She clutched a smaller figure to her, who I was guessing had to be the three-year-old the neighbor had mentioned. Sam hid under a blanket, which almost completely concealed him so that if my gravesight hadn't shown it as moth-eaten and rotted, it would have masked the glow of his soul. The boy glowed a brilliant yellow in the gaps of the blanket, but his older sister's glow was dull, dwindling.

Death waited beside the tub.

He looked up as I burst into the room. Then his eyes closed, his head sagging. "You shouldn't be here, Alex."

"Don't," I said, stepping toward the tub. "Let me take them out."

The girl's head snapped up at the sound of my voice. Her wide eyes were sunken, as if she'd suffered a long sickness, her voice weak as she opened her mouth and screamed. The boy in her arms hunched lower, tucking himself against her without turning to look at the new potential danger.

The girl kept screaming, and I had no idea what her mind saw, but I felt the moment the glamour tried to wrap around me, to twist me into the nightmare she imagined. *She's the Glitter user.* The glamour slid back off me, my own powers rejecting the version of reality her drug-addled mind had tried to cast me into. And her soul dimmed.

The Glitter was fueling the glamour with her life force, and she was running out.

"It's time," Death said, reaching for the girl.

I lunged forward. "No. Wait."

It was already too late. Death's hand was in her chest, his fingers grasping her soul. He gave me a small, sad frown, and said, "There was only one path for her after she took the drug."

He lifted his arm, pulling her dwindling soul free. Her scream cut off, her body sagging. The boy in her arms shifted, but he didn't move. He didn't know she was gone. Not yet.

"At least let me question the ghost." Because I could already feel the hollowness in her corpse—if I could raise a shade, it would be a mere echo, likely too faded to be of use. And we had to find who was distributing this drug. It needed to purged from the street. People couldn't keep dying in these nightmares, or daymares, or whatever.

Death's frown deepened. "She's no restless spirit. She's tired, ready to move on." And to accent his point, he flicked his wrist, and Molly's soul moved on to wherever souls went next.

Damn.

"What about . . . ?" My gaze moved to the boy.

"He's safe," Death said, and tension I hadn't realized had sunk claws into my shoulders loosened. I nodded to acknowledge his words, and he glanced over my shoulder, toward the front of the house.

I finally registered that something about the house had changed with Molly's death. I couldn't tell, not directly, but the flames must have vanished as soon as her life force stopped feeding the glamour. Without the barricade of magical fire and creepy shadow monsters, the firemen were entering the house.

It was time to get Sam out, before his sister began to cool and he realized she wouldn't respond. I stepped forward, approaching the tub. Death reached out, tracing the side of my face, but he didn't say anything. Which was good. I was mad at him. It probably wasn't a fair reaction—he was only doing his job. No, not job. He was fulfilling his function in the world. But I was mad, and a little hurt, unreasonable or not, and I didn't want to talk to him in that moment. So, it was good that after that one, lingering caress, he vanished.

I knelt by the tub. "Hi, are you Sam?"

A tiny hand emerged from under the blanket, lifting it just enough that I could see two brown eyes peering out at me. After a moment, the boy nodded.

"Good to meet you, Sam. I'm Alex, and I'm going to get you out of here, okay?"

The boy emerged a little farther from under the blanket. "This is Lancelot," he said, revealing a teddy bear nearly half his size that he'd been clutching under the blanket. "He's been protecting me from the bad stuff."

I looked down at the bear. I expected it to rot away in my gravesight, but it didn't. Oh, it looked a little haggard, with matted fur and a couple of bald spots, but it looked more well-loved than decayed. He had a small sword made out of tinfoil attached to his paw with an old hair grip, and more tinfoil cupped his head in what I guessed was a makeshift helmet. Curious, I let my ability to sense magic trace over the bear and then the rest of the room—the one and only room in the house to be spared. But there was no magic. No witch magic at least. Just the power of a child's trust and belief.

I forced a smile. "Lancelot did a good job, baby. Now come on, let's go."

Reaching out, I lifted both boy and his brave little bear. Sam wrapped his free arm around my shoulders, but then twisted, looking back at the tub.

"What about, Mol-mol?" he asked, looking at his big sister. "She's sleeping."

I opened my mouth, closed it again. I dealt in a business abundant with grieving loved ones, but I wasn't equipped to explain death to a three-year-old. Or maybe I just wasn't brave enough to tell a child his sister was gone. Either way, as I carried him out of the room, I simply said, "The firemen will come for her."

He nodded, accepting that solution. Then he leaned his small head on my shoulder and hugged his bear close.

Belief magic really was the damnedest thing. It could enact a glamour that killed, but it could also guard a small boy who believed in the protection of a teddy bear.

Chapter 22

"The ledger," I said, bolting upright in my bed. Then a wave of dizziness slammed into me and I collapsed back into my pillows.

"What?" Falin asked as he twisted around to look at me from where he sat on my one barstool in front of his laptop. PC, who was curled up in Falin's lap, lifted his head.

My dog was officially a traitor.

I groaned, closing my eyes against the bright sunlight streaming into the room. I felt hungover. Hell, I wished I was hungover instead of slowly fading from magical withdrawal or whatever. But, no, there had been no drinking last night. Just a lot of creatively evasive statements given to the cops and firemen on how I'd entered the house and why the fire had abruptly vanished. Then an awkward drive home, my blind and shivering stumble upstairs, and my absolute refusal to let Falin share the bed to provide me with body heat—we'd played that game before and it didn't end well for my heartstrings. I had a vague memory of Death kissing my cheek sometime in the middle of the night, but that may have been a dream.

"What about a ledger?" Falin asked again.

I peeled open my eyes and forced my mind to reexamine the first thought I'd had on waking. What was . . . "Oh, yeah. The ledger? The one everyone has to sign going into the VIP area of the Eternal Bloom. We know the alchemist is operating in Faerie, but the drug is being distributed in Nekros. That means our bogeymen have to be traveling back and forth. If we examine the ledger, we might find a pattern to their movements and be able to lie in wait."

Falin nodded, but it was more of a dismissive gesture than one of agreement. "I sent agents to collect the Bloom's ledger after you told me who we were looking for last night. I also have agents stationed both inside and outside the Bloom in case either bogeyman makes an appearance."

Oh. Apparently I wasn't half as clever as I thought I was. I rolled over, sighing, and squinted as light from the open blinds fell directly into my eyes. I stopped. There was an awful lot of light.

"What time is it?"

"Almost noon," Falin said, without looking up from his laptop.

Noon? *Crap.* "I'm late. I'm so late. Why didn't my alarm sound?"

"I turned it off," he said, without the slightest hint of apology. "You looked like you needed the sleep."

I gaped at him. Needed the sleep? I needed to open the office. With Rianna and Ms. B both holding up in Faerie to conserve energy, I was the only one left to run the office. But even more than that, I needed to be up working the case. Sleep wasn't going to make me better—establishing a tie to Faerie was the only way.

Falin shrugged at the aghast look on my face. "I sent an agent to your office to hang a sign stating your office would be closed for the remainder of the week."

Great. Well, that was something, at least. And it freed me up to focus on finding the alchemist. "Must be nice having minions," I muttered, and then swung my legs over the side of the bed. I was still in yesterday's jeans. I shuffled across the room to my dresser, but found my pants drawer empty. I glanced at the pile of dirty clothes beside the dresser. I hadn't done my own laundry since Ms. B decided she was going to be my personal house/office brownie. Now that she was back in Faerie, I was apparently out of clean clothes. I looked down at the clothes I was already wearing. They were likely as good as any of the other dirty clothes. I turned back to Falin. "Didn't the queen forbid you from discussing the case? What did you tell the agents you sent to the Bloom?"

He frowned at me. "I'm the winter knight and the lead agent for the winter court's FIB. I tell my agents that I want them to find and detain two fae, they don't ask me why."

Right. "So now what?"

"Now you eat some food. I made breakfast, but that was earlier. You'll have to nuke it." He pointed to the fridge. "Then change. You smell like a campfire."

Apparently these clothes aren't quite as good as any of the others. I seriously needed to do laundry.

He didn't add anything else to the list, so either his plans extended no further than getting me fed and cleaned up, or he didn't want to tell me, which likely meant he'd decided I was getting too weak and was considering taking me to Faerie. I needed a plan, and now.

"I think we should head to the floodplains," I said as I grabbed the plate loaded with waffles, eggs, and sausage.

Falin looked up, his expression questioning.

I dug my phone out of my back pocket, pulled up the notes I'd jotted down yesterday while reading the enchanted book of folklore, and then slid it across the counter to Falin. "In most of the stories, Jenny Green-teeth is described as a water hag. She traditionally lives in bogs and swamps and drowns naughty children who come too close to the edge of the water," I said between bites of food. "The floodplain isn't exactly a bog, but it's the closest Nekros has to her normal habitat. And it would certainly be easier to search than looking for Tommy Rawhead, who folklore asserts traditionally lives under stairwells."

Falin looked less than convinced, but what did we have to lose?

I popped downstairs to talk to Caleb before we left. He told me that the independent fae were full of gossip about the possibility of the Winter Queen losing her court, but no one would admit to having seen the two bogeymen. *"Would admit."* Those were the words he used.

I repeated as much to Falin, and his lips twisted into a smile I'd never seen on him before. It was darker, sadder than a smile deserved to be, and it made him look like a stranger. "Well, maybe they need someone else to ask the question."

"Are you planning to threaten the fae in the floodplains?" I asked as we walked toward his car.

He didn't answer, but stared straight ahead.

I sighed. I was not exactly sanguine about the idea of threatening local independents for not volunteering information. It was a bullying move. One the courts used quite a lot, and a reason I didn't want to join the courts. I remembered what Caleb had said when I first asked him to talk to the independents for me, about me having too many ties to the courts. I cringed. This would certainly cement that perception. I hated it, but I was also very conscious of my own ticking clock, the number of bodies Glitter was piling up, and the fact that Falin and I couldn't search the entire floodplains ourselves. We'd have to talk to some of the local water spirits.

The drive stretched on in strained silence. The last time I'd visited the Sionan Floodplains Nature Preserve, I'd found a pyramid of dismembered feet. To say it wasn't one of my favorite places was an understatement. Besides, I still didn't have any appropriate footgear, and my thigh-high, wedge-heeled boots weren't made for trucking through the muck.

But what choice did I have?

I pocketed my cell before opening Falin's glove box to stash the purse. My gaze caught on the first-aid kit Falin had used so liberally the day before, and I glanced at him, realizing his movements had been much smoother today. The small lines of pain around his eyes were absent as well. I knew he couldn't be completely recovered, but damn, he did heal fast.

Falin parked in the gravel. Then we both headed into the tree line. At least we hadn't had the rainfall of a few months ago, so for a sometimes–swamp land, the paths we were following were fairly dry.

"How should we go about this?" I asked as we reached the trail.

"I know where several of the locals usually frequent. We'll start there. Ask some questions."

Right.

We walked for nearly forty-five minutes before Falin veered off the path. It was another twenty minutes, this time trudging through sludge that sucked at our feet and undergrowth that entangled our ankles, before Falin held up a hand and ground to a stop.

He looked around, and then up at the sky, as if the midday sun could direct him the way old sailors navigated by the stars. Apparently satisfied, he called out, "Shelly-coat. Show yourself."

I waited, watching and listening. Wind whistled in the trees, birds called to one another, and in the distance the Sionan River churned, but no fae answered. I shuffled my feet.

Nothing.

"I don't think—" I started, but then I heard a very distinct *click-clack*ing emanating from the right. I turned as a tall, rail-thin fae emerged from behind a tree. His foot-falls made no sound, but something under his coat clinked with every step he took.

"You called, Knight?" he asked, straightening to his full height.

The fae looked like a cartoonish caricature of how one might imagine a bogeyman: all sharp angles, willowy long limbs with knobby joints, and a comically large beak of a nose. But he wasn't a bogeyman, and when he spoke, you forgot how he looked because his voice was one of the most soothing, harmonic sounds I'd ever heard—possibly dangerously so. I wasn't sure exactly what kind of fae he was, but if someone told me he was related to sirens, I'd believe them.

"I did. We need information about a fae name Jenny Greenteeth. She may be residing in the area."

The fae's dark gaze slid from Falin to me, and he gave the slightest inclination of his head in greeting. "Alex."

"Malik," I said, keeping my voice carefully empty. The last time I'd seen the fae he'd been a prisoner in Faerie, forced to sing for the queen. Technically I'd freed him, but I was pretty sure he considered it my fault he'd been hauled off in the first place, so I wasn't counting on him being my biggest fan. I'd also just shown up with the winter court's knight and enforcer, which wouldn't win me any points.

"Your green man already asked me about the water hag," he said, addressing me instead of Falin.

I nodded. Green man was what many of the fae called Caleb. The independents didn't have a true hierarchy, but if there had been a leader among the fae in the flood-plains, it would have been Malik. It didn't surprise me that he'd been one of the fae Caleb spoke to on my behalf.

"And what did you tell him?" Falin asked.

The tall fae shrugged. "I have not seen her."

Well, he couldn't lie, so that seemed fairly clear-cut.

But Falin wasn't satisfied. "Have you heard any other fae talking about her, or someone one who might be her?"

"Only you and the green man," Malik said with another shrug, but the movement looked forced, stiff.

I frowned at him. "You know something."

"I *know* nothing about her, planeweaver."

"But you suspect something."

His glance skittered from me to Falin and back, and he wrung his long-fingered hands. "I wouldn't presume to speculate . . ."

"You had better start then," Falin said, taking a step toward Malik. "Or I'll have you hauled to the winter dungeons so that you have plenty of time to think through those speculations."

Malik gulped, his whole body sagging as if he was trying to draw back from Falin without actually giving up any ground. "I don't suppose you're offering anything to trade for the information?" he asked, though he sounded far from hopeful.

Falin took another step toward the other fae. Malik was technically taller, but that was easy to forget with how much more imposing—not to mention dangerous—Falin looked. "I'm offering you the chance to avoid a one-way trip to Faerie."

Malik shrank back further, collapsing in on himself.

"I'm offering trade," I said, stepping forward. "Since you have no direct knowledge, only a small favor, but a favor."

Falin shot a frown at me, but Malik perked up.

"My choosing?"

"No, mine. And the actual value of the favor will be dependent on if your information helps us locate Jenny Greenteeth."

Malik studied me, rubbing the bridge of his long nose with one hooked finger. "You look unwell, planeweaver."

I didn't reply. I wasn't going to tell him how much I

personally had at stake in finding Jenny—it would only give him leverage to sweeten the favor.

"Her offer is on the table for a short time," Falin said, taking another step closer to Malik. "My threat is ongoing."

Malik dropped his hand. "Right. Well, like I said it is nothing definitive, but there are a series of small ponds not far north of here. Recently one of them fouled without obvious cause. The *nixies* won't go near it. It is nothing certain, but last time I met Peg Powler, she preferred hunting in dank, putrid bogs. But that is all I know—I haven't seen the hag herself."

I recognized the name as one of Jenny's aliases, though I couldn't now remember which stories had included which names. Not that it mattered; most of the tales had the same theme.

Falin rubbed his chin, looking for all the world as if he was dissatisfied with Malik's answer. I, on the other hand, had to keep tight control on my feet so I didn't hurry off in the direction Malik had indicated.

Falin asked a few more questions, mostly clarifying the location of the befouled pond and the most direct path to and from it. Then he dismissed the other fae, who was all but quivering by the time he slunk back into the swamp. I would have preferred Malik to guide us to the ponds, but his directions were clear, and I'd take what I could. After all, we finally had a lead.

Chapter 23

"This has to be it," I said, stopping several feet from the dark water. Malik's directions had been easy enough to follow, we weren't even that far off of the main trail. *Easier to eat children if they are likely to wander to your doorstep.* I shivered and edged back a step from the pond. "Now what?"

Falin gazed across the expanse of algae-encrusted water. "Now we knock on her door."

He stepped forward, lifting a blade out of who-knew-where he kept them magically concealed. Dragging the edge of the blade across his palm, he opened a thin slit. Blood welled to the surface and he walked up to the edge of the pond. Fisting his hand over the water, he let several fat drops of red blood fall to the slimy green surface. Then, in a voice that had to be magically amplified, called out, "Jenny Greenteeth, I summon you. As knight of the winter court, I compel your attendance."

"Will that really work? You can compel any fae in winter territory?" I asked, watching the still surface. The pond wasn't large, maybe fifty feet at its widest point. During the summer droughts, all but the deepest sections probably vanished.

"If she was a regular courtier or independent, and assuming she's home, then yes, it would work. But we don't know who she's sworn herself to. I can't compel a noble, nor a fae sworn under a noble."

And Icelynne had said she thought the alchemist was Sleagh Maith. If Jenny was sworn to him, this wouldn't work. Of course, for it to work at all, we had to hope we were in the right place and she was home.

Nothing moved or disturbed the water.

Malik had been spot-on in his assessment that the pond had been fouled. The stagnant water stank, algae covered all but a few murky spots, and the mud around the edges was littered with decaying fish and seaweed. But this was the floodplains. It consistently flooded and then drained back—who was to say this wasn't the pond's natural cycle. *Except that the nixies won't go near it.* From what I knew of them, nixies were harmless and rather childlike water spirits. They did have a propensity to predict deaths while they danced across the water, but they just predicted it, they didn't cause it. They were attracted to all decent-sized bodies of water, so their avoidance of this pond might truly be odd. Malik had certainly implied it was. But then again, fae often relied on implication to skirt the truth. Not being capable of lying meant you had to get creative.

The water remained still.

"Do you think she's out or are we in the wrong place?" I asked, willfully ignoring the possibility she simply didn't have to answer.

Falin wrapped a handkerchief around his palm— people still carried those?—and frowned at the expanse of unmoving water. "I'll have some agents stake out the area, for if she returns."

That was a good idea. I walked a few more feet along the edge of the pond, trying to see if it branched off. Something tugged on my senses, and I stopped.

Falin pulled his phone out of his pocket, and then

scowled at the screen. "No signal." He looked around, as if trying to judge what spot in the nature preserve was more likely to get cell signal. "We'd better head back."

I nodded, but the movement was distracted as I tried to zero in on what my senses were picking up. It wasn't magic, at least not Aetheric witchy magic. But there was something familiar about it. I took a few more steps—in the opposite direction of the path we'd taken to get here.

Falin was still holding his phone up in the air, searching for bars, but he turned when he noticed I wasn't following him. "You coming?"

"Yeah. Yeah, go ahead, I'll catch up in a minute." What *was* that? It tickled along my skin, but it wasn't an unpleasant sensation, and unlike the chill of grave essence reaching for me from the various animal bodies in the area, this felt . . . *warm*.

"I'll be just down the path," Falin said, but a frown claimed his expression, and he didn't head in the direction he'd indicated.

I gave him another nod, barely listening as I reached out with my senses. There was definitely *something* here. It didn't feel malicious, but I still stopped to pull my dagger from the sheath in my boot. After all, I had no idea if Jenny was hiding somewhere out of sight.

Picking my way carefully through the underbrush, I followed the trail of magic like it was a bit of unwound string I could track back to its ball of yarn. It led me away from the edge of the pond, through a small copse of trees, and to a clearing. In the very center of the clearing stood a small sapling, and the trail I'd been following culminated around the thin tree.

I approached it carefully. Despite the fact we were half through October, dark glossy leaves still clung to the branches and flowers bloomed sporadically amid the green foliage.

An amaranthine tree.

I was far from an expert on Faerie flora, but the only other amaranthine tree I knew of grew in the center of the VIP section of the Eternal Bloom, and it acted as the door to Faerie. I didn't know for sure if all of the trees marked doors, and if they did, if those doors randomly sprang up wherever the trees took root, but I did know I didn't like this tree being so close to the fouled pond.

Also, the tree wasn't that far off the path, and in my experience, the flowers had a hypnotic quality. All Nekros needed was for hikers to start disappearing after stumbling into Faerie and becoming changelings. Besides, because of the agreements made after the Magical Awakening, it was illegal for a gate to be unguarded and unrestricted for that very reason. Someone official needed to know about this tree, and hey, I happened to be in the forest with the lead FIB agent—you didn't get much more official than that when it came to fae matters.

I sheathed my dagger and dug my phone out of my pocket. It, of course, had no signal.

Damn.

I snapped a couple of pictures with my phone and then studied the clearing around me, trying to pick out landmarks. I could probably follow the flow of magic back to the tree, but just in case, I wanted some markers rooted in mortal reality. If there was one thing almost all folklore agreed on, it was that finding a door to Faerie once didn't indicate you'd ever be able to find it again. Granted, those stories were about humans interacting with Faerie, but still, better safe than sorry.

I made my way back to the pond's edge, noting anything I thought could help guide me back to the sapling. I was so busy searching for landmarks and checking the phone for signal that the splash of water directly behind me didn't register.

At least, not until a pair of green-tinted arms wrapped around my shoulders, a hand clamped over my mouth, and I was dragged backward, into the befouled water.

*   *   *

I screamed, but the water was already rushing up all around me and the sound emerged trapped in bubbles. The afternoon sun vanished behind a veil of algae. My eyes stung from the dirty water, but I didn't dare squeeze them closed.

And the arms continued dragging me down and down, the light of the surface winking away.

The pond couldn't possibly be this deep, not this close to the bank.

But it was. Somehow.

Thrashing, I struggled to retrieve my dagger from my boot. A slimy strand of black seaweed wrapped around my wrist, pulling it away from my body. Another strand wrapped around my other wrist, then my upper arms, my ankles, my waist, until I was immobilized. Only then did the arms encircling my shoulders release me.

In the dark water, I could only just make out the shape of the figure as she floated up, over my head and then spun so that her upside-down face was inches from mine. Jenny smiled, flashing those pointy green teeth of her namesake.

"Oh my," she said, tutting under her breath. Despite the laws of acoustics in water, I heard her words clearly. She didn't even make bubbles as she spoke. "You're old enough to know better than to play around my bog."

I scowled and pulled at the restraints holding me.

"Why so quiet?" She laughed. "A little smarter than you look, then. But conserving your air won't help. And that scream when you first went under is going to cost you."

She was right. My chest burned, my lungs aching with the need to draw breath. How long had I been underwater already? A minute? A minute and a half?

Jenny twisted upright and floated down until we were face-to-face again. Her dark hair flowed around her, blending into the murky depths of the water as she gave me an appraising once-over. I kept struggling.

"He wants you alive," she said, her smile fading. "I don't see why. But how much more air do you have? Maybe you accidentally drown while I subdue you." She pressed a long-fingered hand over her chest. "There was just nothing poor Jenny could do." She laughed again.

Crap. I had to do something. Fast.

I dropped my shields, looking around. There were dead things aplenty on the bottom of the pond—I could feel their picked-over bones—but thankfully none were human. Unfortunately, deer and hog shades weren't going to do a lot to prevent me from drowning. I glanced at the seaweed holding me, hoping against hope it was simply a glamour I could disbelieve away.

It wasn't.

The seaweed was not only real, but alive, so I couldn't drag it over to the land of the dead and rot it away. Damn. A bubble of exhausted air slipped from between my lips. I needed oxygen, and soon.

Jenny watched me, giggling with delight as I struggled in vain.

I considered trying to pull raw Aetheric energy and shape it into something useful. A fireball to burn away the seaweed? *Underwater—would that even work?* Or maybe a pocket of clean air around me. But even if I knew how to form those kinds of spells, which I didn't, whatever or wherever this pond was, it didn't exist completely in the mortal realm because I could see only the thinnest strands of Aetheric energy.

More expended air escaped my now-tingling lips.

No, I wouldn't die like this. I wouldn't.

But I was out of time. My body took an involuntary breath of water.

The water felt heavy and thick as it rushed into my lungs. Pain spread across my chest and my thrashing turned from struggles to escape into spasms.

Jenny clapped her hands. "Oh, this is my favorite part."

My body heaved, trying to expel the water, but there was nothing but more water to take its place. The pain in my chest was unbearable, but my arms felt numb, heavy. My legs too.

I heard a splash from somewhere in the distance, and a loud, echoing boom. Then there was only darkness.

Chapter 24

The darkness parted to more pain. I coughed up water. Then blessed, cool air rushed into my lungs.

I had less than a moment to savor the sensation before a spasm hit my body and I heaved, hacking up more water. Tears filled my eyes, and I realized I hadn't opened them yet. I coughed and sputtered a moment more before forcing my eyelids to peel back.

Falin knelt over me, one hand still in the center of my chest, and desperation written across his face. I tried to tell him I was all right, but I couldn't stop coughing. My throat was raw, my chest on fire, but my lungs kept attempting to expel every last drop of pond muck.

Falin helped roll me to my side, one of his hands keeping my head tilted back so my airway remained open, the other rubbing my back. I coughed some more, my whole body shaking. Sucking in a deep breath, I focused on holding it a heartbeat before letting it explode back out of my lungs. Then two heartbeats.

After what felt like an eternity, I caught enough of my breath to speak.

"Jenny?" The name emerged as a croak, the effort making my aching throat burn worse.

"I shot her, but she got away," Falin said and I realized the dark object lying in the muck inches from my nose was the butt of Falin's gun.

And speaking of muck, I was ready to be out of it.

"Help me up," I said, struggling to sit.

Falin slid his hands under my armpits and pulled me to my feet, but he didn't stop there. Once I was standing, his arms slid around me and he tugged me against his chest in a tight embrace. I was still shaking, my breath trembling out in wheezing gusts. Add to that the fact that my dip in the pond had chilled me, the October breeze sliding through my wet clothes, and I was more than happy to lean against Falin's warm chest, at least for a moment. I let my exhausted body enjoy the comfort of his strong arms, and maybe, just for a heartbeat, reminisced about the night we'd shared months ago, before everything got so complicated.

But it was complicated, and I couldn't let myself forget that Falin was a danger to more than just my emotions.

Lifting my arms, I pushed against his chest. He didn't release me. His arms protectively encircled me in an embrace gentle but unbreakable. I craned my head back, torquing my shoulders. Only then did I catch sight of the figure behind him.

If the figure had been Jenny Greenteeth or Tommy Rawhead with a weapon, we would have both been dead. Or maybe not. Maybe if the figure existed on the same plane of existence as Falin, the knight would have heard him and would have been armed and in a defensive position in a matter of heartbeats. But this figure wasn't someone Falin could sense, let alone fight.

Because behind Falin, stood Death.

The soul collector looked pale under his tan, and his hazel eyes, cast downward, were haunted. He saw me looking at him, and his shoulders sagged as he shook his head. He looked . . . defeated.

Of course, his girlfriend was currently in the arms of another man.

Damn it.

I shoved against Falin hard enough that when he released me, I stumbled back two steps. He reached out to steady me, but I stepped around his arms, forcing my shaky legs to take me toward Death.

"I couldn't save you," he whispered, squeezing his eyes shut. "You'd lost consciousness before I reached you, so I couldn't touch the plants binding you. *He* had to cut you free." He jerked his head toward Falin without opening his eyes. "I didn't even have breath to offer you to bring you back. All I could have done was take your soul or leave it in your dying body."

I reached for his shoulder but he ducked away from my touch.

"I'm fine," I said. Shaken, definitely. Scared, yeah. But aside from the pain in my throat and chest, I really was fine.

Death caught my hand before it dropped. "Not because of me." He pressed a light kiss against my fingertips. Then he vanished.

"Who is here?" Falin asked, stepping up behind me.

It said something about how well he knew me that he asked which invisible entity I was talking to instead of assuming I was suffering from shock or hallucinating. Yeah, maybe I talked to people on different planes of existence a little too often.

"No one," I said, still staring at the spot where Death had been. Then I forced myself to turn away. "No one else is here." And there were other things I needed to worry about right now than the emotional landfill that acted as my love life.

Like the amaranthine tree. And the fact Jenny was still out there.

*   *   *

"We could cut it down," I said, staring at the sapling. The trunk was no thicker than my thumb, and my dagger was enchanted to slice through nearly any material. It would be easy.

Falin frowned at me. "It's considered taboo to harm amaranthine trees. They are sacred to Faerie."

"So what happens to it then? Will the courts build another bar around it, like the Eternal Bloom?" The tree was deep inside a federal nature preserve—I doubted the government would like it if the fae announced they were commandeering this land. "Any clue what it's doing here anyway?"

Falin appraised the sapling. "There are many different kinds of doors to Faerie, but amaranthine trees are always permanent doors and are epicenters for belief magic to filter in from the mortal realm. A new tree hasn't appeared naturally in recent memory, and from what I've heard, all attempts to propagate one has failed."

We both stared at the tree. Clearly someone had succeeded. We were far too close to the tree in the Eternal Bloom for this one to be natural.

"Is there any way to tell where it leads?"

Falin walked around the tree. I'd considered trying that when I first saw it, but okay, I admit it, I chickened out. Now I held my breath as he rounded the back of the sapling. I waited for him to disappear into Faerie, but nothing happened. He returned to the spot where he'd started and shook his head. "Maybe whatever means was used to create it couldn't duplicate its doorway properties."

"Or maybe it just needs to mature more," I said, because while it might not be a gate we could travel through yet, the tree was definitely syphoning belief magic. I hadn't been able to identify the trail of magic I'd followed to the tree, but now that I knew what I was looking at, it made sense. The Bloom drew in so much magic in a continual stream that it built up around the building in a gradual way; a gradient change that was likely responsible for the mixed realities in the VIP room. This young tree had such a thin stream of magic that it was almost more noticeable because of the thin but concentrated strand I'd all but tripped over.

"You couldn't compel Jenny Greenteeth to respond when you tried to summon her. You said any denizens or independents of winter should have no choice but to respond to the court's knight, unless they were noble or sworn to a noble. I assumed that meant the latter since she didn't appear when you called her, and she's in winter's territory without signs of fading. But with the tree so close to where she made her home . . ." I trailed of, organizing my thoughts. "Could she be tied to another court entirely? Here to guard the tree as a new court establishes a foothold? The tree providing her tie back to her own court and supplying the magic needed to sustain her?"

"Maybe, but it's doubtful. With no gate, all the magic the tree is absorbing is likely fueling its own growth." Falin knelt beside the tree and brushed his thumb over its smooth bark. "Most likely she is tied to a winter noble, possibly one who formed some manner of alliance with another court." Falin frowned down at the sapling. "But this tree's existence makes no sense. Faerie naturally balances the territories when the doors shift. Different seasons wax and wane in power as the year passes, but adding another door would only encourage Faerie to split territory differently the next time the doors moved. The seasons always remain relatively balanced."

"Should the queen have noticed this sapling leaching from her power base here in Nekros?" I asked.

"She's been rather distracted," Falin said.

It was true. And maybe that was the point. I'd been trying to figure out what the alchemist would gain by kidnapping and draining fae, leaving the ghastly display he had with Icelynne's bones, and distributing Glitter to mortals where it caused horrific, high-profile deaths.

Maybe this tree explained all those actions. Maybe they were all distractions.

I thought back to what the nightmare kingling had said when we'd met in my dream. That realms of the imagination were the purview of the light fae. "What if it wasn't a season? What if it was the light court?" *Or shadow? They are certainly dwindling in power and could use a way to gather more.* But Dugan had sworn the bogeymen weren't working for his court. Could he simply not know?

"Light and shadow don't have doors."

"I know. But amaranthine trees don't just appear, either. And like you said, it doesn't make sense for another season to try so hard to establish an extra door—they could lose it at any time when Faerie next rearranges itself."

Falin gave a one-shouldered half shrug that didn't actually communicate anything. And that was likely the point. After a few long moments, he said, "Assuming what you're suggesting is possible, light is the least likely to be orchestrating this invasive takeover. They are the only court that has stood by the queen in her recent . . . troubles . . . and not sent a challenger to duel for her throne. The Queen of Light is the Winter Queen's sister."

My mouth formed a silent O as I let that sink in. The ruling class of Faerie were not a very diverse bunch. Of course, when you lived as long as the fae, alliances through marriages and births were bound to tie a small population together.

I hugged my arms over my chest, trying to quell the shiver threatening to tremble through me. Pond-soaked clothing was certainly not the warmest outfit. Falin glanced up, his gaze lingering over the gooseflesh visible on my arms. Then he stood and without a word, walked to the edge of the clearing. Reaching up, he grabbed a huge hunk of Spanish moss that dangled from one of the bottom branches of a tree.

He shook the twisted gray mat of plant matter and it

grew in his hand, the shape and texture changing as he poured glamour into it. By the time he reached my side, he'd transformed the moss into a gray blanket.

He tossed it over my shoulders, tugging it around me so it covered my soaked clothes and most of my chilled skin. The fabric was heavy, and as velvety and soft as chenille. I tried hard to focus on how it appeared now, and not on the fact that a moment before it had been a tuft of stringy moss, because real or not, it was warm and I didn't want my planeweaving to break the glamour.

"Better," I said, as way of acknowledging the act since I couldn't thank him.

Falin only nodded before turning back to the tree. "I think we should dig it up and take it to the queen."

"Now? We don't have any shovels."

He patted his pockets and pulled out his phone. A few drops of water dripped from the speaker when he turned it upright. Yeah, he wouldn't be making any calls with that anytime soon. Maybe not ever.

I searched for my own phone, but it wasn't in my pocket. I'd had it in my hand when Jenny had grabbed me. If I was lucky, it was in the muck on the edge of the pond. If I was unlucky—and I typically was—I'd managed to hold on to it and it had been dragged into the pond with me. In which case, I'd never see it again. I needed to start paying for insurance on my phones. This was the third one I'd lost or destroyed this year.

We clearly weren't going to be contacting the agents he'd called to come watch the lake. They were likely still on the road and could have stopped to pick up some supplies to help move the sapling, but oh well. I looked down at myself, I was already covered in slime and muck from my trip into the stagnant pond and then subsequent time unconscious in the mud on the bank. How much worse could I get digging up a tree?

I knelt beside the trunk and pulled my dagger from its

sheath. The semicognizant dagger hated being driven into the ground, but despite its protests, it would get the job done. Brushing debris back from the base of the tree, I said, "Let's do this then."

By the time we'd unearthed the tree, I had mud caked under my nails and my fingers felt raw. Who knew such a small sapling would have so many roots? I considered rinsing my hands in the pond, but I doubted that would be much of an improvement. Besides, I didn't want to get any closer to the water than I had to.

We didn't have a bucket or pot for the tree, so Falin turned another clump of Spanish moss into a burlap sack.

"Why not just glamour it into a pot?" I asked, as I helped him wrap the tree's root ball.

He shrugged. "Masters of glamour can create objects from nothing and reality will accept the object, at least until the magic thins at dawn or sunset. But most of us need a base object to change. The fewer changes we make, the stronger the glamoured object's place in reality."

So the fiberlike moss changed into a fiber-based textile was easier for reality to accept. It made sense. And it was something I'd never been told before. Of course, I was still at the stage of trying to learn to use glamour to cover my telltale fae glow, so creating objects was rather out of my ability range. The knowledge did give me an even scarier appreciation for Glitter though. No wonder it burned the user out if the hallucination didn't kill them. The hallucinations-given-life weren't transformations of a base material, but pure glamour fueled by the victims own life energy.

We carried the tree between us, back to where the path and the pond met. I had no doubt Falin could have carried it himself, even with the weight of the soil packed around the roots, but I think having me help was his way of ensuring I was close. It also allowed him to keep his dagger out and bared in his free hand, just in case Jenny made another appearance.

As we walked, I spotted a bit of purple near the edge of the pond. *My phone.*

Falin wouldn't let me approach the water—not that I really wanted to—so I stayed with the tree while he went and scooped the phone out of the muck. It was a little muddy, but it had been spared a trip into the water, so functioning. Of course, it still didn't have signal.

As we waited for the FIB agents, I did the best I could to clean up the phone with the edge of the blanket. While we'd been digging, I'd worked up a sweat, but now that we were standing still in the shadow of the trees, the chill was creeping in again. Thankfully, it didn't take much longer for the agents to arrive. Falin described Jenny to them, and two went into the woods to search for the bogeyman, the third staying to watch for any sign of her at the pond.

After that we were free to leave. Falin wanted to take the amaranthine sapling straight to Faerie, but what I really wanted was a hot shower and a change of clothes.

"You don't need me there to give the tree to the queen," I said as we trudged up the path. The sapling may not be very big, but the longer we carried it, the heavier it got. I was breathing heavy before we made it around the first curve in the path. "Drop me off at home first."

He frowned at me. "The trip to Faerie would be good for you. Nearly drowning took a lot out of you. You'd waste less energy by recovering in Faerie."

And he'd been ordered to drag me back by force if necessary if I seemed to be fading too much. The queen didn't want to risk losing even theoretical access to a planeweaver. I wanted to disagree, but I was both shivering and sweating with the effort of carrying half the tree, and I had no extra breath to argue. Falin sheathed his dagger and took the strap I'd been hauling, lifting the entire weight of the tree alone. He'd been heavily wounded yesterday, but he wasn't even breathing hard.

I didn't fight to help carry the tree. I was too busy keeping my feet from dragging.

We'd reached the parking lot when a shrill beeping issued from my phone.

I had signal.

I dug the phone out of my pocket. The smeared mud residue made it hard to read the screen, but I had a voice mail I'd missed by fewer than five minutes. It was probably a potential client who I wouldn't be able to schedule an appointment for, at least not until this case was solved and I had my independent status secured. Falin was loading the sapling into the car, and I considered listening to the message later, maybe after I felt a little less shaky and had caught my breath, but I didn't have anything else to do.

The signal kept dropping, so it took me two tries to get the message to play.

"Lady Craft," a vaguely familiar voice said in the recording, "you told me to call if the hobgoblin returned to the bar. He's here now," he said. Then the message ended.

I glanced at the time stamp. It had now been ten minutes since the message was left. *Oh please let Tommy Rawhead still be there.* I hit redial on the number.

"Eternal Bloom, come in and let us enchant you," the voice that answered said.

Cute. But hopefully not accurate.

The person who'd answered was male, but I wasn't sure if it was the bartender who'd called me.

"Yes, hi. May I speak to . . ." I trailed off. The fae had never given me his name. Would it be rude to ask for the satyr who tended bar? "Uh, well, that is, this is Alex Craft. I'm returning a call from this number."

"Oh, my lady," the voice on the other side of the line said, confirming that he was the same bartender. "I was beginning to think you didn't get my message." He sounded as if he would have been relieved if his message had somehow gotten lost in the nether-space of cell reception.

"Is the hobgoblin still there?" I asked, ignoring the satyr's obvious discomfort. I put the phone on speaker and climbed into the car, motioning to Falin to listen as well.

"No. He caught sight of the current clientele and turned tail. There are *agents* in the bar today." The way he said agents let me know he was none-too-pleased with the FIB presence.

"Did they go after him?"

There was silence on the other side of the phone for a moment before the bartender said, "One is gone."

So, maybe. I wanted to growl out a frustrated remark about him paying more attention, but that would be rude. He'd kept an eye out like I'd asked and he'd called me. He hadn't had to. I hadn't offered him anything.

I forced myself to take a deep breath so my voice came out calm, even, when I asked, "This hobgoblin, was he wearing a cap that appeared to be leaking blood?"

"Yeah, pretty nasty. He freaks people out when he's in here."

I bet.

Falin had started the car while I was talking, and now he careened out of the parking lot. He dug his waterlogged phone out of his pocket. It was, of course, still not functioning.

"You've been very helpful," I said, taking the phone off speaker so that I could hear and be heard above the roar of wind. Talking on a cell phone in a car with the top down going way too fast on curvy roads was *not* fun, but time was short and I wasn't about to ask Falin to slow down. "If you see him again, call me back. I owe you a boon." As I said the words, I felt the debt take hold, but at least with a boon, I could refuse certain manners of repayment if I didn't agree with the favor asked.

"My lady," he said as way of acknowledging my words, and he sounded amazed. I guessed not too many Sleagh Maiths offered boons to independent lesser fae.

We both disconnected and I passed my phone to Falin. He shot me a frown.

"You have to stop giving away debts," he said as he dialed. I was more than a little nervous with him driving one-handed at the speeds he was pushing the car, but I held my tongue and instead shrugged at his comment. The movement transformed into a shiver, and I sank lower in my seat, dragging the glamoured blanket tighter around my shoulders.

"He was helpful. And if this information helps us catch Tommy Rawhead, it will be worth the boon." And if it didn't, well, it might not matter.

Chapter 25

—✦—◦ ◦—✦—

The agent had, in fact, followed Tommy Rawhead, but it took several calls for Falin to confirm it. Unfortunately, as the agent had been told only to detain fae matching Rawhead's and Greenteeth's descriptions, and as she couldn't get in touch with Falin to clarify her orders, she'd decided to trail Rawhead instead of attempting to arrest him in a place heavily populated by humans. By the time Falin got the agent on the phone and learned she was actively following Rawhead through the streets of the Magic Quarter, we were only minutes away.

Another call got backup headed to her position. While fae typically avoided negative public attention, like a messy public arrest, the FIB would make an exception for this case. Falin pulled onto the main strip of the Quarter. If everything went as planned, the actual takedown would likely occur before we arrived on the scene, but Falin didn't want to take any chances of Rawhead slipping his tail.

My phone rang.

"Sir," an uncertain female voice said when Falin answered. "I think we have a problem."

Oh no.

"The hobgoblin just entered Magic Square," she said. "He changed his glamour again, and I think I've lost him."

Crap. I exchanged glances with Falin. He looked grim as he said, "I want agents scouring that park. I'll be there soon."

He parkcd the car in a loading zone and jumped out. Magic Square, the park in the very heart of the Magic Quarter, wasn't accessible by car. We'd have to walk. Or really, run.

I scrambled out of the car, and nearly tripped over my own legs in my haste. Falin frowned, his eyes cutting a quick assessment over me.

"Wait here," he said.

"Hell, no. Out of the two of us, which can see through glamour?"

I had him there, we both knew it, so he didn't argue. We took off at a run, but he had to slow several times for me to catch up as I wheezed and sucked down air. I almost told him to go on, that I'd catch up, but I hadn't been lying—my ability to see through glamour would be an asset. He had agents swarming the park. We'd be there soon. *I just hope it's soon enough.*

When we reached the gates, I cracked my shields. Wind whipped up around me, blowing across from the land of the dead, and people stopped, stared. Of course, it probably didn't help that Falin and I were both still covered in rancid pond gunk.

I ignored the stares as I scanned the area. We raced through the park, passing several FIB agents. Each gave a quick report to Falin before he sent them back to their own searches.

My feet were all but dragging, my tired legs feeling as if they'd been pumped full of lead, and I was ready to admit defeat when I heard the first scream. It was a high-pitched screech, followed by wailing cries like a child would make. A second child added her voice to the first. Then a third.

I ground to a stop and turned toward the sound. I wasn't the only one who could see through glamour. For bogeymen, at least, young children could always see the fae's true form, as the toddlers at Tamara's wedding had proven.

There was a playground on the far side of the park, and I dashed toward it. Falin was right beside me. He made a gesture over his head, motioning for all the FIB who saw it to descend on the play area as well.

Several children had run to their baffled mothers or were hiding behind playground equipment, and it didn't take me long to spot why. Near the back exit of the park was Tommy Rawhead, glamoured to look like any other jogger out enjoying a run in the brisk autumn air. I pointed to him.

"Gray tracksuit with bloodred piping," I gasped out.

Falin didn't waste time asking questions. He sprang to action, sprinting across the green space, several of his agents on his heels. I tried to keep up.

I couldn't.

I doubled over, gulping down lungfuls of air. Between fading and my near drowning, my chest ached, my breaths making a high-pitched sound with every wheezing inhalation.

By the time I straightened, still out of breath, Rawhead was already in cuffs, Falin dragging him across the park. I didn't bother trying to run to catch up, but set a pace I thought I could manage.

Falin was waiting at the car when I reached it. The other agents were nowhere to be seen, but Rawhead was both cuffed and charmed immobile in the cramped backseat beside the amaranthine tree.

Well, it looked like I was going to Faerie after all.

"How dare you," the queen yelled, stepping down from a throne so melted it barely resembled the majestic seat of power it had been the last time I'd visited the throne room.

I was seriously hoping the queen was talking to the bound hobgoblin Falin had just shoved down into a supplicating position. But she wasn't looking at the bogeyman, her crazed gaze fixed on me, pinning me to the spot like a needle through a bug.

"Your majesty?" My voice came out thin, frightened. I cleared my throat before speaking again. "We've brought you the hobgoblin Tommy Rawhead. We believe he's been distributing Glitter to the humans, and he is likely sworn to the alchemist."

She didn't even glance at the bogeyman. She raised a hand that trembled with rage and pointed at me. "You did this. You are doing this to my court."

I gulped. There was certainly something wrong with the winter court: the ice-crusted walls glistened with dripping water, the floor was little more than a puddle, the seemingly ever-present snow that typically fell from the ceiling without ever hitting the ground had turned to sleet that pelted me, chilling me to the bone, and the distant music that always seemed to filter through Faerie had turned harsh, disharmonious.

"Unraveling a court's magic is certainly possible for a planeweaver," Maeve said offhandedly. Ryese made a sound of agreement from where he leaned against a melting pillar. Lyell only stared straight ahead. Not looking at anyone in particular.

I shot them a collective disgusted glance. Even if the planeweavers of legend could have done this, I most definitely didn't know how to accomplish the task. Besides, while there was no doubt something was wrong with the winter court, if I'd have had to stake my life on the cause—and maybe I was gambling with those stakes—I'd have said Faerie was reflecting the state of the queen.

She was *not* well.

Her dark hair hung in damp, stringy strands that clung to her face and shoulders. Her soaked dress was tattered where she'd pulled at the seams, and lacked any of her normal ornamentation. She was usually as pale as freshly fallen snow, but now that pallor was sickly, like a corpse, and her flesh seemed to be pulled too tightly over her sharp features. And her eyes? Her eyes were fever bright with madness.

No, something was definitely not all right with the queen. And her Faerie court reflected that fact. Of course, I probably didn't look much better. The exhaustion that beat at me weighed me down, even in Faerie, and I'd seen the visible toll fading was taking on my appearance. Add to that the slime and muck encrusted in my hair and clothes—of course the muddy puddle around my boots suggested that sleet had washed at least some of that off— and I probably looked pretty sick myself. But it was more than the queen's body that was unwell. It was her mind.

In the past she'd struck me as manipulative, narcissistic, and cruel. But never mad . . .

"My queen," Falin said, kneeling between the Winter Queen and me. It was unlikely that she had failed to notice the fact he'd physically blocked her access to me, but he hurried on before she could rage about it. "Alex has been a friend to our court. She discovered an amaranthine sapling and has brought it to your court. She's also brought a traitor's conspirator for you to question." He motioned to the bound bogeyman, who had very wisely remained still and hadn't drawn attention to himself while the full weight of the queen's fury had been focused on me.

Now, she finally turned to the bogeyman. Her pale lips curled back in a disgusted sneer as she studied him. "What say you, you repulsive little man? Are you sworn to a member of my court?"

Tommy looked up and smiled at the queen. It was a

disturbing expression with his mouth of pointed teeth and the blood dripping down his face, tinting the water around him.

"I will never say, Queen of Ice."

Her fist balled in her once full skirt, ripping at an already frayed seam. "To whom are you aligned?"

"You may ask until your last breath, but I will give you no names."

If he'd been human, I'd have applauded his bravado, but guessed it wouldn't have held long. But he was fae, and he promised it with such conviction of truth, that I guessed he was bound not to reveal the alchemist.

"There are ways to loosen your tongue, hobgoblin." The queen motioned to Falin, who drew his two wickedly long daggers. They flashed in the unearthly light and I gulped. I wanted answers. *Needed* them to complete my bargain with the queen, to stop the influx of Glitter on the streets, but I hadn't signed on for torture. Of course, what had I really been expecting? An interrogation room with a table, a couple of chairs, and a two-way mirror?

"Shall I take him to Rath?" Ryese asked, making a step toward the bogeyman. "We could start him on the rack."

My stomach flipped and if the late breakfast I'd eaten hadn't been quite so long ago, I might have been revisited by the food. Instead I just felt queasy. The urge to run out of the room and disassociate myself with the whole thing was strong, but I was a part of this. If I wasn't going to protest, I wasn't going to wash my hands of it either.

The queen pursed her lips. "No, I don't think that will do. While I have no doubt he will eventually break, I do not wish to devote that much time in the creature."

"Will you truthseek, Ice Queen?" The hobgoblin asked, still grinning that terrible grin.

"By your gloating expression, I'm assuming that would be a fruitless exercise as you are oath bound to reveal nothing." She leaned down until she was eye level with

Tommy. "Funny things about oaths—they bind only until death. Knight, kill that creature."

Falin, who couldn't disobey a direct command from his queen, jerked the hobgoblin to his feet and pressed a blade against the smaller fae's exposed throat. For the first time, the smile fell from Tommy's face, the whites of his eyes flashing as his eyelids drew back as if he could manage to see more of the danger that would somehow show him a way out of it. But it didn't. Had he so much as breathed hard, the blade pressed against his throat would have bitten into flesh.

While Falin couldn't directly disobey, he could stall. "My queen, are you certain? If I kill him we will not get the answers you need."

"Do not question me, Knight," she snapped. Then she turned and fixed her fever-mad gaze on me. "And we will most definitely get our answers."

Chapter 26

"**K**ill him now, Knight."

I didn't even see Falin's arm move. One moment the blade pressed against Rawhead's throat, glinting in the strange light. Then the blade vanished.

For several long heartbeats, Tommy Rawhead looked stunned. Then his head toppled forward, and tumbled down to roll through the puddles on the throne floor. Falin released Rawhead's body a moment later, and it crumpled to the floor in a lump.

I screamed. It wasn't a conscious decision, the sound just burst out of me as an arc of blood gushed from the now-headless neck. I scrambled back, but the puddles of melted ice and sleet diluted the expanding blood pool, mixing and spreading it far beyond the body.

"Now we will get our answers. Planeweaver?" The queen turned to me, and bile bit at the back of my throat.

I doubled over, my stomach heaving, but nothing but dry hacking came up. Falin was suddenly at my side, his warm fingers brushing my sleet-encrusted curls away from my face.

"Don't show her weakness," he whispered, his hand

moving to the back of my neck and then down, between my shoulder blades.

I stepped away. I didn't want him to touch me. Not now. Maybe not ever. He'd just killed someone in cold blood. I'd seen him kill before—hell, I'd killed in the past—but it had always been self-defense. Yes, Rawhead was a bad guy in folklore. He *ate* children. We knew that. And we suspected he was involved with Glitter, which meant he was at least partially responsible for the deaths of the fae who it had been made from and the mortals who had used it. But we had no proof of his involvement yet. He'd been executed on suspicion alone. He'd already been captured. He'd been no threat to anyone anymore.

I stepped away from Falin, forcing myself to straighten. Wiping the back of my hand across my mouth, I avoided looking at the body. I didn't like blood or gore at the best of times, and I'd seen bodies in much worse condition, but no one had ever been murdered simply so I could question their shade before.

"I can't do this," I whispered, more to myself than anyone in the room.

"What was that, planeweaver?" the queen asked, but the sharp tone of her voice said that she'd heard me.

I could almost feel the stiff stillness of Falin at my back, like a warning. Ryese smiled, but it wasn't a pleasant expression. The look told me that if I refused the queen, he would enjoy dragging me to Rath, the queen's torture room, just as much as he would have enjoyed hauling Tommy Rawhead there. Ryese was an equal opportunity pain dealer. Beside him, Maeve looked away, but Lyell gave a minute shake of his head, a small warning that refusing was a bad plan.

I swallowed and forced my shoulders back. Lifting my head, I met the queen's crazed gaze. "I said, I can't do this. Here." I waved a hand to indicate the throne room. "No land of the dead, remember?"

She raised an eyebrow full of sleet, but she didn't call me on the cover. "Knight, transport that." She gestured to the body. "Ryese, assist him."

"Dearest aunt, perhaps I should stay here and organize the restoration of your throne room?" He gestured to the blood, which had been carried in the puddles to spread across most of the room.

I was going to have to burn my boots.

"Fine." She waved a dismissive hand, and then turned to me again. "After you, planeweaver. I want my answers."

I stared at the body in the center of my circle. I'd considered trying to duck the queen as soon as we'd returned to mortal reality. But, unless I planned to run off and join the shadow court, the only way for me to stop myself and my friends from fading was to find the answers the queen needed. Not questioning the shade due to moral outrage was suicidal. Rawhead was already dead. The damage was done. If he revealed the alchemist, at least some good would come out of this mess. Besides, while Rawhead was almost certainly involved with Glitter, he wasn't the mastermind of the operation. We had to stop the production of the drug.

So here I stood. But there was one major issue. A huge complication that made me hesitate even after resigning myself to performing the ritual.

Rawhead's soul was still inside his corpse.

Just like with Icelynne, because there were no collectors in Faerie, Rawhead's soul hadn't passed on. I was fairly certain that if his body was left in the mortal realm long enough, a collector would eventually stumble over him and take care of the oversight, but we didn't exactly have time to wait for that to happen. I could eject the soul as I'd done with Icelynne. But while she'd emerged scared and confused, she hadn't had any reason to blame me for her demise.

Tommy Rawhead did. I had no doubt he'd hold a grudge.

And I'd be trapped in a circle with him.

"What is the delay, planeweaver?"

I ignored the queen. She was on the outside of my barrier and not my biggest concern, currently, at least. Kneeling, I drew a second circle close to the body, but I didn't activate it yet. If I timed this right, I could eject Rawhead's soul, and then erect the second circle around me and the empty body. The ghost would be left trapped between the two barriers. If I then dropped the outermost circle, Rawhead would be free to leave. The question was, would he? And if he didn't, how long could I keep the smaller circle intact?

I mentally tapped into the raw Aetheric energy stored in my ring. There wasn't much. I prayed it would be enough.

Taking a deep breath, I stepped over the waxy line of my inert inner circle. Then, without releasing my connection with the energy in my ring, I opened my shields, and as the chill of the grave blew through me, I pushed it into the corpse at my feet.

The silver-blue soul of Tommy Rawhead exploded from the corpse. I had hoped he'd be disoriented. That would have given me time to get him away from the body so I could raise the inner circle. But Rawhead lunged toward me before his form solidified.

I stumbled, throwing out my arms to guard my face.

The ghost locked his jaw around my forearm, and cold pain sliced through me as those pointy teeth sank into my flesh. I screamed, blood welling up on my arm.

Outside my circle, yelling erupted, and I felt something slam into my barrier. The force reverberated through my magic. The idea of dropping the circle flitted through my mind, but I couldn't concentrate enough to break the spell—Rawhead was still attached to my arm.

He locked his jaw, and I swore I heard his teeth

grinding against my bones. Screaming again, I pushed against him with my grave magic. The ghost seemed to drink down the magic, becoming more real.

Damn it.

Rawhead released my arm and stepped back. He grinned, spreading his legs and arms like a wrestler preparing to tackle his opponent. Not good, as I was that opponent. He'd manifested exactly as he'd been in life, with blood running down his face from under his hat. But as it was now only an idea of what he'd been, that blood was pale, slightly translucent. The blood running from his mouth was mine, and very real.

I cradled my arm against my chest and backed away, but the circle wasn't large. I had nowhere to go.

Rawhead's bloody grin grew.

On the other side of my circle, Falin, the queen, and her council were yelling. What, I didn't have time to listen to now, but at least no one was trying to break down my barrier anymore.

Rawhead lunged, but this time I managed to duck to the side. He slammed into the edge of my circle, and it shuddered, the barrier sparking. I yelped as the backlash tore through me. If the circle took another hit like that, the ghost would win this fight without even having to catch me because I'd be unconscious. I had to turn the tables.

Ghosts were just will and energy.

There had been nothing I could do about the fact that Tommy Rawhead had been a nasty bogeyman in life, or that he blamed me, at least in part, for his death. But energy? Yeah, that I could affect.

Lifting my uninjured arm, I reached for Rawhead with my ability to touch the dead. But this time, instead of pushing magic at him, I *pulled*.

Energy leapt from Rawhead to me.

Most of the magics associated with the grave were cold, but ghosts weren't actually *of* the land of the dead.

They were souls trapped in the land of the dead when they left their body without transitioning to wherever collectors sent them.

So as the energy slipped under my skin, it was the warm life energy of a soul that I absorbed, not the chill of the grave. I had drawn energy from souls twice before. The first time from Coleman, who'd used so much dark magic his soul was stained black with it, and the second from a creature native to the land of the dead. Both of their essences had been tainted and sludgelike. Rawhead, as reprehensible as he'd been in life, hadn't actually damaged his soul. I drew on his energy and it rushed into me, warm and sweet as a spring breeze. It felt *good*. Which was so wrong.

But I didn't dare stop as he reared back to charge again. He rushed toward me, and I pulled with all my might, drinking down the pure energy. Rawhead faded with each running step he took, his form becoming hazy, less solid. He crashed into me, but it was too late.

He dissolved, like morning dew in the sun. Then I was alone in my circle.

I collapsed to my knees, panting, but honestly, aside from the pain burning along my gnawed-upon arm, I felt better than I had in days. A fact that made me queasy.

I hugged my injured arm to my chest and pushed off the ground. Only then did I look around and take stock of what was happening beyond my circle. The queen was right on the edge of the barrier, Falin physically restraining her from slamming her fists into the circle. It said something about her mental state that she didn't command him to release her. Maeve had backed away from both queen and circle. Lyell had a small scythelike weapon in his hands, but his arms were lowered as his gaze swept around my circle, searching for an enemy he hadn't been able to see.

"What have you done, planeweaver?" the queen asked,

struggling in Falin's arms. "What injury have you inflicted on yourself? Are you attempting to skirt finding the answers I demand? Are you part of this conspiracy against me?"

I looked into her fevered gaze and felt hate, cold and pure, for this queen who regarded the value of others' lives on a sliding scale of what she could gain from them. And yet, I also felt the smallest amount of pity for her. Something was wrong with her. I wasn't sure if she'd snapped under the stress of her position or if something more malicious was at play, but this hateful queen was out of her mind.

"Rawhead's ghost was present. It is gone now." The words came out flat, with no inflection. "I'm ready to raise the shade," I said, and then turned my back on her. I had a job to do and I didn't want to look at the woman who'd ordered the execution of the body in front of me, and so, indirectly forced me to cannibalize a soul.

Or maybe I just wanted to stop thinking because it had been so easy to do this time. And it felt good. Which scared me. After all, even if it was in self-defense, how many souls could I consume without destroying my own?

Chapter 27

With Rawhead's ghost gone, progressing with the ritual was little more than a familiar exercise. After the last several rituals with shades so depleted that I'd had to pour far too much energy into them to raise a mere shadow of my typical shades, the ease of which Rawhead's shade rose from his body was a relief.

I glanced at the shade I'd raised and grimaced. Well, maybe *relief* was the wrong word. Falin had covered the body before I'd drawn my circle, and the ghost had more or less resembled Rawhead in life, but the shade resembled him in death, complete with neck ending in a bloody stump and his severed head in his lap. I looked away.

"What is your name?" I asked the shade.

"We know that already," the queen all but spat from outside my circle.

I shot a frown over my shoulder at her, but she was correct. We knew that information, but I always started my interviews with the question. It was a habit.

Physics—or maybe biology—would insist that a head separated from its body couldn't speak, but Rawhead was dead, a projection of memories, and the magic didn't really care in what condition that projection appeared. So, the shade's response of his name was clear and strong.

Behind me, the queen muttered something about moving on and asking the alchemist's name, but I hesitated before asking my next question. I needed the alchemist's identity, without a doubt, but in the queen's frantic state, she'd likely demand an immediate end to my ritual as soon as we had a name. I didn't want to be called to any more scenes with glamoured fires or homicidal clowns, so I needed a little more information about Glitter before I lost access to Rawhead's shade.

"Have you been distributing the drug Glitter?"

"Yes."

Well, at least I knew we had the right fae. I still felt sick that he'd been killed so that I could question him, but the reassurance that he was responsible for at least half a dozen deaths was something. Oh, and according to legend, he ate children. Major strike against him there.

"How many vials of Glitter did you distribute?"

"Seven."

I blinked. Seven vials? I was expecting the number to be in the dozens if not the hundreds. I had assumed that our victims had overdosed or had a bad reaction to the drug, but if I assumed Gavin Murphy had used the drug—and Death had indicated that he had—I knew where five of the vials had ended up. That left only two vials unaccounted for. They could still be unused, or the results might not have been outlandish enough to warrant attention, the users dying, in seemingly mundane ways. The operation Icelynne had described sounded, if not large, than at least as though more than seven vials had been produced.

"What was the point?" I said under my breath. It wasn't really a question, or at least not one directed at anyone, but the shade answered anyway.

"Fear."

"What?"

"Glitter was distributed to create fear among the humans and disorder in the court," Rawhead said.

"Ask for the name now," the queen yelled from outside my circle. "Or your head will be the next I send my knight to retrieve."

Right. *No more delaying.* I would have liked to get a little more information, but at least I knew the operation was small. Once the alchemist was caught, production would stop. *But where is the rest of the drug now?* Icelynne had seen several other fae in the place where she was held, and she'd been held for days, slowly drained of her glamour. There must have been more than seven vials created.

I was out of time.

I turned toward the shade. "To which court do you belong?"

"I'm sworn to a noble of the winter court."

As expected. "The name of that noble?"

"Ryese."

The world hung for a moment on the silence after the shade spoke. Then a shriek burst from the queen and she threw herself at my barrier.

Pain crashed through my senses as she slammed into the circle. I fell to my knees, trying to ride out the backlash.

"Stop," I said through gritted teeth. Not that she could hear me over her own wails.

"He lies," she screamed, bashing her fist into my circle.

I squeezed my eyes shut as explosions of pain ripped through my psyche. The circle still held, but barely, and each reverberation felt like barbed wire scraping against the inside of my skull. My circles did a good job of keeping out ambient magical forces and keeping my own magic inside and separate from the distracting pull of grave essence beyond my barrier, but I wasn't a strong enough spellcaster to erect a barrier that could withstand an assault by magical entities. And all fae were innately magical. I had to get the circle down before it overloaded and snapped.

"Rest now," I told the shade as I pushed it back into its body.

Falin wrapped his arms around the queen, dragging her back and buying me a moment of peace to reclaim my heat from the corpse. Releasing my hold on the land of the dead, I narrowed the hole in my shields, but I didn't close it completely—I wasn't ready to be blind at the mercy of a raging queen.

Climbing to my feet, I approached the edge of the circle. Reaching out with my good arm, I dispelled the barrier. The haze of blue magic separating the rest of the world from my small circle of protected space popped. The sudden assault on my senses was jarring with my shields still open, but I was prepared for it, and forced my breathing to be measured, controlled, as I adjusted to the magical change.

"Bring him back," the queen bellowed, struggling in Falin's arms.

He held her firmly, but with a tenderness that caught me off guard. Usually it was easy to forget that they had been lovers once. Most of the time, when he looked at her, I saw barely restrained resentment. Now, with his arms crossed over her chest, pinning her back to his front, I saw only concern and pity.

"Bring him back this instant, planeweaver," she yelled again, her voice echoing off the concrete walls of the mostly empty parking garage walls. "He lies."

Now it was my turn to find this mad queen pitiable. Her nephew was behind the plot against her. That had to hurt. "Shades can't lie, your majesty."

"We have only your word for that fact." She leaned forward against Falin's arms, not exactly struggling, but moving toward me. "Maybe you are mortal enough to lie."

I wasn't, but saying as much would prove nothing. Ever try to prove to someone you can't lie? Yeah, it doesn't work. Now proving you can is easy enough, you just have to claim the sky is orange or some nonsense, but proving you can't lie takes years of truths. So, I didn't bother attempting to prove my own truthfulness.

"Rawhead was fae," I said, ignoring the fact I was stating the obvious. "Even if human shades could lie—which they can't—wouldn't it stand to reason that fae shades couldn't because fae can't lie?"

She didn't even pause before retorting with, "Death breaks oaths. Perhaps fae can lie after death."

I sighed. A rational argument wasn't going to work with an irrational person. The queen didn't want to believe Ryese could be behind the plot against her. So she wouldn't believe it.

Falin said something in a lyrical language I didn't know. The language of the fae was beautiful and terrible all at once. I couldn't understand the words he said, but I could feel the power in them. The words slid around my senses as smooth as silk—but with a cutting edge.

The queen sagged in Falin's arms. She released a long breath that sounded wet with tears she hadn't shed. I shot a questioning glance at Falin, but he wasn't looking at me. He was whispering, the words that same language, but they had lost their edge, and now simply sounded gentle, comforting.

"Release me, Knight. Release me," the queen said, her voice level, calm.

Falin had no choice, it was a direct command. Lyell moved to my side. His weapon had vanished, and his posture seemed relaxed, but his eyes betrayed his worry. I wasn't sure if he was showing me support—or just making himself at hand if the queen instructed I be apprehended.

I tensed, but the queen remained still as Falin dropped his arms and backed away. She took several deep breaths before straightening. When she looked up, she appeared more like the distant, frosty queen I'd met during my first visits to Faerie. Oh, she was still disheveled, her skin still sickly and pulled too tight as if from a prolonged illness, but the fevered madness in her eyes had dimmed, her icy gaze cold and calculating once more. She nodded to Falin before scrutinizing both me and the sheet-covered corpse.

"My nephew is spoiled and lazy, but he isn't without ambition," she finally said. "I will carefully consider what has been revealed here, but I will not move forward against my own blood without more substantial proof. You are all forbidden to speak of this until the matter has been resolved." She met the eyes of everyone there—which was difficult, as Maeve had drawn even farther from us and seemed to be avoiding eye contact.

I frowned. Not speaking of it would make further investigation difficult. I was running out of time. Even after consuming the energy of Rawhead's ghost, the short ritual to speak to the shade had taken a lot out of me. I needed my tie to Faerie cemented.

Which meant I needed the queen to accept that I'd completed my task of revealing the alchemist sooner rather than later.

"Your majesty, do you dine with your nephew often?" I asked. After all, seven vials of Glitter couldn't be all Ryese had concocted. Creating a panic among the humans helped damage her credibility and put pressure on her, but what if Ryese had made damn sure she'd break down under that pressure? If a full dose of Glitter caused humans to manifest their fear, what would prolonged small doses of the drug do to a fae? Paranoia, perhaps? A loss of control of the magics governing the court?

The queen bit her full lips, making them disappear into an uncertain line. "I am, perhaps, less than my normal self."

She glanced down at hands that shook slightly. She flexed her fingers, staring at them as if not completely sure they belonged to her. Then the hilt of a sword appeared in her hand.

"Come. I will question my nephew."

Chapter 28

Based on the bargain I'd struck with the queen, all I had to do was identify the alchemist. She was then bound by our agreement to grant me my year and a day as an independent fae.

But only if she accepted my findings.

She stalked through the parking garage, a sword that had to be half as long as she was tall, clutched in her hand. I wasn't sure if it was a purely glamour sword, or an actual magical sword she'd summoned, but it was an intimidating sight. How does one politely broach the subject of completed bargains with a more than slightly mad queen carrying a sword? *You know, without getting skewered.*

To be fair though, whatever spell Falin had chanted, she was significantly less crazed than she had been. But it was still a *very* big sword.

"Your majesty," I started, several steps behind her. Falin was farther back still—he'd had to stop to grab the body after she'd stormed off. Leaving decapitated corpses in parking garages was tacky. Maeve and Lyell had both trailed even farther behind. I got the feeling her council was also trying very hard not to end up on the pointy end of the queen's sword. "About my independent status . . ."

"If we confirm your information, I will grant you your time," she said without slowing her pace.

I didn't think whining that I *really* needed it now would gain me anything, so I held my tongue. But I also didn't want to go to Faerie. Whether the queen found confirmation of Ryese's involvement in the plot against her or proved Rawhead was somehow mistaken—it could happen if his memories had been altered or if he'd only *thought* he was dealing with Ryese—more heads were likely to roll. And the Winter Queen seemed like the type to kill the messenger.

In this case, that would be me.

"You can send Falin to fetch me when you are ready," I said, trying to sound helpful and not overly eager to get out of there.

It didn't work.

The queen whirled around, the sword flashing in her hand. "Where do you think you're going, planeweaver?" she asked, but didn't give me time to respond before saying, "You're weakening. And you're injured. You *will* return to Faerie with me. A healer will see to your arm and monitor your condition until such time as our bargain is complete or you wish to forgo it and join my court."

I didn't mention that her court was a rather miserable place to be currently. My face might not win any beauty pageants, but I was fond of its location above my neck and wished to keep it there. I'm not sure what expression I wore, but the queen's lips thinned and she glanced over my shoulder at Falin.

"Knight, ensure the planeweaver accompanies us back to court," she said before turning and stalking onto the sidewalk.

I grumbled under my breath, but the queen's command didn't surprise me. In fact, the part I hated the most about the whole thing was the stab of betrayal I felt at Falin's "Yes, my queen." He didn't have a choice. I *knew* he didn't. I knew he was her creature. And yet there it was. He'd broken my, admittedly fragile, trust on the night of the Equinox. I'd thought he couldn't hurt me anymore, emotionally at least, but his simple acceptance of a command that was blatantly against my best interest felt like he'd gathered the broken shards and ground them into my chest.

I stepped out of the fluorescents of the parking garage and into the near dusk on the street. Night approached earlier each day this time of the year, and the streetlights hadn't quite caught up yet. Or maybe it wasn't quite as dark out as it appeared to my bad eyes. I'd left my shields cracked, but only enough to make what had been vague outlines in the brightly lit garage into recognizable shapes. Out on the darkening streets, my natural vision failed me, leaving me with only the swirls of color from the Aetheric plane and decaying reflections from the land of the dead. It was enough to prevent me from running into anyone, but not enough to make out details.

I felt vulnerable, unable to truly see the pedestrians on the street, to recognize who might pose a threat—and I took a moment to feel sorry for myself that I'd reached a place in my life that I considered the fact any crowd might contain a threat—but nothing was wrong with my ears, and from the gasps and whispers I could hear, no one was paying attention to me. No, everything I heard pointed to all eyes being on the disheveled woman striding down the sidewalk with a giant sword. Which was probably for the best, as Falin was bringing up the rear with what looked a hell of a lot like a dead body in a tarp. Actually, that was exactly what he carried, so no big surprise. I hoped he had it glamoured because that was the kind of thing that would draw attention, and if we didn't get off the street soon, the police.

Thankfully, we weren't far from the Eternal Bloom.

I'd be able to see once we reached Faerie—for whatever reason, the magical damage my eyes had taken over the years vanished inside Faerie—but there was still more than a block to walk and then there was the Bloom itself. While the bar may hold a pocket of Faerie, I couldn't see there much better than in the mortal realm.

Opening my shields made the world around me pop into focus, even if it was a slightly different version of the world than everyone else on the street saw. There were more planes of existence than I had names for, and while my psyche seemed to naturally focus on the ones I intentionally interacted with on a regular basis, I occasionally caught sight of others that changed the street into an alien world of glittering crystal, or made the buildings bleed color where they'd absorbed strong emotions. I kept the bubble shield that reined in my psyche in place and tried to ignore the less normal aspects—if I focused too much on any one plane, I was more likely to accidentally touch it, and possibly draw it into mortal reality.

We reached the steps of the Bloom without incident. One of the trolls worked the door tonight. I recognized his particular shade of blue skin and hulking size as a bouncer I'd run into several times before. He wasn't the brightest.

"Check iron and sign ledger."

"You're blocking the door," the queen snapped.

The bewildered troll looked around, as if unsure of which door she meant. The queen made a harsh sound, somewhere between a curse and a growl. She lifted the sword, pressing it to the trolls jugular. His large eyebrows knit together, but he shuffled only one step sideways.

"Sign ledger?" he asked again.

"I got it," I said, slipping around his hulking form. The queen made an inarticulate sound, but she didn't say anything else as I jotted my and Falin's names in the ledger. I didn't actually know the queen's name, and she wasn't likely concerned with arriving back in Nekros at this exact time, so I left her and her remaining council members off.

Mollified, the troll shuffled his enormous girth aside until he revealed the door to the VIP area. "Check iron."

"No iron," Falin assured him, and then gestured for me to follow the queen into the bar.

I sighed. With the queen so distracted and Falin injured and carrying a body, I'd hoped they'd both enter the Bloom first, and for a moment I'd entertained the idea of turning around and going home. But Falin had been commanded to ensure I made it to Faerie, and apparently he hadn't forgotten that fact.

In the past few months I'd become something of a regular at the Bloom. In that time, I'd grown accustomed to the kind of crowd that frequented the bar — I could even recognize many regulars on sight. Typically, the patrons were primarily local independents who wanted to feel the homelike resonance of Faerie without actually going to Faerie proper and have to deal with court politics. Occasionally fae from other territories and courts visited since the bar served as neutral ground, but the regulars were locals. The winter court fae who passed through the bar were typically doing just that: passing through from mortal realm to winter court or vice versa. Few ever stopped to dine or gamble or dance or whatever other activities took place in the darkened corners of the bar. Except, apparently, today.

I stopped just inside the door, staring around a room that had gone eerily silent and trying to make sense of what I was seeing. Fae filled every available seat, but not one held a familiar face. Considering most of the faces belonged to Sleagh Maith — the nobility of Faerie — that wasn't surprising. There weren't any noble independents in Nekros. *Well, hopefully I'll be the first.*

The queen had also stopped, taking in the room. Her grip around her sword tightened, and she glared at what had to be a large contingent of her subjects. For their part, almost every head turned downward, avoiding her gaze, as if they'd all suddenly become extremely fascinated by the food in front of them.

I guess they decided the winter court had become inhospitable.

Not that I thought they were all turning tail and planning to suddenly declare independent. At least, I didn't think that was the case. No, more likely they were looking for a dry place to get out of the sleet that was plaguing their home. Still, it had to be a blow to the queen to see her subjects gathered in a small pocket of Faerie that normally was only a pale reflection of the true place. Most likely whatever pocket spaces surrounded the other doors to winter's territory were also packed with court members tonight.

For a moment I thought the queen was going to address her people. To offer reassurance that everything would be back to normal soon, or more likely, to order everyone back to their court regardless of its current condition. Then Maeve approached the queen's side.

"I would deal with this for you, if you would like, my queen." Maeve curtsied as she spoke, her face turned down toward the floorboards.

"Do so," the queen snapped, and then, squaring her shoulders, stalked through the tables toward the amaranthine tree and door to her court.

I didn't start moving fast enough, and Falin gave me the softest shove to get me walking. I trudged forward, catching sidelong glances shot my way as I passed. But no one spoke. In fact, the silence held until I was more than partway around the tree, the world already sliding out of focus. Even then, the sounds of the quickly vanishing bar were subdued. Frightened.

The queen waited just beyond the melting ice pillar that marked the door. The intricate carvings were gone now, replaced by a shiny, wet surface. The queen grimaced at the pillar, and then turned her face upward, into the falling sleet.

The deluge slowed, and then stopped. I glanced up.

Sleet still fell high above us—not the large and majestic snowflakes from before the queen's . . . fall from health . . . but it stopped several feet above my head now, so at least we weren't being pelted with the chilling rain anymore.

Two ice-cloaked guards approached, looking cold and drenched, but they bowed to their queen, making no complaint.

"My nephew, is he here?" the queen asked the first of the guards.

"I believe so, your majesty."

"Good. Bring him to my throne room. We must speak." She started past him, but then paused. "Oh, and take the planeweaver to a room where she can rest, and if there are any healers left who haven't abandoned the court, send one to see to her arm. Knight, attend me."

And with that, she stormed off down the long corridor, leaving me in the care of the two waterlogged guards.

Chapter 29

⊷═══ ◎ ◎───◦

I woke to sleet pelting my face.

I jolted upright, disoriented with sleep, and blinked at the unfamiliar room. It was small, but ornately decorated with furniture carved from some sort of blue crystal that resembled ice—but only resembled, because the actual items of ice were dripping.

The winter court.

Memory washed over me, clearing away the last haze of sleep: Jenny's stagnant pond; Rawhead's death, the fight with his ghost, and his revelation that Ryese was the alchemist; and then the queen's insistence that I recover here, in her court. More sleet fell from the ceiling, sticking to my hair and eyebrows and making a darkening wet spot on the light blanket pooling at my hips. Shivering, I shook the melting ice away, but it was quickly replaced. *What happened?* The queen had managed to stop the sleet from falling, even if she hadn't been able to turn it back into decorative snow. Had she relapsed into the fevered madness?

Pulling the blanket free of the bed, I tugged it around my shoulders and over my head like a cloak. I realized only after I'd bundled myself that I'd used my left arm without any twinge of pain. I held it out and flexed the fingers of my hand as I examined the flesh of my forearm. The healer the queen had sent had done a good job; there wasn't even a scar left where Rawhead's ghost had bit me. But I was tired, so very tired now that the initial adrenaline rush of waking to frozen rain was wearing off.

How long had I slept?

It could have been minutes or hours. One thing was for sure, I hadn't acquired my tie to Faerie yet, and I was running out of time. *I hope Rianna and Ms. B are okay.* How long was it safe to wait for the queen to confront Ryese and decide our bargain was complete? And if I felt this bad, how much worse was it for my friends? As they were sworn to me—in the roundabout way of fae inheritance—self-preservation had apparently cut down the flow of life-sustaining magic to them before I'd even started feeling the effects. And I was definitely feeling it now—just the idea of crawling out of this bed was exhausting.

I had to speak to the queen. One way or another, I had to establish my tie to Faerie. Now.

Sliding out of bed, I stood and looked around. When the healer had left earlier, the doorway had vanished behind her. Now it was back, looking a little like a popsicle on a hot day, but it was a doorway. I stepped up to the edge of it, taking the blanket with me. Like all doors in Faerie, there was no telling what was on the other side before stepping through. I glanced back at the room, making sure I hadn't left anything behind as I'd likely never find this room again. I'd slept fully dressed down to my boots—strange things happened in Faerie and I'd once fallen physically into a nightmare when I'd lost control of my planeweaving ability during sleep. I had no desire to spend the rest of the trip half naked or barefoot, so the decision had seemed prudent. Other than my purse, which I grabbed off the dresser, and the dagger strapped into my boot, I hadn't brought anything else with me.

Well, here goes. With any luck, the queen had already

caught Ryese in a lie, or better yet, found his lab. Then she would have no wiggle room out of our deal.

I stepped through the doorway, wondering where Ryese was now.

And found out much quicker than intended.

I expected to emerge from the doorway into the long ice halls. Instead I stepped into another room, one not much larger than the one I'd just left. But where my room had sported a bed, wardrobe, and other bedroom-like furniture, this one held several chairs bolted to the floor, each chair sporting large leather straps on the arms, legs, and at the waist area. In the corner was a desk cluttered with crystal beakers, tubes, and other chemistry-type equipment. Or really, *al*chemical-type equipment. And leaning over the desk?

Ryese.

Shit.

I tried to backpedal out of the door, but the threshold was gone. *Great. Just great.* The first time I'd traveled through Faerie, Rianna had taken me to the castle I'd inherited. She'd warned me to be careful of thresholds, that I needed to know where I was going before stepping through one. I'd forgotten that particular advice, most likely because every time since, I'd been escorted through Faerie by guards who'd told me which door to take. I'd never known where I was going, but my guides had, and apparently that was enough. This time I'd been wondering where Ryese was as I'd stepped through the threshold. Apparently Faerie had decided to show me.

Ryese hadn't noticed my presence. Moving in slow motion, I fumbled for my dagger, drawing it without making a sound. It buzzed in my hand, reassuring me that we had the element of surprise.

I frowned at the dagger. Unless I was willing to sneak up and assassinate him in cold blood, the element of surprise did me very little good. If I made it across the room without being detected—and that was a big *if*—the dagger would have no qualms against directing my hand into a vulnerable but lethal strike. But I didn't need any more blood on my hands. And I had no idea how to incapacitate an opponent. I seriously needed to start carrying a knock-out charm. Well, okay, those were illegal. But I needed something. In a fair fight I didn't stand a chance. I needed to get out of here. To find Falin and figure out why the queen hadn't done anything about Ryese yet.

With the door behind me gone, the only exit from the room was on the opposite wall. The same wall where Ryese's desk stood. At least it was on the far side of the wall. We were probably equal distances from it. Moving slowly, I edged around the perimeter of the room. The sleet continued falling around me, making soft sounds as it hit the half-frozen puddles on the ground and hopefully covering any noise I made.

I'd reached the halfway point when Ryese looked up. He startled as his gaze fell on me. Then a smile crawled across his face, but the expression was far from friendly.

"Dearest Lexi," he said, his hand dipping into one of the desk drawers.

I didn't wait around to find out what he might have, but dashed for the doorway.

He was faster.

He grabbed the back of the blanket, trying to jerk me off my feet. I released it, so all he got was the soggy material as I kept moving for the door.

Just another yard. Almost there. I could make it.

I'd just reached the threshold as I felt his body collide with mine.

Falin. I thought at the door. *Take us to Falin.*

Maybe, just maybe, Faerie would be kind to me.

It wasn't.

Chapter 30

⸻⟡⟡⸻

Ryese and I crashed through the doorway, him riding me down to the ground where he'd tackled me around the waist. I got my arms in front of me in time to brace myself so my nose didn't slam into the sleet-encrusted floor, but the impact sent the dagger skittering out of my hands. *Crap.* I tried to scramble after it, but Ryese's weight covered most of my bottom half, pinning me to the floor.

I struggled, kicking with my feet. Ryese sucked in a breath as my heel connected with something soft. *Hit.* He drew back with the pain enough for me to crawl out from under him.

I climbed to my feet and scuttled farther away before stopping to take in the room where we'd arrived. I'd been hoping to end up somewhere public, preferably wherever Falin was, but either the door we'd taken had a set destination, or Ryese had had other ideas when we crashed through the door.

The room was small and empty, aside from a pile of debris in the far corner. The only door was the one we'd crashed through, and Ryese was between it and me. Currently he was curled on the floor, cupping his privates and staring at me with hate in his wet eyes. I did *not* want to try to get past him without a weapon. Which meant I needed to find my dagger.

I scanned the floor, finally spotting it a few feet in front of the pile of debris. I darted for it but drew up short as I got closer to the corner. What I had taken for rubble or maybe broken furniture debris was a pile of bones, mostly picked clean but a few with scraps of flesh and hair still attached. Skulls stared at me with empty sockets, most human in appearance, but some had obviously belonged to the less humanoid fae.

Oh crap, where had Ryese taken me? Was this his killing ground?

No, he'd drained the fae in his laboratory. But their bones had been picked clean here.

I shivered and took another step toward the dagger. A soft crunch sounded behind me. A footstep.

Oh crap.

I half turned, torn between diving for the dagger and the need to see Ryese.

Something crashed into the side of the head, just behind the temple. The world shattered—or maybe that was whatever Ryese had smashed against my skull—and pain exploded behind my eyes.

I reeled, my head spinning. The ground rushed up to meet me, knocking my already shaky breath out of me.

Ryese followed me down, planting his knees in my chest. Cold slush soaked into my clothes as Ryese's long fingers wrapped around my throat, denying me air. I thrashed, clawing at his shoulders as I kicked my legs. He'd situated himself higher this time, keeping all his bits and pieces out of range of my flailing legs.

"Do you enjoy the work of the fae you got murdered?" he asked, his hands tightening around my throat until black spots burst behind my eyes.

Work? He had to be talking about Tommy Rawhead, but what work? Distributing the Glitter? I didn't have the breath to ask. My head pounded and my lungs burned, needing air I couldn't draw with Ryese crushing my ribs, my windpipe.

"He was valuable to me." Ryese squeezed harder. "He worked hard as long as I threw him my scraps. Changelings or lesser fae, it didn't matter. Oh, he said they weren't as good as children, but he still accepted with gusto. And bonus, no bodies for anyone to find. Just a pile of bones."

I tried to swallow, but I couldn't do that any more than draw air. That didn't stop my stomach from rolling. Rawhead had *eaten* the fae Ryese drained. This was his . . . lair? Dumping ground?

"But you. You're always in the way." Another flex of his fingers. "You couldn't have just cooperated, could you?" He leaned forward, close enough that spit hit my face as he yelled. "If you'd simply agreed to a union, my *dear* aunt would have officially recognized me as prince of the winter court and the line of succession would have made this all so much easier. But no, you consider yourself oh so much better than me all while swooning over her damn knight."

I was having trouble focusing on him. From the lack of air or the blow to the head, I couldn't be sure, but if something didn't change soon, I'd be unconscious. I tried to buck my hips to dislodge him, but moving was getting hard. My body felt heavy, weakness eating my limbs.

"Why?" I could only mouth the question. I wasn't even sure if I was questioning Ryese's betrayal of his aunt or his hatred of me. It was getting harder to fight, harder to even think.

It didn't matter. He was on a raging tirade with no intention of stopping anytime soon. "Now though, now you've gone and done it. All the cleverly laid plans I'd designed have to be scrapped. So you're going to help me."

Like hell I was.

He studied my face and laughed. "Oh dear, are you having trouble breathing? Here, let me help you." His fingers eased off enough that I managed a shallow breath.

It wasn't enough, but it helped. "Don't worry, dearest Lexi. I don't plan to kill you . . . yet. You still have uses. The queen's grip on the court has destabilized nicely—though I admit I didn't anticipate her descent to make living here quite so miserable." He shook his head, making the gathered sleet fly, several pieces pelted my already frozen cheeks. "Her court has lost faith in her and the other regents are questioning her capability to rule. No one will question me when I usurp her throne—everyone agrees someone must do it."

Ryese switched his grip so only one hand held my throat. I managed a trickle of air, but the world was fuzzy now, my arms not responding. With his free hand, he dug in his coat. I tried to focus, but darkness clung all around me. My blink seemed too long, and I was sure I'd lost seconds.

"Her knight is a problem, though. I had hoped the challengers would soften him up more than they have. As you've probably noticed, I'm no fighter. In a fair duel I have no chance of winning against him. But he has a weakness." Ryese pulled three vials of glittery red liquid from his pocket. "*You* are his weakness."

Ryese uncorked the first vial with his teeth. I had a sinking suspicion I knew what he planned.

No. Oh no.

I pressed my lips together hard. *No. No. No.*

I was hurt, and I hadn't had enough air in some time now. Ryese pulled the corks on all three vials. He smiled at me, all malicious delight. Then he released my throat and pinched my nose with one hand before lifting his weight off my chest.

I needed air. Needed to breathe. It had been too long. My body betrayed me, my mouth splitting. Ryese didn't hesitate, but upended all three vials into my mouth.

I tried to spit. Fought the liquid dribbling into my throat.

I lost.

The Glitter was between me and much needed oxygen. My body swallowed compulsively before sucking in a jagged breath.

No.

Ryese's smile spread further, the poisonous look of a happy snake. Then he rose in one fluid movement.

"I'll leave you to it then, Lexi," he said, striding toward the door. He paused before vanishing into the threshold and turned. "Enjoy your nightmares."

Then he was gone.

Chapter 31

❧━━◦━━❧

I lay on the floor gasping for several ragged breaths. Then I rolled onto my knees. My head spun, nausea sweeping over me. Actually, considering I'd just been force-fed an overdose, getting sick was probably a good idea.

I stoked the nauseated sensation, shoving my finger down my throat. The burn of bile crept up my esophagus, but as I doubled over, only dry heaves shook my body.

No. I couldn't have absorbed the drug that quickly, could I? I didn't know. I'd never used a recreational drug, and this one was a magical drug. Who knew how it behaved. That didn't stop me from trying. But despite the growing sickness crawling through me, nothing left my body.

There was no help for it. I just had to get out of here. Get somewhere safe—which right now probably meant getting the hell out of Faerie. How long would it take for the drug to begin affecting my senses? I tried to remember anything useful from the victims I'd raised—but they'd all died. How helpful was that? Even the victims who hadn't died from their hallucinations had died from some sort of magical burnout. I was fae, I had my own glamour, would that save me?

Three vials.

Shit.

I needed to get up. To get out. My head felt like it had been stuffed full of cotton, my thoughts sloughing through thick syrup to reach the front of my mind. I pushed upright and the world swam.

I swallowed hard, waiting for the dizziness clawing its way through my mind to clear. It took longer than I wanted, the moments passing with the pounding of my pulse in my temples.

My dagger was still several feet in front of me, and I crawled to it, picking it up. The familiar buzz against my hand, my mind, was reassuring. But what the hell could a dagger, even an enchanted, semicognizant one do to protect me from a drug?

Nothing. I had to get out of here. But I didn't put the dagger away, instead I clutched it as I attempted to get my feet under me.

It took two attempts to climb to my feet, and as I finally reached them, a dry crackling sounded behind me. I stiffened, the skin along my spine going tight. I was alone in the room, I was sure of that. Which meant whatever made that sound, was probably created by the drugs.

I twisted, turning in slow motion, feeling like the extra in a horror movie. The stack of bones piled in the corner rustled, the entire pile shaking as if trying to dislodge the icy slush gathering on the bones. A skull tottered and then tumbled down the side of the stack. It rolled across the floor, stopping only a few feet from me, grinning its ghastly smile.

I stared at the skull for several panic-filled moments before my gaze darted back to the pile of bones. They rustled and cracked like dry reeds. Then a meaty hand burst from the center of the pile. A second hand followed, like a zombie clawing its way from a grave.

I backpedaled, trying to ignore the way the room lurched around me. I nearly fell twice, my feet tangling under me, my legs so very heavy.

I reached the far wall and glanced around. Ryese had gone this way, I knew he had. But now there was no threshold, no door.

Damn.

Had Faerie moved it? Or was I hallucinating it away?

My gaze jerked around the room, looking for where the door might have gone. There wasn't a door. Not anywhere. The bone pile continued to shake as the creature in it pulled itself free.

I was so screwed.

I gripped my dagger tighter. It sang in my hand, but even its ever-ready bloodthirst did little to pierce the fog in my head.

"There is a door." I told myself, trying to convince myself, Faerie, the drugged state of my mind—I wasn't sure which—that it was the truth. Despite my words, no door appeared.

A head emerged from under the bones. Blood streamed down the thick, wide face, welling up from the skinned scalp. I recognized the flattened features immediately. Tommy Rawhead.

"You're dead," I told the hallucination.

The hobgoblin smiled at me, his long tongue darting out to lick chapped lips.

"You're not real."

Real or not, the bones tumbled down around him as he freed himself of the pile. He jumped clear, landing predator-soft on the icy floor. Then he turned, studied the pile of bones he'd emerged from and grabbed two thick leg bones, one in each hand. Lifting them, he swung them in front of him like a pair of bleached-white clubs.

He was a hallucination, conjured by my drug-addled brain. I knew he was. He had to be. I'd seen him die.

Then I'd cannibalized his soul.

Oh crap. Could the drug have found whatever was left of him inside of me? Could it have given it form, life?

No. No, that wasn't possible. I'd taken his energy until

his will alone wasn't enough to hold him together. But I couldn't actually absorb his being, just the life force. This was a hallucination. A living nightmare.

That didn't stop a very real-looking Rawhead from stalking forward, lifting the bone clubs.

My grip on the dagger felt slick, but I didn't dare switch hands long enough to wipe my palm as the hobgoblin stalked toward me. He was a hallucination given form by the drug and glamour. I knew that. And glamours could be disbelieved.

I dropped my shields.

The pile of bones glowed with the tortured souls still stuck inside. The hobgoblin, on the other hand, had no inner glow, no soul, nothing that should have given him life. He should have vanished with the confirmation that he was nothing but a hallucination, but Rawhead remained just as solid. Just as real. Glamour couldn't create life, but Faerie had accepted this hallucination as solid, if nothing else. And since it was from my own drug-addled brain, I provided the live feed for his actions and personality.

Which meant I could change it right? Instead of a super-creepy bogeyman determined to rip me apart and suck the marrow from my bones, maybe I could redirect him into something nice. Something harmless. Something fuzzy and cute with a propensity for flower arrangement.

Tommy Rawhead lifted one of the bone clubs over his head.

I scuttled sideways, my concentration shifting to not falling over my own weak legs. The bone whistled through air inches from my shoulder. A miss. But barely. I had to keep moving. To put distance between myself and the glamoured bogeyman.

Rawhead spun, giving chase. And he was faster. A lot faster. Not surprising considering my head still felt a little too heavy.

I couldn't outrun him—not that I had anywhere to go. *Where the hell is that damn door?*

I didn't know. Couldn't remember. The bones had been in the corner, but now I couldn't remember which corner in comparison to the door.

There was no way out. I'd have to fight. I'd often heard that the best defense is a good offense. Unfortunately, I wasn't exactly trained in fighting. With my recent history, I might have to change that.

Of course, first I had to survive now and not end up getting killed by my own imagination.

Crouching, I shifted my grip on the dagger and waited. Rawhead rushed forward, his bone clubs lifted. I didn't know much about fighting, but the move looked more crazed barbarian than anything skilled. I guess that was the only good thing about not having a great imagination. Rawhead was limited to what my waking nightmare could conjure.

I waited for the charging figure to draw close. Then I lunged to the side, slashing out with the dagger as I moved. Unlike my hallucination, I had an enchanted dagger that liked to draw blood and was very good at it. So I let the dagger's mental prodding push me.

The blade sank into flesh, catching momentarily, and then slid free. A hot gush of blood spilled over my hand, and the blade sang in triumph.

But, while the blade guided my arm, it wasn't watching out for the rest of me. The lunge scored a wound in my opponent, but the impact with his body killed my forward momentum. Instead of sailing straight past him, I came down short, slightly to his side. One of the bone clubs slammed against my calf. It was only a grazing hit—not full impact—but pain exploded along my leg.

I rolled aside, a move that was not good for my spinning head, but the next swing of the club missed. When my roll ended, I tried to climb to my feet, but the room lurched, throwing me sideways. Or maybe I just fell.

Rawhead charged. *Shit.* I scooted backward, my butt and boots leaving streaks in the sleet-covered floor like a demented snow angel.

Rawhead was moving too fast, or I was too slow. Whichever way, if I stayed on the defensive, I'd lose. My own damn hallucination would kill me.

No, damn it. I couldn't let that happen. I wouldn't.

I gripped the dagger tight. It sung in my hand. It didn't care if Rawhead was glamour or real, it just wanted a fight. *I hope you know what you're doing,* I thought at it. The dagger, of course, didn't respond. Though, with as much of the drug as Ryese had introduced to my system, I wouldn't have been shocked if it had.

Blood still poured down Rawhead's side, turning his brown pants a sticky crimson color. The wound was deep, maybe mortal for a human. I wasn't so sure for a fae, especially one who was already dead and only a figment of my imagination. Still, it was a lot of blood. If I could keep him occupied long enough to bleed out . . .

He charged again, the clubs swinging. I got my feet under me enough to skitter aside. We'd circled enough that I was now near the bone pile, and I dove around it for cover as a club crashed into the space I'd been a moment before.

Rawhead followed.

I grabbed a long bone from the massive pile and gripped it between both hands, using it to block his next swing. The bones crashed together with a splintering crunch. My arms vibrated with the hit. His club and my makeshift shield both snapped, the top half of his flying off to my side and me left holding two splintered ends. I kept one, dropping the one in the same hand as my dagger.

Having blocked his first blow, I was unprepared for the swing of his off-hand club. It crashed into my stomach, slamming me backward. The air rushed out of me in a loud whoosh, and my back crashed into the bone pile.

Rawhead stalked forward, a short, jagged bone in one hand, a long club in the other, but he was moving slower now, his movements jerkier. Blood still poured from his side, the wound clearly hurting.

If he could be hurt, he could be stopped.

I tried to push out of the pile, but my feet dislodged an avalanche of bones that tumbled down the side, onto the floor. Rawhead kicked them out of his way, never stopping. I grabbed a skull, cupping the forehead with my palm, my fingers in the eye sockets, and then hurled it at Rawhead. He batted it aside with his club, but it slowed him, marginally.

I threw another bone, followed by a third, a fourth. I wasn't doing any damage, just annoying him and buying time, but I kept hurling skulls, arm bones, a whole foot— whatever my hand landed on. Then he was right on top of me, and I was out of time.

He lifted his arm to swing and I pitched myself forward. It was a desperate, almost blind, move, but I had no other options.

The dagger slammed into his chest, sliding through clothing and flesh with no resistance. Rawhead went rigid. Then the rest of my body weight hit him, knocking him off his feet, and I rode him down. My hands were wet, slick with blood, but I didn't let go of the dagger. By the time Rawhead's back hit the floor, he'd stopped moving.

I sat there, straddling his body, panting from exertion. Dizziness swam through my head, leaving black dots across my vision in its wake. When I could see again, I looked down. The dagger was hilt deep in Rawhead's chest, just left of his sternum. I'd hit his heart.

I pulled the blade free, and it slid out with a sickening slurping sound I knew I'd be hearing in my nightmares for months to come—if I lived that long. Rawhead was dead—again—but I was still full of the drug. I tried not to think as I wiped the blade clean on the dead hallucination's shirt. Then I clambered to my feet.

I didn't put the dagger away.

Think happy thoughts, Alex, I told myself. *Rainbows. Bunnies. Unicorns.*

Ever notice how when you try to make yourself think one thing, your brain rebels and circles back to something else?

The image of Rawhead standing back up, coming at me again, kept trying to claw its way to the front of my mind. I kept banishing it, but my gaze moved to the prone figure, half expecting it to jump to its feet and start swinging at me again. I had to get farther away from the body.

I crossed to the other side of the room. The door hadn't reappeared. Damn. I sank into the corner, burying my head in my arms and trying to think happy things. *Puppies. Fast cars. Ice cream.*

"Alex."

I knew that voice. I knew that deep, masculine voice very, very well.

My head snapped up and I found myself staring into the brilliant hazel eyes of Death.

"Hey," he said, flashing his perfect teeth in a smile.

I returned the smile. "Hey back at you," I said, and then stopped. "Wait. I'm in Faerie. You can't be here. Your plane doesn't exist here."

"Are you sure?" He reached out, cupping my face with his hand.

His palm was warm against my skin, gentle. I wanted to sink into the comfort he offered. I was so cold. My clothes were soaked and the sleet kept falling. It was so tempting to embrace the warmth he offered. To let him keep the darkness threatening to spill out of my mind away. To trust he'd guard me from the effects of the drug.

But I wasn't wrong. He couldn't be here. As real as my eyes told me he was, as my skin swore he was, he wasn't real. He was another hallucination. A glamour pulled from my Glitter-addled mind.

Which made him dangerous.

I squeezed my eyes closed. Tried to ignore him.

He made it difficult.

He leaned in, and I could feel his presence along my skin. His breath moved my damp curls. I could even smell the clean fresh-turned earth and dew scent that always clung to him.

"You're not real." I told him.

His lips pressed against my forehead. "I love you."

"No, you don't. The real Death does. You're an illusion."

"I'll break every natural law to be with you. It will put us both in danger, and I don't care."

"You're a bit of glamour."

"I love you. And you don't even know my name."

My head snapped up. The fake Death was inches from me, those hazel eyes so close. But while the real Death's eyes typically held a secret smile that couldn't seem to help but shine through, this one had mocking eyes. Eyes that bore into me.

"It doesn't matter," I told him. "I know Death. I don't need to know his name."

"Do you?" He asked, scooting back slightly so I could see that the haughty, mocking expression covered his whole face, not just his eyes. "Do you know my favorite color? How about the names of my friends? Or how old I am?"

"None of that matters."

"Why have I hung around all these years? Are you anything more than a novelty to me? A reminder of what I lost when I ceased being mortal?"

"Shut up. You aren't real."

The fake Death stood, dragging me to my feet with him. "When your mother was dying, why did I allow you to decide that her soul shouldn't be collected? Why did I allow such a young child to watch her mother's body continue to decay from a disease that should have long since killed her? Collecting her would have been a mercy. Why did I make a five-year-old have to finally ask me to release her soul from the dying prison of her body? Why did I feel that was a lesson that had to be taught just because the same frightened five-year-old had begged me not to take away her mother?"

My blood turned cold, an icy sweat breaking out on my body. "Stop it. Shut up."

"What is my name, Alex Craft?"

"I don't know."

"What is my name?"

"I don't know!" I shoved the fake Death, and he stepped back, laughing. I wanted to scream. I'd thought maybe my brain had spit out a good hallucination this time, but no. This fake Death may not have been attacking me with clubs, but his words pierced me deeper than a sword. They cut into my fears, my doubts.

He laughed again. "What is my name?"

"Alex?" a new voice asked as hands closed on my upper arms.

I twisted away, wrenching my body from the touch, and spun to face the newcomer.

Falin stood behind me, just inside a door that was now visible. Or at least, it looked like it was visible.

"Are you real?" I asked.

He raised one eyebrow in question, the other dropping and bunching in confusion. Then his gaze moved to the fake Death, a frown cutting across his face. "What is going on?"

I backed up another step. He could be an illusion. Just another glamour inspired by the drug. The door could too. Hell, everything in the room was suspect. I had no idea what was real. What wasn't. Death kept thrusting questions at me. Questions I had no answer to but had wondered about.

Falin held up his hands, moving slowly as if approaching a wild animal. "What happened?"

I might be going mad. It was wholly possible Falin was just another hallucination created by the Glitter Ryese had force-fed me. But what if he wasn't?

Ryese was setting a trap for Falin. He'd said as much. For the trap to spring, the real Falin had to show up, right? Was I more or less crazy if I tried to warn a fake Falin on the off chance he was real? I'd already fought a hallucination, and argued with one. Why not try to work with one?

"I've been drugged." I told him everything. Well, almost everything. I told him about the struggle with Ryese and what he'd said, and I summed up the fight with Tommy Rawhead. I didn't explain Death's presence. "He's not real," I said, nodding to the fake collector. "Ignore him."

That statement didn't make the fake Death very happy. He began bellowing his questions, pacing around me as he jabbed at my insecurities.

"Let's get you out of here," Falin said, taking me by the arm and guiding me toward the door. "We need to find the queen. And Ryese."

Chapter 32

—⊶⊷ ⊶⊷—

"Wait," I said, jerking my arm out of Falin's grasp and stumbling backward.

If Falin was another illusion, I couldn't follow him anywhere. Things were dangerous enough trapped in one room, but what would happen if I left? And who else would my hallucinations endanger? And if this wasn't another mirage, what kind of danger was I putting Falin in?

Ryese had said I was Falin's weakness. If I was the bait, where was the trap?

"How did you find me?"

Falin frowned. "I received a note. It said you'd left your quarters and were in trouble. Then it told me how to find you. I'm assuming Ryese sent it and I should watch my back."

Well, that seemed plausible. And coming here was definitely something the real Falin would do, but the fact I thought so meant my imagination could have conjured up the explanation.

"Tell me something I don't know."

Falin's frown deepened. "What?"

"To prove you're real. Tell me something I couldn't know about you."

Falin stepped back, evaluating me, or maybe the request, I wasn't sure which. Then his gaze cut to the fake Death still yelling questions at me. "Why does he keep asking you his name?"

"Because I don't know it."

"But aren't you . . . ?"

He didn't finish the question. He didn't have to. I knew what he was asking. Wasn't I Death's girlfriend? His lover? His *something*, at the very least? Hell, he was my oldest and dearest friend before he was . . . whatever he was now.

And I knew nothing about him.

After several moments of only the fake Death speaking, Falin sighed.

"If I tell you something you don't know, how will that prove anything? You won't know if it's true or not."

Shit. I hadn't thought of that. I pressed my palms against my eyes. Then I stopped.

My eyes. I hadn't been able to pierce the hallucination of Rawhead, hadn't been able to disbelieve him away, but his lack of soul had betrayed he wasn't alive.

I dropped my hands and opened my shields. I blinked, looking around. Death remained exactly the same as I opened my mental sight to the other planes, but Falin had a hazy silver-blue glow haloing his form. A soul.

I smiled in relief. He was real.

Unless of course, my mind could conjure up a soul glow around a hallucination. *Why did I have to think about that possibility?* I hated my brain right now.

Falin watched my thoughts shift with my expressions, and then asked, "You want me to tell you just anything you don't know?" He paused. "You know that I was switched with a human and grew up outside Faerie, right? Well, maybe the spells they wrapped me in weren't quite good enough, or maybe I was just unlucky, because I was abandoned by the family who should have raised me. I don't know. I was too young to remember. I grew up in foster care, but never really fit anywhere. I'd stay in a home for a few months and then they'd send me away, off to a new family. When I reached puberty, the spell began breaking down, my fae nature emerged, and a FIB agent brought me to court. I felt like I belonged for the first time. Faerie felt like the *home* I'd never had. The home I'd missed."

I studied him. I'd asked him for something I didn't know, and he'd given me a doozy. I hadn't known him when he was younger, and I knew very little about his past, but this information fit. In unguarded moments, I'd recognized the part of him that had spent too long without a home, that wanted to belong and be valued. It resonated with me, and had since I first met him.

Well, okay, not when I *first* met him. The first few times we interacted I'd thought he was a major jerk.

But after that.

The story made me want to hug him, even though the pain he'd revealed was decades old and likely well scabbed over. I hadn't grown up in foster care, hadn't bounced around houses, but I'd felt unwanted. I'd felt alienated from my family because of my wyrd ability. Because my father had shipped me off for most of my childhood. Had made a point of disassociating himself from me. So while I couldn't understand exactly what Falin had gone through, I could commiserate on some level.

I could also understand what he meant about Faerie feeling like home. As terrifying as I found the courts, something felt right when I was in Faerie. It was like a drug I knew was dangerous, but craved. Since my awakening, I'd felt Faerie's absence when I was in the mortal realm, but my healthy fear was strong enough to keep me away. So I could imagine what it must have been like for him as a teenager.

And the fact that I could, and my reaction to his story, made me leery.

Wouldn't an illusion my drugged imagination had conjured want to make an emotional connection? And my own mind would be the best to provide the perfect outlet. The fake Death was proof of that fact.

Oh hell. How was Falin supposed to prove if he was real or not? He was acting like the real Falin, my mind's eye told me he had a soul, and he'd given me a believable story when I'd asked. None of it was definitive, but I had to trust *something.*

Yeah, so let's trust the guy who has told you point-blank to never trust him.

But I did. With a healthy dose of caution maybe. But for better or worse, I did trust him.

The sleet continued to fall around us, coating every surface and clinging to my wet, icy hair and clothes. If the drug didn't kill me, I might die from hypothermia before I got out of the winter court.

"Be on the lookout for Ryese," I said, approaching the threshold that had reappeared when Falin entered the room.

"Isn't it usually *me* telling *you* to be careful?" Falin asked, a wry smile touching the edges of his lips.

True. But I didn't say it as I walked through the door, Falin at my heels. We emerged in one of the icy hallways, though at this point, it was more of a slushy hallway. The fake Death followed me a moment later, still yelling.

I scowled at him, hating my own mind that had summoned him and made my insecurity public. Chewing at my bottom lip, I turned to Falin. "That spell you used on the queen earlier . . . ?"

He glanced between me and my illusion. Then shook his head. "It wasn't a healing spell, and it won't help you."

I almost asked him what it was then, but he couldn't lie, and there was no wiggle room in that statement. Hanging my head and doing my best to ignore the verbal barbs from the fake Death, I followed Falin down the corridor.

Ice golems lined the hall. Once before I'd seen them come to life at the queen's whim, but I wasn't sure these particular golems would ever wake again. Their carved ice faces had melted, as had much of their heads and arms. I looked away from the misshapen forms. The winter court was dying.

"Have you seen the queen recently?"

Falin shot a grim look at the golems. "Not too long ago."

"Since the sleet started again?" I asked, and his silence was answer enough. No. He hadn't.

So she might have relapsed. *Or been dosed again.*

"Why isn't Ryese locked up already?"

Falin paused and shot a furtive glance down the long hall. Aside from the melting golems, we were alone. "The queen summoned him, but she didn't ask him directly, so his answers were slippery at best. It didn't matter. He had no blood on his hands, so she wouldn't believe his guilt."

I glanced at my own gloved hands, and at Falin's. I'd killed in defense of myself and those I cared about more than once, and I wore the dead's blood on my hands because Faerie took things very literally. As the queen's knight, Falin was her bloody hands—the one who killed if it must be done but also the one who carried the taint of every unnatural death through the court's history. It made him powerful, but also reviled in the court. Not that other members of the court had never killed—the queen had dueled to the death to gain her position so very long ago—but in the winter court, members passed the blood off to the knight, leaving everyone else's hands lily white—or blue, or green, or whatever color they happened to be naturally. You could cover the blood with gloves, but you couldn't hide it with glamour.

Ryese should have Icelynne's and the other fae's blood on his hands—if not the humans' who he killed indirectly with Glitter.

Of course, just because Faerie tended to be literal, that didn't mean it assigned guilt the same way I would. Ryese had surely orchestrated the kidnapping of the drained fae, but Tommy Rawhead and Jenny Greenteeth might have delivered the death blow to the fae. They'd also chosen to whom to distribute the Glitter. I hadn't seen Jenny inside Faerie, but Rawhead's hands had been saturated with blood.

"So how do we convince her?"

Falin shook his head. "It may not matter. She will not hold the court at this rate."

I stopped. "Doesn't someone have to defeat you in a duel before they can challenge her directly?"

"Yes."

"A duel to the death?"

A muscle bulged above his jaw, but he nodded.

Shit.

"But if her madness deepens and she cannot gain control of this"—he waved a hand to indicate the sleet, the melting walls and golems, maybe even the discordant notes thrumming through the air—"then Faerie itself will reject her as queen. With no designated heir, the scramble will become a free-for-all. The fighting knowledge, speed, and quick healing the court's blood grants me would be a boon to any potential contenders."

"And let me guess—unless you pass it on willingly, the easiest way to acquire that is to kill you?"

Again a tight nod. "After the queen is dethroned, at least. Before that it will revert back to her. A fail-safe to help her protect her seat of power. And as to passing it off, I can only do that with the queen's blessing."

And no queen, no blessing. Great. So there was a higher than average chance any change in power would involve Falin's death.

Reaching out, I squeezed his hand. He glanced down at where my gloved hand touched his, and the smallest smile tipped the edges of his lips as he squeezed back.

Behind me, the fake Death began screaming again. "Are your emotions so fickle, Alex Craft? I've proven willing to sacrifice my everlasting soul for you, and your heart still wanders?"

I jerked my hand out of Falin's as if a snake had lunged at me. Then I whirled on the fake Death.

"Shut up, shut up, shut up!" I yelled at him. "You aren't *real.*"

The fake Death smiled his very un-Death-like mocking grin. Anger washed through me, tinged with guilt. A second fake Death appeared, this one spouting off rhetoric about my inability to commit as the other returned to goading me about how little I knew about my own lover.

Dizziness crashed over me with the second hallucination's appearance, and I swayed. Only Falin's hands steadying my shoulders kept me from falling to the sleet-encrusted floor. That gave the Deaths even more fuel to work with.

"Alex, stay calm," Falin whispered. "The drug is triggered by your anxiety and fear and it's feeding off your energy. You don't have much to spare. So try to stay calm."

I nodded, knowing he was right. But even knowing something was true or for my own good didn't make it easy.

Taking a deep breath, I turned my back on the two fake Deaths and tried to ignore them. Falin watched me a moment longer, as if afraid I'd collapse if he looked away. Then he also turned, striding through the slush once more.

We'd rounded two corners in the seemingly never-ending corridors when I drew up short. Falin stopped, studying me with one cocked eyebrow. The question in his expression was clear, as was a hint of irritation. Me and my hallucinations were slowing us down and Ryese was out there. Somewhere.

Still, I waved him off, trying to concentrate. I felt . . . something. A kind of change in the space around me. It was similar to the magic trail I'd followed when I'd found the amaranthine tree. But that trail had felt warm, good. The disturbance I felt this time was . . . wrong.

Like a wound cut into the very fabric of Faerie.

I glanced around. There were doors on either side of the corridor. I'd stepped into the trail, and it led forward, so whoever or whatever had caused the disturbance in reality had originated from behind one of the two doors.

"Where do these go?" I asked, pointing from one to the other door.

Falin frowned at me. "Currently?"

Right. Faerie and its shifting doors. I sighed. Then I started forward again, motioning Falin to lead on. There was no telling if the disturbance I felt was even real.

The sleet fell harder and faster as we walked. I balled my fists and tucked them under my armpits, trying to get some warmth back into my fingers. The disturbance also seemed to grow rawer the farther we walked. I wasn't sure if we were actually following a trail or if my hallucinations were damaging Faerie. Or maybe it was another symptom of the queen's loss of control.

Maybe the queen is also hallucinating.

If Ryese had been dosing her with Glitter, and he got an opportunity to slip more to her, he may well have given her the critical amount to reach hallucinations.

The sleet-slush had built up to ankle-deep by the time we turned the next corner, but soggy paths had been trod through it already. Falin frowned at the indistinct footprints, but I tried to keep my steps in line with those who'd cut the path—my boots were water resistant only up to the point the laces started, and as my feet were the only part of me still dry, I wanted to keep them that way.

Falin paused in front of one door. Based on the runnels in the sleet, a lot of fae had passed this way, and recently. The trail dragging across realities was stronger here as well. Sharper, almost, and deeper.

And oh so very wrong.

If it had been something I could see, I would have expected an infected wound, open and dripping with pus. The trail led directly into the doorway Falin was about to step through. I grabbed his arm, making him hesitate.

"If Faeric rejects the queen's right to rule the court, would that cause a wound in the fabric of Faerie?"

He tilted his head slightly, his gaze moving over my face as if he'd find the answer there. "What kind of wound?" he asked, his voice low, cautious.

I tried to think of a way to describe the raw sensation, but I was cold and exhausted, and I wasn't even sure it was real and not another Glitter effect. Instead of answering, I shook my head and dropped my hand from Falin's arm. He studied my face one more moment before his gaze shifted to the screaming Deaths behind me and then back. Reaching out, he pressed a hand to my forehead.

"You're burning up."

"I promise you, I'm freezing," I told him, wrapping my arms around my middle in an effort to slow my trembling.

Falin didn't argue, he just gave me a look—a sad, knowing look—and said, "Let's get you your tie to Faerie."

Then he stepped through the doorway.

Chapter 33

I'd grown accustomed to the bone-chilling sleet that had accompanied me since I woke in Faerie. I was not prepared for a full-on blizzard, but that's what awaited us through the doorway.

The throne room was a blur of white. A howling wind tore around the room, pelting me with wet snow from every direction. Fae huddled in clusters around the door, snow piling up on their hunched shoulders and bowed heads. Sleagh Maith and lesser fae alike clung to one another, fear all but radiating off their trembling forms. But as close as they were to the door, they didn't move, didn't dare bolt. Some sense of self-preservation telling them that the first to move wouldn't be moving for long.

And the reason for all that fear raged in the center of the storm. The queen, sword in hand, stalked across the center of the room, raving in one of the fae languages. A body at her feet.

Dark blood stained the hem of her gown, splashes of the blood dotting the tattered garment up to her high waistline. More blood soaked into the icy snow all around the body, like the nightmare version of a snow cone.

The queen whirled around as we entered. More blood

had spattered her pale skin, momentarily distracting me from the madness burning in her eyes. Until that gaze landed on me like a hot iron in the blizzard.

"You." She pointed the sword at me, and I froze. "Are you satisfied now? I've killed him. I. Killed. Him."

I glanced at the body again, I couldn't help it, couldn't stop myself. It was at an angle, the face turned away from me, blood mixing with hair that glistened even in the storm. I couldn't positively identify the bloody shape from this angle. Not by sight. But by her words, I knew who it had to be.

Ryese.

Relief flooded through me, despite the queen's growing rage, but something nagged at my senses. I tried to chalk it up to the drug, or my exhaustion, or maybe the impending hypothermia, but it persisted, drawing my eye back toward the body even as the queen stomped through the mounds of ice and snow, straight toward me.

Ryese wore a flamboyant court outfit, similar to how he'd dressed at the ball when I'd first met him. The shirt with its frilled collar and sleeves was soaked in blood all across the chest and up over the shoulder, but the flowy sleeve closest to me was hardly touched. Despite that, blood coated his palm.

Blood that hadn't been there when I'd last seen him.

It was possible that he'd touched his own blood as he died, but Falin had said seeing Ryese's bloody hands would likely be the only way the queen would believe he could be behind the plot against her. She'd killed him before I even presented what I'd learned. Something had changed her mind.

I peeled back my shield, gazing across layers of reality. The body changed. A soul glowed from within, but the form was no longer Ryese. The form slimmed and curved into feminine lines. The hair darkened to a chestnut brown, twined with bits of mistletoe.

Maeve.

I saw both images overlapping. The glamour that wrapped the dead fae kept trying to push forward, make itself true. I'd seen fae disguised with glamour inside Faerie before. While Faerie tended to accept strong glamour and make it part of its reality, it couldn't change a sentient being from one thing or person to another, but this one was trying to in a way glamour never should have done.

Which I guessed meant Ryese had finally given the queen enough Glitter that her fears were taking form. She stalked forward, clearly unaware that she'd slaughtered her council member by mistake.

But if the butchered form in the middle of the courtroom wasn't Ryese, he was still in the court. Still waiting to spring his trap.

Someone in the huddled mass of fae straightened, and Faerie buckled, a new gash tearing open in reality. It felt like something cut straight through the magic of Faerie, draining it away in the areas it touched. And I could think of only one thing that would do that.

Iron.

The queen was still striding toward me, sword pointed at my heart. Falin had edged forward, not quite putting himself between us, but trying to draw her attention. The wound in Faerie grew.

I had no special fear of iron. It hurt when touched, and I knew it was dangerous, but I wasn't afraid of it. Which meant, this wasn't likely my drug-addled imagination.

It was Ryese's trap.

A hooded figure lifted a small blowpipe loaded with what had to be an iron dart. My first instinct was to yell to Falin. But even as the warning rose in my throat, I realized what Ryese had meant when he'd said I was Falin's weakness: it wasn't that I was the key to defeating Falin, but that Falin would defend me. He stood now, in front of half the court, between the queen and me. Everyone was watching them, watching him lift his blades to a defensive position to fend off her sword.

And when Ryese's iron dart took the queen in the chest, all would assume Falin had turned on the queen. In one blow, Ryese would take out both queen and knight.

My scream of warning still only just beginning to bubble out of my throat, I dove forward, tackling the queen like a demented linebacker. The move was sloppy, but she wasn't expecting it, and I knocked her off her feet, taking her to the ground.

Heat exploded across my back as I felt Faerie rip apart in the space we'd occupied. The queen hit a snowdrift with a loud *ooaf*, her sword dropping beside her. I landed on top of her, and tried to roll away, but dizziness exploded in my head, filling my vision with dancing black dots.

"What is the meaning of this, planeweaver?" the queen bellowed, but she wasn't doing much better at regaining her feet than I had.

I couldn't catch my breath, couldn't even get close. "Ryese," I managed to get out between wheezes. "Iron."

"Impossible. I killed my nephew with my own hands."

I shook my head. "Glitter," I said, not sure she'd understand. But Falin would. Then I turned, trying to touch the burning line radiating across my shoulder blades. My gloves came away with a thin band of blood. My blood.

The dart had grazed me, nothing more, but the pain clawed at my back, the burn much more than was warranted by the grazing cut.

A cut made by an iron dart.

Shit.

Iron disrupted Faerie's magic. It could kill a fae exposed to it for too long. In the mortal realm, touching it cut off a fae's connection to Faerie, and drained the life-sustaining magic from their body. What happened to an already fading fae?

I had the feeling I already knew. I was so exhausted. So cold. I hurt, and not just my back. As if the iron had poisoned my very blood, the pain traveled through me like daggers dragged against my skin. And the two Deaths kept yelling at me. Or were there three now? Yes, a new one had appeared, telling me it was time for him to take my soul. At least he didn't scream.

I could curl up in a ball in the snow and let go. Give in to the fuzzy feeling in my head, close my eyes, and sleep.

But no, if I did that, what would happen to Rianna? To Ms. B? The garden gnome? No, I had to get up. To do . . . something.

Thoughts were getting harder to string into coherent ideas. I needed to stop Ryese. I needed the queen to grant me a tie to Faerie. I needed to protect Falin. I needed to make Faerie stop screaming. . . .

That last one made me stop. The Deaths were screaming. Some of the gathered fae—those not frozen in shock— were screaming. But Faerie itself wasn't, was it?

Not exactly, but it was in pain. I could *feel* it, sense the pain in unraveling layers of reality.

The dart.

I could feel the trail it had sliced through Faerie. More than that, I could feel the disturbance it still made, like a festering wound, blistering reality around it. The blowgun Ryese had smuggled the iron into Faerie in must have had some hard-core spells on it, because the iron hadn't been doing this much damage before. Now the layers of reality felt like they were withering.

I twisted, looking for the projectile, and beside me, the queen sucked in a breath.

"Planeweaver, what? No. Someone send for a healer." She reached for me, but her hand stopped before she touched the bare skin on my shoulder.

Falin stepped closer, his eyes wide, fear reflecting in his gaze. Then his jaw clenched and he whirled around, marching through the huddled fae and shoving them aside.

I couldn't see the graze the dart had cut across my back, but it was barely bleeding, and couldn't have been much more than a scratch. Still, I twisted, trying see what they saw. Unfortunately, I could. Gray tendrils spread under my skin, crawling over my shoulder.

Iron poisoning.

I stared at the graying skin. The third Death, the one that wasn't yelling, knelt beside me.

"It's time, Alex," he said, holding out his hand.

I looked from him to my shoulder and then back. "You're still not real."

With that, I concentrated on searching for the dart again. The blisters in reality were right in front of me. It had to be in that snowdrift.

Behind me, I heard a loud yelp, and I twisted around in time to see Falin's hand clasp around the throat of a fae. He hauled the fae off the ground, one-handed, and the fae's hood fall back to reveal Ryese's crystalline hair.

"Don't kill him, my knight," the queen said, an edge of panic in her voice as she pushed herself out of the snow. "I killed him once already today. I can't see it again."

Rational or not, desperate or not, a command was a command, and Falin's killing dagger thrust stopped, inches from Ryese's chest. The man in his arms sagged, a smug smile slithering across Ryese's face. Oh no, he wasn't just walking away from this.

I thrust my hand into the snowdrift, searching. More than the feel of something harder than snow, it was the sudden stabbing pain that rushed down my fingers, even through my gloves, that told me I'd found the dart. Trying to insulate it with inches of snow, I scooped it out.

The dart looked innocuous enough. Just a bit of thin, dull metal no longer than my pinkie nail. But it was far from harmless. If Ryese had managed a clean shot at the queen, and she had died, the small dart could have easily been missed, the blame for her unknown cause of death easily falling on her feared bloody hands.

Patting it into the center of a small snowball like a deadly core, I climbed to my feet. Then I had to wait a moment as my vision swam. I braced my feet, trying to avoid crashing back to my butt in the snow. Deep breath. Two.

"Falin," I yelled.

He stopped, looking up from where he was in the process of dragging Ryese in front of the queen. The slighter man thrashed in Falin's grasp, the smugness now absent from his face as more and more bloody, dead versions of himself appeared around the queen. For her part, the queen seemed to have forgotten everything but the multiplying bodies, her distress feeding the drug and hallucinations.

"Catch," I yelled, tossing the snowball to Falin as gently as I could. It still crumbled as he caught it, but the dart remained cushioned in a small layer of snow.

I'd been working without a plan, thinking only that the dart needed to get back inside the dampening effect of the blowgun.

Falin had other ideas.

He drove the thin bit of metal into Ryese's palm. The other fae screamed, the sound a high-pitched cry of pain and fear.

The skin around the dart immediately darkened, the glow in his skin dampening. Whereas the tendrils crawling under my flesh were a cloudy gray, his spread out in ink-black lines. Falin had once told me he'd been switched during infancy so that he'd not only learn about the human world, but also gain some resistance to all the metals, especially iron, found in mortal reality. I'd also grown up outside of Faerie, so I had some resistance as well. But Ryese was a pampered noble, and the iron poisoning shot through his flesh, creating an elaborate spiderweb of darkness across Ryese's palm.

"I'm removing this poison from our court," Falin told the queen as he hauled the howling man to his feet.

The queen's fevered gaze swept over Ryese, taking in the darkness spreading over his skin. Then she nodded and leaned closer. "If you are alive, my favorite nephew, blood of my blood, my Ryese, then you are banished from this court and all my territory. As long as I rule here, no door will open for you in winter. Here witness it, all of you."

Ryese's pitiful cries took on a new level of frenzy, but the words had the ring of a binding oath to them, and I felt the magic of Faerie shift, acknowledging the queen's proclamation even as the huddled fae murmured their witness to her words. Falin gave no heed to the other fae's pleading, but dragged him to where two winter guards stood waiting.

"See him to the edge of our territory in the mortal realm," he told the guards. They nodded, and then hauled Ryese out of the room. As soon as he passed through the doorway, the sound of his cries fell off abruptly.

Falin turned back toward me. I tried to smile at him, because we'd won. The alchemist had been caught and dealt with. The queen couldn't deny me my tie to Faerie now. But my face seemed frozen, unable to respond to my prompting.

I realized I wasn't cold anymore. I didn't even hurt, though the gray tendrils were now circling down to my elbow. All I felt was tired. So very bone-weary tired.

I tried to sit, not caring that the only place to do so was the snow, but my legs gave out halfway down and I crashed onto my butt. I didn't even have enough energy to yell.

I lay where I fell, my eyes fluttering closed. The last things I saw were the three Deaths hovering over me. Then the world went dark.

Chapter 34

I drifted in and out of a fevered sleep. Sometimes the Deaths were there, yelling at me. Other times I woke to Falin curled around me, clutching me tight. More than once the world was lost in endless snow. Others I was burning alive from iron spikes driven through my back.

Or maybe all were dreams.

When I opened my eyes, finally sure I was truly awake, I sat up. I was in a large four-poster bed I'd never seen before, wearing a silky gown I knew wasn't mine, but at least it wasn't sleeting.

"Well, I guess this means I survived."

"Astute observation," a voice said from the other side of the room.

I jumped, whirling around. Falin leaned against the doorframe, watching me, a small crooked smile touching his lips. He pushed away from the wall, striding toward the bed, and I became very aware of how thin and airy the material of the gown felt. Was it see-through?

"Where are my clothes?" I asked, gathering the royal blue comforter and clutching it to my chest, which earned me an amused—and knowing—smile. Okay, yes, he'd seen all I had to display, but we were just friends now, and I was dating Death.

The thought of Death made me shiver as I remembered the three fake versions the drug had conjured from my fears. And they were my own fears. Magnified maybe, but the issues they addressed were real. Death and I needed to sit down and have a long talk.

But first I needed my clothes.

"They were ruined. I convinced them to spare your boots." He nodded to a spot on the floor near the foot of the bed. "And it looks like your brownie has visited while you were sleeping, because they were not in that good of a shape when the healers peeled them off you. And that gown is spun from spider silk; it is a lot more substantial than it feels."

Oh. I dropped the comforter and slid to the edge of the bed to reclaim my boots. He was right—they were in better shape now than the last time I'd put them on. Which had to mean Ms. B had stopped in. And if she'd left the castle . . .

I realized I felt better than I had in weeks. I was more than just healed and free of the drug, I was energized. "Did the queen grant me my tie to Faerie?"

Falin nodded. "You have a year and a day of independent status."

A year to figure out what to do next. It wasn't a long-term solution, but it bought me time.

"So are you guarding the door for my protection or to prevent me from leaving?" I asked, and Falin winced, but it was a legitimate question.

"Maybe I'm hiding, avoiding more duels?"

"Have you been fighting a lot?"

He gave a half shrug, as if the answer wasn't important, but said, "In the days immediately following Ryese's banishment, several opportunistic fae both in our court and in others thought to take advantage while the queen was both emotionally off balance and still mentally and magically impaired by Ryese's drug. Since the effects of the Glitter have worn off and the court has begun to recover, the challenges have dropped off."

Days? Oh, no. How many days had I already lost of my year and a day of independent status? "How long was I recovering from the drug?"

As if reading my thoughts, Falin shook his head. "Don't worry. Your time is calculated in the mortal realm, as that is where you'll reside. You signed in at the Bloom, right?"

That seemed like so very long ago. But I had. As long as the doors weren't completely evil, I'd lost no more than an evening. Smiling, I pulled on my boots and checked the placement of my dagger in its holster. As I did, a glimmer of silver on my inner wrist caught my attention.

I lifted my hand to eye level. An intricate, silver snowflake twinkled from under my skin just below where my hand and arm met.

"Uh . . . ?"

"Your tie to Faerie," Falin said, noticing my dismay. "It marks you as an independent of the winter court. And before you ask, no, it can't be covered with glamour."

I scowled at the very noticeable snowflake. "Caleb's an independent. I've never seen a mark like this on his wrist."

Falin winced. "Yeah, well, usually the queen places the marks in more discreet locations, and typically they are smaller."

I stared at him. The Winter Queen had visibly *claimed* me. The snowflake may as well be an ownership tag.

At my look, Falin lifted his hands. "Hey, I did stop her from putting it in the middle of your forehead."

Okay, yeah, that would have been worse. I'd have to find a way to cover it. I'd never been big on any jewelry except the charm bracelet carrying my shields, but maybe

I'd have to find a nice cuff bracelet to avoid having to explain why I had a magical snowflake tattoo.

I sighed and stood, stretching. My stomach gave out a low growl, informing me it had been neglected for far too long.

"So your earlier response wasn't actually an answer. What kind of guard are you?" My stomach rumbled again. "And is there somewhere to get food?"

Falin laughed and threw an arm around my shoulders, leading me to the door. "We'll get some food at the Bloom before I take you home."

Sounds like a plan to me.

We had a companionable meal, which was laid out like a lavish feast. I didn't know the last time I'd eaten—though I had vague memories of being spooned some sort of gruel while in my drug and iron-fevered sleep—so I dug in with relish. Now that the queen was sane—*sane-ish?*—and the winter court was hospitable again, the court fae were no longer hiding out in the pocket spaces that connected to winter's territory. Which in turn meant the regulars were back in the bar. I didn't talk to any of them, but it was good to see the familiar faces. And, I guess I was one of them now. Just another independent getting a sip of Faerie's nectar before slipping back to the harsh mortal reality.

While we ate, Falin filled me in on what had happened after I'd lost consciousness. Only two things of importance had occurred: the queen granting me independent status, which I obviously already knew about, and the amaranthine sapling had disappeared. No one was sure if Faerie had moved it, or if someone had stolen the young tree. Falin and his FIB agents had been looking into it, but so far no leads. They also hadn't been able to track down Jenny Greenteeth.

That worried me. Both because the bogeyman creeped me out, and because I had to wonder if there was more going on in this situation. Had she been guarding the tree? And if she had been, where was it supposed to lead? If Ryese had simply planned to take over the court from his aunt, he wouldn't have needed another door to Faerie in territory that already belonged to winter.

Was he working with another court? Falin had mentioned that the Queen of Light was the Winter Queen's sister—was she Ryese's mother? Hers had been the only court not to provide challengers for the winter throne. Falin had indicated that had been a show of loyalty between the two rulers, but maybe the Light Queen hadn't needed to as her son, her ace, was behind the issues and working on positioning himself onto the throne with none the wiser?

Falin looked more than a little troubled by the idea when I suggested it. Neither of us believed Ryese had been clever enough to create Glitter on his own. Had he received help from the light court? Was that why the user's imagination influenced how the glamour manifested in reality? The imagination was the domain of the light fae.

It was a troubling thought, but one for another day. Today I wanted to go home, see my dog, and check on my friends. I'd sent a message to Rianna when I first entered the Bloom, but she hadn't answered, which likely meant she wasn't currently in Faerie. Maybe she'd gone to the mortal realm once my tie to Faerie solidified and she started feeling better? At least I hoped that was the case.

After so long in Faerie, it felt odd to walk through the VIP door and into mortal reality, but it wasn't the draining sensation it had been before I'd been granted independent status. I rolled my shoulders and turned toward the bouncer. It was the same slightly dim troll who'd been working when I'd entered with the queen.

"What's the date and time?" I asked.

He gave me a confused look, and held up his wrist

where he wore a small clock as a watch. I couldn't help but smile. I'd lost only four hours in Faerie. Sometimes the freaky doors actually worked for me. Grinning, I all but skipped as I made my way to the front door.

My phone beeped as Falin and I walked out of the Bloom, indicating a new voice mail message. I dug it out of my purse and glanced at the display.

Caleb.

I played the message as I followed Falin toward his car.

"Al, what did you do now?" Caleb's agitated voice asked in the message. "Why did Rianna just walk out of a castle that materialized in my backyard?"

Oops. Apparently, now that I had my independent status, Faerie had moved my castle out of limbo and into my new territory: the mortal realm.

This was going to take a little explaining. . . .

Read on for a special preview of the next
Alex Craft novel by Kalayna Price,
coming from Roc Books in 2017.

The first time I realized I could feel corpses, I had nightmares for a week. I was a child at the time, so that was understandable. These days I was accustomed to the clammy reach of the grave that lifted from dead bodies. To the eerie feeling of my own innate magic, responding and filling me with the unrequested knowledge of how recently a person died, their gender, and the approximate age they'd been at death. When I anticipated encountering a corpse, I tightened my mental shields and worked at keeping my magic at bay, but usually that was only necessary at places like graveyards, the morgue, and funeral homes—places one might expect to find a body.

I never expected to feel a corpse walking across the street in the middle of the Magic Quarter.

"Alex? I've lost you, haven't I?" Tamara, one of my best friends and my current lunch mate, asked. She sighed, twisting in her seat to scan the sidewalk beyond the small café. "Huh. Which one is he? I may be married and knocked up, but I know a good-looking man when I see one, and, girl, I *don't* see one. Who are you staring at?"

"That guy," I said, nodding my head at a man in a brown suit crossing the street.

Tamara glanced at the squat middle-aged man who was more than a little soft in the middle, and then she cocked an eyebrow at me. "I've seen what you have at home, so

I take it this is business. Did you bring one of your cases to our lunch?"

I ignored the "at home" comment, as that situation was more than a little complicated, and shook my head. "My case docket is clear," I said absently, and let my senses stretch. When I concentrated, I could feel grave essences reaching from corpses in my vicinity. All corpses. There were decades of dead and decaying rats in the sewer below the streets and smaller creatures like insects that barely even made a blip on my radar, but like called to like, and my magic zeroed in on the man.

"He's dead," I said, and even to me my voice sounded unsure.

Tamara blinked at me, likely waiting for me to reveal the joke, but when I pushed out of my seat as the man turned up the street, she grabbed my arm. "I'm the lead medical examiner for Nekros City, and I can tell you with ninety-nine point nine percent certainty that the man *walking* down the street is very much alive." She put extra emphasis on the word "walking," and on any other day, I would have agreed with her.

My own eyes agreed with her. But my magic, that part of me that touched the grave, that could piece together shades from the memories left in every cell of a body, disagreed. That man, walking or not, was a corpse. Granted, he was a fresh one—the way he felt to my magic told me he couldn't have been dead more than an hour. But he was dead.

So how the hell had he just walked into a shop specializing in high-end magical components?

After dropping enough crumpled dollars on the table to cover my portion of the bill and tip, I sprinted toward the shop across the street. Behind me, Tamara grumbled under her breath, but after a moment I heard her chair slide back as she pushed away from the table. She hadn't quite caught up as I reached the door to the shop.

The shop's wards tingled along my skin as I stepped

through the threshold. I'd never been in this shop before. The types of magic I could create didn't require any outside components aside from the occasional storage vessel, like the silver charms dangling from my bracelet—not that I'd created most of those either. I sucked at traditional spell casting. But my ability to sense magic was acute, and the wards on the doors had some hard-core theft deterrents that prickled at the edge of my senses. Of course, most magic that used components required items that were rare or hard to acquire, or were just plain dangerous, so it probably wasn't surprising that such extensive wards were in place.

Not everyone could feel wards though. Clearly the corpse I'd followed in didn't comprehend the extent of the shop's theft-deterrent system.

I'd entered only minutes behind him, but he almost barreled into me as I stepped through the door. His shoulder brushed me at the same moment he hit the antitheft wards, and several things happened at once. The wards snapped to life, blaring a warning to the shopkeeper to let him know something was being stolen. Simultaneously, a theft-deterring paralytic spell sparked across the would-be thief, locking his body—and the merchandise—in place.

Unfortunately, while the wards were powerful, they weren't terribly specific. Where his shoulder touched mine, the spell jumped from him to me, immobilizing me as well. Under normal circumstances, that would majorly suck. Under these circumstances? It was so much worse.

My magic still identified him as a corpse. I could feel the grave essence lifting off him, clawing at me. My mental shields were strong, but my magic *liked* dead things. A lot. And I hadn't raised a shade in nearly a week, so my magic was looking for release. Typically I made a point not to touch the dead. Now I couldn't get away.

My magic battered against the inside of my shields, looking for chinks in my mental walls that it could jump through. Fighting the spell holding me was a waste of energy—I was well and truly caught—so I focused all of my attention on holding back my own magic. But I could feel the chilled fingers of the grave sliding under my skin, worming its way into me and making paths for my magic to leach into the animated corpse frozen against me.

I wanted to open my shields and *See* what the thing in front of me was truly made of. But if I cracked my shields to gaze across the planes of reality and get a good look at the body, more of my magic would escape. And too much was already whispering through my shields, making fissures where more could follow. Sweat broke out on my paralyzed brow as I poured my focus into holding my magic at bay.

But I was touching a corpse.

The grave essence leaking from the body clawed at the fractures my magic was chewing through my shields, and it was too much. If I could have stepped back . . . But I couldn't.

All at once a chunk of my mental wall caved, and the magic rushed out of me. Color washed over the world as the Aetheric plane snapped into focus around me. A wind lifted from the land of the dead, stirring my curls and chilling my clammy skin. I could see the network of magic holding me in place, as well as the knot of magic in the sprung ward, but more important, I could see the magic coating the corpse in front of me. And it was a corpse, no doubt about it, the dead skin sagging, bloating.

But under the dead flesh, a yellow glimmer of a soul glowed.

Which meant the body was both dead and alive. Considering it was up and walking around, it was a heck of a lot more alive than a dead body should have been.

The soul inside was the color I associated with humans, so this wasn't a corpse being worn and walked around by something from Faerie or one of the other planes. I'd never seen spellwork like what shimmered across the dead flesh, but whatever kind of half-life the man existed in wasn't going to last much longer if I couldn't get ahold of my magic.

The hole in my shields wasn't huge, but I could feel my magic filling the body. And the grave and souls didn't get along. I couldn't stop the hemorrhage of magic, but I managed to slow it to a trickle.

I'd barely noticed the crowd gathering around us until one of the shopkeepers began releasing the spell holding us. If the antitheft paralyzing spell was dropped, I'd be able to get my distance from the corpse.

But either he wasn't a very good witch, or he was stalling—likely to wait for the cops—because he was taking his sweet time, and more and more of my magic was flowing out.

I'd ejected souls from bodies before. While souls didn't like the touch of the grave, they tended to cling to their flesh pretty hard, and it took directed magic to pry them free. I was actively fighting expelling the soul, and only a small portion of my magic had filled the corpse, but the soul's connection to the body felt weak, tentative.

I couldn't shift my gaze to the shopkeeper, but I could see him out of the corner of my eye. *Oh please, release the damn immobility spell.*

Too late.

In a burst of light, the soul popped free of the corpse.

Nothing about the body changed. It had already been dead and it was still held immobile by the spell, but the soul was free. For a long moment it was almost too bright to look at, a shimmering crystalline yellow. But souls can't exist without a body, and in a heartbeat the glow dimmed, the form solidifying as the soul transitioned to the purgatory landscape of the land of the dead.

If I could have stumbled back in shock, I would have, but I couldn't even blink in surprise. Not because the soul transitioned—that I had expected—but because the ghost now standing in front of me was that of a young woman.

I glanced from the balding middle-aged man to the woman who may not have been old enough to drink. Ghosts weren't like shades. While shades were always an exact representation of the person at the moment of death, ghosts tended to reflect how a person perceived himself. Appearing a little younger or more attractive was common. I supposed it was even possible that if someone identified across gender lines, their ghost might reflect that discrepancy. But this ghost was a drastically different age as well as being a different gender and ethnicity. And that was unheard-of.

The ghost-girl looked around, no longer inhibited by the spell still holding the body she'd been inside. Her dark eyes grew large and round, and her motions took on the frantic quickness of panic.

A panic that didn't last long, as a figure appeared beside her. He was dressed from head to toe in gray and carried a silver skull-topped cane. The Gray Man. A soul collector.

I wanted to scream *No*. To run between him and the girl, who clearly hadn't belonged in the dead body. Things didn't add up here, and I wanted to talk to the ghost.

But I still couldn't move.

I stood silently frozen in place as the Gray Man reached out, grabbed the soul, and sent her on to wherever souls went next. Then he turned and looked at the body she'd just vacated. His expression gave away nothing as his gazed moved to me. He gave me one stern shake of his head, which could have meant anything from the fact that he also didn't know what was going on or that he knew but it wasn't any business of mine.

Then he vanished.

Of course, that was the moment the shopkeeper released the spell. I stumbled back as the now truly dead body collapsed.

I barely registered the gasps and screams. I was far too busy staring at the spot where the Gray Man and the ghost had been. She hadn't belonged in the wrongly animated body. So the question was, how the hell had she gotten into someone else's body? And why?

ALSO AVAILABLE
FROM
Kalayna Price

GRAVE DANCE

An Alex Craft Novel

After a month of down time, Grave Witch Alex Craft
is ready to get back to solving murders by raising the
dead. With her love life in turmoil, Alex is eager for
the distractions of work. But when her new case
forces her to overuse her magic, it might be the last
mystery the Grave Witch ever gets to solve...

"Fascinating magic, a delicious heartthrob,
and a fresh, inventive world."
—Chloe Neill, *New York Times* bestselling author of *Hard Bitten*

Available wherever books are sold or at
penguin.com